An Angel's Touch

"*Heavenly Persuasion* is a perfect novel...a tender, heartwarming tale....Don't miss it!"

—Barbara Cummings, Bestselling Author Of *Fortune's Fire*

PARADISE IN HIS ARMS

Benjamin looked into the depths of Jessica's eyes and saw the anguish that matched his own. Tentatively, he rubbed his hand along her arm, then reached up and gently touched her cheek. But instead of giving her the comfort he'd hoped, the gesture made her cry. A moment later, she was in his arms, sobs racking her body. He held her close, wishing he could absorb her pain.

"Jessica...Jessica," he said as he rocked her gently in his arms.

She looked up at him with red-rimmed eyes, her cheeks glistening with tears. "Why? Why did she have to die, Benjamin?"

As Jessica's sobs slowed, her eyes held his. And suddenly, inexplicably, her arms were around his neck, her lips on his lips, and he was returning her gentle kiss with the passionate fury that she'd released with her first touch.

Heavenly Persuasion

LORRAINE HENDERSON

LOVE SPELL NEW YORK CITY

LOVE SPELL®

Published by
Dorchester Publishing Co., Inc.
276 Fifth Avenue
New York, NY 10001

Cover Art by John Ennis

Printed in the United States of America.

In loving memory of my mother, Frances Zydanowicz, who always believed...in angels and my book.

For Dar, a special friend, whose unflagging faith and encouragement kept me writing.

For Polly, Jan and Donna R., who believed in this book from beginning to end. And the other Big Ten members—Ann, Colleen, Donna V., Edna, Joy, Kit, Lee and Shelley—whose friendship means so much.

And for the thirteen angels in my life who give special meaning to the word family.

But most of all, for George, who loved me through it all and never doubted.

To the people of Put-In-Bay on South Bass Island: I ask your indulgence.

I fell in love with your island many years ago and have always wanted to write a book using it as the location. I have studied your history and much of what is found in this book is exactly as I've found it in the history books. However, since my book is a fictional work, I have taken the liberty of changing some names of people and places as well as altering some events. I sincerely hope these changes will not deter you from enjoying the story.

Heavenly Persuasion

Prologue

South Bass Island, Lake Erie, 1868

Jessica Campbell felt a prickle along the nape of her neck and instinctively knew someone was watching her. She turned, and Benjamin Whittaker's dark eyes instantly caught her gaze and refused to let go. Jessie blamed the rapid increase of her heartbeat on the surprise of finding him staring at her. But she'd been unable to explain away the warmth she'd felt at his touch earlier, when he'd escorted her out of the church after Frannie's wedding. At the time, her conscience had quickly admonished her. *Ignore this attraction, Jessica, you are promised to another.*

It hadn't been too difficult to push Benjamin from her thoughts. All she had to do was remember her sister Frannie's warning about how cynical the man could be at times, his pessimism a result of a disastrous marriage that had ended six years earlier.

Jessie had managed to get through the rest of the afternoon by avoiding Frannie's new brother-in-law. But now he continued to hold her with his intense gaze as surely as if his arms held her to him. Without so much as a blink, he came across the room, and Jessie knew she could avoid him no longer.

The broad smile he displayed softened his rugged features and captivated Jessie. He looked nothing like the bitter man Frannie had described.

The lilting music of a waltz flowed across the dance floor, and Benjamin held out his hand. "I believe it's proper for the best man and maid of honor to dance. May I?"

She willed her heart to slow down, certain he would be able to hear its rapid thumping as she went into his arms. Heat accompanied the pressure of his hand on hers, and a second jolt shook her when his other hand encircled her waist.

Benjamin felt her stiffen and couldn't help but wonder if it was because she'd noticed his immediate attraction for her when they'd first met. She'd intruded on his every waking moment and invaded even his dreams since the first moment he'd seen her on the ferry a week earlier.

He'd gone down to the dock in order to escort her to his brother Jonathan's home, and had watched as the boat came toward shore, pitching and rocking in the rough waters of the lake. Despite the buffeting, he had seen Jessica stand her ground, peering out at the churning water. The waves had sprayed a fine mist up over the prow, and the wind had tugged tendrils of her long black hair from the knot at the nape of her long, slender neck. Even if she hadn't been the only woman on the ferry, Benjamin would have recognized her. She looked exactly as her sister Fran had described her. Jessica Campbell was an exceedingly beautiful young woman.

During the week that Jessica had been on the island helping her sister prepare for the wedding, he'd had some difficulty keeping his distance. He'd noted her warm, caring nature many times and had marveled that her beauty was more than superficial. But he'd done his best to keep his feelings at bay since his brother had told him that Jessica was betrothed. It hadn't been easy, since no woman had affected him in this way since Helene had deserted him six years before.

Now he wondered if he could continue to ignore his attraction to Jessica. Could there be a chance for them? Engagements had been broken before. There might be a possibility if she felt the same.

How could he overlook the exciting tension that vibrated between them when he'd slipped his arm around her and taken her hand in his.

Gently he smoothed his thumb over the soft skin of her hand, hoping to help her relax. Even that light touch stirred his senses and made him want to know her better.

A tremor of pleasure spread through Jessie's body as Benjamin's callused thumb caressed her skin. She found it difficult to understand these tingly sensations. They were so different from the rather comfortable feeling she experienced at her fiance's touch. And although looking into Michael's eyes filled her with a warm, secure feeling, it was nothing like the fire that burned with Benjamin's glance.

In order to quell the disturbing, and exciting, emotions she'd felt since their first meeting, Jessie looked up into Benjamin's smiling face and without preamble announced, "I'm leaving for Indiana in the morning, and I'm to be wed there next month."

"So soon?" he said, trying not to betray his disappointment. "You seem too young to be ready for marriage."

"I'm nineteen, and Michael and I have been betrothed for nearly two years."

"Then you must know him well," Benjamin said.

"Our families have known each other for many years, but Michael and I haven't been able to spend much time together. He's worked long and hard to save money for the farm we both want. That's the reason he's not here. Why he was unable to attend the wedding with me," she added, unable to stop the flow of words—afraid if she did she would reveal her attraction to Benjamin. "He had to leave for Indiana to sign the final papers for our land. I'll be meeting him there and we'll be married immediately."

The thought of her in another man's bed caused Benjamin's jaw to clench. The thought was coupled with a strong suspicion that the young woman in his arms felt the magnetism between them as intensely as he did. Yet she was making it very clear that her allegiance was to her fiance. His earlier hope that she might be willing to break her engagement seemed a bit farfetched. And in his heart Benjamin knew he could not bring himself to interfere with her betrothal.

With a sense of sadness that surprised him, he mouthed some appropriate words. "I'm sure you're pleased to be marrying a young man who is not afraid of hard work."

"Michael isn't as young as I. He's quite . . . mature, and he is indeed hard working and very responsible. I know we'll be happy."

"Will you?" Benjamin asked, knowing he shouldn't have.

"Yes," she answered, stubbornly meeting his gaze. "I'm *certain* we will."

Benjamin stopped dancing and released Jessie's hands. "Then I'm certain our dance is over," he said. And with a courtly nod he turned and walked away.

Chapter One

South Bass Island, Monday, October 4, 1875

Jessie felt the grit from her long journey settling into her shoes and stockings as the movement of her skirts swirled miniature dust clouds at her feet. She eyed the heavy clouds that had darkened the afternoon sky, and stepped up her pace. Beginning to wonder if she'd gone in the wrong direction, she suddenly spied, through the almost bare trees, the decorative cupola atop her sister's house. Her feet virtually flew the last few yards, and she was on the porch of the white battenboard house seconds later, rapping on the door.

Waiting for a response, she couldn't help but remember the telegram that had brought her to this island. The blunt, brief message was imbedded in her mind. *Jonathan Whittaker dead in boating mishap. Frances in coma.* The message had come from Benjamin Whittaker.

Impatiently, she knocked longer and harder as fear began to grip her heart. *What if Frannie's dead?* As quickly as the morbid thought came to mind she dismissed it, and peered through a long window near the door. Despite the impending darkness, there were no lamps lit and her panic grew. She tried the knob, and was relieved to find it unlocked. When the door swung inward, the first thing Jessie saw was the silver candelabra she'd given Jonathan and Frannie as a wedding gift. It pained her to remember how happy her sister had been on that day. Even if Frannie recovered completely from her physical injuries, the tragedy of losing Jonathan would surely affect her deeply.

"Frannie," she called out. Then, realizing her sister would be unable to respond if she still lay in a coma, she called to her niece. "Maria, are you here? Maria, it's Aunt Jessie."

The silence terrified her. Jessie dropped her satchel in the entry and, lifting her skirt, she raced down the hall to the large kitchen in the back of the house. No one was there. The cookstove was cold to her touch. There was no sign of life. The coldness overpowered the cheery atmosphere Jessie recalled from her last visit.

She rapidly retraced her steps to the entry and started up the wooden staircase, still calling out, "Maria . . . Maria." Quickly she covered the distance from the stairs to Frannie's bedroom, but she threw open the door only to find the room empty.

"Who's up there?" A booming male voice startled Jessie, and she instinctively backed against the wall as she heard heavy footfalls on the stairs.

"Who's there?" the voice called out again.

As the man came to the top of the stairs, his rugged profile and dark hair became visible and Jessica's heart skipped a beat as she recognized him as Benjamin Whittaker. She stepped into the hall and called out, "It's Jessica McAllister, Mr. Whittaker . . . Frannie's sister."

He'd reached the top of the landing by then and turned to face her, his hands on his hips, legs spread wide. His dark eyes bored into hers, and she stopped abruptly, stunned by the angry look on his face and in his eyes.

"What are you doing here?" he asked gruffly.

"You must have known I'd come to take care of Frances and Maria."

"There's no need for that. My housekeeper and I are managing well. You shouldn't have come."

How dare he? Jessie pushed back the words, trying to hold her temper at bay. "I'm pleased to hear they're being cared for. But where are they?"

"I've had them moved into my house. It was easier than traveling back and forth across the island every day."

Jessie nodded, still a bit overwhelmed by the man's angry stance and obviously belligerent attitude. So this is the cynical, angry man Fran warned me about six years ago, Jessie thought. This was a side of Benjamin Whittaker she'd not seen on her previous visit. He was nothing like the charming, polite man she remembered. Unable to deal with the hostility emanating from him, she said, "I'd like to see my sister."

"Didn't the telegram explain she was in a coma? She can't speak to you."

Jessie could not understand why he appeared so antagonistic. As he continued to glare at her she found her usually passive nature being put to the test, and responded with more authority in her voice. "I have traveled two long, arduous days to be with my sister and I wish to see her now, Mr. Whittaker. Will you take me to her or shall I find my own way?"

"Humph," he mumbled, starting back downstairs.

"Sir, I'll not be ignored. I am family and wish to see my sister—immediately!" Jessie had raised her voice enough to make Benjamin turn around. His eyes looked black as coal, although Jessie knew they were a velvety brown. She remembered distinctly how they'd gleamed during his brother's wedding ceremony and how warmly he'd gazed at her during the reception afterwards. Now, though, as he continued to stare at her, she felt like an insect being studied at the end of a pin.

Benjamin Whittaker looked up at the woman on the landing above him and tried not to remember the attraction he'd felt for her so many years before. She was even more beautiful now, strands of dark hair curling about her oval face, obviously having been blown free from the long braid that hung down her back. Her eyes were a shade unlike any he'd ever seen—aquamarine—clear as the sea itself. She wore a black dress topped with a cape of wool the very color of her eyes. Jessica McAllister had matured from a lovely young girl into an extremely beautiful woman, making it difficult for him to pull his gaze away from her.

An instant later, though, he remembered why she'd come, and he forced those thoughts from his mind. His brother Jonathan had told him how it distressed Fran to know her own sister was unable to bear a child. Now, here she was, after almost seven years' absence. With her sister on her deathbed, she'd come, like a vulture, to snatch Maria away from him. But he had promised his brother to care for the child, and he would rather die than break that promise.

Jessica continued to hold his gaze and, despite the angry thoughts that flowed through his mind, the passionate feelings her eyes suggested unsettled him. He turned abruptly and stomped down the stairs while at the same time saying, "You'll have to ride with me. There's no other horse available here."

Jessie followed. She hadn't remembered him being such a dark, angry man. Perhaps it was because of the loss of his brother. Jessie was well aware that some men covered their grief with anger.

As they moved down the path toward his steed, Jessie said, "I'm sorry about the loss of your brother. This must be a very painful time for you."

There was only the briefest hesitation in the man's stride, but Jessie saw his shoulders slump forward. "Thank you for your concern, Mrs. McAllister."

A moment after helping Jessie up on the horse, Benjamin had also mounted and they were on their way down the road along the lake. Jessie tried not to think about the fact that they were on an island. Being surrounded by water gave her a rather strange, disconnected sensation. She looked away from the vast expanse of water and turned her eyes inward, concentrating instead on keeping herself upright behind Benjamin.

He rode fast, pushing the stallion onward, clouds of dust kicking up in their wake. With her hands around Benjamin's firm body, Jessie could feel the movement of his taut muscles beneath his clothing. On several bumps and turns her head jostled against his back and the pungent leather smell from his vest invaded her nostrils.

She was glad she'd positioned the tapestry bag on her lap between them. It was embarrassing enough to have to clutch him with both arms without having her entire body bumping against his. He'd given her no time to look for her sister's riding habit, and her skirts were pulled up high in order to sit astride the horse. The satchel was a welcome buffer.

With her arms around him, though, Jessie couldn't help but recall the last time they were this close, when they'd danced a waltz at her sister's wedding reception. He had been smiling then, and she remembered how his smile had softened his rugged features. She also recalled his touch and how it had aroused her. She'd countered it with the announcement of her upcoming marriage, and he'd been surprised that it was to be so soon. There was also the vivid recollection of her sense of loss when Benjamin had ended the dance and walked away from her.

During her marriage she'd often wondered why she had been unable to respond to Michael's loving gestures with the same sensations Benjamin Whittaker had evoked in her with but a touch and a gaze. Her guilt at having such thoughts always banished them quickly, though, and knowing how much Michael loved her enabled her to push thoughts of Benjamin out of her mind. Now, as she felt his body moving beneath her hands, those same sensations threatened to overtake her. The mere thought of his dark eyes on hers sent a quiver through her body. Yet she knew she mustn't let such emotions distract her. She had to concentrate on her sister and her niece, not on Benjamin Whittaker.

Benjamin wondered what Jessica could be thinking as she tightened her grip around his waist. The constriction was almost unbearable, but he wasn't sure if it was because he found the woman so attractive, or because he wished she'd never come.

If only I'd gone with my first instinct and not sent the telegram, he thought, she wouldn't be here now. But his housekeeper had insisted, and after some consideration he'd realized Fran's sister had to be notified.

Now that she was here, she'd awakened all the haunting memories he'd thought were long buried, and she continued to stir conflicting emotions within him which he was not prepared to deal with. He didn't want to feel the desire that crept into his being with her every glance. The passion she aroused with her touch was something he couldn't handle, not when he had Fran and Maria to think about.

When she'd brought up Jonathan it had only made things worse. It was best not to think—not to remember. His brother was gone, lost at sea, and no one could ease the pain that gripped him. He had to concentrate on Fran, lying there so helpless, and on Maria and his promise to take care of her, to see that she had her rightful place in the winery when she grew up.

The chilly autumn winds blew Jessie's hood back off her head as Benjamin's horse galloped up a narrow path carved into a steep, rocky hillside. The sight of an enormous house at the top of the cliff surprised Jessie. She hadn't been to this end of the island on her previous visit, and she'd never imagined Benjamin's home would be so ostentatious.

The house stood three stories high and was built with blocks of gray stone. Mullioned windows lined the first two stories, and the oddly angled roof and eaves seemed to go on forever, with turrets at each of the four corners jutting into the somber gray sky. She couldn't help but wonder at the difference in the two brothers' homes, especially since they'd been business partners, as Frannie had told her.

They slowed considerably going up the hill, and Benjamin stopped his horse in front of a short path that led to the house. He was off the saddle in one fluid motion, extending his hands up to her. She looked hesitantly into his eyes for a moment before slipping into his waiting arms. As his strong hands slid under her cape, encircling her waist to lift her down, she drew in a sharp breath . . . it had been a long time since a man had held her.

She could feel the heat from his hands right through her heavy wool dress as it stirred the embers of a flame he'd lit years before. As though he too felt the fire between them and was anxious to douse it, Benjamin hastily withdrew his hands and was astride his horse a moment later. Looking down at her he said, "Go inside. Mrs. Cochran will see you to your sister." Then he spurred his stallion onward and was gone.

As Jessie proceeded up the fieldstone walkway that led to the massive, intimidating front door, she marveled at the brilliant yellow and rust-colored chrysanthemums lining the path, still blooming despite the early October chill. The thought also crossed her mind that they were the only visible signs of warmth around the huge mansion.

When she reached the house she used the ornate metal door knocker to announce her arrival. Waiting for someone to respond, Jessie listened to the rhythmical sound of the waves below the house, letting the sound wash over her, soothing her agitation.

Until she'd stopped at this door, she hadn't noticed her exhaustion. She'd barely paused to rest since receiving the telegram from Benjamin two days earlier. There'd been the long wagon ride out of Chalmers, and then the strange excitement of riding on a train for the first time in her life. Now, even the recent crossing on the ferry seemed a bit hazy. It had been such a hurried trip and she had been fraught with anxiety over Frannie.

The only bright moment in the whole trip had been meeting Ann Weldon and her son Willy—a playmate of Maria's—on the ferry. Mrs. Weldon had been very kind to Jessie, assuring her that everyone was praying for Frannie's recovery. Mrs. Weldon's husband, a minister, had arranged for a wagon to be at the dock waiting for his wife and son. Ann had insisted that Jessie ride along to East Point, where both the Weldons' and Frannie's houses were located. The elderly driver, John Thomas, had kindly agreed. When they'd parted at a fork in the road, Ann had promised she would stop by to visit the next day.

Jessie suddenly realized her new friend would not find her at Frannie's house.

She sighed and knocked again, weariness beginning to seep into her body. At least now she knew her sister was still alive, and the knowledge that she would be seeing her momentarily buoyed her wilting spirits.

A moment later the door opened and a thin, pink-cheeked, gray-haired woman smiled out at Jessie. "Good evenin', miss. May I help you?"

"I'm Jessica McAllister, Mrs. Whittaker's sister."

"Oh, my dear, do come in. I'm Mrs. Cochran—Margaret Cochran—Mr. Benjamin's housekeeper." She bustled about, closing the door firmly, taking Jessie's cape, and fussing about the chill in the house.

Jessie couldn't help but shiver, not only from the frigid temperature in the hall but from the cold, austere look of the place. The drab block walls were not warmed by tapestries or paintings. No carpets softened the relentless expanse of gray stone. She couldn't help but compare the place to a prison . . . or a mausoleum.

"I'll have my husband Samuel stoke up the fire in the parlor for you, ma'am. And I suppose you'll be stayin' the night with us?"

"Thank you, Mrs. Cochran, but there's no need to bother your husband. I'd like to go directly to see my sister. I've come a long way to see her and Maria."

For a moment, Mrs. Cochran stood there blinking her eyes and clutching at the waistband of her crisp white apron, making no move to escort Jessie anywhere.

Jessie repeated her request. "May I please see my sister *now*, Mrs. Cochran?"

"Of course, of course, Mrs. McAllister. I just hope you're prepared for her . . . her condition. It's disconcerting to see her lyin' there like she was goin' to speak to you any moment yet never a move does she make." The apple-cheeked woman rubbed her hands nervously up and down her apron, avoiding eye contact with Jessie. Then she turned abruptly and picked up one of two oil lamps that rested at opposite ends of a long wooden table near the stairs.

"Come along then," she said, starting up the wide spiral staircase, lifting the lamp high to light the way.

The echo of their footsteps bounced off the stone walls, and Jessie couldn't help but think of her young niece living here. The child must be terrified of this horrible place, she thought, recalling the cozy warmth of her sister's home. Jessie knew she must take Frannie and Maria back to their own home—and she would do it as soon as possible. This harsh, somber environment couldn't be good for the child, and it certainly wouldn't be conducive to her sister's recovery.

"Where is Maria?" Jessie asked as they proceeded up the stairs.

"Samuel . . . Mr. Cochran, that is, has taken her for a walk down by the lake. The little one loves to walk along the shore. Bless her soul, I don't think she's aware of the fact that her beloved sea took her father from her."

"You mean no one's told her?"

"Oh, yes. Of course, miss. Mr. Benjamin and I both spoke with her. She understands about heaven and she knows her daddy went there to be with Jesus, but at times she seems to be watching for his boat to come back into the bay.

"They never found his body, you know," Margaret said as she stopped on the step above Jessie, looking down at her with sadness in her eyes.

"No . . . no, I didn't know. That must be difficult

for Mr. Whittaker. Not being able to bury his brother."

The housekeeper nodded. "Indeed, very difficult."

"Is Maria's room near her mother's?" Jessie asked, trying to get the housekeeper moving again.

"No," she said, proceeding to the top of the landing and gesturing down the long corridor. "Maria has the room at the end of the hall next to her uncle's. He says he likes to keep an eye on her . . . but I must tell you, miss, it's been upsetting for him."

"How so, Mrs. Cochran?" Jessie asked, hoping to discover some clue to Benjamin's sullen demeanor.

"It's just that the man's so busy workin' the vineyard in order to try and recoup the losses he's had this past year that he barely has time for the poor lass."

"The winery is losing money?" Jessie asked, as they continued across the landing.

"I'm afraid so. A large new wine company with many financial backers came onto the island a few years ago. They're able to sell their wine cheaper than a smaller company like the Whittakers', so it's been sustaining constant losses of revenue. He and his brother had been struggling to overcome their problems when the accident took Jonathan's life."

"I see," Jessie said, thinking perhaps his business difficulties had added to Benjamin's black mood.

At the same time, she couldn't help but think that this depressing house could affect anyone's temperament. She glanced both upward and downward trying to imagine the place with some feminine touches. The walls could be warmed with woven tapestries and framed seascapes or floral scenes. Carpets would soften the harsh echoes and make the place much more livable. But no matter, she would be taking her sister and niece back to their own comfortable home soon.

Mrs. Cochran stopped in front of the second doorway on the right. "Here we are," she said, opening the door for Jessie.

Upon entering her sister's room, Jessie drew in a ragged breath. Frannie looked like a corpse, lying still as a rock in the enormous four-poster bed that dominated the room. As Jessie stepped closer, she saw Frannie's eyes—open and unblinking—fixed on a point somewhere far beyond the ceiling above her.

"Dear God, no," Jessie gasped. "I'm too late. She's dead."

Chapter Two

"Oh, no . . . oh, Missus McAllister, she's not dead." Margaret Cochran put her arm around Jessie's shoulders. "I thought I warned you. Her eyes . . . they just won't close. We've tried. Sometimes they stay closed for a bit, but then they just open again."

"Thank God," Jessie murmured, still shaken. Needing a moment to regain her composure, Jessie pulled her gaze away from the cold, vacant eyes of her beloved sister.

She took in the spacious room, and was pleased to see that an attempt at warmth was evident. A huge bouquet of fall flowers stood in a vase on the bedside table, and a thick carpet softened the floor under Jessie's feet. Flames flickering in the fireplace at the far side of the room cast a rosy glow, and four golden candlesticks with tapers burning brightly stood at each end of the wooden mantelpiece. Sounds of the sea were muffled by heavy green velvet drapes at the windows. The draperies also served to add some warmth to the cold, gray walls.

Somehow the attempt at brightening this room made the sight of Frannie's still form not quite so terrible.

With a final pat on Jessie's shoulder, Mrs. Cochran stepped away. "Call down if you need anything," the housekeeper told her as she left and closed the door behind her.

Slowly Jessie walked over to the bed and took her sister's hand in hers. "Frannie, it's me, Jessie. Frannie, can you hear me?"

Jessie squeezed her sister's cold, lifeless fingers, but there was no answering movement, no warmth, no feeling of life.

Tears came unbidden to Jessie's eyes and she blinked furiously trying to still them, but they slid down her cheeks, dropping onto the white muslin nightgown her sister wore.

"Oh, Frannie, please try and hear me. I've come quite a way to see you and it's been such a long time since we've talked."

"At least you admit that." Benjamin's voice boomed from the doorway, and Jessie whirled around to face him. The man certainly had a startling way of making his presence known.

"Please leave us alone Mr. Whittaker," Jessie said through clenched teeth.

"It's been almost seven years since you've seen your sister, Mrs. McAllister. Why did you feel you had to travel all this way now when she can't even talk to you?"

"I came because I was needed. I'm her sister and I'm going to take care of her and my niece."

"Now we get to the truth. You have no child of your own, so you've come to take Fran's child. Well, be it known, madame, that you'll not take the child while there's still a breath of life in Fran or me. Maria's a Whittaker, and this island is where she belongs."

A sudden, violent throbbing in Jessie's temples caused her to feel faint, but she knew she couldn't let this bully see any weakness. How dare he speak to her in such a way? She'd often wondered if she was indeed barren, but for him to allude to that fact set her on edge. And how could he even think that she would take Maria away from her mother?

Resolutely, she stood, still clutching Frannie's hand, and raised her voice just enough to make him listen. "This is my sister, my own flesh and blood. She and Maria are my only living relatives and I will take care of both of them . . . in their own home."

"I promised my brother I would care for them, and I'll not break my promise," he responded angrily.

"I have not asked you to break your promise. We will be happy to accept any help you care to give, but it shall be given in my sister's home, where I know she will be more comfortable."

"I don't think it's wise to move her," Benjamin said, his dark eyes warring with Jessie's.

"You moved her here and it didn't make a difference, did it?"

When he didn't answer, Jessie decided to soften her stance. A bit more calmly she added, "Mr. Whittaker . . . Benjamin, Frannie needs to be in familiar surroundings if there's any hope for her to wake from this stupor."

Benjamin glanced away from Jessica and

looked down at his sweet sister-in-law. Fran had always been good and kind to him, including him in their family as though he were her own brother, and he loved her as dearly as if she'd been his own sister. She'd been a good wife to his brother and had borne Jonathan a beautiful child. Benjamin knew he would deny Fran nothing if she were able to ask it. Could Jessica be right? Would the familiarity of her own home help bring Fran back to them?

Not wanting Jessica McAllister to see the tears that moistened his eyes, Benjamin kept his head inclined toward Fran and asked, "Do you really believe she would be happier in her own home?"

"I do," Jessie answered simply.

"Then we'll move her in the morning. You are welcome to spend the night. I'll have Mrs. Cochran prepare a room for you."

Jessie was amazed at the change in his demeanor. Despite the turn of his head, she'd seen the tears in his eyes and the tender way he'd looked at Frannie; she could only assume he cared deeply about his sister-in-law.

At that moment a tiny replica of Frannie burst into the room, tears streaming down her pink cheeks, fists balled at her sides. "Uncle Ben, why did you take away my kitty?"

"That is no way to enter a room, young lady. As you can see, we have a guest."

The little girl began crying in earnest as she looked up at Jessie with Frannie's green eyes. "I loved my kitty."

Jessie felt an enormous lump form in her throat at the sight of her adorable niece. She hunkered down to the child's level and looked at her for a moment. "Maria, I'm your Aunt Jessie and I've come to take care of you and your mother."

The small child looked hesitantly from her uncle to Jessie. Then she met Jessie's eyes and took a tentative step forward. "Are you really my Aunt Jessie?" she asked.

"Yes, I am. Your momma is my sister and I love you both very much."

Maria's arms wound around Jessie's neck. "Oh, Aunt Jessie," she murmured. "Momma always told me you'd come some day. She told me you loved me."

"Yes, I do, my sweet Maria."

The little girl moved back a bit, one hand still around Jessie's neck. "I wish you'd come sooner. Maybe you could have made Uncle Ben let my kitty live here."

"Why did you take away the child's pet?" Jessie asked Benjamin.

"It is no concern of yours, madame, and I will thank you to keep your meddling words out of my home." He took two giant strides toward Jessie and Maria.

"Maria, it's past your bedtime. Please go to your room," he said sternly.

The tender man Jessie had briefly encountered only moments before had disappeared. She could see Maria's alarm at Benjamin's raised voice. "Maria, don't be frightened of your uncle," she said. "He's just had a difficult day and is taking it out on us."

Jessie looked up at Benjamin, who at that moment appeared much taller than the six feet she judged him to be. With her eyes, she dared him to say another word to the child.

Benjamin stood rock still, looking down on them, his arms crossed over his chest, his jaw clenching and unclenching as he scowled at Jessie.

Without taking her eyes from his, Jessie spoke tenderly to Maria. "Maria, you do have to get ready for bed, though, because I'm going to take you and your momma home tomorrow and you need a good rest."

Maria immediately began to smother Jessie with little-girl kisses. "Oh, thank you, Aunt Jessie. I've been wanting to go home and see all my dollies and Peter too and I know Momma wants to be at home, even though she can't say so right now."

Jessie could see the excitement in Maria's green eyes, and couldn't help but notice how her dark curls framed the tiny features so like her mother's.

"Who's Peter?" Jessie asked.

"He's a bunny rabbit Momma and I saved from a trap in the woods and we're taking care of him. Momma said we would make him all better and he could be my pet."

Jessie looked up at Benjamin and he shook his head. Once again, Jessie saw the compassion in his eyes, and she wondered how the man managed to spring so quickly between anger and tenderness.

"Well, we'll see, sweetheart," Jessie said. "Sometimes bunnies just can't get better."

"Oh, he has to, Aunt Jessie," the child wailed. "When Momma wakes up I want her to see that I took good care of Peter. Momma's going to be awfully sad when we tell her Daddy's gone to heaven, and I know if Peter gets well it will help Momma feel better too." Tears flowed down the child's cheeks as she slipped out of Jessie's arms and went to the side of the bed. Tenderly, she reached up and wrapped her small, slender fingers around her mother's hand. "Peter's going to be all right, Momma . . . and so are you."

Jessie's heart almost broke at the sight of her niece's distress. She went to Maria and gently placed her hands on the child's shoulders. "Let's get some sleep, sweetheart, and wait and see what tomorrow brings."

In Maria's room, Jessie helped the little girl get ready for bed. When she was tucking the covers up under her chin, the child reached up and hugged her once more and kissed her cheek. "Momma always told me you were very special to her, Aunt Jessie. When you wrote me letters, she read them to me and told me stories about when you were both little girls. She told me I'd love you the minute we met and I do."

Tears brimming in her eyes, Jessie hugged her niece and whispered, "I love you too, Maria. Good night."

Benjamin watched the tender scene from the doorway and wondered why the child had never said those words to him. Of course, he had never been given to hugging and kissing little children. Perhaps nearing 40 and being alone had made him a bitter man.

His parents had died 15 years earlier, and two years later Helene had left him, just months after he'd finished building this monstrosity of a house for her.

He was aware of his brother Jonathan's love for him, but they never spoke the words to one another. For nearly half his life, Benjamin had never heard anyone say those words to him.

And at that moment, watching Maria with Jessica, he remembered his mother's sweet voice as she'd so often said, "I love you." Benjamin ached to hear someone voice that sentiment once more.

The longing reached deep within him like icy fingers closing around his heart, and he wondered if there would ever be someone who could love him enough to say those three words to him again.

After Maria finished her prayers, Benjamin stiffly escorted Jessie to her room. With a rather gruff "Good night," he strode away leaving Jessie to wonder what had set him off again. His demeanor seemed to leap from hot to cold with barely any reason.

Although Jessie found her bed quite comfortable and the fireplace cast a warm and friendly glow, she was restless and unable to sleep.

Usually thoughts of Michael helped her in the silence of long sleepless nights, but tonight when she closed her eyes all she could see were Benjamin's brown eyes. As her arms wound around her pillow she thought of her arms around Benjamin's broad chest as they'd ridden to this house together. When she tried to remember Michael's touch, she could only think about the warmth of Benjamin's hands as he'd lifted her down from his saddle.

Jessica's mind also played back the feelings that Benjamin had stirred in her nearly seven years earlier when they'd danced at Frannie's wedding. If she hadn't been betrothed to Michael, she knew she would have been open to those feelings.

Abruptly, Jessie climbed out of bed.

What in heaven's name is wrong with me? she thought. I've never doubted my love for Michael before.

"I did love you, Michael," she murmured into the silent room. "But I wonder if I cheated you from a stronger love . . . a love you deserved. Perhaps, meeting Benjamin and feeling the passion he aroused in me kept me from loving you as I should have. Yet we did have tender moments. We did share a bed for three years."

She lowered herself into an armchair near the fire and stared into the dancing flames, forcing herself to remember amorous times with Michael. As she thought about those times, though, it only reinforced the feelings she'd always had. Their love was a warm, comfortable closeness—nothing more, nothing less.

Possibly, a child would have helped their love grow stronger. Michael had never voiced his concern, though, and she preferred not to think of herself as barren—the word Benjamin had implied when he'd accused her of coming to steal Maria away. Perhaps that was why she'd been so angry with him. He'd brought up a fact that still pained her deeply. With Michael dead there was no one to carry on his name. She'd borne the guilt of that fact silently, never voicing it to anyone . . . except in a letter to Frannie. Had her sister talked to Benjamin about such a private concern?

Jessie shook her head, knowing her sister would not betray such a personal confidence to anyone, except perhaps her husband. Jonathan might have carried the tale to his brother. But Benjamin still had no right to insinuate that because she was childless she would be so heartless as to take Maria away from her home.

Jessie sighed and tried to think of more pleasant thoughts . . . thoughts more conducive to sleep. Again she called memories of Michael to mind and smiled. She recalled early mornings when they held each other before the sun came up. Sometimes they'd just snuggle against each other; other times they made love. Their lovemaking had always been a sweet, tender interlude, and Jessie had often wondered about the passion associated with lovemaking that she'd heard other women hint at.

Perhaps she and Michael had never known such passion because she'd been so young. And there hadn't been an opportunity for their love to grow into passion. They'd been married less than three years when Michael died. Influenza had moved swiftly through their small rural community, cruelly picking and choosing its victims from family after family. Not one family had been spared—some had been wiped out completely. At the time, Jessie had wished she'd died too.

During lonely nights exactly like this one, she longed to have strong arms hold her, longed to have a home, to be part of a family again.

Perhaps if . . . when Frannie was herself again, she would ask Jessie to stay on South Bass Island with her and Maria. The three of them would be a family. She wished now that she'd come when Frannie had invited her after Michael's death. But she'd been so sure she could manage the farm. Even with her two farmhands, though, the work had been too much, the profits too little.

She shuddered remembering the awful man she'd had to go to work for in the general store in Chalmers. If only she hadn't been too proud to come here to her sister, she wouldn't have had to endure Mr. Neuman's lewd advances.

The sound of the waves battering the rocks below interrupted Jessie's musings and drew her to the window. She moved aside the heavy damask draperies and stared out into the darkness.

The thin sliver of moon that remained from September barely cast any light, and only occasionally, between passing clouds, could Jessie make out its silvery splinter of reflection in the lake below. In less than a month, though, the full moon would once again shine, reflecting over and over in the waves that washed up against the cliff beneath Benjamin's house. It would be a lovely sight to see.

Abruptly her pleasant reflections were replaced by the image of Benjamin taking Maria's kitten away. *No. I'll not be in this house to see the full moon. In fact, I shall not pass another night here unless absolutely necessary.*

With those words ringing in her mind, Jessie moved away from the window, leaving the pounding surf muffled behind the heavy draperies. She climbed back under the quilts Mrs. Cochran had piled on the bed, secure in the knowledge that she was doing the right thing by moving Maria and Frannie out of Benjamin's house.

Yes, Jessie thought determinedly, Frannie will get better and together we'll give Maria a loving home. This island could well feel like home to me if the three of us are together—united, as a family should be.

Warm thoughts of a loving family finally lulled Jessie to sleep.

Down the hall from Jessie's room a soft slice of light seeped out from under Benjamin's door. He too was having difficulty sleeping.

Being the sort of man who was unable to waste a moment's valuable time, he had risen and lit a lamp in order to do some work on his accounts. Benjamin sat in a straight-backed wooden chair at a small table near the window. He had pulled the draperies back earlier and opened the window a crack in order to better hear the sound of his beloved sea.

For several minutes Benjamin dipped his pen and, in his flamboyant scrawl, managed to pen notices to two restaurants on the mainland who'd been ignoring his requests for payment. He would tolerate no more delays, writing that he himself would come to collect the money due the company if he did not receive payment within three days.

It was essential that he collect every debt owed, in order for the winery to be able to process and bottle the new grapes. Even then, without new business, they might not survive this drop in revenue. A trip to the mainland to bolster their sales was a necessity, yet he was needed to supervise the work in the fields and do his brother's work as well. If only he could split himself in two.

As Benjamin prepared to write yet another notice, his mind drifted from the work at hand, drifted right down the hall to where Jessica McAllister slept.

He need only close his eyes to imagine how lovely she would look asleep. Her thick, dark lashes would softly brush her rosy cheeks; her dark hair would flow over the pillow where she rested her head, and her long, perfectly proportioned legs—which he had glimpsed as he'd helped her off his mount earlier that day—would be stretched out invitingly on the pristine white sheets of the bed.

Benjamin shook his head, attempting to eliminate these images from his mind. Brushing an annoying lock of hair back off his forehead, he stood abruptly, knocking his chair to the floor. "Damn!" he said as he bent to retrieve it. "Why did you come to my island, Jessica McAllister? And why do you have to invade my every thought?"

Extinguishing the lamp, Benjamin got back into bed knowing he had to get some sleep if he were to manage his business affairs in the morning. Two of his biggest customers on the mainland were considering the new wine company's bid at getting their business, and Benjamin would need his wits about him to show his wine to be the superior product. He could only hope thoughts of his business losses wouldn't cause him nightmares.

An hour later, still awake, Benjamin punched his pillow angrily, then got back out of bed and paced the floor. It was not his business affairs that kept him awake—it was Jessica McAllister's face that appeared each time he closed his eyes. And once, afraid to close them again, he stared into the darkness, and still her image came floating towards him like a ghostly visage he was unable to halt.

Again he lit the lamp beside his bed and at last banished her countenance from his room. Yet once her image was gone, Benjamin felt a pang of loneliness pierce him deep inside and he longed to see her face again.

A low moan escaped his lips as he rolled over and buried his face in his pillow. "Why did you have to come back, Jessica?" he murmured aloud. "No woman except you has tempted me since Helene left me."

Benjamin rose and again extinguished the

lamp. The waves pounding on the rocks below summoned him. Standing at the window, he spoke aloud as though Jessica stood before him, as though saying the words would be a catharsis, ridding him of the spell she'd cast over him.

"At my brother's wedding you made me remember I was a man . . . and then told me you would wed another. I forced myself to forget you and forget about love. I vowed that no woman would ever hurt me again.

"You and Helene are alike in many ways, Jessica. Neither of you cared for this island. My venomous wife couldn't wait to get off it and neither could you. My brother told me how you hated being surrounded by water, just like Helene. So you'll be leaving sooner or later just as she did. But you won't take Maria with you. That little girl loves this island just as her father and I, and our father before us. No one will take her away from it while I still live and breathe."

With those angry words ringing in his ears, Benjamin went back to bed. His fury now filled the lonely spot in his heart and effectively blotted Jessica's image from his mind.

Chapter Three

A warmth on Jessie's cheek brought her awake from a dream of Benjamin. Without opening her eyes she put her hand up to her face, hoping it was indeed Benjamin's warm touch . . . but her fingers brushed only her own smooth skin. Blinking her eyes open, she saw the warmth came from a patch of sunlight. Evidently, she'd not closed the draperies tightly after her late night wanderings, and a stream of golden sunshine poured into the room, warming even the cold gray walls.

Luxuriating in the sun's comfortable light, Jessie suddenly found herself daydreaming about what it would be like to have Benjamin's arms around her in the early morning. As quickly as she became aware of her thoughts, she dismissed the fantasy from her mind and climbed out from under the covers.

Frannie was the only reason she was in this

house. Jessie knew she must keep this thought foremost in her mind.

She shivered as her bare feet moved over the cold stone near the fireplace. Taking kindling from the basket on the hearth, Jessie placing the pieces on the smoldering coals as her father had taught her years before. Almost instantly the slivers of wood ignited, and Jessie added two solid logs to the flames. When satisfied that the fire had taken hold, she pulled back the draperies in order to allow the warmth of the sun to fill the room as well.

Soon the blazing fire and the bright rays of the sun dispelled the chill. With the room adequately heated, Jessie slipped out of her nightgown and went to the small alcove where her dress and undergarments hung on wooden pegs next to the washstand. She poured water from the porcelain pitcher into the gold-rimmed basin. As she washed, she couldn't help but wonder why there were a few lovely pieces in the house, such as this washbasin and the golden candlesticks on all the mantels, yet the walls and floors were empty of any adornment. It was as though someone had begun to furnish the house, then stopped abruptly.

That thought brought to mind what she'd heard of Benjamin's ex-wife. Perhaps the woman had just begun to furnish the house when she left him.

When Jessie had first met Benjamin, she could recall wondering why a woman would leave such a handsome husband. But seeing his change of moods yesterday, she could well understand.

Vowing to stop thinking about the man, she took the linen towel from the rack to dry her face, rubbing her cheeks briskly to add some color . . .

rubbing Benjamin from her thoughts. Then, anxious to see Frannie, she dressed quickly and put on her shoes. Just as she'd started lacing them, she heard a soft rapping at the door, followed by Mrs. Cochran's voice saying, "Breakfast is ready, Mrs. McAllister."

Jessie opened the door and smiled at the woman, who once again wore a spotless white apron over her gray cotton dress.

"I'll be down in a few minutes, Mrs. Cochran. I'd like to look in on my sister and check on Maria."

"Maria's already gone off to the vineyard with her uncle, ma'am."

"The vineyard? Shouldn't she be in school?" Jessie inquired.

"All the children are out of school for nearly two weeks this time of year. Almost every able-bodied man, woman, and child helps with the picking before gettin' back to their own chores."

"I see," Jessie murmured, realizing how little she knew of life on the island. Frannie had written her about the vineyards and even about the quality of their wines, but Jessie never gave those things much thought after she'd put the letters away.

"You go ahead and see your sister. I'll keep your breakfast warm." The housekeeper smiled broadly and hurried back down the hall.

Jessie sighed, suddenly aware of the fact that Benjamin had removed Maria from the house, despite his agreement to let her take her sister and niece home today. Although, as she recalled his words, she realized he'd only agreed with her about the possibility of *Frannie* getting better in familiar surroundings. They'd never discussed

Maria. But surely he wouldn't expect her to leave the child with him.

After pinning her hair back into a knot, Jessie went to look in on her sister. It was extremely disconcerting to see Frannie lying there exactly as she had the night before. No movement, no blink of an eye or a twitch, no answering squeeze when Jessie clasped her hand.

She kissed Frannie's forehead and spoke softly to her, exactly as she would have if Frannie could hear. "I'm going downstairs and have some breakfast now. I'll bring you a cup of tea when I come back up, and we'll see if you can sip it at least."

Wonderful aromas led Jessie into the dining room. A blazing fire warmed the room, but the sight of the single place setting at the enormous table only reminded her of all the lonely breakfasts she'd had since Michael died. Jessie wished she'd wakened earlier so she could have shared breakfast with Maria . . . and Benjamin. She was a bit surprised at the disappointment she felt at his absence.

Jessie noticed the envelope on her plate as she sat. Opening it, she was pleased, yet rather astonished to find a printed note from her niece in rather neat block letters for a child so young.

Dearest Aunt Jessie,
I am pikking grapes this morning. I will see you soon.
I love you.
Maria

Mrs. Cochran smiled as she served a thick slab of ham, boiled potatoes, and eggs to Jessie, then placed a basket of freshly baked biscuits on the table. "I see you found the child's note."

"Yes, and I must admit I'm quite amazed. I had no idea a child Maria's age could print so well."

"I'm sure most six-year-olds don't," Mrs. Cochran said. "Your sister's worked with Maria from the day the child could hold pen in hand, hoping to encourage Maria to enjoy writing as much as she herself does."

Jessie nodded, remembering Frannie's long letters. "Of course, and Maria had often added a printed note of love at the bottom of Frannie's letters to me, but I had no idea she could put sentences together."

"Well, as you can see, she doesn't always spell everything correctly, but does a fair job for one so young. Now, eat your breakfast before it gets cold."

"I will," Jessie said, picking up a fork. "It looks wonderful."

"Will you be needin' anything else, Mrs. McAllister?"

"Please . . . call me Jessie."

"Oh, no, ma'am, it wouldn't be proper," the woman said, looking down at her feet. Then she raised her head and with a smile said, "But I could use Miss Jessie. I've always called your sister, Miss Fran."

"Why Fran?" Jessie asked. Since she'd always been Frannie to friends and family and Frances in public, Jessie was curious.

The housekeeper shrugged. "It's the name Mr. Benjamin always used."

I wonder what he'll call me? Jessie thought, as she turned to the breakfast Mrs. Cochran had set before her.

"You're a good cook," Jessie remarked when the

housekeeper came back later to clear the table.

"Thank you. Would you care for more coffee, ma'am . . . er, Miss Jessie?" she asked.

"Thank you, I would."

The housekeeper poured her another steaming cup, then bustled about filling a tray with used tableware and dishes.

"Mrs. Cochran, could you sit and have a cup of coffee with me?"

"Oh, I don't think so, Miss Jessie. I have my chores, you know."

"Please. I'm just a farm girl and not accustomed to sitting at such a large table—and especially not alone. I feel rather lost here."

The elderly woman's pink cheeks creased with a smile and she said, "Just a moment," as she hurried through the doorway into the kitchen. A few seconds later she returned bearing a crockery cup rather than a china one like Jessie's.

"Ahh," the housekeeper murmured as she sat to Jessie's right. "It's quite nice to get off my feet for a bit."

"Good," Jessie said, returning Mrs. Cochran's smile. "I'd like us to be friends, even though I won't be staying here very long."

"Mr. Benjamin said you'd be leaving today," Mrs. Cochran said as she poured coffee for herself. "Along with Miss Fran and Maria."

Jessie concealed her relief, secretly pleased that he'd not changed his mind about letting them go without an argument. She was especially relieved to hear Maria's name included.

"That's right. But I'd still like to know I have a friend on the island and could come to you for advice or to answer any questions I might have."

"Anytime you've a need," Mrs. Cochran said, "I'd

be delighted to try and help." She sipped her coffee, then continued. "Your sister is a fine woman and from all she's said about you, I know you are too—and a hard worker from her description."

Jessie nodded, recalling the back-breaking labor on the farm. "Thank you for your kind words and your offer of help. Perhaps you'll be able to give me some idea on how to go about getting a wagon to take my sister back home."

"Mr. Benjamin's already arranged all that, miss. He told me John Thomas would be by with his wagon around noon. He'll have Maria home by then, and John will be bringin' a friend to help carry Miss Fran down the hillside to the wagon."

"I hadn't even thought of how we'd get her down off this steep incline," Jessie remarked.

"I've found Mr. Benjamin usually thinks of everything, miss."

Jessie nodded, then remembered Maria's kitten. "Mrs. Cochran—"

"You'd do me an honor if you'd use my Christian name of Margaret."

"Of course." Jessie smiled, pleased by the woman's friendliness. "Margaret, if what you say about Mr. Benjamin is true and he thinks of everything, what was he thinking about when he took Maria's kitten away from her? The child needs—"

The housekeeper interrupted. "Mr. Benjamin did exactly what was right in this case. The animal was sickly. Samuel, whom I hope you'll soon meet, he saw the cat takin' on a raccoon not long ago, and when the poor thing started actin' like they do when they're rabid, the men did the only thing they could."

"But he didn't tell Maria that."

"No. He thought it better for her to be angry

with him for not allowin' an animal in his home, rather than suffer another loss so soon after her father."

Jessie sat, momentarily silenced by this news.

The man wasn't as heartless as she'd come to believe. These actions, and his tears last night at Frannie's bedside, reminded her much more of the man she'd met many years before. Evidently, beneath Benjamin's rough exterior did truly beat a kind and caring heart.

As Jessie thought about his cruel words from the previous day, she wondered if he had indeed been frightened that she was going to try to take Maria away from the island. She would have to show him he needn't fear anything from her. As long as Fran lived—conscious or not—Jessie would never take Maria from her home.

Jessie's brow furrowed with concern as she thought about her sister. "Margaret, what has the doctor said about Fran's condition? If she stays like that, not eating or drinking—"

"Now, don't be thinkin' the worst. We've managed to get a few sips of water and tea down her throat. We still have some time to rouse her from her stupor. With love and prayers I'm sure she'll come round."

A loud knocking reverberated down the hall, and Mrs. Cochran almost spilled her coffee as she rushed off to answer the door. A minute later, she was back. "It's Rev. Weldon's wife, ma'am. Would you like to see her in the parlor?"

"Oh, I'm so glad she came. Could you show her in here, Margaret. I'm sure she'd appreciate a cup of coffee or tea on such a chilly morning. And I'd like to repay her for her kindness to me on the ferry yesterday."

"Yes, ma'am," Mrs. Cochran said, moving out into the hall.

After the housekeeper had shown Ann Weldon in and gone off to get her some tea, Ann sat down with Jessie at the long wooden table.

"I'm so glad you came, Ann."

"I told you I'd be by to see if you needed anything, although I was a bit surprised when no one answered my knock at your sister's home."

"I understand," Jessie said. "I was quite alarmed myself."

"Well," Ann said, "I immediately realized Benjamin must have moved Frances and Maria here. And I knew you'd be well cared for. I'm sure you've found Mr. and Mrs. Cochran to be good people."

"Mrs. Cochran has been very kind, but I've yet to meet her husband."

"Samuel is a good man. If you need anything, Jessica, ask him, and I know he'll do his best for you."

"Did I hear my husband's name?" Mrs. Cochran asked as she carried in a tea tray.

"You did indeed, Margaret," Ann said. "I was telling Mrs. McAllister what a good man he is."

The housekeeper nodded, pouring tea into a china cup.

After Mrs. Cochran left the room, Ann turned to Jessie. "Is your sister improved at all?"

The question brought to mind the picture of Frannie lying upstairs staring at the ceiling with unseeing eyes, and tears sprang to Jessie's own. She shook her head, unable to speak.

"I'm sorry," Jessie murmured after a moment of silence.

"No need to apologize," Mrs. Weldon said. "I

can imagine the shock you had seeing her in such a state."

"I'm taking her back to her own home—I know it will help."

Ann Weldon nodded in approval. "I agree. Familiar surroundings can do wonders for a person. Benjamin's home . . ." She stopped herself, looking uncomfortable, then continued. "I'm sorry, I have no right to speak out of turn."

Jessie shook her head. "No, please. I believe I know exactly what you were about to say." Her eyes scanned the length of the enormous table and the stone walls surrounding them. "The place is . . . cold. There's no warmth here."

"Not only that," Ann said. "I was concerned about Maria being away from her home as well. Having lost her father, and with her mother in this condition, she needs something familiar to cling to."

"I am Maria's uncle, Mrs. Weldon . . . and quite familiar to her." Benjamin's gruff voice seemed to echo from corner to corner in the cavernous room. He walked toward them, boot heels clicking on the stone floor.

And once more he's managed to make a grand entrance, Jessie thought. She wondered if he was in the habit of eavesdropping, making his presence known at just the precise moment of his choosing.

When he got within three feet of the table he spoke again. "I have known Maria from the day of her birth, and I am, at this moment, the most *familiar* person in her life."

"Of course, Mr. Whittaker," Ann said. "I only meant the child would most likely be more comfortable in her own home with her own things around her. And as Mrs. McAllister has said, I do believe your sister-in-law might benefit from being in more familiar surroundings."

Benjamin cleared his throat and, sounding a bit more normal, said, "That is why I have arranged for her to be moved back there today."

"For her sake, I'm glad you made the decision," Ann said, then turned back to Jessie. "Could I be of any help to you, my dear?"

"Oh, yes," Jessie answered. She'd been dreading the ordeal of getting her sister prepared for the move and welcomed the offer of help.

"We appreciate your kindness, Mrs. Weldon," Benjamin said, looking straight at Jessie. "But I came home to help get Fran ready for the move."

Jessie stood, trying not to be intimidated by the dark man towering over her. "I believe I would prefer another woman to help me dress my sister, Mr. Whittaker," she said firmly, despite the trembling she felt inside.

He held her gaze for several moments, and Jessie wondered how she could ever have dreamt that this man could mean anything to her. Michael had been tender and sweet. He had never looked at her with such . . . animosity, no matter what she said or did that might have upset him.

"Where's Maria?" Jessie said in order to break the silence that bound them.

"Mr. Thomas will bring her home in an hour. He was working in the vineyards this morning and told me he would be happy to bring her back since we'll be using his wagon to take Fran home."

"You don't own a wagon?" Jessie asked, wondering why a man of his stature would need to use another man's wagon.

"I own many wagons. But they are all being

used in the vineyards and at the winery during this busy season."

Jessie felt her face color and turned away. He had put her in her place, as well she deserved this time. "Come, Ann," she said. "Let's get Frannie ready."

By the time John Thomas and his friend arrived, Ann and Jessie had dressed Frannie in warm clothes and Mrs. Cochran had packed the few things Maria had brought with her.

"Good day," the men said in unison as they came into the room.

"Good day, Mr. Thomas," Jessie answered. "It seems I'm going to owe you my thanks again for the use of your wagon."

"No need, ma'am," he answered. "I was more than pleased to give you a lift from the ferry yesterday, and I'm glad Mr. Whittaker asked me to help in taking your sister back to her home."

"John's always willing to help," Ann said. "And so is Arthur," she added, smiling at the younger man standing next to Mr. Thomas. "Jessica, may I introduce you to Arthur Conners. He also lives on East Point. His house is on Chapman Road not far from your sister's home."

"Pleased to meet you, Mrs. McAllister," the tall blond man said, nervously fingering the hat he held in his hand.

"The pleasure's mine, Mr. Conners, and I thank you for helping with my sister."

"Mrs. Whittaker's a good woman. She helped me with my children when my wife died, and I'd do anything to repay her."

Jessie felt a pang of sympathy, knowing how this young man must have felt losing his wife. But at least he had children. Jessie had had no one to comfort her when Michael died.

While the men discussed the best way to move Fran, Mrs. Cochran went to find her husband and Jessie proceeded to gather up the rest of her sister's belongings. She was bent over, packing her sister's toilet articles, when Benjamin's harsh words caused her to whirl around abruptly.

"Mr. Conners, I will not stand for your disrespectful appraisal of Mrs. McAllister. I'm sure if she'd seen you ogling her from behind, she herself would have asked you to stop."

Jessie's cheeks flamed as she glanced from Arthur Conners to Benjamin, then to the gray-haired man standing beside him.

"I apologize, sir," Arthur said. Turning to Jessie, he said softly, "I meant no disrespect, Mrs. McAllister. You are a beautiful woman, and my eyes betrayed my good manners. Please, accept my apology."

Jessie nodded, too mortified to speak.

Benjamin ignored her embarrassment. "Mr. Cochran, this is Fran's sister, Jessica McAllister."

"Pleased to meet you, ma'am," the tall, older man said, looking rather embarrassed himself.

"Mr. Cochran." Jessie offered a brief nod to acknowledge the introduction, then turned away, wishing she could dissolve into the floorboards.

As though nothing had happened, the men worked together and quickly dispatched their precious burden down the steep hillside to John Thomas's wagon, where he'd prepared a soft bed of straw and blankets. Jessie climbed in back with Frannie and they were soon on their way.

Since Ann had her husband's wagon, she followed behind with Maria and the rest of their belongings. Mrs. Cochran also insisted on going along to help get the kitchen in order and cook them a hot meal. Benjamin, however, had gone back to the vineyards without even a good-bye to Jessie.

As she rode along in silence beside Frannie, her anger at Benjamin Whittaker grew. *How dare the man embarrass me that way?* Her cheeks flamed once again with the remembrance. Then a sudden notion crept into Jessie's mind. Could Benjamin have been jealous that another man had looked at her? Jessie quickly pushed the conjecture from her mind. Benjamin Whittaker didn't give a hoot about her. There would be no reason for him to react with jealousy.

Perhaps Arthur Conners had been ogling her the way her old employer Mr. Neuman had often done. The remembrance of her obese, bald employer leering at her sent a tremor of disgust through her. If Mr. Conners had looked at her in that way, Jessie should have thanked Benjamin for his intervention.

She decided that was exactly what she would do the next time she saw him. And abruptly, she realized she could hardly wait to see Benjamin again.

The ride to Frannie's house was pleasant. Although a brisk breeze blew in from the lake, the sun shimmered brightly overhead. Jessie looked out over the water and imagined this would be a rather lovely place to spend the hot summer months. It didn't seem nearly as foreboding as it had on her first visit. Being surrounded by water had bothered her then. Perhaps, being older, she now appreciated the solitude more.

When Jessie saw the cupola of her sister's house

through the remnants of the autumn leaves, she was amazed to find herself looking forward to settling into Frannie's home. Jessie had a good feeling about bringing her sister back where she belonged.

As soon as they arrived, Arthur Conners carefully carried Frannie upstairs, while John Thomas went ahead and laid a fire in the room. Mrs. Cochran busied herself in the kitchen, building a fire in the cookstove and setting things to order there.

After the men were finished upstairs they headed outside to gather more firewood, and Maria asked if she could help them. "We have to keep Momma warm, Aunt Jessie."

"Of course, Maria. I'm sure Mr. Thomas and Mr. Conners would appreciate your help."

Ann and Jessie then settled Frannie into her own bed with layers of quilts and comforters to warm her. Just as they finished, Ann cried out, and Jessie looked up to see her staring at Frannie. Slowly Jessie turned toward her sister, unsure of what Ann had reacted to. She could hardly believe what she saw.

Frannie's bright green eyes shifted from Ann to Jessie and back again. For a moment Jessie was too stunned to react; then she quickly moved to the side of the bed and took her sister's cold hand in hers. "Frannie, it's me, Jessie. I've come to take care of you and Maria. You have to get better, Frannie. Maria needs you . . . and I miss you."

Frannie's eyes remained on her sister's as Jessie spoke, and for several moments afterward, but there was no answering movement in her hand, no words spoken. And as abruptly as the eye contact began—it ended. The brightness left her eyes, and they suddenly moved straight out and upward; her sight once more locked on the blank ceiling above.

Jessie's eyes filled with tears, and she turned to face Ann. "I didn't imagine it, did I? She saw us."

Ann reached out and clasped Jessie's hand in hers. "Praise God, your sister did indeed see us. I'm certain she did."

"She's going to be all right," Jessie murmured with relief. "I'm sure this is a good sign. She's coming back to us, Ann."

A faint smile appeared on Ann's face as she squeezed Jessie's hand reassuringly. "I pray that she is, Jessie. But let's wait before we tell Maria. We wouldn't want to build the child's hopes up too soon. It could take some time before her mother truly returns to full consciousness."

Jessie nodded, but her smile grew wider as she looked down at her sister with eyes filled with love and tears. "Please come back, dearest sister," she whispered. "Your daughter needs you . . . and so do I."

A few seconds later, Maria came running into the room squealing in delight.

"What is it, Maria?" Jessie asked, smiling at the little girl's apparent pleasure.

The child took a moment to catch her breath, then talked so fast Jessie could hardly understand her.

"He's still here. He's all right. There's nothing at all wrong with—"

"Maria, slow down. I don't understand what you're talking about."

"Peter!" she shouted. "Peter's all right." Then, with skirts flying, she was out the door and gone again.

"That's not possible," Jessie murmured as Mrs.

Cochran walked in the door smiling broadly.

"That's certainly one happy little girl," the housekeeper said.

"But . . . but Margaret, Peter can't be all right. I'm sure Mr. Whittaker indicated to me that the rabbit had died."

"True enough, miss, but he also knew the child would be inconsolable if she lost the kitten and the rabbit, so . . ." She shrugged.

"So he found another one and replaced Peter," Jessie finished. "And doesn't he think Maria might notice the difference?"

"The animal's quite a match, miss, and Maria's been away. She seems too happy to make any comparisons."

Once more Jessie found herself perplexed. The man was impossible one minute and did something exceptionally kind the next. She would have to learn to deal with this changeable nature of his if they were to have any kind of relationship . . . for Maria's sake. After all, Maria was his niece too.

The men carried in the women's satchels and sacks of food, and Mrs. Cochran fed everyone a hearty lunch before John and Arthur started back to the vineyards to continue picking grapes.

The rest of the day passed quickly as the women helped Jessie and Maria get settled.

By late afternoon, Jessie was satisfied with their progress. Fires glowed in the sitting room next to the kitchen and in two of the upstairs bedrooms. A hearty stew bubbled on the stove, a pan of biscuits had just come out of the oven, and the teakettle added warmth to the cozy kitchen with the steam curling from its spout.

Mrs. Cochran continued to empty sacks, and

Jessie finally protested. "There are only three of us, Margaret. How much food have you brought?"

"Well, ma'am, we took most of Miss Fran's perishable items up to the house when we moved her, and I'm mostly replacin' all those things . . . and addin' a few," she said with a twinkle in her bright blue eyes.

"A few?" Jessie said. "I've checked the cellar. It's filled with sacks of potatoes, apples, and carrots, and there are two smoked hams and several ropes of sausage hanging from the rafters down there. And the kitchen cupboards are brimming over with sacks of flour and sugar, and cannisters of coffee and tea and Lord knows what else."

Margaret muffled her laughter behind her hand as Jessie continued.

"And," Jessie added, "I believe there's a jug of milk on the service porch, along with a crock of butter and two blocks of cheese."

"And don't forget," Margaret said as Jessie slowed down. "There's some of Mr. Benjamin's best wine in the back of the cellar."

"Margaret, I can't imagine how we'll ever use all the food you've brought."

The housekeeper smiled broadly. "You'd be surprised how much that little one eats, and before you know it you'll have to be fattenin' up your sister."

Impulsively, Jessie hugged Margaret. "Thank you for saying that."

"Only sayin' what you're hoping for, miss."

"I have more hope today than I did yesterday."

"Well, you should. Mrs. Weldon told me about Miss Fran lookin' right at you both. It's a good sign."

Ann poked her head in the kitchen. "Do you want to go upstairs with me and show me where to put the rest of Frannie's things?"

"Of course. I believe Margaret has the kitchen well tended to."

Jessie helped Ann unpack Frannie's clothing and personal things and put her sister's bedroom in order. Then, while Ann finished up in Frannie's room, Jessie took her own things into Maria's room and unpacked. Earlier, she and Maria had decided the two of them would share a room for the time being so they wouldn't have as many fires to tend.

Maria came in just as Jessie finished emptying her bags. "It's going to be fun sharing a room with you, Aunt Jessie," she said.

Ann came in as the child spoke and smiled at her, then taking Jessie aside, she asked, "Are you sure there's enough room for two of you in that bed?"

"It'll be fine, Ann. She is, after all, only a small child."

"Besides," she added, as Maria skipped over to stand beside her, "I'll be spending most of my time sitting with Frannie."

"And I can sit with Momma too," Maria added.

Jessie marveled at how grown up the child was for her short six years of life. "Of course you can. I'll need you to do that when I'm getting meals ready or running errands."

"There's no reason for you to leave the house to run errands," Ann said. "Anytime you need help, I can send my older son James over. Maria can easily walk to our house and fetch him. Please don't hesitate to ask."

"Thank you so much, Ann. I'm truly glad we

met. I feel as though you've been my friend much longer than two days."

Ann took Jessie's hand in hers. "I'm glad too. I think you'll need a friend here."

"That she will," said Mrs. Cochran, who had just come in with a tea tray. "And she has another right here in me."

Jessie looked from the chubby blonde woman to the thin gray-haired housekeeper. "I'm very fortunate to call you both friends."

Mrs. Cochran looked a bit flustered, then quickly composed herself, as she usually did, by rubbing her hands on her apron.

"By the way, Miss Jessie," she said, "I forgot to tell you. Mr. Benjamin brought a mare for you and a pony for Maria to use."

"Is he still here?" Jessie asked, hoping her rapidly beating heart would not betray her excitement at the thought of seeing him.

"No, ma'am. He just left the horses and went back to the vineyard. But he did say if you needed any instruction in riding, he would provide someone for that as well."

Jessie tried to hide her disappointment that Benjamin had not come in to see her. She quickly pasted on a smile and said, "You may inform Mr. Benjamin that I am quite capable at handling a horse . . . and thank him for his thoughtfulness." Perhaps she'd get to show off—or show up—Benjamin sometime in the future.

An hour later, despite Ann's objections, Jessie insisted both she and Mrs. Cochran get back to their homes before dark.

"Maria and I will be perfectly fine. The house is warm, Mrs. Cochran has prepared enough food for days, and I am confident that Frannie is already progressing. You've both been so kind, but I'm sure your family is waiting for you, Ann. And I'm sure Mr. Benjamin is looking for his supper, Margaret," Jessie added.

"I left instructions with Samuel for their evening meal, Miss Jessie. I could stay till morning if you'd like."

"No, please. I thank you both for your kind offer, but I think Maria and I should be alone with Frannie tonight. Perhaps if we sit and talk to her we'll prod her once again from this stupor."

After the two women left, Jessie and Maria had a light supper in Frannie's bedroom. Maria carried the dirty dishes downstairs and when she came back, Jessie asked the child to sit with her mother for a few minutes.

Maria started forward eagerly, then suddenly glanced at her mother's face and seemed hesitant. Jessie had never given a thought to the fact that Maria might be frightened by her mother's appearance. She opened her arms and Maria ran to her. "Sweetheart, there's no reason for you to be frightened. Your momma is resting from her injuries. I know it's strange to see her with her eyes open like—"

"No, Aunt Jessie," Maria interrupted. "I wasn't afraid of Momma's eyes being open." The child hesitated, then leaned against her aunt and whispered, "Her eyes are closed."

Chapter Four

Jessie's head whipped toward the bed. Indeed Frannie's eyes were closed. Dear God, Jessie thought, don't let her be dead.

"Maria, sweetheart," Jessie said as calmly as possible, "Would you go downstairs and get your momma a glass of milk? Mrs. Cochran left a crock out on the service porch."

"But—"

"Please," Jessie said trying not to panic. "I think she might be thirsty."

Maria nodded and started for the door, pausing once to look back at her mother. "Is she all right, Aunt Jessie?"

"Of course, and she'll feel better when she has a nice soothing sip of milk."

As soon as Maria shut the door behind her, Jessie rushed to her sister's side. "Frannie . . . Frannie, are you all right? Can you hear me?"

No movement, no sound. Jessie leaned closer, and was relieved to feel the breath coming from her sister's nose. She then put her ear to Frannie's chest and heard the steady pounding of her heart.

"Thank God," she whispered. "Thank God."

Maria came back with a glass of milk, carefully carrying it to the bedside table.

Jessie put a finger to her lips and smiled. "Your momma is sleeping, sweetheart. We'll just leave the milk here in case she wakes up."

Maria looked from her mother to Jessie with solemn eyes. "Do you really think she'll wake up, Aunt Jessie?"

"I believe it with all my heart. I think her eyes being closed is a good sign. It means she's truly resting and once rested, she will wake up and I think the first words she'll say are, 'Where's my little girl?' "

Jessie's words brought the hint of a smile to the girl's lips. "I'd like that." Maria moved closer to the bed. After studying her mother's face for several seconds she turned back to Jessie and whispered, "She is sleeping. Maybe if I pray really hard tonight she'll wake up in the morning just like always."

"We'll both pray. But Maria, you must be patient. If she doesn't wake in the morning she may just need more rest."

Maria nodded her head somberly. "I understand."

"Will you stay here with your mother while I go in and change?"

"All right. I like knowing Momma's sleeping. I'll stay here till you come back." The little girl slid up onto the rocking chair Jessie had been sitting in.

When Jessie went back a few minutes later, Maria was sitting exactly as she'd left her. As Jessie approached the bed, the child hopped down from the rocker and hugged her aunt.

"Good night, Aunt Jessie."

"Good night, Maria."

Then the child walked up to the side of the bed and gently patted her mother's hand. "Good night, Momma."

"I'll be in soon to tuck you in," Jessie said.

"I can tuck myself in, Aunt Jessie. I did at Uncle Ben's, unless Mrs. Cochran wasn't busy, then she'd do it."

"Well, this isn't Uncle Ben's, this is home, and I will come and tuck you in. You go ahead and say your prayers and by the time you're finished I'll be there."

Jessie watched the little girl leave the room.

She was opposed to listening to the child's prayers, just as her father had been with her. "Whatever you say's between you and God," he'd told Jessie when she'd asked why he never listened to her prayers. And only as an adult did she understand how right he was.

Ten minutes later, Jessie leaned over and listened to her sister's regular, even breathing, then went to check on Maria.

The little girl was still kneeling beside her bed as Jessie opened the door. ". . . and bless Uncle Ben too 'cause he loves me and Momma even though he doesn't love kittens. Amen."

Jessie's heart lurched at the child's words. If only she knew how much her uncle loved her, taking the blame for the kitten in order to protect her, and replacing the rabbit to shield her from more hurt. Although Jessie had never seen the man hug or kiss the child, she had no doubt that Benjamin

Whittaker did indeed love his niece.

"It's about time you got some sleep, young lady," Jessie said as she neared the bed.

As if to reinforce her aunt's words, Maria yawned.

Jessie leaned down and kissed the child's soft cheek. "You must get a good night's sleep so you can help me take care of your mother tomorrow, all right?"

"But I have to pick grapes in the morning, Aunt Jessie."

"I don't think you have to go tomorrow. I'm sure your Uncle Ben will let you have one day off."

"But we all have to do our share. Momma told me that when she went . . ." Maria stopped suddenly, her eyes wide.

"When she went where, sweetheart?" Jessie asked as she sat on the side of the bed.

"I'm not supposed to tell. It was a secret. Only Poppa, Momma, and Uncle Ben knew."

"Your mother told you the night she went out on the boat, didn't she?" Jessie probed gently.

"Uh-huh. But the storm came so fast and . . . and Uncle Ben said Poppa couldn't keep the boat on course. Everybody said I was lucky that Momma was still with us. And they all wondered why she went out on the boat with Poppa. But I didn't tell."

"Why was your momma on the boat, sweetheart?"

Maria looked down at her hands, folded in her lap, then back up at her aunt.

"I don't know if I should tell you."

"Maria, I know you made a promise, but your poppa was Uncle Ben's brother and your uncle knows the secret, and I'm your momma's sister, so it's all right for me to know the secret too. I promise I won't tell a soul."

Maria's forehead crinkled up as she gave Jessie's words some thought. Then she smiled and said, "I think it's all right for you to know.

"Poppa and Uncle Ben had to go to the mainland. They said it was . . .'perative."

"Imperative," Jessie corrected with a smile.

"Uh-huh. Poppa said that meant it was very important. When Momma heard them planning the trip, she told them they couldn't both leave the winery . . . this is such a busy time of year, you know, Aunt Jessie."

"I know, sweetheart."

"So Momma offered to go in Uncle Ben's place. That's when she told me we all had to do our part." Maria's lips curled upward in a half smile. "I remember Poppa and Uncle Ben were pleased with her suggestion. They said a beautiful woman could probably sell more wine than either of them."

Maria's smile faded as other thoughts evidently replaced that happy moment in the child's mind. "Mrs. Cochran came and stayed with me," she continued. "She was still here when Uncle Ben came to tell me about . . . Poppa."

Maria's eyes filled with tears, and Jessie pulled her close. "Don't cry, sweetheart. I'm glad you told me the secret, but I didn't mean to make you cry."

Jessie sat and held Maria for several minutes, rocking her until she felt the child finally relax in her arms.

She kissed her forehead, then laid her back on the pillow. Maria's eyes blinked open once, and then closed as she sighed deeply.

"Good night, sweet angel," Jessie whispered.

"Sleep well." She pulled the quilts up and watched her niece settle into sleep.

Observing the peacefulness on the child's face as she slept, Jessie marveled at how much she'd grown to love Maria in so short a time.

If only God would answer her prayer; if only Frannie would wake up in the morning. It wouldn't bring Maria's father back, but at least the child would have her mother to help her through her loss.

Jessie turned the lamp down low, then went back in to check on her sister. Frannie still seemed to be resting quietly, so Jessie went downstairs to make sure the doors were securely shut. She remembered Mrs. Cochran telling her to lock up before retiring, but it seemed so strange as they'd never locked the doors on the farmhouse.

It seemed even stranger to do so here on this small island, but she thought it must be a good idea if her new friend Margaret suggested it. So she slid the latch on the front door and the back door, and made sure all the windows were shut securely and latched as well.

Jessie banked the cookstove and sitting room fires for the night, then extinguished the kitchen and hall lamps before going upstairs. It had been a long day and she suddenly found herself quite tired.

She looked in on her sister once more before retiring for the night. She thought it might be easier to sleep tonight, here in Frannie's home, without Benjamin's presence to disturb her. Jessie climbed into bed alongside Maria and turned the lamp down until the flame was extinguished.

The last thing she remembered was how terribly dark it was, even though there were only lace curtains at the windows. Not even a sliver of moonlight cut through the black sky.

The ship's mast was outlined by brightly flashing bolts of lightning as it rocked violently back and forth in the lake. Waves crashed over the sides of the ship as Jonathan vainly tried to grip the wheel, which spun wildly out of his control.

Thunder crashed so fiercely overhead that the very planks of the ship reverberated with each boom from the sky.

Another lightning bolt flashed and in its light, Frannie stood, her long, white nightgown billowing around her in the raging storm, her arms outstretched as though reaching for Jonathan.

Then Jonathan gave up the battle. He released the wheel and tenderly took Frannie in his arms.

"Aunt Jessie, Aunt Jessie wake up. Please wake up."

Maria's voice pulled Jessie from her nightmare, but when she opened her eyes the storm of her dreams still raged outside the windows. Thunderbolts crashed one after another, shaking the very foundation of the house.

Maria's little arms were wrapped firmly around Jessie's waist, and her head was burrowed beneath Jessie's breast.

"Maria, sweetheart, it's only a storm. We're safe here in the house. Don't cry, my sweet." Jessie stroked the girl's soft curls reassuringly, as much to comfort herself as the child. The image of Jonathan taking Frannie in his arms was still with Jessie, and she found it unsettling. She didn't especially believe in premonitions, but the dream had disturbing connotations.

"Maria, I must look in on your mother."

"Don't leave me, Aunt Jessie, please don't leave me."

"I have to see if your momma's all right. If you don't want to stay in bed, come with me."

The child never let go of Jessie's long flannel gown. Jessie lit the lamp, then moved slowly toward the door with Maria right on her heel.

As Jessie opened the door to Frannie's room a monstrous bolt of lightning lit the entire room and a fierce clap of thunder shook the house. Maria whimpered and clutched Jessie's nightgown.

The repetitious flashes of lightning marched across the darkened room, giving Frannie the eerie appearance of movement. Jessie had to blink twice before she could be certain it was only an illusion.

Still holding Maria's hand, Jessie made sure her sister was breathing. Slowly, she released a breath she hadn't been aware of holding. The nightmare had been just that—a nightmare—nothing to do with reality. She'd merely incorporated the storm into her dream along with two people she loved dearly. Remembering Maria's arms around her when she'd awakened, she realized she'd put that movement into her dream as well when Jonathan had put his arms around Frannie.

Jessie pulled the rocking chair close beside the bed and lifted Maria into the chair. "I want you to sit here and hold your momma's hand so she won't be afraid. Do you think you can do that for me?"

Maria nodded, a look of determination on her face. But when another bolt crashed into the lake beyond the windows, the child flinched. "Where are you going, Aunt Jessie?"

"I'm just going to check the doors and windows. There seems to be a draft coming from somewhere and I want to make sure the rain isn't blowing in."

Rain pelted the bedroom windows so violently, Jessie wondered if the waves themselves had reached the house. She went and looked outside. The waves were breaking up and over the rocks, crashing onto the roadway below. The fury of the storm was frightening. She went back and gave Maria a hug, noticing the child still clasped her mother's hand in hers.

"That's a good girl. You take care of your momma until I come back upstairs, all right?"

Again, the child nodded, but her eyes were wide with fright, and Jessie wasn't sure if she should leave her there.

A rhythmic banging caught Jessie's attention. It was a different sound from the crashing and rumbling of thunder and the roaring of the sea. Then another sound joined the banging. It sounded almost like . . . it was . . . someone was calling her name.

"Maria, someone's at the door."

"Don't go, Aunt Jessie. Please don't leave me and Momma."

"Your mother's asleep. Come." Jessie reached down and gathered the trembling child into her arms.

There was no need to carry the lamp as the lightning was so ferocious the illumination from it was almost constant.

Jessie moved cautiously down the stairs, keeping a tight grip on her niece.

A looming shadow was outlined behind the glass of the front door by bright flashes of lightning, and if Jessie hadn't immediately recognized the voice, the image would have frightened her. Silently she thanked God that Benjamin had come.

She slid open the latch and moved back immediately as the wind and rain battered the open door. Benjamin strained against the ferocity of the storm to close the door and slide the latch back into place. Then he leaned back against the door for a moment, rain dripping onto the carpet and running along the floorboards.

He seemed to be taking long, gulping breaths of air, until at last he pulled off his rain-soaked hat and coat and looked directly into Jessie's eyes. For a brief moment she thought he was going to put his arm around her, but instead he took Maria's hand in his. "Are you all right, Maria?"

The little girl nodded as she appraised him with solemn eyes. "You shouldn't be out in such a terrible storm, Uncle Ben," she admonished. "You could catch an awful cold."

As suddenly as a clap of thunder, Benjamin leaned his head back and began to laugh. The laughter just bubbled up out of him like a pot boiling over, and Jessie found herself smiling. Slowly he wound down to a soft chuckle, and Maria added, "It's not funny, Uncle Ben."

"You are right, my little one. I should not have been out in the storm. But, I was worried about you . . . and your aunt." Again he sought Jessie's eyes, and in the next flash of light Jessie felt certain she saw a look of affection there.

"How are you?" he asked softly.

"Fine. We're all fine. Maria was a little frightened, but together we calmed each other. And

Frannie is sleeping . . . really sleeping, with her eyes closed."

"Her eyes are closed?"

Jessie nodded.

"May I see her? I've gotten so used to her being at the house, I find myself missing her terribly."

"Why don't you get out of those wet things first. I'm sure there's something upstairs you could wear. The coals in the sitting room fireplace should still be hot. Go and put on some logs and I'll get dry clothing for you."

Jessie started toward the stairs with Maria still in her arms, but the little girl tugged at her sleeve. "Could I stay down here with Uncle Ben?"

Glancing down the hall, Jessie saw Benjamin blink several times. Then he nodded and held out his arms. Jessie set Maria down and she ran to Benjamin, her bare feet padding on the carpet.

He scooped her up in his arms and she squealed, "Put me down, Uncle Ben, you're all wet."

Jessie saw him hesitate, holding her close for another moment before setting her down and taking her small hand in his. It was the closest thing to love this man had displayed since Jessie had arrived, and it warmed her heart to witness it.

After Benjamin had dressed in the dry clothes Jessie brought him from Jonathan's closet, he again asked to see Fran.

"Of course," Jessie said. "Why don't you carry Maria up to her bed on your way?" The child had fallen asleep on the sofa in the sitting room, and now that the thunder rolled slowly off in the distance, Jessie thought she would be able to sleep through the night.

Jessie walked into Fran's room behind Benjamin, and watched as he went down on one knee beside the bed in order to see Fran's face.

"How long has she been . . . sleeping?"

"Since shortly after sundown." Jessie sat in the rocking chair near the bed, which put her at Benjamin's level.

"Benjamin, there's something else you should know. When Ann and I got Frannie into bed this afternoon . . . she . . . she looked at us. Her eyes moved from my face to Ann's and back again. It was astonishing, and I believe that movement and her closing her eyes this evening are good signs for recovery."

Benjamin leaned his head on his hands on the edge of the bed and murmured, "You were right." Then, still on his knees, he lifted his head and turned toward Jessie. "And if that's true and Fran needed to be here to get well, I delayed her recovery by moving her. God knows what might have happened if you hadn't come."

When Jessie saw the tears in his eyes, her heart ached for him. She couldn't help but reach out to console him, her hand cupping his cheek.

He took her hand in both of his and kissed it tenderly.

She watched with fascination as his large, rough hands dwarfed her slender one, and she almost flinched as the heat from his lips seared her skin like a hot branding iron.

"Thank you for coming, dear Jessica. I thank you for Fran's sake and for Maria's." With those words he released her hand and turned back to Fran.

Jessie sat, staring at the back of his head, astonished by her strong reaction to his touch. She could not pull her eyes away from him as he continued to kneel beside her sister's bed. His coal-black hair, still damp from the rain, curled along the collar of his brother's white shirt, and his broad shoulders, obviously wider than Jonathan's, strained the fabric. His hands now held Frannie's, but Jessie could still feel the warmth of his rough yet tender touch.

As she sat, her eyes absorbing every detail, she recalled the words he'd just spoken. He'd called her "dear Jessica," but his thanks had been for Fran and Maria's sake. He'd said not a word with regard to how he felt about her coming.

Aren't you glad I've come? Jessie silently wondered.

Then she touched her hand, still warm from his kiss, and wondered if she might feel the heat of his lips there forever.

Chapter Five

As Benjamin looked down at his sister-in-law he prayed for her recovery. He wanted her to be well again, for Maria's sake and for his own.

He bore so much guilt for what had happened to Jonathan and Fran.

"I should never have let them go on that trip, especially not Fran," Benjamin murmured.

Not wanting to give away Maria's confidence, Jessie pretended curiosity. "Why did they go?"

"Jonathan and I both felt it was necessary to talk to the restaurateurs on the mainland who've been persuaded to buy the new winery's product because it's cheaper. We felt if they compared the wines they would see we had the superior product." Benjamin shook his head sadly. "But Fran shouldn't have been on the boat," he said. "I shouldn't have listened to her. I shouldn't have stayed here on the island."

"Why did Fran want to go? I'd always believed, from what she wrote me, that she preferred staying on the island."

"She did. She rarely went to the mainland. But this time she insisted that I was needed here to supervise the picking and pressing." He smiled ruefully. "She said she wanted to help, that everyone had to do their share. And now here she is, without her husband, her health in jeopardy, and I'm to blame."

Pleased that Benjamin was finally confiding in her, Jessica wanted to help alleviate his guilt. "No, Benjamin," she said. "It's not your fault. Fran wanted to help, to do her share. I know my sister. Once she made up her mind to go, you could not have dissuaded her."

"You're probably right, but I still wish it had been me on the boat instead of Fran."

"You musn't talk this way. Everything happens for a reason, Benjamin," she said, putting a comforting hand on his shoulder. "If it were you in this bed, who would be running the winery right now? You must accept what's happened and go on from here, no matter how deep your sense of loss."

He knew she spoke the truth for she too had suffered loss. Her words, no doubt, came from her own experience in dealing with sorrow.

Benjamin sighed and placed Fran's hand gently back at her side. When he turned to face Jessica, her gaze met his head on. For a moment he was lost in the clear blue-green depths of her eyes, but presently he found his voice.

"I'm grateful that you've come to care for your sister and Maria. And I would like to apologize for my behavior upon your arrival."

"There's no need for your apology. I understand

that grief affects us each in different ways. I know it was your sorrow that caused you to be so abrupt with me."

"Abrupt is hardly the word for my ill manners. Please, accept my apology." And with those words he again took her hand in his own.

"Of course, I accept."

For several silent seconds they held each other's gaze, and Jessie's hand grew hot in his large palm. When the intensity was almost too much to bear, she cleared her throat, stood, and pulled her hand from his. "We should get some sleep," she said. "It's very late."

Benjamin smiled up at her for a brief moment, then stood himself. "Yes, we should," he repeated, even then knowing that thoughts of Jessica McAllister would most likely keep him awake yet another night.

After Jessie saw that Benjamin had a blanket and pillow, she left him in the downstairs sitting room, where he'd decided to sleep.

"It's always been my favorite room," he said. "Frannie made it a place where anyone could sit and talk and feel comfortable."

Jessie agreed that it was indeed a pleasant room, yet the furnishings did not lend themselves to sleeping. There was a low divan in the corner, a padded rocking chair near the fireplace, and two easy chairs near a large table which was used for many activities, including sewing and writing. None of these seemed suitable for overnight accommodations.

But Benjamin assured her that if he had a problem sleeping on the divan, he would stretch out on the carpet in front of the fire.

Later, as Jessie tried to get to sleep, she kept

hearing his voice in her head. There'd been no reason for his words to affect her as they had. But his eyes and lips, as he'd spoken, had somehow stirred her even more than his touch.

"I'll be fine," he'd said, his deep brown eyes piercing hers. Then, trying to pull away from his gaze, Jessie had lowered her eyes and found herself focused instead on his full, sensuous lips as he'd drawn-out his next words. "But if I should have a problem sleeping on the divan, I'll just . . . stretch out . . . on the carpet . . . in front of the fireplace."

With each pause, Jessie's pulse grew more rapid as she'd pictured the movement he described.

And an hour later, as the grandfather clock in the upper hall struck three, the image of Benjamin stretching out on the floor in front of the fire still stirred a flame deep within Jessie.

"Aunt Jessie, Aunt Jessie, hurry, Momma's awake!"

Maria's voice jarred Jessie from a deep sleep. She tried to think, but the child was bouncing on the bed and she had to sit up quickly.

She recalled the clock striking four, so sleep had evidently come between then and dawn, which was just now breaking with a brilliant pink glow outside her window.

"Maria, calm down. You know your mother's eyes open and close now, so you mustn't get excited by each movement."

Maria was pulling on Jessie's hand as she shouted, "No, it's not just her eyes. Momma's awake—she talked to me. She told me to come and get you."

Jessie was stunned, but recovered in an instant

and immediately raced with Maria out of their room and across the hall into Frannie's.

Frannie was indeed awake, and managed a weak smile when Jessie came through the door.

"Thank God!" Jessie cried as she ran to her sister's side. She kissed Frannie's cheek gently and as she leaned close, felt her own tears mingle with her sister's.

"Oh, Frannie," she said, raising her head to look into her sister's eyes. "Don't cry. Everything's going to be all right now. You're going to be just fine, I know it."

Jessie took her sister's hand, and Frannie squeezed it in return. Jessie's heart swelled with joy—she'd waited so long for that answering movement.

Maria was up on the other side of the bed, curled against her mother, with one small arm around Frannie's waist.

Frannie turned her head toward her daughter and kissed the top of her head. "Maria, could you . . . get . . . me . . . a drink?" Each whispered word seemed a struggle for Frannie to say.

"Hush, Frannie," Jessie said. "Try and rest. Don't talk. I'll go and make you some tea."

"There's the milk I brought you last night, Momma," Maria said pointing to the bedside table.

Frannie clutched Jessie's hand as she shook her head slowly. "Want . . . water."

"I'll get it," Jessie said, and started to move away. But Frannie held tight to her hand.

"No. Stay. Maria . . ."

"I'll go, Momma." Maria slid off the bed and was gone in a second.

"Oh, Frannie," Jessie said, as she fought to keep

the tears from falling once again. "I'm so happy to see you awake. We've been so worried. And Maria has been so patient, waiting for you to return to us."

Frannie's eyes began to droop, then fluttered open again. Her head moved weakly back and forth on the pillow, and Jessie couldn't help but notice how dull her sister's usually bright green eyes looked. "No . . . Jess," she whispered.

Jessie sat on the bed beside her, moving closer to hear what she said. "What do you mean . . . no?"

"Not good. I . . . hurt, Jess."

"It'll be all right. I'll send for the doctor. Benjamin's here—he can go and get him."

"No . . ." Frannie whispered hoarsely. "Listen to me . . . please, Jess."

"All right. I'm listening. But take your time. You've been through so much. You need your rest."

Frannie sighed deeply, a rasping sound that made Jessie recall her husband Michael's last breaths. Fear clutched Jessie's heart in an icy grip.

"You should try not to talk, Frannie. I'll send for the doctor. He may be able to help."

Frannie shook her head slowly. "No time . . . want to tell you . . ." She swallowed and her eyes closed again.

Jessie tightened her grip on her sister's slender fingers. "Frannie?"

The green eyes opened again and Frannie spoke a little more firmly. "Jess . . . I want you . . . to promise that you'll take care of . . . Maria. She needs you, Jess. You have . . . to promise . . ."

"Shh," Jessie whispered, putting a finger to her sister's cold lips. "No need to waste your breath saying such things. I'm here. I'll not leave as long as you or Maria need me."

As Jessie watched, a solitary tear spilled from Frannie's eye and traced a wet streak down her pale cheek.

"Don't cry," Jessie said, wiping the tear from her sister's cheek. "I love Maria almost as much as I love you—and you know how dear you are to me."

Frannie gave an almost imperceptible nod of her head. "Will you stay here . . . after . . . after I'm . . . gone?" Frannie asked.

Again, Jessie felt an icy twist inside. "You are not going anywhere, sister," she said, forcing a smile.

"Promise me . . . Jess . . . please."

"I'll stay here forever if Maria needs me, but I don't want you talking foolishly. You're better now and you're going to continue to improve."

"I'm . . . so . . . cold." As if to emphasize the fact, a chill ran strongly through Frannie's body. Jessie felt it in her own fingers, which still gripped her sister's hand.

"Let me get some wood on this fire," Jessie said, and started to stand.

"No," Frannie said, holding onto Jessie with more strength than Jessie thought she had in her.

"But you're so cold. I need to make the room warmer for you."

"Ben . . . he'll take care . . ."

At the moment his name was mentioned, the door opened and Jessie heard Maria's voice. "See, I told you she was awake, Uncle Ben."

Maria moved much more quickly than her uncle, who seemed stunned to see his sister-in-law looking at him.

"Here's your water, Momma."

Jessie took the glass and helped Frannie take a sip.

"Fran?" Benjamin's voice was tentative as he approached the bed. Jessie moved back a step so he could move closer, and watched as he leaned forward and kissed both of Fran's cheeks. "Dear sister, thank God you've come back to us."

He glanced at Jessie, and she could see the warm look of affection in his eyes before he turned back to Frannie again, smiling. "It was Jessica who insisted you be brought back here to your own bed. She said you'd get well if you were at home."

Frannie nodded weakly. "Glad . . . to be home."

"Benjamin," Jessie said, touching his arm. "Frannie's cold. If you could fix the fire, I'll go and make some tea to warm her inside as well."

"Of course," he said. But she saw him glance downward, and instantly became uncomfortably aware of her bare feet peeking out from beneath the ruffled bottom of her nightgown—under which she wore nothing.

She'd jumped up so quickly, she hadn't even pulled on her robe. Suddenly anxious to be out of Benjamin's scrutinizing gaze, she made her escape. "Come, Maria, you can help me with the tea tray," Jessie said, giving Benjamin the opportunity of a moment alone with Fran, and giving herself time to put on a robe and slippers.

Benjamin was already at the fireplace when Jessie and Maria left the room.

Jessie saw Benjamin and her sister exchange yet another warm glance before she closed the door. Once again it was obvious that Benjamin cared deeply for Frannie, and from the fond look in her sister's gaze she could see the feeling was reciprocated.

She quickly made her way across the hall to get her robe and slippers before going down to make tea.

Benjamin added kindling to coax flames from the red-hot coals in the grate, then stacked on logs and turned back to Fran's bed.

"There. You'll be warmer in a minute," he said as he sat gently beside her. He took her hand in his. "My dearest Fran. I've missed you."

Fran blinked her eyes, and Benjamin could see her struggle to keep them open.

"Perhaps you should try and rest," he said, standing.

But Fran grasped his hand and he immediately sat back down. "I don't want to tire you," he said softly.

Her dark hair accentuated the pallor of her usually rosy complexion, and Benjamin couldn't help but notice how deathly cold her hand was, as were her cheeks when he'd kissed her.

"Dear Ben, you . . . have been . . . like the brother . . . I never had."

Benjamin patted her hand and smiled. "And you like a sister."

Her eyes closed again, but Fran continued to speak in a hoarse whisper. "You must . . . care for . . ."

"Of course. You don't even have to say it," Benjamin said, squeezing her hand to reassure her.

And once more a whispered plea. "Help her . . ."

"I will," Benjamin interjected, trying to keep her struggle to speak at a minimum. "I promise you, Fran. Maria will be well cared for always."

Frances could feel consciousness ebbing away again, but she fought against it. She had to make Ben understand that she wanted him to help Jess care for Maria.

She hoped he understood. It was important for Maria to live in her own home with Jess caring for her. Jess was the only person Fran would ever trust to raise her daughter.

And she prayed that Ben would be a brother to Jess as she raised Maria without her parents.

It seems so strange, she thought. To think of death so calmly. For despite her brief return to consciousness, she was certain that death was near at hand.

Maria opened the door to her mother's room so Jessie could carry in the tea tray. But Benjamin hurried over to intercept them. "She's asleep," he whispered. "I think she needs sleep more than tea right now."

Jessie nodded and turned back into the hall. "Maria," she whispered, "could you sit very quietly next to your mother while your uncle and I have a cup of tea?" Jessie felt the need of something in her queasy stomach. "We'll just be across the hall in your room so you can call us if your mother wakes up, all right?"

The child nodded, her dark eyes serious. "I'll be quiet as a mouse," she whispered. "And I promise I'll call you the minute Momma wakes up."

Jessie went across the hall with Benjamin following. And although she knew it would do Maria some good to have a few minutes alone with her mother, Jessie was a bit concerned about being in the bedroom with Benjamin while still in her nightclothes. Yet she knew they had to be nearby when Frannie awakened.

Benjamin reached around and opened the door for her, then took the tray and set it on the small table in front of the windows. He pulled over two chairs from near the fireplace, and when they were seated Jessie picked up the teapot.

"Would you rather have coffee, Benjamin? I could go down and—"

"No. Tea's fine."

Jessica started to pour, and Benjamin saw her hand trembling. Gently he took the teapot from her hand. "Let me," he said, quickly filling two of the cups. "You've been under a strain ever since you learned of the accident, Jessica. This trembling in your body is most likely a reaction to the relief you feel now that you know your sister's going to be all right."

Jessica didn't answer, but appeared deep in thought. She sipped her tea, and Benjamin couldn't help but notice how her long hair glistened in the early morning sunlight. Her hair was still tousled from her night's sleep and gave her an endearing childlike appearance.

Speaking to her sister had obviously moved her deeply, and he wished he could take her in his arms and still her trembling. But since they were in her bedroom, he thought it best to keep his distance. As he looked out the window, he wished Jessica could find some comfort in the rhythmical movement of the waves surrounding the island.

She seemed so far away despite the fact that she sat across from him. Benjamin needed to bring her back from wherever her mind had wandered.

"You were right in bringing her home, Jessica."

Jessie nodded, but couldn't help thinking of the brief conversation she'd had with her sister.

"Did you notice how terribly cold she was, Benjamin?"

"I'm sure it's just the result of being so still for such a long time," he answered. "When she awakens again, I'll rub her hands and feet and try to get her circulation improved."

"That's a good suggestion," Jessie said, feeling better about the thought of actually doing something to help Frannie.

Jessie set her teacup down, and noticed Benjamin's eyes focused on the lake beyond the window glass. From what he'd said, she knew he thought Frannie was going to be all right. She had to say something or he'd be unprepared.

"I'm afraid," she said.

"Of what?" he asked.

She shook her head, and her hair moved in soft ripples down her back.

"Something's terribly wrong with Frannie," she said.

"But she was conscious," Benjamin said. "She spoke coherently. She—"

Jessie interrupted. "She's so terribly cold and her eyes are dull . . . and . . . she sounded so . . . strange."

Reaching across the wicker table, Benjamin took Jessica's hands in his. "Fran's been unconscious for nearly a week. She's lost her husband. She's bound to have problems stemming from that."

"That's not it," Jessie said, shaking her head again. "And she never did ask about Jonathan."

"I'm sure she knows," Benjamin said.

Jessica slipped her hands from his, and Benjamin was aware of an electrifying sensation as her fingers brushed his palms.

He watched as she slowly raised her teacup to her soft, pink lips and sipped from it. After setting her cup down again, Jessica said, "I think the doctor should see Frannie."

Benjamin nodded. "Of course. I'll ride out to Dr. Rittman's and bring him back." Benjamin could see how deeply disturbed Jessica was about her sister's condition. "Especially if it will ease your mind," he added as he stood.

"Yes, it will. I hope and pray I'm wrong, for Maria's sake. I don't want to think about the child losing both her parents."

"Then don't think it," Benjamin said. "It would be too unfair, and so terribly painful for Maria."

He started for the door, but Jessica called out, "Benjamin, would you like breakfast before you go?"

"No. The tea was fine."

"I'll have breakfast ready when you return with the doctor then."

He shook his head. "No. You stay up here with Fran. I'll take care of breakfast when I get back." Then he turned and was gone.

Jessie went back into her sister's room. Maria sat next to her mother as still as a statue.

"Has she wakened at all, sweetheart?" Jessie whispered.

Maria shook her head.

Jessie bent and kissed Maria's forehead. "Would you like some breakfast, angel?" she whispered.

"I'm not hungry, Aunt Jessie," she whispered in return.

Frannie's voice startled Jessie. "You . . . don't have . . . to whisper," she said hoarsely. Then she cleared her throat and her next words seemed less strained. "Water, please?"

Jessie held the cup to her lips, and Frannie took several sips.

"Would you like some nice, hot tea, Frannie?" Jessie asked.

Frannie seemed to have trouble focusing her eyes, and finally closed them, but she nodded her head.

"Tea . . . would be nice."

"Maria, you stay here with your mother and I'll be right back."

Jessica quickly moved across the hall, and although the tea was not as hot as it had been, she decided against getting a fresh pot. Frannie needed some sustenance right now. Jessie poured a cup and added twice the amount of sugar Frannie would normally put in her tea, hoping it would give her some strength.

A minute later, she was helping her sister lean forward to sip the warm brew.

"Oh . . . that tastes wonderful, Jess."

Frannie's voice seemed a bit stronger. Perhaps the tea is helping, Jessie thought.

She continued to help her sister until Frannie had drunk the last drop. "Frannie would you like more? Or perhaps a piece of buttered bread? Or a boiled egg?"

Jessie felt the gentle touch of her sister's hand patting hers. "Sit down, Jess. Please. I don't . . . believe I could swallow food right now. But the tea . . . the tea . . . was wonderful."

For a moment Frannie closed her eyes, and Jessie was afraid to move, unwilling to disturb her rest. But her sister's eyes opened again only seconds later.

"Maria . . . come . . . sit here . . . next to me . . . and your Aunt Jessie."

The little girl got up on the bed between Jessie and her mother and snuggled up against her, resting her head near Frannie's shoulder.

Jessie watched as Frannie took the child's hand in her own. Maria responded by rolling toward her mother and wrapping her other little arm around her mother's waist.

Reaching out with her other hand, Frannie stroked Maria's head gently. When she spoke, her voice was once more a mere whisper. "Maria, my sweet, I want you to always remember how very much . . . Poppa and I love you."

Maria raised her head and looked up into her mother's eyes. "Poppa's . . . gone," Maria said sadly.

Frannie nodded, and stroked her daughter's head again as Maria leaned against her mother's bosom.

"You understand that Poppa is in heaven, don't you?"

Maria nodded without raising her head. "Mrs. Cochran told me he was."

"Do you remember . . . when you went to Bible school last summer . . . and Rev. Weldon told you . . . about heaven?" Frannie's voice was hesitant, but her words were clear.

Maria sat up and looked into her mother's eyes, and as Jessie watched the two of them, she had to blink back the tears that threatened to spill from her eyes.

Cocking her head to one side as though concentrating, Maria finally said, "Poppa is an angel in heaven and he'll wait for us until we get old and die."

Frannie smiled down at Maria and said, "Sometimes, people die before they are old, my sweet."

She knows, Jessie thought, as a lump formed in her throat. Somehow, Frannie knows she's going to die. And the very thought of it made Jessie's own heart ache.

Maria's little chin trembled as she raised her head. "I don't want us to die before we're old, Momma."

Frannie continued to stroke Maria's head, smoothing her dark curls down across her shoulders. "I'm sure you . . . will live to be . . . ninety-seven years old, my darling Maria."

The child sighed, but didn't speak.

When Frannie continued, her voice was more strained. "Momma doesn't think . . . she's strong enough . . . to stay with you."

"I don't want you to leave me, Momma," Maria said, clutching her mother's hand. Tears sprang to her eyes and she cried out, "It would be awful if you were gone. I miss Poppa, especially at night when he used to come and read me a story. But he was away so much, sometimes I can pretend he's just at work or on a trip."

Maria shook her head back and forth, tears streaming down her cheeks. "But not you, Momma. You're always with me. You can't go to heaven."

Jessie saw the tears and felt helpless, knowing there was nothing she could do. This was between mother and child.

"Shh . . . don't fret, baby," Frannie crooned.

"Please don't leave me, Momma," Maria whimpered.

"But I'm getting . . . so weak, baby. I don't think . . . I can stay much longer."

"No!" Maria shouted. "We'll help you get strong, won't we, Aunt Jessie?" The child swung around, her green eyes blazing as they met Jessie's.

Then, just as quickly, she turned back to her mother without waiting for Jessie to answer. She began to cry and shout at the same time. "We'll cook you chicken broth and tea and feed you until you're strong again, just like you did last spring when I was sick. We'll sit you in your rocking chair by the fire so you'll be warm and you'll get all better . . ." Her last words were muffled until nothing could be heard but her sobs as she leaned against her mother and cried.

Frannie continued stroking her child as tears glistened in her own eyes. Jessie could only stand there, powerless to say or do anything to comfort them.

At last, Frannie spoke. "Maria, my baby . . . I love you so much. I don't want to leave you and . . . if your aunt weren't here to take care of you, I would be in agony at the thought of it. But . . . your aunt loves you, Maria. She'll take care of you always because she's my sister and we love each other very much . . . and that's why she loves you so much."

Jessie could no longer hold back the tears that had filled her eyes. They streamed down her cheeks and dripped onto the ruffles of Maria's soft white nightgown. She leaned down and embraced both her sister and her niece. The three of them held each other until Maria's sobs finally softened to a whimper. Then Jessie sat up again and Frannie continued.

"Poppa's waiting, Maria, and since he's alone, I'll go and wait with him. Aunt Jessie will watch you grow up into a beautiful young lady, and she'll be here for you when you have children of your own."

"I want you, Momma," Maria wailed.

"Now, Maria, look at me." Frannie tipped Maria's chin up with her hand. "You love Aunt Jessie, don't you?"

The child nodded her head.

Frannie managed a weak smile. "Good. I know you'll be sad for a while, but you have to remember that Poppa and I will be looking down on you from heaven. You can talk to us any time you want to . . . but you might not be able to hear us answer. If you . . . have to have an . . . answer . . . then you ask your Aunt . . . Jessie.

"Do you understand, my sweet?"

"I understand, Momma," she said, then threw both arms around her mother and held on tight.

"I love you, baby," Frannie whispered as she wrapped her own trembling arms around her child.

"I love you, Momma, and I love Poppa too."

Frannie's eyes met Jessie's then. "Take good care of my little girl, sister."

"I'll do the very best I know how."

Frannie nodded, then said, "I love you, Jess."

Jessie reached out and clasped her sister's hand. "I love you too."

Frannie began to softly sing a lullaby that Jessie recognized as one their mother had often sung to them.

"Hush, little baby, close your eyes, Momma's gonna . . ."

Jessie listened with tears streaming down her cheeks, and when she realized that Frannie had stopped singing, she slowly finished the refrain. ". . . sing you a lullaby. Dream of angels and don't you cry, 'cause we'll all be together by and by."

When Jessie felt the gentle pressure on her

shoulder, she realized Benjamin was there and the doctor with him.

"Come, Jessica, let Dr. Rittman see to his patient."

Jessie watched Benjamin lean down and gently take Maria in his arms. The child was exhausted from her crying, and didn't resist as he carried her from the room. Jessie stood, but could not move away from the bed. She looked on as the doctor opened his bag and examined Frannie's lifeless body.

When he straightened up and looked at Jessie, he shook his head, then closed his bag and left the room.

By the time Benjamin came back, Jessie's tears had dried. He came up behind her, his hands gently squeezing her shoulders as he murmured, "I'm so terribly sorry, Jessica."

Then he knelt beside the bed, his elbows leaning on the edge, his head bowed as though in prayer.

Jessie placed a hand on his shoulder. "Thank you for being here for her when I wasn't." Then she turned slowly and left the room.

Minutes later Benjamin found her in the kitchen, powdery white blotches all over her deep green robe as she frantically dumped cup after cup of flour into a large bowl.

"There are things that must be done, Jessica," he said softly, taking the cup from her hand.

"Dr. Rittman said he'd see that the grave is opened," Jessie said without looking up.

Benjamin nodded, then asked, "Would you like me to have Mrs. Cochran and Mrs. Weldon come over and help you get Fran dressed?"

She didn't answer, but instead poured milk from a pitcher into the flour mixture.

"I know you're friendly with both of them, and they've helped prepare others for—"

"Yes, that'll be fine," she said. "Margaret and Ann are good people. I'm sure Frannie would be pleased to have them help."

"I'll send Mrs. Weldon over right away, but you might want to check on Maria before she gets here and . . . perhaps you'd like to get dressed before anyone comes?"

Jessie looked down at her nightclothes as though unaware of the fact that she was not dressed. She glanced back at Benjamin and nodded, then set the pitcher down and wiped her hands on a towel that hung alongside the stove.

"I'll get dressed and sit with Maria until Ann gets here," she said as she walked past him.

Benjamin put a hand on her shoulder, stopping her. "Are you all right, Jessica?"

Her eyes were deep as the sea itself when she looked up at him. "My mother and father and husband are dead and I've learned to deal with that. I mourned for Jonathan on my way here and now I'll mourn for my sister. I'll deal with my pain and I'll survive . . . despite the fact that everyone in my family is dead except for my niece.

"It's because of Maria that I must deal with this sorrow and go on."

Benjamin continued to search her eyes, unsure of her mental state, despite her calm demeanor. "Will you be all right while I'm gone, Jessica?"

She blinked once and looked him straight in the eye. "I'll be fine, Benjamin."

And with the regal bearing of a queen she turned and left the kitchen.

Benjamin watched her go, but he knew she wasn't fine at all. He knew that Jessica would need him in the days ahead. And despite the grief that engulfed him at Fran's loss, Benjamin was glad that he was here, that he would be the one Jessica turned to in her sorrow.

Chapter Six

For the rest of the day, the house settled into a somber flurry of activity. Ann and Margaret came and helped Jessie wash and dress Frannie. Close friends and neighbors began coming by shortly afterward to offer condolences.

Jessie soon discovered the island ways weren't much different from those back home. People still gathered round, some because they truly cared and wanted to give comfort, some because they liked to pry into other people's lives.

Then Maria woke from her nap. Jessie was sitting in a chair near the window, and wasn't prepared when Maria raced across the hall shouting, "Momma, Momma." Her eyes lit up with joy when she saw her mother. "Momma's well enough to get dressed," she shouted gleefully.

Jessie's heart constricted, and she saw Ann and Margaret's look of sympathy as she caught the little girl up in her arms and held her close. "No, my sweet. Don't you remember your mother saying good-bye to you?"

"Yes, but that was before my nap. Momma was just in my room, Aunt Jessie. She must be all right if she came in my room."

"You must have been dreaming, sweetheart," Jessie said, gently running her hand over the child's head, wanting to comfort her.

"No, it wasn't a dream," Maria insisted. "She talked to me, she told me not to be sad. But she was in a white robe, not those clothes she has on now."

Margaret went to Maria and laid a hand lovingly on her shoulder. "Perhaps you're just remembering your momma in that lovely pale blue robe your poppa got her last Christmas, Maria."

"No, Mrs. Cochran," she said, shaking her head. "The robe she had on was white, even whiter than new-fallen snow with the sun shining on it."

Benjamin came into the room, and when he heard the last part of the conversation, his heart ached for his niece.

"And you love the snow, don't you, Maria?" he asked, trying to get the child's mind off her imaginary visit with her mother.

"Uh-huh, and so does Momma. She always said it was the only time you and Poppa got to rest, Uncle Ben."

"Indeed," he said. "Now, why don't you come along with me. Mrs. Whitfield and Mrs. Snyder are here and they've brought something they made especially for you."

Taking Maria from Jessica's arms, he carried the child downstairs into the warm kitchen. He was grateful for the women who were there, ready to try to diminish his niece's sorrow by filling her with cookies and milk.

Knowing nothing about rearing a child, especially a little girl, Benjamin was thankful for all the women who'd filled the house this day, especially Jessica, who'd been so helpful with Maria. Perhaps, after the burial, he would talk to Jessica about remaining on the island. Maria would, after all, need a woman's touch in her formative years, and who better to provide it than her own mother's sister.

There was always the possibility that he could convince her the island was a good place to live. Quite different from her fields in Indiana, but with its own splendid beauty. He could make her understand that the sea was not to be feared, but to be enjoyed. He must do his best to make her love the island as he and Maria loved it, because there was no better person to care for Maria than her own aunt.

In fact, he could think of no one else he'd trust to help him raise the child. Margaret was getting along in years and had enough duties to keep her busy. Ann Weldon had her own family to care for, plus her involvement in her husband's church affairs. There were probably other women on the island who would be capable of caring for Maria, but they could never love her as Jessica did. She was Maria's flesh and blood. She was the logical choice.

The thought of seeing Jessica on a regular basis warmed the coldness that had descended on him with Fran's death. It would be good to have her nearby to share the pain of their mutual loss. Yet he knew he must not concentrate on his own pain.

He had, after all, promised both his brother and

Fran that he would care for Maria, and the best way he could do so was to have Jessica stay on the island. Of course, he thought, she may have a life she wishes to continue in Indiana. Perhaps she even has a man waiting for her there. He found the notion disturbing, and was uncertain if it was because he cared for Jessica or because she might try to take Maria with her when she went back to her home in Indiana. That had been the one fear he'd had when she came.

Jessica picked that precise moment to enter the kitchen. She had changed into a black silk dress that he recognized as one of Fran's older dresses.

He could still remember Fran's dismay when she'd tried it on shortly after Maria's birth. Jonathan had been away on business, and Benjamin had come to the house to take Fran to the burial of an elderly neighbor. She'd been crying because she couldn't fasten the dress at the waist, and he'd had to coax her out of her depression.

And now Benjamin stood in Fran's kitchen, staring at Jessica in that same dress, unable to pull his gaze away. The black silk clung to her, accentuating her firm bosom and slim waist, but the color only emphasized her pallor. He saw that she'd once again bound her hair—which was as silky as the dress she wore and almost as black—into a knot. He couldn't help but think it should never be so bound, but left to freely ripple down her back as it had this morning when she was still in her nightgown . . . her slender, bare feet peeking out from beneath the hem.

With that image in mind Benjamin knew he wanted Jessica to stay—and it wasn't just for Maria's sake.

Jessica's voice pulled him from his thoughts.

"Benjamin . . . Benjamin, I said she's ready."

He nodded. "The men are out back. I'll tell them."

The smell of the sea mixed with the autumn winds that swept across the ridge at the cemetery and swirled golden and bronze leaves into the open grave that held Fran's coffin.

A sudden gust of wind blew the hood of Jessica's borrowed black cape off, and Benjamin watched as the stiff breeze continued to tug and pull strands of hair from her carefully arranged knot, twisting them into long spiral curls around her face. He could see she was totally unaware of her hair blowing about her face, or the cold winds that continued to fling the dying leaves onto the lid of the wooden coffin.

They stood side by side as friends and neighbors bade them good-bye. One by one the wagons pulled away from the hillside cemetery until there was but one remaining.

Benjamin hesitated, unwilling to disturb Jessica as she stared into the gaping hole in the earth. She hadn't even budged when Mrs. Cochran had told her she'd take Maria back to the house with her.

Ann Weldon had offered to remain at the cemetery with Jessica, but Benjamin had insisted she go on home. The days had grown shorter, and Benjamin wanted everyone to be on their way before nightfall. People had come to Crown Hill Cemetery from both ends of the island, and those from East Point especially had a good distance to travel back to their homes.

Two workmen waited nearby, leaning patiently on their shovels. Benjamin imagined they were anxious to finish their task and go on home to their families as well. That thought made him move toward Jessica and grasp her elbow, hoping to nudge her into movement.

She looked at him with blank eyes, then shrugged her arm from his.

"Jessica," Benjamin said quietly. "These men are waiting to finish here. They have families and . . ."

Those words finally broke through the silent barrier that had surrounded her. She looked over at the men who were standing under a nearby maple tree which had been stripped naked by the wind.

She nodded, then pulled up her hood, holding it firmly with one hand under her chin while taking the arm Benjamin offered with the other.

As they walked down the winding path, Benjamin also acknowledged the workmen standing nearby with a nod. Both men removed their hats and as Jessie walked by them, she stopped. "I'm sorry we've kept you from your work, gentlemen," she said softly.

"Quite all right, ma'am," said the older man. "We're sorry for your loss. Mrs. Whittaker was a fine woman."

"Thank you," Jessie said. Then she and Benjamin continued down the hillside.

For several minutes Jessie sat next to Benjamin in the wagon without speaking a single word. The horse's hoofbeats, the wagon wheels turning, and the shrill whistling of the wind were the only sounds that breached the silence between them.

Finally, Benjamin could not bear to see the forsaken look on Jessica's face a moment longer. He pulled the wagon off the road near a stand of pines. The trees cut the wind, and Benjamin felt it was a good place to talk before they got back to the house and had to face Maria.

Benjamin turned toward her and said, "Jessica, you aren't alone. I'm going to miss her too."

He looked into the depths of Jessica's eyes and saw the anguish that matched his own. He felt the need to touch her, to hold her—to try to offer comfort. Tentatively he rubbed his hand along her arm, then reached up with his gloved hand and gently touched her cheek. But instead of giving her the comfort he'd hoped, the gesture made her cry.

Watching the tears stream down her pale cheeks, he realized he'd not seen her do more than blink away a few tears. Jessica had never given in to her grief completely—not at the house or at the cemetery.

A moment later, she was in his arms, sobs racking her body. He held her close to him, wishing he could absorb her pain.

"Jessica . . . Jessica," he said as he rocked her gently in his arms.

She looked up at him with red-rimmed eyes, her cheeks glistening with tears. "Why? Why did she have to die, Benjamin?"

The tears intensified the extraordinary color of her eyes, and Benjamin could only return her gaze, unable to answer her unanswerable question.

As Jessica's sobs slowed, her eyes held his. And suddenly, inexplicably, her arms were around his neck, her lips on his lips, and he was returning her gentle kiss with the passionate fury that she'd unleashed with her first touch.

As suddenly as it began, Jessica pushed Benjamin away. "Dear God," she cried. "What are we doing? What have I done?" Again a tremor shook her body as tears flowed from her eyes.

"It's all right, Jessica," Benjamin murmured, pulling her back into his arms.

"No!" she said, pushing him away again. "I must be depraved to behave this way after my sister's burial. Dear God, what's happening to me?"

"Jessica, it's not unusual for people to draw closer during their grief."

"Draw closer? Perhaps. But that's not what I call what just happened here." She pulled a handkerchief from the pocket of her cape and wiped the tears from her face.

She sat up straight and squared her shoulders, adjusting the hood over her hair once more. The tears had stopped and her voice was stronger. "I don't blame you, Benjamin. It was entirely my fault and I apologize."

"There's no reason for you to apologize. We are grieving. We needed and offered each other comfort."

"That was not comforting—it was disturbing. Please take me back to the house, Benjamin, immediately!"

From the set of her jaw, he knew there would be no further discussion, so he reined the horse around and got back on the road to East Point.

He felt badly to have caused her more distress—but he did not regret the kiss. It had been right and good no matter what she felt right now.

During the rest of the silent ride home, Jessie tried to understand what caused her to act as she had with Benjamin, but instead found herself confused by conflicting emotions, and totally distraught by her sister's death.

She found herself unable to speak to Mrs. Cochran when they returned to the house because of the shame she felt at her actions.

"Would you like a cup of tea, Miss Jessie?" Margaret asked as Jessie hung her cape on the coat rack in the hall.

Jessie merely shook her head, brushed past the housekeeper, and went straight upstairs to check on Maria.

Opening Maria's bedroom door as softly as possible, not wanting to wake the child, Jessie was surprised at finding the bed empty. She glanced across the hall at the door to her sister's room. Would Maria have gone there trying to find comfort?

Jessie went to Frannie's room and gently opened the door. A lamp burned low on the bedside table, casting a soft glow on Maria's still form. Jessie looked down at the child, who lay so serene in sleep.

The little girl appeared even smaller on the enormous four-poster bed. She was curled up in a ball, her knees almost touching her chest, her head bowed, her whole body sunk down into the feather coverlet. She looked very much like a newborn babe—in the very bed where her parents had most likely conceived her.

Jessie tucked a quilt around her, leaving the lamp burning low in case Maria woke in the middle of the night. For tonight, at least, she and her niece would sleep separately. The child most likely needed the comfort and security of her parents' bed, and Jessica felt the need to be alone.

She bent to kiss the little girl's forehead, realizing how vulnerable Maria was—an orphan now. But not for long. Jessie knew exactly what Frannie had wanted. She would take no chances with her sister's child. First thing in the morning she would draw up a petition for adoption and send it off to the county seat on the mainland.

For now, though, Jessie wanted only to sleep. It had been a very long day.

Maria wakened, snuggling down in the soft bed. The sweet smell of lilacs drifted from her mother's pillow, and she smiled remembering how Momma had loved the fancy lilac soaps Poppa had bought her on her last birthday.

Remembering the way Momma had looked in her dream made Maria happy. She'd been shiny bright, almost sparkly, like the way the sun sparkled on the waters of the lake.

As Maria opened her eyes, though, she thought about her mother and the things Momma had told her. The more she thought about it, the more sure she was that it had been more than just a dream. In fact, she'd felt her Momma's touch wakening her. It couldn't have been a dream. She remembered the lamp glowing softly on the nightstand and her Momma standing there beside the bed.

Maria pushed herself up on one elbow, looking around the room, almost certain she'd be able to see her again.

"Momma?" she called out softly. "Momma, are you here?"

There was no answer, but Maria was sure she had not been "imagining things" as she'd heard Mrs. Cochran tell Aunt Jessie the day before.

Maria lay back down, thinking about how Momma had looked as she stood by the bed smiling at her.

Suddenly, she knew why her mother's clothing had seemed so familiar. The shimmery white robe

Momma had worn looked exactly like all the angel robes she'd ever seen . . . like the ones portrayed on Christmas greeting cards, and even the ones worn by the angels in the Christmas pageant at church.

The robe hadn't been like hers or Aunt Jessie's with a tie holding it together in front. The one Momma wore, the shiny white robe, appeared to be all one piece . . . long and flowing all around her, rather like a long cape with no opening in the front.

A knowing smile spread across Maria's face as she realized what had happened to her mother. Aunt Jessie was right, she thought . . . and so was I. Momma really did die, but she was here too. Momma's an angel now.

She called out again, as softly as she could, anxious to share this exciting knowledge with her mother. When there was still no answer, Maria used her child's logic to determine exactly where she could go to find her mother.

"Miss Jessie . . . Miss Jessie . . ." The sound of Margaret's voice, added to the pounding, woke Jessie with a start.

"Come in, Margaret." Jessie sat up, noting that the sky beyond her window was just beginning to lighten—daybreak was near.

"I'm sorry to bother you so early, miss, but when I woke this morning, I came up to look in on Maria and I can't find her anywhere. I've checked."

It took only a second for Jessie to come fully awake. "What do you mean you can't find her?"

"Well, she was asleep in her mother's bed—"

"I know. I tucked her in myself." Jessie glanced at the mantle clock. "It's not even six o'clock, Margaret. Where could the child be? And how did you discover her missing?" Jessie knew it didn't matter, but she had to say something to stem her panic.

"I got up early," Margaret said. "I couldn't sleep, and decided to put some dough in the oven to rise. It was after my mornin' cup of tea that I came up to look in on the child. When I saw she wasn't there . . ."

While Margaret went on about her distress and her search, Jessie hurried into the dressing room and pulled on her old black cotton dress, not even bothering with her undergarments.

"Where have you looked, Margaret?" she asked, slipping on her shoes and lacing them haphazardly.

"I've checked all the rooms, miss, and the root cellar and the service porch, of course. I called out back and off the front porch, but it's still rather dark and I couldn't see her anywhere . . . nor was there any answer to my call."

Jessie's mind worked frantically as she rushed down the stairs with Margaret behind her. "The closets . . . under the bed . . . did you search under her mother's bed? Perhaps she's frightened . . . hiding . . ."

"What is it?" Benjamin came out of the sitting room rubbing his eyes, his hair rumpled from sleep. He wore no shirt, only a pair of trousers that had obviously been pulled on hastily.

"I didn't realize you were still here, Benjamin," Jessie said.

"I thought you might need some help today, and from the looks of the two of you, I'd say that's exactly what you do need."

"Maria's missing," Jessie said.

"Missing?"

"Margaret, you explain it, I'm going to look out back. She may be with her rabbit."

Benjamin stood and listened to the housekeeper after Jessica rushed past him and out the back door.

"All right . . . Margaret, calm down." Benjamin placed his hands on her shoulders and found her trembling. "We'll find her. She's just an unhappy little girl and probably is out with Peter, just like Jessica said."

Even as he said the words aloud, inside his soul cried out to God. Don't let this be. Dear God don't let anything happen to Maria.

Margaret moved toward the stairs. "I'll look under the beds and in the closets like Miss Jessie said."

Back in the sitting room Benjamin hurriedly donned his shirt and leather vest. He pulled on his boots, and was headed out the back door when he heard Jessica cry out, "Her pony's gone . . . Benjamin, the pony's gone!"

Benjamin raced out the door and almost collided with her. He grasped her arms to steady them both. "Slow down, Jessica. I'll saddle a horse and head out. She can't be far."

"Saddle one for me too."

He hesitated for a moment. She could slow him down.

Seeing his indecision, she quickly added, "We can cover a larger area if both of us go."

"All right. But get your wrap. You'll freeze in that thin dress."

A few minutes later Jessica returned with her long woolen cape over her shoulders. Benjamin had just finished saddling the second horse.

He turned to help her up, but in one swift movement she was on her mount and heading out of the barn.

"Jessica, wait!"

She pulled up on the reins and turned, her long black tresses billowing out from the sides of the hooded cape. "Which way are you going?" she called back.

He mounted as he spoke. "I think she may have gone to my house to find that kitten she believes I put out."

"Why?"

"Because she needs something familiar to hold on to and I'm sure she knows that you'd let her keep it."

"You could be right. Then I'll head in the opposite direction. I have an idea too."

Before Benjamin could ask what her idea was, she was gone. He started down the road behind her, and was stunned by the speed she'd gained. He had only a moment to pause and wonder where she'd learned to ride so well.

The wind swiped viciously at Jessie's body, cutting through even her heavy cape as she rode down Bay View Road, along the lake. Although the wind off the lake was frigid, Jessie knew this was the quickest route to Catawba Road.

As she rode, she prayed her instincts were correct. She fervently hoped that Maria had gone to talk to her mother at the cemetery.

Dawn was breaking, and the sun brushed the lake with wide swaths of bright orange and pink stripes as Jessie neared Meechen Road. From a distance she could see that the heavy iron gates were closed, and her heart dropped. Little Maria would never be able to open the gates—the handle was much too high.

Jessie held her mare to a trot until she reached the gates, wondering where to look next. She was ready to turn away when a sound . . . a voice . . . something beyond the fence made her dismount. After securing her horse she opened the gate and entered.

Moving up the hillside, Jessie could feel her heart hammering. "Please, God," she murmured. "Please let her be all right."

As Jessie circled to the other side of the cemetery she saw a break in the fence she hadn't noticed the day of the funeral—and it was open. The sun broke through the clouds, and in that glorious moment with the sunshine as a brilliant backdrop she could see the darkened silhouette of a pony.

Jessie's breath came in ragged gasps as she raced to the crest of the hill. As she got closer she could make out the tiny figure near the place where they'd laid Fran to rest. She slowed her pace so as not to frighten the child, and when she was almost at the grave site she called out, "Maria . . . Maria, it's me. It's Aunt Jessie."

By the time she reached her, Maria was standing and looking up at her with a pixie-like smile. Jessie hugged her, and was glad to see she'd worn her woolen cape and bonnet and even had gloves on. Not many children would have thought of the cold.

"Maria . . . do you have any idea how frightened I was when Margaret told me you weren't in your bed?"

The child's smile ebbed a bit as she shook her head.

"To find a child you love missing in the middle

of the night is terribly—"

Her tiny voice interrupted, "It was almost morning, Aunt Jess."

Hearing the child use the shortened version of her name startled Jessie, and she tried not to show how much it had unnerved her. She moved closer to her niece, while looking at the grave from the corner of her eye. She'd never liked thinking of her loved ones under all that dirt.

"Why did you call me Jess?" she asked.

"I didn't. I called you *Aunt* Jess."

"But you've always called me Aunt Jessie before."

The little girl glanced lovingly at the grave of her mother and smiled. "Momma told me she called you Jess, and I like that name for you too."

Jessie's heart lurched. Her sister had been the only person to ever use the shortened version of her name. Could it be? No. Jessie's mind rebelled. A moment later she realized the child had obviously heard Frannie use the shortened version of her name before her death.

She sighed and bent over to hug the child. "Oh, Maria, I wish I had told you, you don't have to come to the cemetery to talk to your mother. You can talk to her anywhere—in your room, out in the backyard, or even the front porch. She'll hear you wherever you are."

"I know that now, Aunt Jess."

"You do?"

"Uh-huh. Momma told me I just have to be patient when I want to talk to her. She said if I'd waited in her room, she would have come back to talk to me again."

Jessie was afraid the dear child was suffering some sort of shock from the loss of her parents, so she decided not to argue the point and just ignore what Maria had said.

"Well, we better get you home before poor Margaret and your Uncle Ben call out the marshal to find you."

Maria looked properly repentant. "Momma told me you'd all be worried about me."

Again, Jessie ignored the comment. "You musn't ever leave the house without letting someone know, sweetheart. Will you try and remember that?"

The little girl nodded, and her pony whinnied at that moment, causing her to laugh. "Pony will remember too."

"Is that what you've named him?"

"Yes. I talked it over with Momma and she agreed that it was a good name too. She told me I could talk to her about anything, anytime I need to."

I'll have to see Dr. Rittman soon, Jessie thought, and ask if there's any harm in this fantasizing. Perhaps it's nothing to be alarmed about. Just a little girl's reaction to too much loss.

"Well, let's get you on Pony and go back home," Jessie said.

When Maria was mounted, they started down the hill, and Jessie was surprised to hear Maria's cheerful voice call out, "Bye, Momma. I'll talk to you later."

Tears moistened Jessie's eyes, but she forced herself to blink them back. Whether the child was imagining her mother talking to her or not, at least she was happy.

The ride back to the house took considerably longer with Pony carrying Maria, but Jessie was content with trotting along slowly in the sunshine.

The air had settled into a calm breeze, and the sun took away the chill that had settled over Jessie as she'd ridden to the cemetery. It was turning out to be an extraordinary October day—the kind that makes one recall summer despite the almost bare branches of the trees overhead. The wind had blown all the clouds away, and only clear blue sky was visible as far as the eye could see.

As they trotted along side by side, Jessie looked down at her niece with love. No matter how you fare because of your parents' deaths, my little one, Jessie thought, I'll always take care of you as your mother asked. Love will always bind us, but we'll take no chances where you're concerned. Soon you will be legally mine.

Halfway to the house, Maria called out, "Here comes Uncle Ben!"

Jessie had seen the rider in the distance, but hadn't recognized Benjamin—still didn't. "How do you know it's your uncle?"

"Can't you tell, Aunt Jess? There's not another man on the island that has curly black hair that shines in the sun like Uncle Ben's—even Poppa's wasn't that black or that shiny. Besides," she added with a smile. "That's the jacket Momma and Poppa gave him for his last birthday."

She was quiet for a few seconds, then asked, almost in awe, "Did you know Uncle Ben's thirty-eight years old?"

"I don't think I did," Jessie said, trying not to smile at the child's obvious look of wonder.

"Don't you think that's old?" the child asked.

"How about if I let you know in ten years or so?"

"Why?"

"Because I'll be nearly thirty-eight by then."

Jessie had to smile at the quizzical look in Maria's eyes as her forehead crinkled up in thought.

"Are you trying to figure out how old I am?" Jessie asked.

She nodded and said, "I'm not so good at 'rithmetic unless I have a pencil and tablet."

"You do know it's not polite to ask a lady her age?"

"I know. Momma taught me that, but I didn't ask you."

Jessie had to laugh. "You're right, you didn't. But if you keep it a secret I'll tell you anyway."

"Okay."

"I'm twenty-six, but I'll be twenty-seven on my next birthday."

"And your birthday is one week before Christmas."

Jessie registered a surprised expression. "How did you know that?"

"'Cause I remember Momma getting your birthday gift and your Christmas gift ready at the same time, and I told her I was glad my birthday was in the summer 'cause I wouldn't want to get all my presents in one week."

Once again the child made Jessie smile. Oh, little one, Jessie thought. It's going to be good to have you here to help me through this difficult time.

Benjamin must have seen Maria about the same time she'd seen him, and he closed the distance between them rapidly.

"You're all right," he said, pulling up on the other side of Maria.

"Yes, Uncle Ben," she said with a contrite voice. "And I'm truly sorry I worried everyone. I've promised Aunt Jess I will never leave the house without telling somebody—and Pony promised too."

Jessie could see the relief pass over Benjamin's face.

"How did you know where she was?" Benjamin asked Jessie.

"Woman's intuition, I suppose."

"Aunt Jess knew I went to talk to Momma."

At Benjamin's surprised look, Jessie quickly added, "I told Maria that she could talk to her mother right at home, and from now on that's what she's going to do."

Maria was nodding her head vigorously. "Because Momma's an angel now," she said. "And I can talk to her anytime."

Benjamin again glanced at Jessica, but she shook her head, and he didn't question Maria any further.

Although the ride back to the house was at a leisurely pace and the conversation was rather casual as Maria pointed out her favorite places and things to her aunt, Benjamin's mind raced.

When he'd first heard Margaret and Jessica's concerned voices this morning as they told him of Maria's disappearance, he'd immediately prepared to be the child's savior. Without even thinking about asking her opinion, he'd told Jessica he would go and find the child. If Jessica hadn't insisted that the two of them searching would be better, he would have gone off on his own . . . and in the wrong direction.

Jessica, in the short time she'd spent with their niece, had come to understand Maria better than he, who'd known the child since the day of her birth. He would never have considered the fact that Maria might have gone to the cemetery. What had Jessica said? "Woman's intuition." Indeed, this episode with Maria reconfirmed Benjamin's inclination toward having Jessica raise Maria. He would have to talk to her soon. Hopefully, he would be able to convince Jessica that the child needed her here.

"Look, Pony," Maria cried out, her voice bringing Benjamin out of his reverie. "There's Margaret waiting for us. I'll bet she'll have a carrot for you and breakfast for us. And I'm so hungry."

Benjamin smiled at the child, then glanced up at Jessica. Her appearance was so somber, it made him realize she must still be concerned about Maria's conversation with her mother. But he didn't find it all that unusual. Children had vivid imaginations, and with all the talk of heaven, it didn't seem odd that she would imagine her mother as an angel. But he'd best listen to what Jessica had to say on the subject, since she appeared to be more sensitive to the child's frame of mind.

Benjamin helped the women dismount, and watched Margaret enfold Maria right into her crisp white apron.

"Praise God, you're safe, child," she said.

Leaving Margaret and Jessica to fuss over Maria, Benjamin took their horses and headed for the barn.

"Come back quickly, Mr. Benjamin," Margaret called after him. "Breakfast is ready."

As they went into the kitchen, Jessie explained where Maria had gone, and although she saw Margaret brush a tear from her cheek, the housekeeper quickly regained her composure and insisted they all sit down and have a good hot meal.

Though she had no desire to eat, Jessie knew there was no use arguing. And in truth, she was glad to be back in the comfortable warmth of her sister's kitchen with Maria safe and sound.

This was her favorite room in the house. Knowing from Frannie's letters that it was the center of their daily life, Jessie often thought of the three of them here. Although it was a large room, Frannie's homey touches gave it a cozy feeling. Red-checkered gingham curtains, which Jessie knew her sister had sewn, hung at the windows that flanked the back door. And Frannie's whimsical embroidery added fanciful designs of sea horses and wildflowers to the tea towels that hung on a rack near the sink. A large, round oak table sat in the center of the room, and as Jessie glanced around the table she tried to picture the happy family times Frannie and Jonathan had shared there with their daughter.

As Margaret bustled to the cookstove for the coffeepot, Jessie couldn't help but think of the many meals her sister had prepared there. And the opposite wall was lined with shelves that not only held everyday dishes and cooking supplies, but several items from their childhood home. A large blue-and-white crockery bowl that had been their mother's caused a swell of nostalgia to rise up inside Jessie. She'd licked batter from that bowl more than once in her young life.

The back door swung open, pulling Jessie back to the present. Again, her eyes connected with Benjamin's. She was glad they'd cooperated in the search for Maria. It boded well for their mutual efforts to secure Maria's future.

As Benjamin stepped inside, Margaret's voice stopped him. "Mr. Benjamin," she called out from her post at the stove. "Would you please get the crock of butter off the porch? I know Miss Jessie likes butter on her biscuits."

"Oh, please don't bother if it's just for me," Jessie said. "I honestly couldn't eat anything right now.

"But you have to eat," Margaret said. "At a time like this—"

"It's important to keep up your strength," Benjamin said, finishing Margaret's sentence.

"You might as well eat," he added, "or the woman will give you no peace."

Jessie did manage to eat a little, while Maria and Benjamin scraped their plates clean.

Before the meal was finished, though, Maria started yawning, and when Jessie suggested a nap, the little girl agreed.

"Uncle Ben, would you carry me? I'm so tired."

"Well," he said, smiling across the table at the child, "that's what a long ride at dawn will do for you. I'm a bit tired myself."

Jessie watched as he took Maria in his arms. The little girl wound her arms around his neck, and her head nestled on his shoulder. And the look in his eyes as he kissed her cheek was one of pure love.

After they left the kitchen, Mrs. Cochran shook her head and murmured, "Well, I'll be . . ."

"What is it, Margaret?"

"Mr. Benjamin . . . he's never kissed that child before."

"Never?" Jessie couldn't believe her words.

Margaret shook her head. "Oh, she's often enough run up to him and put those loving arms around his neck and kissed his cheek, but never once have I seen the man kiss her on his own, or even return her kiss."

Margaret looked over at Jessie and smiled.

"Something . . . or somebody must be turnin' him into a softie."

"I rather doubt that a kiss on the cheek would automatically give a man the distinction of being a 'softie.' And I have no idea why you're looking at me that way."

Jessie silently wondered if the attraction she'd felt for Benjamin was visible.

"I'm sorry if I've spoken out of turn, Miss Jessie. I just think you might be bringin' out the best in him, that's all."

Wanting to put an end to the talk about her and Benjamin, Jessie didn't comment on the housekeeper's statement, but instead asked, "Margaret, do you know of someone who could take some papers to the courthouse for me?"

The woman knitted her brows for a moment, then cheerfully announced, "John Thomas is going to the mainland on this afternoon's ferry. He mentioned it when he stopped by here yesterday, after the . . . after we laid Miss Frannie to rest. I'm sure he'd be more than happy to do it for you."

She wiped her hands on her apron, then said, "And Mrs. Weldon's sendin' her boy James over shortly to pick up some of this extra food the neighbors sent over. I hope you don't mind my taking the liberty, but I'm not one to see food spoil, and there's a poor family over there near the church that Mrs. Weldon says could use some."

"That's fine, Margaret."

"And, what I meant to say was, James, he could take your papers to Mr. Thomas."

"Good, then I'll go and get them ready. And Margaret, why don't you go on home. I'm sure Mr. Cochran's missing you."

Margaret's pink cheeks grew even pinker, and

she fidgeted with the edge of her apron, rubbing it between the thumbs and fingers of both hands. "All right, miss, if you're sure you won't be needin' me anymore today."

"No, you go right ahead, and thank you for everything. I don't know what I'd have done without you and Ann these past two days."

"No need for thanks. I'll just wait till James comes, then tell him that you'll be giving him some papers to take back to Mr. Thomas."

Jessie nodded, then left the kitchen.

Benjamin came down the stairs just as Jessica started up. He paused a step above her and held a finger to his lips. "She's sound asleep."

"Thank you so much for your help today, Benjamin."

He shook his head, looking down at her for several very long moments. Jessie glanced downward to break the connection. She would not have a repeat of yesterday.

"No, Jessica," he said. "Once again, your instincts were right. I went off in the wrong direction. You have a way with the child and . . . a way with horses as well, judging from the technique you exhibited as you rode off this morning."

Jessie had to smile. "I've been riding for years, Benjamin. I've even competed in some riding contests and won."

"You must have found it quite humorous when I offered riding lessons then."

Another smile played on Jessie's lips. "It was a lovely gesture."

"Is there anything else I can do for you this morning?"

Jessie shook her head. "I have some papers I must attend to right now, and I've told Mrs. Cochran she can go on home and take care of things there."

"If you're sure you'll be all right, I would like to check on things at the vineyard. We'll have so little time to finish if the weather turns cold."

"Please, do go and take care of your business. You've spent too much time away from it already. Maria and I will be fine. I'm sure we both can use some extra rest. We'll have an early supper and perhaps I'll read to her tonight."

"Maria loves books. Fran always read to her."

"Then I'll continue to do so. She's going to need some stability in her life—some things that remain unchanged, despite all she's lost." She paused. Then looking into Benjamin's eyes, she said, "Thank you for everything, Benjamin."

He nodded, then left without another word.

Jessie sighed. He probably felt the strain too. An unsettling tension stretched tautly between them, and it was getting more difficult to deal with each day. It also left Jessie exhausted. Of course, she'd been through so much since she first opened that dreadful telegram, it could be that she simply needed to rest.

But first the petition. Once Maria was legally hers she would rest much easier.

Abruptly, she realized she'd not mentioned the adoption to Benjamin. "No matter," she murmured aloud. "The man has enough on his mind."

Chapter Seven

Jessica carefully folded the sheet of paper and placed it in an envelope. She had painstakingly worded her request to adopt her sister's orphaned child, praying as she penned each word that the court would understand how much she loved Maria and how much Maria needed her.

As Jessie held the envelope, she wondered if she'd said everything that needed to be said. Nervously she took the paper out and scanned it once more.

Yes . . . she mentioned that she was one of only two living relatives . . . she told of the deathbed request her sister had made of her . . . and she wrote of her love and affection for the child.

She sighed and again folded the paper, replacing it in the envelope.

A tentative knock came at the door, and Jessie got up to open it.

She'd seen James Weldon at a distance, but had not met him before. He was big for 16, very muscular and long legged too, like Willy. And they both had the same blond hair and crooked smile. "You must be James," she said.

"Yes, ma'am. Mrs. Cochran says you have something for me to take to Mr. Thomas."

"That's right, James, and it's very important that he receives it before he leaves on this afternoon's ferry. He'll be taking it to the courthouse, and I've marked that right here on the front."

James nodded, and a lock of blond hair fell in a soft wave across his forehead.

"And this is for your trouble," she said, reaching into her pocket for a ten-cent piece.

"No, ma'am, it's no trouble."

"I'm sure a young man like you can find somewhere to spend a dime."

He smiled broadly and accepted the coin.

"And give this fifty cents to Mr. Thomas with my thanks. I believe Mrs. Cochran said it would more than cover his fare from the ferry to the courthouse."

"Yes, ma'am. I'll see that he gets it right away."

Once the envelope was dispatched, Jessie felt calmer. She went back upstairs and sat in the rocking chair in Frannie's room. There she found herself really looking at the room for the first time since her arrival. The four-poster bed was the focal point of the room. With Fran gone now, Mrs. Cochran had made up the bed with the covering of antique lace over pale blue silk that had been a wedding gift to Jonathan and his bride.

The thought of their wedding brought back a memory of Frannie as a bride. Jessie had helped her sister dress right here in this room. She had brushed her sister's hair and plaited it into a long braid because Jonathan loved her hair braided. Then Jessie had taken the wreath of daisies that Jonathan himself had woven together and attached a white bow with ribbons streaming down the back. They'd chosen white and pale yellow ribbons to match the white daisies with their yellow centers.

When Jessie had set the wreath atop her sister's head with the ribbons cascading down her back, it had been as though they were characters in a fairy tale and Frannie was the princess.

Jessie sighed at the remembrance. Her sister and Jonathan had been so in love, and now, seven years later, they were both dead, the child conceived of their love left behind for Jessie to raise.

"I'll do the best I can, Frannie, the best I know how to do." With those words Jessie stood and walked to the double window that faced the lake, unaware that her words had brought an unseen presence into the room.

Jessie ran her fingers along the delicate Belgian lace curtains that hung at the windows. They too had been a wedding gift. She recalled how Frannie had cried when she opened the package.

They'd come from Aunt Libbie, the wonderful woman who'd cared for them after their parents had died, and Frannie had cried that day because Aunt Libbie couldn't travel to the island for the wedding.

It had never occurred to Jessie until that moment that she would be to Maria what Aunt Libbie had been to her and Frannie. Of course, they'd been older than Maria—Frannie 15 and Jessie 13—and there'd been no adoption. Aunt Libbie had been appointed their guardian. If Jessie could leave Maria with as many wonderful memories as Aunt Libbie had left her, she would be quite happy.

A floorboard creaked before Jessie realized Maria had tiptoed into the room.

"Hi. Why are you being so quiet?" Jessie asked.

"You were talking to Momma and I didn't want to interrupt."

For a moment, Maria's words puzzled Jessie, until she recalled she had spoken her sister's name aloud. A smile came unbidden to Jessie's lips as she realized she'd done exactly what she'd been so concerned about Maria doing—she'd talked to her sister.

She took Maria into her arms and sat down on the rocking chair again. "I suppose I was talking to your mother . . . just like you did this morning."

Maria nodded, rubbing her eyes with one balled-up fist.

Jessie sighed, feeling better about Maria's talks with her mother. "You know, Maria, even though your mother's gone, part of her will always be here with us . . . the memories we carry in our heart are special and will keep her close."

Maria looked up at her aunt with a quizzical expression on her tiny features. "You didn't see her, did you?" she asked rather sadly.

Jessie's heart lurched in her chest. "No, Maria. Your mother's not here. She's in heaven with your poppa."

"Don't you know angels can come down from heaven to see us, Aunt Jess?"

"Well, I suppose that is possible. We do, after all, have guardian angels, don't we?"

Maria nodded enthusiastically.

Jessie tried to think of the right words to say,

words that would help Maria differentiate between reality and imagination. She uttered a quick, silent prayer for help.

"Maria, I'm not sure you understand. There's a difference between—"

"All right. I understand," Maria said, without letting her aunt finish.

"What do you understand?" Jessie asked.

Maria looked up at her aunt. "I understand why you can't see Momma standing over there by the window."

"You can see your mother . . . here . . . now?" Jessie asked.

Maria nodded. "And she told me why you can't see her."

"What did she tell you, Maria?"

"Momma said you can't see her because you don't believe."

"Oh, Maria," Jessie said, wrapping her arms around her niece. "Don't you see, sweetheart. This is all in your imagination. Because you want to see your mother so much, you're imagining her presence."

The child glanced at the window and her smile was so radiant, Jessie found herself looking up . . . almost wishing she could see Frannie too.

Once again, she decided to let Maria's fantasy go until she spoke to Dr. Rittman about it.

She kissed Maria's forehead. "Why don't you run along and get your shoes and stockings on, and I'll go down and see what Mrs. Cochran left us for a snack."

"All right." As Maria scrambled down off Jessie's lap, she stopped and reached up and kissed her aunt's cheek.

The gesture touched Jessie's heart, and she

hugged Maria and murmured, "I love you, little girl."

"I love you too, Aunt Jess, but I'm not so little."

"I'll try and remember that. Now go ahead and get your shoes, and I'll go down to the kitchen and find something for us to eat."

They were still in the kitchen when Willy Weldon came to the back door.

"Could Maria come over to my house and play with me for a while?"

"Oh, could I, please, Aunt Jess? Willy has wonderful puppets, and we have such fun. And I want to tell him about Momma's visits too."

"How can your mother visit?" Willy asked, his eyes widening in surprise.

"I'll tell you in a minute," she said, then turned back to Jessie. "Is it all right to go, Aunt Jess?"

Jessie didn't want to let Maria out of her sight. The way she kept talking about her mother was bound to cause her problems. She could already see the confusion on Willy's face.

Then Jessie decided she was being overprotective. It might be good for Maria to talk this out with another child. Besides, Maria had been through so much tragedy, she deserved to have some pleasure playing with her little friend.

"All right, you go on and enjoy yourself, but promise you'll be back before dark."

"My mother said she'd bring Maria home, Mrs. McAllister, so I'll tell her it should be before dark," Willy said, sounding exactly like a little adult.

"How old are you, Willy?" Jessie asked.

"I'll be seven on October twenty-eighth, ma'am," he said with a bright smile.

"My, my, Maria, we'll have to go shopping for a birthday gift."

Maria clapped her hands. "I know just what to get."

"Don't tell," Jessie cautioned.

The little girl shook her head, her curls twisting from side to side.

"Now run along and get your cape and bonnet—take the gray one, it's warmer. There's a definite nip in the air today." Although the breeze coming in off the lake was always refreshing, Jessie had noticed the air this afternoon definitely had the smell of winter behind it. She'd not be surprised to see an early snowfall, despite the lovely weather they'd been enjoying.

With the two youngsters gone, the house was much too quiet. Jessie walked through the hall and slid open the doors into the parlor. The room was quite formal, and although the furniture was lovely, none of it looked as comfortable as the pieces in the sitting room. Jessie admired the deep red velvet settee and armchairs framed with dark, carved wooden backs and legs.

She walked slowly to the other side of the red-and-black patterned rug and let her fingers slide across the marble-topped table that held an ornate oil lamp. A pattern of green flowers adorned the outer glass, and crystal teardrops dangled from the center ring that held the glass in place.

A tall grandfather's clock stood like a silent sentinel in the far corner, and Jessie wondered if it had wound down or was inoperable. Not wishing to damage the internal workings, she decided to ask Benjamin about it the next time he stopped by.

The very thought of him still set off a tingle inside. She knew it wasn't appropriate to have such feelings, especially the day after her sister's death, yet she also had an inkling that Frannie would be pleased if she and Benjamin became close.

A banging on the front door startled Jessie from her daydreaming, and she hurried out to the entry.

"I'm coming!" she called out, afraid the caller would batter the door down.

She unlatched the bolt and opened the door.

"Benjamin!"

He strode past her, and she had no problem identifying the look on his face. It was anger or quite possibly rage.

"What's wrong?"

"What's wrong, the woman asks!" As suddenly as he began to shout he lowered his voice, "Where's Maria?"

"She went over to the Weldons' to play with Willy."

Benjamin looked at her with such loathing Jessie backed away.

"I've learned what you've done, and I can't believe I was taken in by your sweet words and kind ways. What a sham!"

His voice rose again, and he pushed past her and stomped into the living room.

"Benjamin, I have no idea what you're talking about, but I think you owe me an explanation for your rude behavior."

"*My* behavior, madame, is impeccable—it is you who've gone beyond the boundaries of decency. How could you? Fran is barely cold in her grave, and you're plotting to take Maria away from her family—her heritage. Maria is a Whittaker! What right have you to file for adoption?"

"Is that what all this is about? I would have told you. I planned to—"

"No more lies! If I didn't have a friend in the courthouse, I'd not know about your deceit. I was right about you the first day you came. I should never have let my guard down."

"Benjamin, I don't know what you're talking about. There was no plot. I had no plan. When Fran was dying she asked me to take care of Maria always."

"Liar!" Benjamin took a step forward as he shouted the word, and Jessica was suddenly frightened.

Where was the kind, tender man who'd held her yesterday? Where was the compassionate man who'd stood beside her at Fran's grave . . . who'd carried Maria so gently . . .

His next words were not shouted, but strained through tight, angry lips. "Fran asked *me* to take care of Maria. So you are a liar. How dare you file for adoption when Fran wanted me to care for the child? How dare you go behind my back . . ."

Jessica could not believe her ears. Either she had lost her mind or this man had. Either way she would not stand by and be called a liar.

"Stop it!" Jessie yelled. And he did, just long enough for her to have her say.

"I will not be called a liar. I loved my sister more than life itself, and when she lay dying I made her a promise to care for her child. If you have deluded yourself into thinking she said the same words to you, then you have lost your mind. And before you even think of saying another word, I want you out of this house!"

Benjamin looked at the woman he had held in his arms yesterday. The woman who had cried for her dead sister. Where was the loving, compassionate woman he had thought he could care for?

"I'll go. But you've not heard the last of this."

He slammed the door so violently Jessie thought the glass might shatter, but a moment later silence had once more settled over the house.

Only then did Jessie sink down on the settee, her body trembling both inside and out.

"Damn you, Benjamin Whittaker," Jessie whispered into the silent room. Then she broke down and cried for what might have been.

By the time Maria got back from the Weldons', Jessie had composed herself once again, but the emotional turmoil of the past week had evidently left its mark.

Ann Weldon took one look at Jessie, sitting at the kitchen table in a room as cold as the outside air, and asked Willy and Maria to go up to Maria's room and read some books.

As soon as the children were upstairs, Ann went to Jessie and put her hands on Jessie's shoulders. "What's wrong? And don't say nothing. I know you've just lost your sister, but that's not all of it. What is it, Jessie?"

"Oh, Ann. Maybe it's me. Could I have misunderstood? Why would he lie? I thought it was the right thing to do—"

"Stop this right now," Ann interrupted. "You're not making any sense. Start at the beginning."

Ann went to restart the fire in the stove and Jessie began apologizing for the cold, for letting the fire go out. "Dear Lord, look what's happening to me, Ann. That man drives me to distraction, I can't even keep my mind on necessary tasks. How can I take care of Maria if I can't even remember to add logs to the fire."

"Don't worry about the fire. I can get it started while you tell me everything that's happened. You'll feel better if you get it out."

Ann worked at the stove, but listened attentively as Jessie told her all about Frannie's last request, about the adoption, and about Benjamin's rage when he found out about it.

The flames were already igniting the logs Ann had added to the coals as Jessie finished her tale, and Ann went and sat beside her, patting her hands reassuringly. "There is obviously some misunderstanding here. Benjamin may not be the most gracious man I've ever known, and perhaps he is a bit opinionated, but he would not call someone a liar without believing it."

"Then why me?"

"As I said, my dear, it's most likely a misunderstanding. Be patient and I'm sure everything will work out. After all, he too has Maria's well-being in mind."

Those words finally got through Jessie's anger. "You're right, Ann. And I should have thought about that before making him leave in anger as I did. He is Maria's uncle, and I musn't come between them."

"Then go and talk to him. Willy and Maria are busy upstairs, and I'll be happy to stay until you come back. And I'll keep the fires going too," she added.

Jessie glanced out the window and saw the long shadows of the trees along the drive. "I'll have to hurry if I'm to get back before nightfall."

"I'm sure if you stay past dark he'll accompany you home."

The thought of riding alongside Benjamin at night intrigued Jessie. "Of course. He is—usually—a gentlemen."

Ann smiled. "He is that. And I'm sure you'll see that he's just concerned about his niece. I'm also certain that you'll sleep much better tonight if you get this cleared up."

Jessie spurred her horse onward, watching the sun move toward the horizon. Sunsets on the island were particularly glorious, the sun appearing to sink into the water while setting it aflame, tipping each wave with fiery sparks of color.

She would prefer to think only of the beauty of the sunset, but knew she must plan the words she would say to Benjamin. It was up to her to set things right between them—for Maria's sake.

Jessie rode hard, determined not to let the sun set on their anger. Her mother had told her long ago that the best way to keep any relationship on an even keel was to settle any minor disputes before the sun set each day.

The stone house still appeared uninviting and oppressive as Jessie rode up the hill. Mr. Cochran, Margaret's husband, happened to be walking between the house and stable, and was kind enough to see to her horse.

"I won't be long," she said as she started up the path.

"Just let Margaret know when you're ready to leave, ma'am, and I'll have the horse waiting for you."

Jessie knocked, and Margaret answered a moment later.

"Miss Jessie," she exclaimed. "Whatever are you doing out? It's getting late."

"I had to speak to Benjamin, Margaret. Is he at home?"

"Of course. Come sit in the parlor and I'll go and fetch him."

Jessie paced in front of the massive stone fireplace, hoping she'd say the right words. When Benjamin walked in moments later and looked at her, though, she felt very much as she had the first day she'd come. There was no kindness in his glance. A cold, dark-eyed stranger stood before her.

"Mrs. Cochran tells me you wish to speak to me, so get on with it. It will be dark soon, and I'll not be maneuvered into seeing you back home."

Jessie's temper flared, but she bit her tongue to keep from answering angrily. She had made a promise to herself and meant to keep it.

"I would not expect you to go out tonight, Benjamin. I'm sure Mr. Cochran could see me back . . . if our conversation keeps me until dark."

Jessie sighed wearily and asked, "Could we please sit down and talk—for Maria's sake."

She could see him struggle to maintain his hostility, but a flicker of indecision crossed his face before he motioned to the two wing chairs that flanked the fireplace.

Jessie gratefully moved to the one on the right, and Benjamin settled in the other. While she uttered a silent prayer to say the right words, Benjamin spoke first.

"Why did you do it, Jessica . . . and why so quickly?"

Jessie leaned forward a bit and tried to express her views sincerely. "My only concern was for Maria. I didn't want to take any chances of the state making her a ward of the court or some other preposterous thing."

"And how could that happen?" he asked. "No one on the island was running to the court to inform them of your sister's death."

"Things have a way of getting out," she said. "Surely news of the accident has reached the mainland, and when Frannie's death is made known there will be questions about her child."

"Especially in view of the fact that Maria stands to inherit half of the winery," Benjamin added, his voice harsh.

"I hadn't even thought of that," Jessie said.

"Oh, hadn't you?" he asked sarcastically. "Then why not apply for guardianship—why adoption?"

As he said the word "adoption," his suppressed rage was quite apparent.

Jessie swallowed, then continued, maintaining her composure. "I felt that Maria needed to know she belonged to someone. I think she needs a parent more than just a guardian."

"I've often heard Fran talk of your Aunt Libbie," Benjamin said, his mouth a taut line as he spoke. "Who, I believe, became a guardian to you and your sister after your parents' death."

"Yes," Jessie answered. "And we loved her dearly. But we were in our teens when our parents died, Benjamin. Maria is so young. I think . . . I believe she needs to know she belongs to someone, that she has a legal parent who will not be taken away from her."

He stood, his face contorted with anger as he glowered down at her. "It's just as I said the day you arrived, Mrs. McAllister—you cannot have a child of your own so you would steal Maria from me."

Jessie could not remain seated another minute, and as she stood her voice rose as well. "She is not *yours*."

"She is a Whittaker, and I swore to my brother and to his wife that I would see that she remained a Whittaker. She deserves her inheritance. Jonathan always saw Maria as taking over the wine company when she was older. I won't have you take that away from her!"

"You mention promises, Benjamin. You talk about Maria's name and her inheritance and about the winery. And despite what you think, I do not wish to take any of those things from her. But my dear Mr. Whittaker, what I have not heard you talk about—not one word—is about love and caring and what's best for a little girl who's just lost both of her parents!"

Jessie stood as she finished her tirade. "Good day, sir, and please don't bother to see me out. I am perfectly capable of finding my way out of this cold, impersonal house."

With those words Jessie turned away and marched out of the parlor, down the hall, and out the door without a backward glance.

"The woman is a damnable witch!" Benjamin sputtered.

"Sir?" Mrs. Cochran had come down the hall and stood agape in the parlor doorway, obviously startled and confused by her employer's words.

"Margaret, come in here," he shouted.

The housekeeper wiped her hands on her white apron, as she was prone to do when nervous, and approached him cautiously. "Yes, sir?"

"Do you know what that woman's done?"

Margaret shook her head, trying to imagine

what Miss Jessie could have done to cause him to be so furious.

"She filed a petition to adopt Maria. Can you believe it? She wants to raise her and she's not even a Whittaker."

"But . . . but she does love the child, sir."

"Are you defending her?"

Margaret grew more flustered, bunching up the bottom corners of her apron in her fists as Benjamin stepped toward her.

"I . . . I don't . . . know if you'd call it a defense, Mr. Benjamin, sir . . . but I must say I've seen her with Maria. She truly loves her sister's child."

"But does love give her the right to adopt her—to replace Fran in the child's eyes?"

"Sir!" Margaret gasped. "I cannot imagine Miss Jessie trying to replace the child's mother. She loved her sister and would never let Maria forget who her mother was."

"Then why did she do this? And why so quickly? It could have waited a day or two. She could have spoken to me first. It seems devious being done as it was, sneaking the petition off the island—"

"Begging your pardon, sir," Margaret interrupted. "Miss Jessie didn't sneak . . . in fact, when she asked me how she could transport the papers to the mainland, I told her John Thomas was going over on the ferry, and even arranged for young James Weldon to take the papers to him."

Benjamin stared at his housekeeper for several seconds before he spoke. "You . . . you were the one who made the arrangements. Margaret, how could you do this to me?"

"I did nothing I thought was wrong. In fact, although I suspected the papers had to do with Maria, I didn't know the actual content. I'm sorry if you feel I did wrong, sir, but you asked me to be of help to Miss Jessie and that's exactly what I did."

Benjamin sat back down in the chair and leaned forward on his elbows, chin on balled-up fists, and shook his head as he stared into the flames leaping from the grate in the fireplace.

Margaret stood silently, continuing to twist her apron.

"I'm sorry, Margaret," Benjamin said. "You did exactly what I asked, and I don't blame you for what happened."

"Thank you, sir, but I hope you won't look on this as somehow meant as a disparagement. I'm sure Miss Jessie was only thinking of Maria's welfare. She's a good woman, Mr. Benjamin."

Benjamin did not comment on her statement, but instead dismissed her. "I won't be needing anything else if you'd like to retire early."

The housekeeper sighed and murmured, "Good night then."

"Margaret, wait."

"Yes, sir," she said.

"What do you think she meant when she called this a 'cold' house? Do you think it's . . . cold?"

Margaret cleared her throat but didn't answer, looking down at the floor as though she wished it would swallow her up.

"Well, do you? Don't be afraid to speak up. I need your honesty right now."

"Yes, sir, begging your pardon, sir, but this is a cold house, especially the downstairs."

"Cold how? And what can be done to improve it?"

Margaret looked around, then turned to face the doorway into the hall.

"There, for instance. The entry and stairs. They're grand in dimension yet nothing but a vast expanse of cold, rigid stone. Carpets would soften the entry. Tapestries or watercolors along the walls there and going up the stairs might help. Or perhaps wall sconces with candles that would light the way without carrying lamps up and down."

Margaret's face lit up as she described it. "This could be a grand house, sir," she said, continuing with her thoughts. "Flowers on the entry table and at the landing atop the stairs would be a lovely touch as well."

"Why haven't you told me any of this before, Margaret?"

"Mr. Benjamin, I've been in this house since the day you and . . . since the day you moved in. When I first came, I did try, but . . . but I was told it was not my place to make suggestions."

Benjamin sighed. "My wife kept you from doing these things?"

Margaret looked down and nodded her head.

"Thank you, Margaret. I appreciate your candor. Go ahead and get some rest now."

"Yes, sir. Good night."

After Margaret left, Benjamin sat staring into the dying flames. Every now and then an orange tongue of fire would lick up around the last of the logs, and it reminded him somehow of Jessica's kiss. Had she been brazenly trying to seduce him? No, he thought. It was she who had pushed away, then avoided him for the rest of the day.

"Of course," he murmured aloud. "That might have been part of her plan. Making me want her even more." As Benjamin recalled the kiss and the desire he'd felt afterward, he was well aware of the fact that, if indeed it had been a plan to interest him . . . it had certainly worked.

"But that won't help you, Jessica McAllister," he whispered into the empty room. "You won't steal Maria away. I won't let you.

"I've dealt with manipulative women before and I've learned my lesson well." He looked around the room and thought about Margaret's words.

The woman he'd brought to the island as his bride had been a master manipulator. First seducing him with all her womanly charms. Then, after the wedding, she'd turned into a frigid woman who'd rarely let him sleep in her bed, claiming one illness after another.

Even so, she'd cajoled and wheedled him into building her this house—a pretentious thing that he'd never wanted. But even the stone couldn't keep out the sea air that she claimed gave her the many illnesses that kept her in her bed—alone. So she'd left him.

"No, Jessica," he whispered into the empty room. "I will never be manipulated by another woman . . . never."

With those words he stood and banked the fire for the night, then went upstairs.

At his desk, Benjamin lit a lamp to chase away the shadows that fell with the nearness of nightfall. He wondered if Mr. Cochran had escorted Jessica home, then decided it shouldn't concern him.

Taking paper and dipping his pen in the inkwell, he quickly began to word his own petition for adoption, citing his ability to care for the child and the fact that she was the only heir to her father's holdings in the Whittaker Wine Company. He carefully worded the appeal to assure the court that he would see to her well-being, both financially and personally.

He also stressed the fact that although there was indeed one other living relative, he, as a Whittaker, could adopt the child and still leave her with her rightful name.

Benjamin thought a moment longer, and added a postscript. He wrote the court that he would indeed consider guardianship if the court felt that would be in the child's best interests—then added Jessie's own words, that *he* sensed the child needed a parent more than a guardian. She had, after all, lost both her parents within a week, and would be known as an orphan if she were not adopted.

The lamplight magnified Benjamin's sarcastic smile as he spoke aloud. "Two can play at this game, madame. No doubt you worded your letter carefully as well, but I can offer Maria much more financially, and I have no doubt that the court will take that into account."

Benjamin sealed the envelope and put out the lamp.

He pulled off his shirt and walked to the window, opening it to hear the sound of the surf below.

After several minutes, listening to the calming effect of the sea, Benjamin murmured softly into the night air.

"I believe you've lost this round, Mrs. McAllister."

Darkness fell swiftly after Jessie galloped away from Benjamin's house, and the long shadows had now turned into ominous blackness. She had refused Mr. Cochran's offer to ride along with her, telling him she was not afraid of the dark.

He had accepted her refusal, assuring her that since the summer people were gone and the island once more belonged to the native islanders, she had nothing to fear. "People who live on the island are good people," he'd assured her.

Jessie had no reason to doubt his words, but when the wind whistled through the bare treetops and the small sliver of moon was eaten by an enormous cloud, a shiver of apprehension shot through her.

She had started out on this ride with optimism, but had met with obstinacy and cruel words from Benjamin. The warmth of the day was gone and as his harsh, cold words repeated in her head, a bitter chill crept into her body.

Jessie prodded her mount forward, picking up speed as she moved away from the hilly terrain near Benjamin's home. As she rode, though, the unmistakable sound of another set of hoofbeats came from behind her.

Could Benjamin have had a change of heart? Perhaps he was riding to tell her that he'd been wrong and would gladly have her raise Maria. Or could Margaret have sent Mr. Cochran to see that she got home safely?

Rather than worry needlessly about the solitary rider, she slowed her horse and turned in the saddle to see who approached.

At first, she indeed thought it was Benjamin because of the man's height in the saddle and the breadth of his shoulders. He was also wearing a vest that appeared to be like Benjamin's. Her heartbeat quickened at the thought that he might have realized his mistake and was coming to apologize. Whether or not he apologized, Jessie was relieved that there would be someone to ride along home with her. There'd be no need to fear the night with Benjamin by her side.

But when the man galloped closer, she was disappointed to see that he appeared to have light-colored hair and was not as muscular as Benjamin. In fact, despite the darkness, as he reined his horse in alongside her and removed his hat, she immediately recognized Arthur Conners, the young man who'd helped her move Frannie back to her home.

"Good evening, Mrs. McAllister."

"Good evening to you, Mr. Conners."

"It's a rather dark night," he said. "If you'd like an escort home, I'd be happy to ride along with you."

"I'm not afraid of the dark, Mr. Conners, but I must admit I'm not as familiar with the road as I thought. I'd be pleased to have you show me the way."

He replaced his hat and they started down the road side by side, just as Jessie had imagined riding alongside Benjamin.

"It's very nice of you to take the time to see me home," Jessie said.

"No problem at all, ma'am. If the truth be known, I still feel the need to do something to show you I'm not the scoundrel Mr. Whittaker believes me to be."

The remembrance of his "ogling" her, as Benjamin had put it, brought a flush to her cheeks and she was grateful for the lack of light. "I'm sure you're not. Mrs. Weldon told me you're a fine man."

"I hope you'll remember that as we continue our talk."

"That sounds rather ominous, Mr. Conners."

"If you don't mind, ma'am, I'd be honored if you'd call me Arthur."

"Only if you stop calling me, ma'am. It makes me feel ancient."

"You certainly aren't that, ma . . . Mrs.—"

"No, no," she interrupted. "Not Mrs. either. Just Jessica or Jessie will do. Now, Arthur, perhaps you should tell me what you want to talk to me about."

"I'm not exactly sure how to say this, but I would like to offer you my assistance," he said. "As I told you, your sister helped me with my children after my wife's death and I never had a chance to repay her kindness. I'd be pleased to repay that debt by doing something for you."

"And you are, by escorting me home," Jessie said, a bit curious about this lengthy explanation of his offer to see her home.

"Oh, no, you misunderstand. I mean, riding home with you is no problem, Jessica. Let me start over. I understand you've filed a petition to adopt your young niece, and I'd like to assist you in that regard."

"Do you have a friend at the courthouse too?" she asked rather brusquely, recalling the way Benjamin had learned of the adoption.

"No, ma'am. I just stopped at the house to take Mrs. Cochran some late fall apples as she wanted to make some apple butter, and she appeared distressed about you riding off alone. She rather blurted out the little skirmish you had with Mr. Whittaker over the adoption.

"And please don't think it was idle gossip. I don't hold to intruding into another's affairs, but Mrs. Cochran was upset and the words came out in her concern over you."

"All right, Arthur, I understand. But how in heaven's name do you think you could be of any assistance in the matter of Maria's adoption?"

Jessie waited with curiosity while Arthur cleared his throat, then hemmed and hawed, starting at least three times before he finally said his piece.

"Mrs. McAllister . . . Jessica . . . I'd like to . . . I mean, I'd be more than willing to marry you, if it would help solidify your claim to little Maria. With my name and a ready-made family in my three boys, it might be of some benefit when the court looks at your circumstances."

They'd been riding at a slow trot, but by the time Arthur had said his piece, Jessie had drawn her mount up short. He was several paces ahead when he evidently realized Jessie was no longer beside him. He stopped and turned back, their horses now turned in opposite directions. Removing his hat, Arthur focused his eyes on Jessie. His face was clearly visible now in the fragmented light of the crescent moon, partially uncovered as a cloud drifted away from its face.

She could only return his gaze, so stunned by his proposal that she was unable to speak. Arthur blinked once, then cast his eyes downward as though finding something interesting to look at on his hat band.

"Arthur . . . I'm at a loss for words. Why would you make such a proposal to a woman you barely know?"

"I told you, ma'am . . . Jessica, your sister was a fine woman who did so much for me when I had nowhere to turn. My wife's death devastated me and I . . . I couldn't properly care for my boys in my grief. Truth be known, I drank myself into a stupor for quite a few weeks. Mrs. Whittaker cared for my sons all that time, then took it upon herself to come into the tavern and bodily drag me out and sober me up.

"She then issued me an ultimatum, telling me to get hold of myself for my boys' sake or she'd see that they were given to a family who cared about them."

"Frannie said that?" Jessie asked, surprised by such a stern portrait of her sister, who was usually a sympathetic person.

Arthur looked up at her again, a grin on his face. "Oh, she didn't mean it. She just used the words to scare the livin' tar out of me—and it worked. I stayed sober, got back to my farming, and have managed to make a good home for my boys ever since. But as I said earlier, I never had a chance to return her kindness. Helping you would be my way of doing that."

Jessica smiled at the thought of marriage to this man as his way of relieving his debt to Frannie. She was certain her sister would be smiling down from heaven at this interesting turn of events.

"Arthur, I appreciate your offer, and I know my sister would be pleased at your willingness to help . . . but I believe two people who marry should have at least a fondness for each other, or perhaps share some part of one another's lives."

He looked down at his hat again.

"Do you understand what I mean, Arthur?"

"Yes, ma'am."

Then his head came up and his gaze locked on Jessie's. "I might say, though, that a man most likely wouldn't need much time to form a fondness for you, Jessica. You're a beautiful woman and one any man would be proud to call his own."

This declaration from Arthur Conners surprised Jessie much more than his chivalrous offer of marriage. Yet, she probably shouldn't have been surprised, recalling how Benjamin had censured the young man for the way he'd looked at her just days before.

"Thank you for your kind words and your generous offer to help, Arthur, but I believe the court will take into consideration the fact that I'm Maria's blood kin. I see no reason for you to give up your freedom when there could be a woman somewhere on this island right now destined to be your bride."

Jessie might have imagined it, but she believed she saw a flash of relief cross Arthur's face. "Now, why don't we stop dallying," she said. "I should be home with Maria. Care to race me?"

She didn't wait for his answer, but galloped off, getting a good head start. Jessie had no desire to continue their conversation, somehow feeling like an old maid who'd just turned down her last chance at marriage.

Arthur's steed quickly caught up with hers, and they sped along side by side the rest of the way. With the sound of the surf, the wind whistling through the overhead branches, and the horses' hoofbeats, conversation would have been impossible, even if Jessie had wanted to speak. When they neared the road to Frannie's home, Jessie slowed to a trot and turned. "Thank you for your kindness in seeing me home, Arthur. I'll be fine now."

Again he tipped his hat. "It was my pleasure. As was the race," he added with a smile. "You ride well. And please, Jessica, do keep in mind my offer. If you have any problem with the adoption, my proposal stands." He looked at her for one more long moment. "Arranged marriages often result in love . . . it could easily happen in this case as well."

With those words said, he turned and galloped off, leaving Jessie to ponder his provocative statement.

Moments later, though, she had no doubt that what he'd said could never happen between them.

No, Arthur, she thought. I married once without passion. I'll not make the same mistake again.

No matter what might happen between her and Benjamin, she'd experienced the pleasure of his impassioned kiss, the excitement of his touch. Jessie would settle for nothing less before she married again.

Then her thoughts turned to her niece and the remote possibility of losing her. Jessie uttered a silent, prayerful plea that there would be no reason for her to take Arthur Conners up on his proposal . . . because if it meant keeping Maria, Jessie knew she would do anything to achieve that goal.

Even if it meant marrying a man she didn't love.

Chapter Eight

Jessie went in the back door and found Ann sitting at the kitchen table reading.

Ann immediately set her book aside. "Well, was your visit with Benjamin productive?"

"Now that's an interesting question, Ann," Jessie said. "My visit with Benjamin ended in angry words with me walking out of his house . . . but on my way home I received a proposal of marriage."

Ann's eyes widened in surprise. "He came after you and proposed?"

Jessie shook her head, unable to keep the laughter out of her voice. "It was Arthur Conners who proposed."

"Arthur?"

"I'm sorry," Jessie said, stifling her laughter. "I should not be laughing, but it suddenly struck me as quite funny."

"Why would Arthur propose? He barely knows you."

Jessie removed her cape and sat down at the table. "He was actually being quite thoughtful. Margaret happened to mention the adoption to him, and he thought it might bode well if I were married."

"Surely you didn't consider his proposal."

"No. I told Arthur I thought the court would take into consideration the fact that I'm Maria's aunt, but he did say his offer still stands if I run into difficulties. And to be truthful, Ann, I am concerned."

"About what, Jessie?"

"What if Benjamin fights me? I have nothing to offer Maria. No money in the bank . . . not even a home of my own."

"This house belongs to Maria," Ann said firmly. "And I'm sure the court will be more concerned with a loving parent raising her here in her own home than the finances involved."

"I would hope so. But Benjamin loves her too. If things should go his way . . ."

Ann shook her head. "No. Jessie, you musn't think of marrying without love."

Jessie sighed deeply. "That's what I told Arthur. But he left me with his thought that arranged marriages often result in love."

"Are you telling me you are seriously considering marriage to Arthur?"

"Not seriously, but if need be, I might."

Ann suddenly smiled.

"What do you find so amusing?" Jessie asked.

"I was just thinking, perhaps it's your angel who's sent Arthur Conners to your aid."

Jessie shook her head. "Maria's been talking to you too."

"Not directly, but I did hear her telling Willy about her Momma-angel."

"Do you think this is something I should be concerned about, Ann?"

"I don't think so. It's not all that strange for the child to want to see and talk to her mother. If her imagination is strong, she might very well be able to do that." Ann stood and closed her book. Then she looked at Jessica. "You know there is the possibility that it's not her imagination."

"Oh, Ann, I know you're a minister's wife, but surely you don't think the dead just sprout wings and come back to earth?"

"Perhaps, if something has been left unsettled, they come back until their mission is complete."

"And what, pray tell, might Frannie have left unsettled?" Jessie asked.

"The way you and Benjamin are arguing over her child would be enough to bring a mother back."

"I don't believe we're having this conversation about heavenly beings. It's Maria's imagination. That's all it is."

"It probably is," Ann agreed. "But you must keep in mind that through the ages, children have been more attuned to spiritual things, simply because they are still innocent enough to believe anything is possible."

"Maria told me that's why I couldn't see Frannie," Jessie said. "Because I didn't believe."

Ann put her arms around Jessie. "Don't dwell on it anymore tonight. You're exhausted, and it's time we all got some rest. Besides," she added with a half smile, "you have to reconsider Arthur's proposal. That might put an end to Maria's uncertain future."

The children's appearance brought their conversation to an abrupt end.

After Ann and Willy went home, Jessie got Maria ready for bed. But long after the child slept, Jessie sat and thought about what Ann had said.

"Dear Lord," she whispered before crawling into bed, "please help me to adopt Maria without having to consider marrying a man I don't love."

Jessie woke early after a restless night tormented by horrible dreams of Benjamin trying to pull Maria from her arms, while Arthur attempted to keep Benjamin from doing so. The dream ended with the two men fighting and Jessie running away with Maria.

The dream left her more exhausted than when she'd gone to bed, but she couldn't go back to sleep. Jessie checked on Maria, who continued to sleep in her mother's bed, and tucked the quilt over her shoulders. She then stoked the fire and added wood before going downstairs.

In the chilly kitchen, she quickly opened the firebox of the cookstove, shook down the ashes, and added kindling to the remaining coals. She put the teakettle on, then got busy mixing biscuit dough until the water finally boiled. After brewing herself a pot of tea, she put a pan of biscuits in the oven. The smell would probably rouse Maria from her slumber since there was almost nothing she liked better than biscuits with her mother's strawberry jam.

Jessie picked up the jam jar she'd set out on the table, and thought about her sister picking the berries in the warm summer sunshine. "Oh, Frannie," she said aloud. "I wish I'd come for a visit. If only I had been here just one summer to help you pick berries or take Maria swimming in the lake. What a joy it would have been if I'd been able to share a Christmas here with you and your daughter, or gone together on a sleigh ride.

"All those things you wrote me about. Your descriptions were so vivid, I felt as though I were here with you—but I wasn't—and the opportunity is lost forever. Nevertheless, I'm here now and I will do these things with Maria, and through her your memory will be with me always."

Jessie drained her teacup and got up to check on the biscuits.

"Aunt Jess." Maria's voice sounded tentative as she padded into the kitchen on bare feet.

"Maria, haven't I told you to put slippers on before you come downstairs? It's not summer anymore, and if you don't start wearing slippers, you're going to get—"

Jessie stopped, noticing that the child wasn't listening but looking around the kitchen as though searching for something.

"Maria, what are you looking for?"

The little girl glanced up at Jessie and blinked her eyes, the long, dark lashes brushing her cheeks like butterflies. "Who were you talking to, Aunt Jess?"

"I wasn't talking to anybody."

"But I heard you. When I walked down the steps I heard you talking."

Jessie walked over and gave Maria a big hug. "Oh, now you know my secret."

"A secret?" she asked, her eyes wide.

"I talk to myself sometimes," Jessie whispered conspiratorially.

For the first time since she'd arrived, Jessie

heard the little girl giggle. Not just a smile or a bit of laughter—this was out-and-out giggling—just the way little girls had done all through the centuries.

Just the way she and Frannie had done together.

And Jessie suddenly felt sad because Maria would never have a sister with whom she could share giggles and other precious moments.

When Maria finally stopped laughing, she sat down at the table and matter-of-factly said, "I thought you might have been talking to Momma, because she was upstairs before."

"Well, actually I was talking to your mother, but it's just my way of keeping her memory alive. I don't see her and she doesn't answer me."

"She wasn't here when I came in," Maria said. "That's why I was wondering if she might have left before I got here."

"She didn't leave because she was never here, Maria."

"Maybe she was and you just didn't see her."

Jessie debated whether or not to push the issue, then decided to let it drop. She turned to the stove and got the fresh biscuits from the pan. "Why don't we have some of your momma's strawberry jam on these biscuits I just took out of the oven."

"Yummy," Maria said. "I love Momma's strawberry jam. It's even better than Mrs. Cochran's."

As they ate, Jessie enjoyed listening to Maria talk about Willy's puppets and the books he had at his house. Having been alone for so long, Jessie found it a joy to have someone at the table with her, especially this child of her sister's who was so dear.

* * *

After breakfast, Maria again asked Jessie if she could go to the vineyard to pick grapes.

"Is it important that you do this, Maria?" Jessie asked, honestly trying to understand this business with the wine company.

"Of course it is, Aunt Jess. That's why we have a holiday from school, to help with the picking. Everyone goes, even Mr. and Mrs. Cochran and Willy and James."

"Is this your way of telling me that I should be going too?"

Maria nodded her head vigorously, emphasizing her words. "You live on the island now. Aunt Jess and Momma always said that every able-bodied man, woman, and child on the island was needed at grape-picking time. But whether you go or not, I have to go. I am, after all, a Whittaker, and Poppa told me as his firstborn child the wine company was a part of my birthright."

Hearing these strong words from her young niece, Jessie knew if she was to be a part of Maria's life, she too must adjust to the island ways. If grape picking was such an important part of island life, then Jessie too must become involved. She smiled down at her niece. "All right, we'll both go. I want to do my share too."

"Yea!" Maria shouted, jumping up and down and clapping her hands, looking more like a child again.

Jessie's lips curved into a wide smile. This was the second time she'd heard Maria act more like a little girl than a sober adult.

An hour later they were both in the vineyard. Maria had gotten her aunt a stool, basket, and shears and had shown her what to do.

There were three to four people working in each

row of vines. Jessie, Maria, a friendly woman named Alice, and her little girl Joanna worked in one row. The sun had come out from behind the early morning clouds, and the warmth of the sunshine added to Jessie's enjoyment of her outdoor work. It had been a while since she'd worked in her own fields back in Indiana, and it felt good to be working outside again.

She hadn't realized how much she'd missed farming. The sun was warm on her back, and the smell of the earth mingling with the sweet fragrance of the grapes tantalized her. She could almost taste the sweet grape juice Maria had promised they would get to drink when they stopped for lunch.

Glancing further down the row, she saw Maria and Joanna talking as they worked. Alice caught her eye and smiled broadly.

All in all, Jessie thought, this is the best morning I've had in a long, long time.

"What are you doing in my vineyard?" The words were whispered, yet so harshly and so near her ear, Jessie jerked back and almost fell from her stool. But Benjamin's strong arms caught her and set her upright.

"You scared the wits out of me," she whispered back angrily.

"I doubt if anyone could frighten you, madame."

Jessie looked up into Benjamin's eyes, wondering how he could hate her so much. She'd done nothing to hurt him. Why did he look at her with such loathing?

"Benjamin—"

"Uncle Ben . . . Uncle Ben." Maria was up off her stool and racing between the two rows of vines till she stood in front of her uncle, wrapping her arms around him.

"Well, good morning, Maria," he said, bending down to return his niece's hug. "It's good to see you back."

"It feels good to be back. And did you see—I brought Aunt Jess!" Then she motioned Benjamin closer and whispered, "She's new at this, but she's a good worker."

Benjamin cleared his throat and said, "Well, we need good workers, don't we, my little one?"

"Uh-huh. I told Aunt Jess that Momma said everybody had to do their share."

Benjamin beamed down at Maria. "You're going to be a grand winery manager someday, child."

"I know," she said. "Poppa always told me that. But right now, I better get back to work or Joanna's going to pick more grapes than me."

Benjamin and Jessie both watched her go, and waved in unison when Maria turned back to wave at them. With a fake smile still on his face, he turned back to Jessie. "I hope you don't think I'm fooled by this ploy, madame. Working in my vineyard and putting on a friendly face is not going to make me change my mind about you."

She too smiled at him as she spoke. "Oh, I'm not doing this for you, Benjamin. Maria asked me to come, explaining how important it was for everyone to help. Since it will be her vineyard someday, I decided to come for her sake. But surprisingly, I'm enjoying it immensely. I did work a farm for three years, you know, so outdoor work agrees with me."

"You're very good, Jessica. I'll give you that. But if you think your little speech will soften my attitude toward you, you're wrong."

"I have no reason to want you to like me, Benjamin . . . though it would be nice if we could at least pretend to get along so Maria didn't have to choose between us."

"She won't have to choose," Benjamin shot back, his smile suddenly vanished. "When the court receives the request I sent on the first ferry this morning, they will choose for her. And I, madame, will be their choice."

Jessie's heart hammered in her chest. "What do you mean? You also sent a petition for her adoption?"

He crossed his arms and glared at her. "That is correct."

"Benjamin, why are you doing this? Why hurt that child any more than she's already been hurt?"

"She won't know about this. Only when the final decision is made will she have to be told."

Jessie shook her head sadly. "I had hoped we could at least be good friends and together see that Maria was raised well, but I see now it's not to be."

"You won't get her, Jessica. She's a Whittaker and the court will agree that I am best suited to adopt her."

Jessie couldn't bear to see the animosity in his eyes another moment. She turned back to the vines and continued cutting.

Benjamin clenched his jaw, knowing he couldn't raise his voice here. How dare you turn your back on me? he thought. Then he glanced down the row of vines aware of someone watching him.

When he saw Maria looking at him with a puzzled expression on her face, he immediately forced a smile. After she returned his smile and a wave, he left the vineyard.

Benjamin had much to do. He'd been surprised when the man who'd carried his request for adoption to the court telegraphed him that an official would arrive on the last ferry of the day to investigate the two petitions received. He'd assumed it would be weeks before anyone would come.

A smile came to Benjamin's lips as he realized Jessica would not be at home to receive the official. Maria had done well in bringing her to the vineyard.

Benjamin went into the office of his company manager, Henry Monroe, to let him know he would be leaving for the day.

"But Ben, you've been gone so much and it's such a busy time. You handle the men better than I. My proficiency is here with the accounts and managing the supplies. The men need your authority. Our production is always off when you're not here to supervise the pressing."

Benjamin listened attentively, and was torn between his concern for the company and his need to keep Maria from Jessica's clutches.

"I'm sorry, Henry. This is something that can't be set aside. I apologize for giving you the additional work and promise to make it up to you."

"You don't need to make it up to me. I know how much you care about this company and your employees. I am well aware that you work harder than most men here, so whatever you have to do today must be important. Just get back as soon as possible."

"I will," Benjamin said. "On that you have my word."

Before going home, Benjamin stopped to say

good-bye to Maria. He was pleased to see that she and her friend had moved further down the row, so there was no chance of Jessica hearing what he told the child. "Maria, I have to go and tend to some business. I hope you'll see that your aunt gets some of our grape juice with her lunch—you did bring a lunch, didn't you?"

"Oh, yes. Aunt Jess brought us some ham and biscuits left over from breakfast, and we have apples too."

Benjamin smiled smugly. "Good, then I'll see you both when I get back later."

He turned and saw that Jessica was looking their way, so he smiled broadly and waved. He could see the indecision on her face before she finally raised her hand to wave in return. But she didn't return his smile, and Benjamin wondered how he could possibly miss it so much.

At the house, Benjamin could see his plans had been set in motion. Some of the men he'd hired were just finishing the outdoor work, and when he stepped inside the house he could see Margaret had done wonders.

Shopkeepers from town had opened their doors to him early that morning, and he had surprised Margaret by giving her free rein with the purchases. He'd also requested and received help from some men in his employ, who'd offered to transport everything from the shops to his house.

As Benjamin entered the hall, a floral-patterned carpet in shades of green and blue muffled his steps. Brass sconces were already affixed to the walls, and the crystal teardrops dangling from them glowed in the candlelight.

Margaret had just finished lighting the candles when he entered.

"It's beautiful, Margaret."

The woman whirled around, smiling nervously, rather like a little girl with her hand caught in the candy jar. "I couldn't wait till nightfall to see how they looked, Mr. Benjamin. Doesn't the glow of the candles brighten the staircase?"

"Not only that," Benjamin said, "the little crystal bobs shimmer like the sun on the lake. The sconces are perfect."

Margaret beamed with the praise. "Samuel's helping Mr. Shenkle finish hanging the mirrors in the sitting room and parlor. Oh, wait till you see them, Mr. Benjamin. They have lovely gilt frames, and the reflected light does wonders for the rooms. And I've also taken the liberty of hiring Mrs. Mills to help me with a few things. She's just finishing in the living room.

"We've pulled back the heavy drapes in the parlor and hung lace curtains at the windows. It allows sunlight to enter, and there's a lovely view of the lake from there."

"With the pleasure I derive from looking at the lake," Benjamin said, "I'm amazed I've never thought to do that."

Margaret continued to smile, obviously relishing his approval.

"Well, I won't keep you, Margaret. I'll just go on and see what other wonders you've wrought in my home."

"I could never have done it alone, Mr. Benjamin. The owners of each of the stores where I made purchases offered to have one of the boys in their employ come and help with the installation of the various items I acquired. They've done an enormous job."

"Good, I'll be sure to thank them all for their help." Benjamin left Margaret to her work and continued along the hall, inspecting each room. His housekeeper had indeed done what she'd set out to do. There were warm, homey touches everywhere, and Benjamin finally understood why Jessica had said the house was cold.

There were grand seascapes with elegantly carved wooden frames in both the hall and sitting room. Sconces on either side graced the one in the hall, and the one in the sitting room brightened the bare stone wall opposite the fireplace.

In the parlor, the lace curtains were a wonderful change, in addition to lovely statues and brass candlesticks on the mantle. Margaret had evidently resurrected numerous objects from the attic, as he recognized many of his mother's belongings in the rooms.

In the upper hall, he marveled at the magnificently framed portraits of his grandparents. The portraits had once hung in his parents' home, but his wife had refused to display them in her house.

Benjamin moved from one room to the next, staring in wonder at the many vases of fall foliage and bright yellow and orange mums that adorned mantles and tables everywhere.

As he entered the library, his amazement continued. The empty shelves were filled with the books that he'd stored away when he and Helene had moved into the house. His wife had hated books and refused to unpack them. He had brought a few down over the years when he'd had time to read, but had never consider putting them all in place. And on the table in the center of the room was the carved ivory chess set his father had bought for him and Jonathan.

Benjamin picked up one of the exquisitely carved pieces—a white king he'd often used to trounce his brother—and rubbed his thumb over the surface. The sight and feel of the piece brought a warm feeling of nostalgia as Benjamin recalled the many rainy days spent at the chess table with Jonathan.

He slumped down in an armchair. "I miss you, brother," he murmured aloud. "How I wish you and Fran were still here." Benjamin leaned forward, his head in his hands, suddenly overwhelmed by emotion.

"Oh, dear," came a startled gasp from the doorway. "You don't like it," Margaret said. "We can put it back the way it was, sir. I thought the books were so lovely, but if you'd rather—"

Benjamin shook his head. "No, no . . . Margaret, it's magnificent. Everything you've done is perfect. You've changed this house into a home. You've replaced the coldness with warmth. I'm grateful to you."

"But you seemed so . . . sad."

"It was seeing the chess set," he said, still fingering the piece. "My brother and I had many wonderful times together over that board."

"Would you like me to put it back in storage?"

"No." He stood and placed his hand on her shoulder. "Memories are good to have. I don't want to forget my brother nor the special times we shared. Thank you for bringing it out."

Margaret nodded, and Benjamin thought he detected a tear in her eye. When she turned and dabbed at her eyes with her apron, he knew he'd been right.

"When will our guest be arriving?" she asked after she'd composed herself.

"On the four o'clock ferry."

"Then we must hurry so all the workers are out of the house before our guest arrives. Would you like me to prepare something to serve before dinner?"

"Perhaps a light snack. I'm sure coffee and something sweet would do when he arrives."

"Yes, sir." Margaret stood there for several moments, and he finally asked her if there was something on her mind.

"I guess I can't help but wonder who we're doin' all this for. I know it's none of my business, but to make all these changes for one visitor is a bit of a puzzle to me."

"Ah, but this is a most important visitor. The man who will be coming to look at this house is an official from the court on the mainland. He is going to judge who is best qualified to adopt Maria."

The happiness that had lit Margaret's face since he'd arrived home abruptly vanished, like a flame doused by water.

"You don't approve?"

"It's not my place to approve or disapprove, sir."

"But you think this is unfair of me, don't you?"

Margaret sighed and shook her head. "My only thought is how sad that you would change this house only to impress some official from the court. If you'd made the improvements with Maria in mind, it would have meant so much more. If you'd made the changes in order to make this place more like a home for the child, then your gesture would have meant something."

Margaret stared at him, her blue eyes darkening

with disappointment, making Benjamin recall how she'd made him feel as a boy when he'd gotten into some sort of mischief.

"But you weren't thinking about Maria when you arranged for all this to be done," she said, gesturing expansively with both arms upraised. "You were thinking only of winning—of beating Miss Jessie. And that takes all the warmth away. This house feels cold again." With those words she turned and walked away.

"Margaret."

For the first time in all her years with Benjamin, the woman did not turn, did not come back, did not even acknowledge that he'd spoken her name.

"Dear God," he murmured. "Now that witch has turned my own housekeeper away from me."

When Samuel saw his wife in the upstairs hall, he could see her mood had changed dramatically. "My dear, what's wrong?"

Margaret shook her head sadly. "Mr. Benjamin has turned bitter, Samuel. I'm afraid for him and for little Maria. She needs warmth and caring, and instead she's goin' to be in the middle of a tug of war."

"We can do nothing, Margaret. We are, after all, only employees in this house."

Margaret nodded. "I know. But I don't like to see this happen. Miss Jessie was good for Mr. Benjamin. I could see the change in him after she came. If only they could have become closer before this adoption issue came up."

Samuel smiled and shook his head. "You are nothing but an old matchmaker."

She looked up into his clear blue eyes, returning

his smile. "I just want everyone to be as happy as I am."

The old man put his arm around his wife's shoulder and said, "I know, my dear, but this time, I don't think you can change the course of events. Perhaps Maria herself will somehow bring them together."

"She needs them both, Samuel. If only the two of them could see that."

"Mrs. McAllister made an effort in coming here last night," Samuel said. "It was Mr. Benjamin who turned her away."

Margaret agreed. "He's a stubborn one, and it's the fault of that woman he married so long ago. She left him cynical and with an unyielding nature where women are concerned."

Samuel patted her shoulder and reassured her. "He may learn yet. Mrs. McAllister is a lovely woman and Maria could still bring them together. Benjamin knows her sister was a good woman. Perhaps he'll finally be able to forget that woman who left him, divorcing him without a second thought."

"I don't know." Margaret sighed. "Sometimes he seems so bitter, I'm not sure he'll ever get over it."

"Margaret? . . . Samuel? . . . Where the devil are you?" Benjamin's voice drifted upstairs, and the old couple quickly rushed to the landing to answer.

"Coming, Mr. Benjamin," Margaret called down.

Benjamin met them at the bottom of the stairs. "Aren't you two finished upstairs?"

"Yes, sir," Samuel said. "We were just checking to make sure the workmen didn't leave anything behind."

"We want everything to look just right for your important visitor, sir," Margaret said, a tad sharply.

"Margaret, I realize you are not happy with my conduct. But I am doing what I feel is necessary to fulfill a promise made to my brother and his wife. I vowed to care for Maria and I'll do anything to keep that vow. Do I make myself clear?"

"Yes, sir," Margaret answered.

"She's just concerned that Maria will be caught in the middle of a battle," Samuel said, coming to his wife's defense.

Benjamin shook his head and put a hand on Margaret's shoulder. "Margaret, I know you mean well, and I wish there didn't have to be a battle, but—"

"There doesn't have to be," she interrupted.

"Margaret, I know what I'm doing. Jessica McAllister wants that child for her own and I won't stand for it. Maria's a Whittaker and a Whittaker she will remain!"

Margaret shrugged off his hand. "If you'll excuse me, sir, I have work to finish." She did not wait for a reply before turning and hurrying away.

Benjamin saw Samuel's struggle as he looked from his employer to his departing wife and back again.

"Please, sir," he finally said. "Forgive her. She means well."

"I know Samuel. You've both been more like friends than employees, and I don't like hurting Margaret's feelings, but I have to do what I feel is right where my brother's only child and heir is concerned."

"Yes, sir. I only hope you realize that Mrs. McAllister is most likely thinking she must do right by her *sister's* only child."

Without another word, Samuel turned and followed his wife into the kitchen, while Benjamin was left to ponder all that had been said.

Could I be wrong? Benjamin wondered. Yet when he recalled Fran's words, he was certain she'd asked him to take care of Maria.

A loud knocking interrupted his thoughts, and he hurried to the door.

A tall, slim young man with bright red hair and a mustache to match stood on the threshold. Large spectacles and a rather ill-fitting woolen suit made him look very much like a stern teacher Benjamin had once despised. "Mr. Whittaker?"

"Yes, I'm Benjamin Whittaker."

The man extended his hand. "Robert Talbot, sir. I'm here in regard to the letter you sent the court about your niece."

"Oh, of course," he said, shaking the young man's hand. "Do come in, Mr. Talbot. We weren't expecting you until the four o'clock ferry. In fact, I had someone going to pick you up at the dock."

He smiled crookedly at Benjamin and said, "We like to surprise people. Catch them off guard, so to speak."

"Of course. A wise idea, I'm sure. I was actually quite surprised to hear you were coming so soon. I imagined it would take some time to get to my petition."

"Normally, it might take a bit longer, but my superiors thought it warranted a faster response since we received *two* petitions in two days for the same child. That rarely happens—in fact, it never does.

"I tried going to your brother's home to speak with Mrs. McAllister first, since she too filed for adoption, but no one seemed to be at home," Mr. Talbot said.

"Well, I'm glad you found your way here then."

As they'd spoken, Benjamin took note of Talbot's observation of the entry, his eyes going up the stairs and back down the hall to the new wall arrangement.

"Lovely seascape. Is it one of Adele Thompson's?"

Fortunately for Benjamin, Margaret came through the hall at that moment and answered for him. "No, sir. That one's by a local artist here on the island—Oliver Cooper. Mr Whittaker likes to support the local people, don't you, sir?"

She smiled at him with a cherubic look in her blue eyes as she took Mr. Talbot's hat.

"Of course," Benjamin said with a broad smile of his own. "We all depend on each other on the island. Rather like one large family."

Benjamin hoped Mr. Talbot didn't see the look Margaret gave him when he said those words.

"That's quite commendable, Mr. Whittaker," the man said, pulling a small leather-bound notebook from his suit pocket.

"Would you gentlemen care for coffee or tea in the parlor?" the housekeeper asked.

"Coffee would be quite nice," Mr. Talbot said. "The crossing was rather brisk despite the sunshine."

"Coffee for me as well, Margaret," Benjamin said, "But we'll take it in the library. Much less formal . . . if you don't mind?" he said to the bespectacled young man.

"That would be fine. No need to be formal with me, sir."

After Margaret left them, Benjamin led Talbot

into the library. Once again he noticed the man's eyes taking in every detail of the room. Talbot walked to the far wall and scrutinized the shelves filled with countless volumes.

"Quite a collection you have here, sir. I am personally fond of all of Shakespeare's works."

He turned abruptly and caught Benjamin's eye. "Do you have a favorite author?"

Well, Benjamin thought, Margaret can't save me this time.

"Unfortunately my business keeps me so busy I rarely have time to read. But when I do, I usually choose Dickens."

"Ah, very good choice." Again Benjamin watched as the man made notes in his little black book, and he couldn't help wondering what he had written—"likes Dickens," perhaps, or "is hard worker." Benjamin wondered if working long hours would make him less fit to be a parent. *Perhaps I should address that right now.*

"Although I do work long hours, I want you to know that I spend as much time as possible with my niece. In fact, we were in the vineyards together this morning."

"Your niece does not attend school?"

"Of course, but we have a two-week grape-picking vacation here on the island twice a year since many hands are needed to harvest the grapes."

"I see. Quaint custom."

"It's more a necessity than a custom, but as I was saying, I do spend time with my niece and when I am unable to be here, Mrs. Cochran is quite capable of caring for her."

"Your housekeeper?"

"Margaret is truly more than a housekeeper,

Mr. Talbot. She and her husband Samuel have been with our family for more than thirty years. They came to the island with my parents and remained with me after my parents died.

"They are friends as well as employees," Benjamin finished.

Additional notes in the book. Then the young man removed a handkerchief from his pocket and took several seconds to clean his spectacles.

"You have a lovely home. I would like to see the child's room before I leave."

"Certainly."

Margaret entered with the coffee tray, and the next few minutes were taken up with her pouring and offering the little jam cakes Benjamin liked so well.

"These cakes are quite delicious, Mrs. Cochran," the young man said after sampling a raspberry one.

"Thank you, sir. They're a favorite with Mr. Benjamin—have been for quite a few years."

Benjamin's mind drifted back in time as Margaret talked with Mr. Talbot. He could still recall the first time she'd made those jam cakes. He must have been near Maria's age when he first tasted them. And he remembered licking his lips and declaring them "the most delicious sweets I've ever eaten."

"Isn't that right, sir?" Margaret asked, bringing him back from his reverie.

"I'm terribly sorry, Margaret. I'm afraid I was lost in thought—remembering the first time you served the jam cakes in my mother's home."

Margaret smiled up at him, her pink cheeks taking on more color. "I remember. You said they were the most delicious sweets you'd ever eaten."

Benjamin nodded, feeling again the pull of nostalgic reminiscence. When he looked up again, Mr. Talbot was scribbling furiously in his notebook once more.

"Quite nice to see a relationship like this," Talbot said.

"If you gentlemen will excuse me, I should be getting back to the kitchen."

"Of course, Margaret," Benjamin said. "And when we're finished with our business, Mr. Talbot will want to see Maria's room—that is, the room she stayed in when she was living here."

"And the rest of the house, if it wouldn't be too much trouble?" Mr. Talbot interjected.

"No trouble at all, sir," Margaret said. "Just let me know when you're ready."

With the notebook open, Mr. Talbot said, "You mentioned, 'when the child was living here.' When was that?"

"It was before her aunt came. After her father—my brother Jonathan—was drowned in a boating mishap, her mother was in a coma. I brought them both here to care for them."

"Then Mrs. McAllister came?"

"Yes. I believe it was four or five days later. I'd sent her a telegram and she came shortly after that."

"Is Mrs. McAllister close to the child as well?"

"They get on quite well for just having met one another."

One of the young man's red eyebrows arched up. "They'd never met before?"

"No. Jessica's residence is in Indiana. She and her husband owned a farm there, and evidently there was never an opportunity for her to come for a visit."

Mr. Talbot pushed his spectacles up his nose and riffled through the pages of his notebook, then looked back up at Benjamin. "The child is six years old?"

Benjamin nodded. "Correct."

More notes. Benjamin suppressed the smile that came to his lips. He was certain he knew what the man had written that time.

"And where is *Mr.* McAllister at this time?"

"Mrs. McAllister is a widow. Her husband died over three years ago."

Again Talbot's arched eyebrow preceded his question. "Do you know the reason she didn't come to see her sister and niece after she was widowed?"

"I believe she tried to keep the farm going after her husband's death."

"Commendable," Talbot said, jotting down more notes.

Damn, Benjamin thought. I have to watch what I say, or she's going to look like a saint.

"Does she still have the farm?"

"No, she lost it about a year ago."

Benjamin walked to the window, hands clasped behind his back, trying to compose his next words. "Fran, that's Maria's mother, asked Jessica to come and stay with them at the time. My sister-in-law had fond memories of her younger sister and was quite excited about the prospect of having her come here to live."

"But she didn't?"

"No. I believe she decided against it because she didn't care for life on the island. As I recall, when she came for her sister's wedding seven years ago, she couldn't wait to get off the island."

"Strange," Mr. Talbot remarked, his bushy red

eyebrows knitting together. "It seems to be a rather attractive piece of land, and quite peaceful away from the city."

"I agree with you and I felt badly for my dear sister-in-law. Fran had counted on Jessica coming and was quite disappointed. I believe the reason Jessica gave at the time was that she was uncomfortable being surrounded by water and being at the mercy of the elements."

"Yet," Mr. Talbot said, "the child knows only life here on the island, and I assume she loves her home."

"Yes," Benjamin agreed with a smile. "Maria loves everything about the island. She is well versed in its plant life and loves to swim and fish and watch the waves lap at the shore. I can't imagine her living anywhere but here on the island."

And that warranted another note in Talbot's book.

Benjamin smiled. *Let Jessica try to get out of that one.*

Chapter Nine

After Margaret and Samuel showed Mr. Talbot the house and stables, Benjamin took him on a tour of the wine company and the vineyards.

"Quite impressive, Mr. Whittaker," the young man said as they stood on the balcony of Benjamin's office looking out over the vast fields of symmetrical rows of vines—workers busy at their task of harvesting the grapes.

"Thank you. My brother and I worked hard to make it profitable, and of course it will all be Maria's someday."

Talbot nodded. "Indeed, I read that in the report I received." He looked out at the vineyard, glancing at the many workers. "You mentioned that Maria was working here today. Perhaps I could meet her."

"Certainly. Come inside and I'll send one of the men out to fetch her."

While they waited for Maria, Benjamin served Mr. Talbot a glass of their best wine.

"Excellent . . . excellent, Mr. Whittaker. I have tasted some fine wine in my time, but this Catawba is outstanding."

Benjamin beamed. "The combination of the limestone soil here on the island along with our superior climate is conducive to the growth of a superb grape," he said.

"If those are the reasons, then you do indeed have the perfect place for a winery," Talbot said. "I must take a bottle home to my father. He enjoys a good bottle of wine."

"You will take two then, with my compliments."

Mr. Talbot smiled, which made him look even younger. "No. I'll be delighted to pay. In my job there can be no hint of favoritism, so we accept no gifts or monetary contributions."

"I assure you bribery was not my intent," Benjamin quickly said.

"Of course not. I did not take it as such."

Maria came in, looking tentatively from her uncle to Mr. Talbot. Benjamin smiled and extended his arms. Maria hesitated only a moment and ran to him. He scooped her up in his arms, and glancing back at Mr. Talbot, she said, "Henry said you wanted me to meet somebody."

"Yes I did, my sweet. This is Mr. Talbot, and this, Mr. Talbot, is my niece, Maria Whittaker."

Benjamin set her back down, and Talbot took the child's hand and bowed low, kissing it as he did so.

Maria giggled. "That tickles."

"Mustaches often do, Maria," he said with a smile. "Would you mind sitting and talking with me for a few minutes?"

Maria shook her head and climbed up on a chair across from her uncle's desk. Talbot pulled another chair over and sat beside her.

"Maria, do you know anything about the courts?"

She shook her head and said, "No. I'm only in first grade, so we're learning how to read and write . . . and do some 'rithmetic. But the older kids are learning about somethin' like that. I heard Willy's big brother James talking about justice in the courts one day in school, but I didn't understand when he tried to explain it to me."

"All right, then I'm not going to try either, except to say that there are good people in the courts who try and make laws that help people be nice to each other, or to keep them from harm."

"You mean like when the marshal doesn't let somebody steal something from the store or when you aren't allowed to swim if a storm's coming?" she asked.

"Yes," Talbot said with a broad smile. "You're a smart little girl."

"That's what my momma always told me."

Talbot leaned forward in his chair, putting himself eye to eye with the child. "And your momma's gone now, isn't she?"

"She did die, but I can still talk to her anytime I want."

Talbot glanced at Benjamin, a wary look on his face. Benjamin shook his head, indicating that the man should not pursue this line of questioning.

Mr. Talbot nodded and cleared his throat, then looked back at the little girl with a smile firmly planted on his face. "I see. Well, Maria, as I was saying I come from the court where good people make those laws I was telling you about. And the court that I come from back on the mainland sent me to find out where the best place is for you to live and who you should live with."

Maria tipped her head to the side, her dark curls falling across her shoulder. She looked at Talbot for several seconds, then wiped her hands on her apron and looked at him again.

Benjamin could see the man was biding his time and letting Maria think about what he'd said.

When she finally spoke, she sounded very cautious, as though suddenly aware of the fact that her world might not be as secure as she thought. "You don't have to find out anything because I already have a house and my Aunt Jess is there, so I don't need to live with anybody else."

"I know your aunt has been taking good care of you, but your Uncle Ben here loves you too and thought you might like to live with him."

Maria made a face, then shook her head. "I love you too, Uncle Ben, but I don't like your house."

Mr. Talbot leaned even closer to Maria. "Why not, Maria? It's a beautiful home."

"I like my house better. It's not so big and it's not made out of that gray stuff."

Talbot nodded and made more notes in the little black book.

"May I say something?" Benjamin asked.

"Please do," Talbot answered.

Benjamin scooted down next to Maria's chair. "What if I would move into your house and take care of you there?"

"Oh, Uncle Ben, it would be fun having you and Aunt Jess there together . . . and Momma would be so—"

"No, no, Maria," Benjamin interrupted. "I

meant just me . . . and maybe Margaret and Samuel."

She looked at him quizzically. "But where would Aunt Jess live?"

"She might want to go back home to Indiana, Maria."

Maria shook her head vigorously, her long curls twisting to and fro. "No. Aunt Jess never talks about Indiana. She's staying here with me. She promised Momma she'd take care of me."

Benjamin started to speak, but Mr. Talbot held up a hand. "Just a minute. I'd like to hear what Maria has to say."

As Maria told Talbot that she had been in the room the morning her mother died and heard her ask her aunt to take care of her, Benjamin began pacing back and forth in front of his desk.

"Momma told me I'd never have to be afraid, 'cause Aunt Jess loved me and would always take care of me. She . . . she said . . . forever. That's it, she said Aunt Jess would take care of me forever!"

Furious scribbling in the little book at those words.

Benjamin again got down to Maria's level and said, "Sweetheart, are you sure you heard your mother say those things?"

The little girl nodded her head firmly.

"But you see, she told me to take care of you too," Benjamin said. "That very same morning before she . . . went to heaven."

Marie scrunched up her mouth, her forehead furrowed. Then her features became placid once again as she cried out, "Maybe she wanted you both to take care of me!"

The door burst open at that precise moment and a disheveled Jessica came storming through.

"Is this some sort of conspiracy?"

"Excuse me, madame?" Mr. Talbot said, rising from his chair.

Maria went running to her aunt. "Aunt Jess, Mr. Talbot's from a court. He wants to find out the best place for me to live, but I told him I live at my house."

"Mrs. McAllister, I presume?" Mr. Talbot asked.

"Yes, I am, and I can't believe you would speak to Benjamin before me. I'm quite sure my petition arrived first."

"What's a 'tition, Aunt Jess?"

"Maria," Jessie said calmly. "Why don't you go back outside. Joanna doesn't like working without you."

"All right," she said, sliding off the chair. She shook her head and added, "And I'll have to catch up with her now too. I was ahead by two baskets. Bye, Aunt Jess, Uncle Ben. Bye, Mr. Talbot."

"Good-bye, Maria," both men and Jessie said in unison.

Benjamin could hardly look at Jessica. Her turqoise eyes blazed with angry blue sparks.

"What is the meaning of this . . . this interrogation of a child with one of the two parties seeking adoption? I venture to say this is not standard procedure."

"Mrs. McAllister, please sit down," Mr. Talbot said. "You misunderstand. I did go by your sister's house first, but you weren't there, so I visited Mr. Whittaker's home instead."

"You call that cold, stone mausoleum a home?"

Mr. Talbot blinked as though he'd heard her wrong. "Why, I would not term Mr. Whittaker's home a mausoleum. It is in fact quite warm and homey. Why, the library itself would be a joy for any youngster who enjoys reading and—"

"The library?" she interrupted.

"Yes, a most charming room. Actually, from the very moment I entered, I felt a welcoming warmth surrounded by all those wonderful volumes of prose and poetry. And Maria's room is certainly a place any little girl would be pleased to have for her own."

Jessica looked at Benjamin, who could not meet her gaze. He turned and looked out the window, leaving Jessica to wonder how he'd managed to make his drab house appear so inviting.

"Mr. Talbot, I heard Maria herself tell you she lives at her house. Why don't we go there and talk? Knowing how Benjamin feels about me, I'd prefer talking to you alone."

"Certainly. If you'll excuse us, Mr. Whittaker?"

"I'll have a wagon take you," Benjamin said.

"Can you spare a wagon during such a busy time, Benjamin?" Jessie asked sarcastically.

"Of course," he shot back. "You could hardly expect Mr. Talbot to ride behind you on your mare."

His words brought back the image of her astride Benjamin's horse, her arms around his body . . . and she cursed her own womanhood for still responding to that thought.

Benjamin could see his words had gotten to Jessica, but she deserved it after her sarcasm. Benjamin could also see the young man writing in his infernal book again and immediately adjusted his demeanor. "Please, Jessica, allow me to accommodate you and Mr. Talbot, and I'll see that Maria and her pony as well as your horse get home safely after she's finished in the vineyard and you've had time to talk to Mr. Talbot."

Jessie turned and left the room without thanking him. She felt betrayed, and even though he sounded sincere in his offer of a wagon, she refused to thank the man who'd betrayed her.

On the ride home, through talking with Mr. Talbot, Jessie learned that Benjamin had evidently redone his home to suitably impress this official of the court.

She could only hope that he would see the warmth of Frannie's home was much less contrived.

The house wasn't as warm as usual since she'd banked the fires when they left for the vineyards. Jessie wished she could have prepared for Mr. Talbot's arrival as Benjamin evidently had.

Jam cakes, indeed, she thought, recalling Mr. Talbot's description of the sweets Margaret had served.

"Would you mind coming to the kitchen until I start a fire in the parlor, Mr. Talbot? It will be warmer in there from the cookstove."

"No need to bother with the parlor, Mrs. McAllister," he said, peering into the room. "It is a beautifully appointed room, but there's no need for formality."

Jessie sighed. "Good. Come along then and I'll make us a cup of tea, or would you prefer coffee."

"I do have a preference for coffee if it isn't too much trouble."

After building up the fire in the cookstove and putting coffee on to brew, Jessie excused herself.

She quickly rekindled the fires in Maria's room and the sitting room, then splashed water from the washbasin over her face and changed into Frannie's black silk dress. As she brushed her hair back she was aware of her appearance when she met Mr. Talbot, and knew she had not made a good first impression.

When Jessie went back into the kitchen, the young man rose and said, "You look lovely."

"Thank you. I'm afraid I didn't make a very good appearance at our first meeting."

"I understood completely. You'd been working in the vineyards, and I commend you for your hard work."

"I wanted to spend more time with Maria and it seemed like a good opportunity," she said as she prepared a tray. "The child is quite committed to the wine company, as was her father. And I myself have never been afraid of hard work, Mr. Talbot," she added.

He nodded, and took out his small leather-covered book, which he laid on the table. Jessie assumed it was to take notes on her and the house, and couldn't help but wonder what he'd written about Benjamin.

By the time Jessie sat down at the table with Mr. Talbot, the kitchen had warmed and the aroma of freshly brewed coffee lent a homey touch. She had placed several biscuits from breakfast in the warming oven, and as she served them with Frannie's strawberry jam, Jessie prayed they would not be too dry.

"This jam is delicious," Mr. Talbot exclaimed after his first bite.

"My sister made it."

He nodded, then finished his biscuit and coffee while talking about how he'd picked strawberries with his grandmother as a child.

Growing impatient, Jessie interrupted. "Mr. Talbot, I'm not sure what Benjamin told you—"

"Please," he interrupted. "Let's not talk about

Mr. Whittaker. I want to hear about you. About why you want to adopt Maria; how you will take care of her; what your plans are for her future."

Jessie smiled. "Now those, sir, are easy questions. I want to adopt Maria because I feel she needs a parent after all she's gone through. I loved my sister very much, and when she asked me to take care of her daughter I made a solemn vow that I would.

"As for your second question. I will take care of her just as I am now. Caring for her daily needs, seeing that she is well schooled and loving her to the best of my ability. Thus far Mr. Whittaker has seen to our material well-being, but I am not averse to working. If necessary, I will find work on the island and earn a living for myself and Maria."

Jessie took a sip of her coffee and waited. She noticed Mr. Talbot jotting things into his small book, and tried to look away.

"I like to keep notes on things so I can review them when I make my report," he explained.

"I understand."

"All right, now let's see . . . her future. What plans do you have for that?"

"Well, from what I understand, Maria is to inherit the wine company, so I would assume she will be trained to run the company by her uncle as she gets older."

Mr. Talbot stared at her for a moment through his thick spectacles, and when he spoke again, she noticed his tone was not as friendly.

"Mrs. McAllister, are you aware of the fact that this house and Maria's share of the wine company will be under the direct control of Maria's guardian or adopted parent?"

"I hadn't thought about it one way or the other."

"But you do plan on living here with your niece?"

"Of course. It's her home."

He nodded, then riffled through the pages of his book. "I have been made aware of the fact that you do not have any property to speak of, Mrs. McAllister. Is that correct?"

"It is." Jessica could see exactly what he was leading up to, but she saw no use in trying to stop him. And she seethed inside at the thought that Benjamin had told this man about how she'd lost her farm.

Talbot looked around the kitchen, then back at Jessica. His tone once again warm, he said, "I can see this is a lovely home, and it has been Maria's home since her birth. The court will naturally take that into consideration. And the fact that you've taken such good care of her since your arrival will also bode well."

He paused before continuing, absently stroking one side of his mustache. "But I do have a concern, Mrs. McAllister. You never saw the child until last week—Monday, the fourth of October—if my dates are correct."

"They are, sir, but I hope you do not subscribe to the theory that love cannot grow with distance between loved ones. Because I assure you, my love for Maria has grown from the day of her birth. My sister wrote me regularly about her growth, her accomplishments, her joys, her illnesses. I love Maria as much as anyone who has been with her from the day she was born."

"I did not mean to imply that you did not."

They sat for several silent moments, magnified green eyes staring into fiery turquoise ones.

When he spoke again it was with quiet determination. "Why do you feel you are better suited to caring for the child than Mr. Whittaker?"

"Because I'm a woman. I'm her mother's sister and I know how my sister would want her raised."

"Even though you did not see either Maria or your sister for the entire six years of the child's life?"

"I thought I explained to you—"

"Yes, yes, I know, love still binds you." He glanced down again into the pages of his book, then looked back at Jessica. "Are you acquainted with Mr. Whittaker's housekeeper, Mrs. Cochran?"

"Yes. Margaret is a fine woman. Kind and compassionate and loving."

"And you are aware of the fact that if Mr. Whittaker adopted Maria, his housekeeper would be in charge of Maria when her uncle is at the wine company or otherwise occupied?"

Jessica tried to keep in mind that the man had said "if," and kept her voice on an even keel, despite the turmoil she felt brewing inside her.

"I would assume so, but Mrs. Cochran has many other duties and—"

"And you have no other duties except to take care of the child in your sister's home?"

Jessie did not answer. She did not trust herself to say a word. The man obviously favored Benjamin and he was baiting her into an argument.

After several silent moments, Mr. Talbot spoke again, and this time he made no effort to keep the contemptuous tone from his voice. "Are you quite sure, madame, that you are thinking only of the child in this proceeding?"

Jessie felt her frustration building. "Maria's well-being is the *only* issue here, sir. What else could there be to think about?"

"Perhaps your own well-being, madame. This is, as you pointed out, a lovely home, and since you have no home of your own . . ."

Jessie rose abruptly. "How dare you! I will not listen to such insinuations. Please leave this house, sir . . . now!"

She'd held her temper, tried to be diplomatic, but he'd gone too far.

Without a word, he picked up his notebook, stood, and slid his chair back under the table, then looked at her again.

"I asked you to leave."

"If I've misjudged you, I apologize, Mrs. McAllister, but try and see this from my viewpoint. You have no home, no means of income, and suddenly you rush to see a child you've never seen in six years." His eyes bored into hers as he continued. "And I also know that you refused an offer from your sister to come here and live with her after your husband died."

"I did not refuse," Jessie said, anger gripping her because of Benjamin's obvious interference. "I merely wanted to try and save our farm, sir. I spent three backbreaking years trying to save it."

"And failed," Talbot added. "Then, once more, refused your sister's offer of a home here with her. A refusal that hurt her deeply."

"How dare you presume to know how my decision affected my sister?"

"Mr. Whittaker told me of her disappointment when you once again turned down her invitation . . . and he appeared to be telling the truth. Can you deny that she wanted you to come here?"

Jessie felt beaten, yet her anger kept her from falling apart. "I won't deny that. Yes, Frannie invited me to come here, but I did not want to impose, to be a burden, to—"

"Are you sure it wasn't because you disliked the island?"

"It appears to me, sir, that you've listened only to Benjamin's side of this rather than hear me out."

"Put yourself in my place, madame. You ask me to believe that love for your niece keeps you on an island you yourself professed to hate on your only visit here seven years ago. Then your sister dies, and immediately you file a petition for adoption. It would appear to me that you have put aside your dislike of this beautiful island in order to gain for yourself a home."

"Get out of this house . . . now."

Mr. Talbot looked as though he were going to say something, but instead he picked up his hat and left without another word.

By the time the front door slammed behind him, Jessie was out the back and headed for the barn, ready to ride to the wine company and confront Benjamin. Too late she remembered her horse was at the vineyard.

She slammed the barn door shut and went back inside the house, pacing from the kitchen into the sitting room, down the hall and back again. Over and over she walked through the two rooms and hall, tracing over her own words as she paced.

She knew she'd made a dreadful mistake in throwing Mr. Talbot out of the house, but she couldn't bear his accusations. How could he believe her only reason for wanting to adopt Maria was to find a home for herself?

Probably because of what Benjamin told him, she thought. Damn that man's meddling.

"Oh, Frannie, why did you have to die?" Jessie cried out. Tears pooled in her eyes and one blink sent them cascading down her cheeks.

A minute later she heard horses approaching. When she looked out the front window and saw Benjamin leading her horse with Maria and her pony alongside him, her tears dried instantly. A savage fury took over at the sight of this arrogant man who was determined to take Maria away from her.

She went back through the house and out the kitchen door, meeting Maria halfway between the house and the barn. Jessie hugged her niece, holding her close for several seconds before telling her to go in the house and get washed up for supper.

Maria evidently sensed her aunt's distress, and without hesitation, did as she was told. Then Jessie marched out to the barn, where Benjamin was putting up her horse and the pony.

"How dare you?" she shouted.

Benjamin spun around, obviously surprised by her appearance.

"What do you—"

"You're a monster. You have done everything in your power to sway that man toward you. To change your house into a warm home in a day must have taken considerable effort . . . and money. But you weren't satisfied with just impressing him with your home and business, were you?"

Jessie came and stood right in front of Benjamin, almost toe to toe, and without waiting for him to answer, she continued her tirade. "I wouldn't put it past you to have plied him with wine as well."

She was so close, Benjamin could feel the heat

from her body as she looked up at him, rage in her eyes, in her stance. She was coiled like a snake ready to strike.

"It wasn't bad enough to have given him reason to believe I was trying to procure a home for myself by using Maria as a ploy—but to make him think that I don't love her as much as you was just too much. Even for you, that was a cruel blow."

As abruptly as she'd begun, she whirled around and left the barn. It took Benjamin a second to move after her, and he caught up with her between the house and barn.

"Hold on, woman!" he shouted, and when she didn't stop, he ran to catch up with her, grasping her by her shoulders to turn her toward him as he yelled at her. "How dare you berate me when it was you who started this whole ugly mess. You came here and insinuated yourself into my life, you accepted my help, you . . . you even . . ." Benjamin could not bring himself to mention the kiss. It would place too much importance on it.

"You could have spoken to me, Jessica, and we might have worked things out, but you had to have her all to yourself. You had to sneak behind my back to try and take her away from me. You're the one who's cruel and untrustworthy—you're the one who—"

"Stop it!" Jessie shouted, pulling away from him. "I have been insulted enough for one day. Go back to your *warm* home and leave me alone."

"Give up, Jessica. I'll fight you on this to the bitter end."

Jessie looked right at Benjamin and in a menacing tone spat out, "You will live to regret filing those papers, Mr. Whittaker."

"Is that a threat?"

Without an answer, she turned and walked rigidly back to the house.

Once inside the kitchen, Jessie tried to control her fury. The man had forced her into saying things she'd never meant to say. A threat, she thought. How in God's holy name could I be a threat to you, Benjamin. I haven't a thing to fight you with—nothing at all.

The house seemed terribly quiet, and Jessie forced herself up the stairs, wondering what Maria was doing.

The door to the child's room was open, but Jessie couldn't see her anywhere. Then she saw the door to Frannie's room ajar. As she approached she heard Maria crying.

Once again, as on the day her mother died, Jessie found Maria curled up on her mother's bed, but this time she was awake and crying as though her heart had been broken.

"Maria, what's wrong, sweetheart?" Jessie asked as she sat down beside her.

The child raised up and threw herself into Jessie's arms. Her hiccuping sobs were heart wrenching.

"Please tell me, sweetheart."

Jessie remembered the open bedroom door. Maria's window overlooked the backyard. Dear Lord, Jessie thought. She heard us. What have we done, Benjamin? What have we done to this poor child?

"Maria, look at me," Jessie said softly, tilting the child's head up with a hand under her quivering chin.

"You heard your uncle and me arguing, didn't you?"

The answering sobs shook both Maria and Jessie.

"Oh, sweetheart, don't cry. It's just a silly grown-up discussion and you musn't be concerned about it."

Jessie rocked Maria in her arms, trying to offer some comfort. After a time the sobbing ebbed to deep sighs. When Maria eventually spoke, her words were barely audible between breaths.

"Why . . . is Uncle Ben . . . so angry? Do you . . . really want to . . . to take me . . . away?"

"No, no, sweet. Your uncle misunderstood. All I wanted was for the court to give me a paper saying I could stay here and take care of you—to give you a home. That's where the misunderstanding came in. Your Uncle Ben thought I wanted to take you away from him, and that's not true. I know he loves you as much as I do."

A shuddering sigh went through the little girl's body, and Jessie held her closer as she tried to speak. "But . . . he said . . . he said he'd . . . fight you. Wh . . . what did he . . . mean?"

Jessie tried to remember the angry words they'd hurled at one another. "He didn't mean an actual fight. It's just that he wants those same papers saying that he can give you a good home."

"But I don't want to . . . to live at Uncle Ben's house. I want to live here . . . I want to live in my own house, Aunt Jess. Uncle Ben knows that. He even told me he would come here and live with me, but not with you. He said you might want to go back to Indiana." The little girl looked up at Jessie. "I don't want you to go away, Aunt Jess. Please don't leave."

"Sweetheart, I'm not going to leave you, not ever. I have no idea where your uncle got such an idea. We'll just have to explain that to him. And I'll do my best not to get angry and shout at him ever again. Shouting only makes matters worse. I should have known that."

Maria didn't say anything, but clung tightly to Jessie. After a few more minutes, Jessie said, "Why don't we go down and get something to eat?"

Maria still didn't move.

"Come on now. I know you've got to be hungry."

The child moved back a little and looked up at Jessie with red-rimmed eyes. "I don't want you and Uncle Ben to fight anymore."

"I know. And I'll try my best not to. All right?"

Jessie eventually got Maria something to eat, and after she read her a story the little girl, exhausted from crying, fell sound asleep.

For a long while, Jessie sat and looked at her, knowing she and Benjamin could easily destroy the child.

She promised herself and her sleeping niece that she would go and talk to Benjamin in the morning. Tell him about their niece's pain. Offer to do anything that would be agreeable to him if they could do it together—to keep Maria safe from any more hurt.

Morning came sooner than expected, though, as a loud banging woke Jessie. She rushed down the stairs, hoping to prevent her early morning caller from waking Maria.

Benjamin was at the door, looking angrier than he had the day before. "I can't believe the lengths you would go to, woman!" he shouted.

Jessie stepped outside, pulling a shawl from the rack near the door to cover her nightgown. "Please lower your voice. Maria is sleeping and we musn't—"

He didn't let her finish, although he did lower his voice. His rage hissed from between clenched teeth. "I don't know how you managed to do it, but I'm not going to back down, Jessica. And whoever you got to help you do your dirty work will pay for this too."

"Benjamin, I don't have any idea what you're talking about."

"Your threat . . . you said I'd regret having filed for Maria's adoption and you meant it. I just didn't think you'd go this far."

"Tell me what you're talking about."

"As if you didn't know. I'm not sure how you convinced someone to try and destroy me, but it didn't work. They did manage to break into my warehouse, but only axed one barrel before my manager, who just happened to be working late, heard the commotion and ran them off, stopping them from doing any more damage on your behalf, Mrs. McAllister."

Jessie gasped when she understood what he meant.

"Benjamin, for God's sake, I didn't do anything."

"Liar!"

"It's the truth. Even if I were so devious—which I'm not—who in heaven's name would I have gotten to do this terrible deed? I don't know anyone on the island except Ann and Margaret—"

"How about your new friend Arthur Conners? From what I hear, you and he have gotten very friendly, taking late night rides together across the island."

"Our 'late night rides together,' as you call it, was two nights ago when I came to your home to try and make peace and got slapped in the face again. You allowed me, a woman alone . . . a woman new to the island, to ride off at night without an escort. I thank God that Arthur Conners heard of my plight from Margaret and, being much more a gentleman than you, followed after me and escorted me home."

"Don't try to put the blame back on me, woman. You set out to destroy me, and if Henry Monroe hadn't been in the office late, you might have succeeded. It wouldn't take much to push me over the edge, and I'm sure Margaret's let that slip too. For some reason the woman likes you, can't see your evil side."

"Benjamin, stop it. I'm not evil. I'd never ask anyone to do anything to bring harm to you or your wine company."

"I won't listen to any more of your lies, woman. I just wanted to let you know your plan didn't work."

"Benjamin, think about what you're saying. What good would it do me to have your barrels of wine axed?"

"You're a clever woman, Jessica. You know if I'm put out of business, I'd lose my leverage in this battle over Maria. If I lost my wine, my sole means of income, I'd be no better off than you. And if we were on equal footing, the court might decide a woman is better at raising a child. But you didn't succeed—you didn't destroy me as you set out to do."

"Please, Benjamin, for Maria's sake, you have to believe me. I—"

"Stop with your pleas," Benjamin shouted. "I won't listen anymore. Maria will be better off without a scheming witch taking care of her. I will adopt her and when I do, you'll have no right to remain in this house. Once I have custody of Maria, you won't be welcome anywhere on this island, Jessica McAllister—I'll see to that. I'll have you driven off this island forever.

"And you'll never see Maria again!"

Chapter Ten

Though shaken by Benjamin's outburst, and troubled by the prospect of having Maria taken from her, Jessie slipped quietly back into the house and tiptoed upstairs. When she peeked in the bedroom and saw that Maria was still asleep, she thanked God for sparing the child another scene.

Watching her niece sleep, so vulnerable, so defenseless, Jessie wanted only to keep her safe and help her heal from her terrible loss.

The odds for adoption appeared to be in Benjamin's favor, especially after the way Jessie had shouted at Mr. Talbot yesterday.

I must have sounded like a shrew, Jessie thought, not at all like a good maternal figure. She'd actually helped Benjamin's case by her behavior. And if Benjamin did succeed in adopting Maria, Jessie had no doubt that he'd make good on his vow to see her off the island.

How could she keep her promise to Frannie if she weren't even on the island? It would be bad enough if she couldn't raise the child . . . but how could she survive separation from Maria, now that she'd come to know and love her?

Yet the more Jessie thought about her dilemma, the more she realized that Benjamin himself had suggested a solution. Returning to Indiana might be the one way she could fulfill her promise to Frannie and still keep the promise she'd made Maria to never leave her. By taking her niece back to Indiana with her, both promises would be kept.

It's the only logical solution, Jessie thought.

Jessie refused to let herself consider that the act could be termed kidnapping. It didn't matter. Only Maria's well-being mattered . . . and the promise Jessie had made to Frannie.

When Maria woke and came downstairs for breakfast, Jessica began to set her plan in motion. As she cooked oatmeal and cut thick slices of bread, she talked to the little girl about Indiana, telling her of the wide-open fields and the many farms with all sorts of animals.

Maria listened and remembered her uncle's words. "Your aunt may want to go back home to Indiana." She also knew that Aunt Jess had promised never to leave her.

Making herself pay attention, Maria heard her aunt describe the pigs and chickens she'd had on her farm. And as her aunt continued to talk about Indiana, Maria noticed a look in her eyes she'd not seen before. Could Uncle Ben be right? Maria wondered. Is Aunt Jess homesick?

"Why do you like Indiana so much, Aunt Jess?"

"I guess it's because it was my home for so long, sweetheart."

"Just like the island's my home."

Jessie nodded. "Exactly."

"But don't you like it here on the island?" Maria asked.

"Of course I do. Sometimes, though, knowing I'm on such a small piece of land in this huge lake makes me a bit nervous, but it truly is a lovely place."

"Didn't you have a lake in Indiana?"

Jessie had to laugh at the very thought of Sweeney Lake. "As a matter of fact we did. But it was quite small. Just a place to go fishing sometimes. Nothing like Lake Erie."

Jessie wanted so much to make Maria understand that life could be good elsewhere. "Don't you ever think you'd like to visit other places, Maria?"

"Sometimes I do, especially when we have a lesson from our geography books. I'd love to see the mountains someday and the ocean."

"Do you think you'd like to see where I live in Indiana?"

"Could I see the pigs and chickens?"

"Well, I don't have the farm anymore, but I'm sure we could go and visit a farm near my . . ." She couldn't bring herself to call the boardinghouse her home.

"Near your house?" Maria finished.

Jessie nodded and instantly knew how unfair it would be to take Maria to Indiana and raise her in a boardinghouse. The idea of taking her away from her home had been ridiculous. The child loved the island. Knowing that, Jessie decided she'd have to come up with another plan. She also immediately came to the awareness that if she did succeed in adopting Maria, she'd have to come to terms with living on the island . . . and loving it as much as Maria did.

"Maria, what do you like best about the island?"

The child cocked her head to one side and thought for a minute, scrunching up the corner of her mouth as she so often did in thought. The gesture made her look so much like Frannie it tore at Jessie's heart, making her even more cognizant of her responsibility to her sister's child.

"The best thing about the island is the part you don't like," Maria finally said. "I love the lake. Swimming and fishing are so much fun, Aunt Jess. I think fishing with Poppa was one of my most favorite times. And if we caught any fish, Momma would fry them up for supper, and they tasted better than any meat I ever ate . . . especially the perch."

She paused for a moment, then went on. "I like everything about the lake, especially just sitting on the shore or up on the cliff and watching the water. Sometimes, Aunt Jess, I look at the foam the waves leave on shore and I see pictures there . . . that's fun. And sometimes when there's a high wind or a storm's brewing, the calm water becomes like an ocean with waves crashing up over the rocks, almost as though it's angry at being disturbed."

"You're quite right, sweetheart," Jessie said. "But I thought you'd never seen an ocean."

"I haven't," Maria answered. "Not for real, but I've seen pictures in books that Poppa showed me and in our geography book at school too."

"Of course," Jessie said. "Go on now, tell me more."

Maria sighed, leaning her chin on her hands, and Jessie could almost see her mind working as she gazed straight ahead. "The most special times I had with Momma and Poppa were when we'd go to West Shore Cove and watch the sun set." The child's face lit up much like the very sun she was talking about. "You know," she said, looking up at her aunt, "when I was little, I thought the sun went right down into the lake. You know how the water gets all orange and red or sometimes pink or even deep purple when it's going down?"

Jessie nodded. Maria's excitement was infectious, making Jessie recall the many brilliant sunsets she herself had already observed here on the island.

"I thought the sun must sit there under the water until morning when it slides right out the other side." The child smiled so brightly at the remembrance that Jessie couldn't resist leaning over and giving her a hug.

"And what else do you like besides the lake?" Jessie prodded.

Maria shrugged her shoulders and said simply, "Everything, Aunt Jess."

"Well, that's a lot. Try and break apart the everything and tell me about some of the things you like."

After a moment's silence, Maria smiled again. "I really like going down by the shore to see the blue herons, and the little egrets that come pecking for food. And I like sitting under the maple trees in the park in the summer and picking wildflowers for Momma. . . . " She paused only a moment, then added, "I can pick them for you now, can't I?"

"Of course, sweetheart."

As if she hadn't even paused, Maria went on

with a longer list than Jessie ever dreamed possible.

"I love collecting pretty rocks along the shore, and watching the big boats come into the town dock, and skipping flat rocks in the waves like Poppa taught me, and gathering cattails, 'cause they're fuzzy just like a real kitty's tail. And I like summer here on the island too.

"Going into town is such fun in the summer, Aunt Jess. Momma always said our little village of Put-in-Bay becomes like a city on the mainland come summer. So many people come here for the summer!" Maria looked hesitantly at her aunt, who smiled encouragingly. "And, oh, how pretty it is in town at night when Mr. Gascoyne lights all the street lamps. It's such a special time with so many people vacationing here . . . and it's good for business," she added, exactly as the future owner of a winery should.

"But it's nice when summer's over too. Then the island becomes our own again. Soon the leaves change colors and it's time to harvest the grapes, just like now. And I really enjoy my days in the vineyard, Aunt Jess. You know how you can smell the grapes when you're getting close?"

Jessie nodded.

"That yummy sweet smell always makes me hungry, and I can hardly wait to get there and pick a bunch so I can start eating them." Maria closed her eyes and licked her lips. "And what I really, really love is being there at the press when the first juice comes out. It smells so fruity and sweet and it tastes sooooo good."

"That good, huh?" Jessie asked, laughing at the drawn out word.

"Didn't you think so when we had some for

lunch yesterday?" Maria asked.

"I must admit, it was exceptionally delicious."

"Oh, I almost forgot. Going out on the boat is another of my favorite things . . . being right out there in the water, moving up and down, then up and down again . . . it's such fun."

"Anything else?" Jessie asked, marveling at the list Maria had compiled.

"Yes! The caves. You haven't seen any of the caves yet, but Momma and Poppa took me in one—just a little ways so we wouldn't get lost, and then when Momma and I were taking a long walk last summer we found one of our own. We were picking flowers, and I bent down and there was this grand opening in the hillside, sort of covered up with long vines and ferns growing all around. Poppa was so surprised when we told him, because he never knew of it and he's lived here longer than me or Momma."

Jessie couldn't help but smile as Maria described all the wonderful places on her island, and the things she loved to do. "Well, now that I've heard so much about your island, I can see there's a lot more to this place than I thought. It'll take me a long time to see and do everything you've described to me."

"I can start showing you around right after the grape harvesting is over, Aunt Jess." Maria was beaming from ear to ear. "And wait until the first snow. The island's so pretty when it's covered with snow. And when the lake's frozen over you can even take a sleigh ride across to the mainland. I know you'll love it."

"I can hardly wait," Jessie said. "And after winter, there'll be spring again, and then summer, and we'll pick flowers together and sit under the maple trees in the park and watch those summer ladies sashaying by in their fancy silk dresses."

"And," Maria added happily, clapping her hands, "we'll pick strawberries and go swimming too. You are staying, aren't you, Aunt Jess?"

"Of course I am. I promised you I'd never leave you and I don't break my promises, Maria."

"And you aren't homesick for Indiana, like Uncle Ben said?"

"It's a funny thing about home, sweetheart. My mother once told me that home isn't always a house or a certain part of the country. She said that home is a place where your heart truly is. If you love someone, your home is wherever that someone is . . . and since I love you—"

"Your home is on the island too," Maria finished.

"That's exactly right. My home is here with you. Now you go on upstairs and get dressed or Joanna will have so many baskets of grapes picked you'll never catch up."

As soon as Maria was ready Jessie took her to the vineyard, bypassing the warehouse so as not to chance seeing Benjamin. Jessie explained to her niece that she'd be unable to work because she had to attend to some business matters. Promising to pick Maria up later that afternoon, Jessie continued on to Benjamin's house.

Having listened to Maria's loving description of her island home that morning, and promising the child that she would stay, Jessie knew she had to take some drastic action to win the child's adoption.

At first, in a bit of a panic, she'd considered going to Arthur Conners, but upon further thought, another tactic came to mind. Benjamin's own words in his tirade earlier this morning had given her the idea, and she was now on her way to talk to Margaret about her plan.

If anyone could give her the information she needed, it was Benjamin's housekeeper. But would Margaret be willing to go against her employer in order to help Jessie?

Knowing this might be her only chance, Jessie took a deep breath and tethered her horse to a tree near the kitchen door. She'd decided against going to the front door, and knocked tentatively at the back door, uncertain of her welcome, hoping Benjamin hadn't turned Margaret against her.

Margaret's smile, when she opened the door, was welcome enough and her first words warmed Jessie's heart.

"Oh, Miss Jessie, I'm so glad you came. And," she said, lowering her voice, "it's wise you came to the back door with him out there in the library."

"Benjamin's still at home?"

"No, he's at the warehouse, supervising repairs. It's the skinny young man with the red hair who's out there . . . the one who's bound and determined to make trouble here."

Despite Jessie's same thought yesterday, she said, "I suppose he's just doing his job, Margaret."

"Well, I think he should have stayed in town at the hotel if he's doin' a job and not socializing with one of the parties fightin' over a poor little child."

"I agree, Margaret. The man should not have stayed here in this house. But I want you to know it's not I who wanted this fight. It was Benjamin who—"

"Hush now," Margaret interrupted. "I know you tried to talk to my bullheaded employer, but you have to understand—I probably shouldn't talk out of turn, but Mr. Benjamin had a bad experience with that wife of his and he's not trusted another woman since—except me, of course, and your sweet sister."

"Frannie wrote me a little about his bitterness and lack of trust, but I don't understand why he would allow something that happened so long ago color his judgment of all women to this day."

Margaret shrugged. "Lord knows, I don't understand the way the man thinks even after all these years. Although his wife was a strange one; and it's taken even me some time to get over her deceitful ways. She was cold, Miss Jessie, and unfeeling, and her treachery affected this entire house and all of us who lived within its walls."

"Perhaps that explains some of Benjamin's actions," Jessie said. "But it doesn't give him the right to jeopardize Maria's future."

"I agree," Margaret said as she lifted the teapot off the stove. "I was just about to pour myself a cup of tea. Will you join me?"

"I'd love to," she said, sitting down at the small round table. "I do need to talk to you, Margaret, and it's quite important."

Margaret's blue eyes met Jessie's head on. "It's about this adoption, I suppose?"

"Yes, and I know your first loyalty is to Benjamin. But I've promised Maria I'd stay here, and if Benjamin adopts her, he's vowed to see that I'm not welcome anywhere on the island."

Jessie paused, almost unable to say the next words. "He told me I'd never see the child again."

"Dear Lord," Margaret exclaimed. "The man's completely daft." She reached across the table and patted Jessie's hand. "Now, you mustn't worry too much. I'm certain the court would consider a woman to be the better choice at raising a child, especially a little girl."

"I'm not so sure of that, Margaret. After all, Benjamin does have you here, and Mr. Talbot was quite taken with you and your jam cakes."

Margaret blushed and shook her head. "I had no idea who Mr. Benjamin was preparing for until the man was on our doorstep, Miss Jessie. I only did what I would for any guest."

"Oh, Margaret, I wasn't criticizing. After all, who could resist your cakes and your hospitality. But for whatever reason, Mr. Talbot is on Benjamin's side. He thinks I'm just seeking custody so I can have a house to live in."

"Dear Lord," Margaret said. "Can neither of these men see how much you love the child? You are, after all, her mother's own sister."

"I wish you were the one making the judgment," Jessie said with a wry smile.

"Well, why don't I just go out and talk to that young whippersnapper and tell him a thing or two."

Jessie shook her head. "No, he's only interested in facts. And I'm hoping you can help me with some of those."

"I'll do anything I can, Miss."

"I'm sure you've heard about the damage at the warehouse?"

"Oh, my yes—such a shame. And I'm sorry to tell you who Mr. Benjamin's blamin'."

"I know. He came over before dawn to accuse me."

Margaret shook her head. "How could he think a sweet young woman like you could do such a thing? Especially when Henry Monroe is sure it was just some young boys looking to get into mischief . . . or a wine barrel."

"You mean Benjamin knows who did this, yet is blaming me?"

"Oh, no, he's too stubborn to listen to Henry, Miss Jessie. He keeps saying it must have been your friend Arthur Conners. I told him you barely know the man, but he has this idea that the man's sweet on you and would do anything for you."

"Arthur did ask me to marry him, Margaret."

"My stars, I had no idea you and Arthur had gotten so close," Margaret said.

"We haven't. I never saw him after that day when he helped take Frannie home. But the night I left here so angry with Benjamin, it seems you mentioned my predicament to Arthur."

"Perhaps I did. I was upset that Mr. Benjamin let you ride off in your state of mind, but I wasn't—"

"Arthur assured me the two of you weren't gossiping. I know you were truly concerned about me. And Arthur was too. He told me Frannie had been good to him when his wife died and he wanted to help me if at all possible. It would be his way of repaying the debt he felt he owed my sister. He offered to give me his name if it would be of benefit in adopting Maria."

"Surely you wouldn't—"

"No, I wouldn't, Margaret, not without love. A marriage without love would do Maria more harm than good. But you must understand, in light of Benjamin's early morning visit, I was so distraught after his dreadful accusations, I was actually reconsidering Arthur's proposal . . . and then I even considered taking Maria home to Indiana."

"Oh, no, Miss Jessie."

Jessie shook her head, putting a hand on Margaret's arm. "No, don't worry. I'm not going to be so foolish. I have nothing to offer the child there. If I still had the farm, I might have thought about it more seriously, but . . . Maria loves this island so much, I could never take her away. And I won't marry Arthur either."

"What will you do then?"

"I am trusting you with what I'm about to say, Margaret. As I said, I'm well aware of your loyalty to Benjamin and I only ask that you hear me out."

"Certainly, miss."

"Do you agree that the best thing for Maria would be to stay in the house where she was born and have me care for her?"

"I most certainly do."

"Then you must see that I have to do whatever I can to adopt her."

Margaret nodded.

"I didn't want this conflict between Benjamin and me. All I intended was to file the petition, legally adopt Maria so she would not go through life as an orphan, and raise her in her own home. I never wanted to part her from her uncle. She loves him and I would do nothing to come between them."

"I believe you."

"As I said, I didn't *want* a fight—but I've got one now—and I have to win."

Margaret shook her head and sighed deeply. "I understand. Do what you must. The breach can be healed afterward."

Jessie smiled. "That's exactly what I thought. Thank you for understanding."

"Now, what can I do to help?" Margaret asked, leaning forward eagerly.

"I need to prove that I can be as good a parent as Benjamin. Since Mr. Talbot seems to be so influenced by Benjamin's home and business, the only chance I have is to discredit Benjamin in some way. I know you will not say anything against him, but if you could answer some questions for me . . ."

"If I can."

"This problem at the winery with declining revenues, it's because of the large wine company that opened on the island a few years ago, isn't it?"

"Of course," Margaret said. "They can sell wine much cheaper because of their volume. Unfortunately, they also continue to court the restaurants on the mainland, and Mr. Benjamin's lost several accounts there. The summer season helped considerably because the island's hotel and restaurant owners are loyal to Mr. Benjamin. But now that the summer people are gone and vacation time is over, he doesn't have the local sales to get him through the next few months."

"How do you know sales are down? Benjamin seems to be a private man where his personal affairs are concerned."

"That he is, Miss Jessie." Margaret looked down into her teacup for several seconds before continuing. "I must admit it. I'm a snoop. Sometimes my curiosity just gets the best of me and I snoop."

"And that's how you know about the profits being down?"

Margaret nodded. "According to the papers I've seen, there are no profits, and if things get much worse, I don't know if he'll be able to continue operating the winery."

"Margaret, where are these papers?"

"He keeps them in his room in that big desk of his."

Margaret hung her head and twirled the bottom hem of her apron in her fingers, obviously embarrassed at having intruded on her employer's private affairs.

Jessie leaned across the table and gently tipped Margaret's head up. "Margaret, I have to see those papers. You don't have to get them for me. Just tell me which drawer they're in and I'll go on up. If anyone catches me, I'll take full blame."

There was a moment's hesitation, and then Margaret said, "They're in the large center desk drawer in a brown leather binder."

"Thank you." Jessie kissed the woman's wrinkled cheek.

"Be careful of that Talbot person," Margaret warned.

Jessie nodded, then moved quietly out the kitchen door.

Slowly she made her way along the hall, breathing a sigh of relief when she saw the library doors were closed. She continued on, pleased that Benjamin's new carpet muffled her footsteps.

Jessie marveled at the change in the place, and could see why Mr. Talbot had thought it so lovely.

When she got to Benjamin's room, her chest constricted. Even though she knew he was at the warehouse, the very thought of going into his room momentarily immobilized her.

But with Maria's welfare in mind, she turned the knob and entered. The draperies had been pulled back and although it was a cloudy day, there was enough light to see that the room was very much a man's room. Lush shades of forest green and burnished wood tones were the only colors used there. The ornate mahogany desk to the right of the fireplace immediately beckoned to her.

As Jessie walked toward it, though, her gaze was drawn to the enormous bed in the corner with its tall, carved wood headboard, and she could not help but think of Benjamin lying there. She could almost smell his musky scent as her imagination drew an earthy image of him there beneath the covers. The possibility of lying there with him, against his body, sent a tremor of desire through her entire being.

She shook her head, trying to dislodge the erotic sight from her mind, wondering how she could even consider such a notion after all he'd done. Forcing herself to focus on the reason she was in Benjamin's room, she resolutely made her way to the desk. With bated breath, she slid open the center drawer.

There it was. A brown leather cover that held all the papers she needed.

Quickly she glanced through the contents. Even as a novice at accounting, Jessie could see there was trouble. And in Benjamin's own hand a phrase was scribbled in the margin of one paper: *Will sell house if necessary*.

Moments later, Jessie was downstairs knocking at the library door.

"Come in."

"Good day, Mr. Talbot."

Jessie enjoyed the look of surprise and consternation on the young man's face.

"Good day, Mrs. McAllister. What can I do for you?"

Jessie shook her head. "No, no. It's what I can do for you, sir.

"Please do sit," she said, gesturing to the wing chair to the right of the fireplace as she took the one to the left. After a quick appraisal of the room, Jessie thought to herself that the books certainly made a difference in what was once a hollow-sounding, empty-shelved room. The chess table was also a fine addition.

Mr. Talbot settled himself in the chair she'd indicated, looking a bit uncomfortable, and Jessie began presenting her case. "I'm sure you're aware of the break-in at Benjamin's warehouse?"

"Yes I am. And I've heard—"

"Forget what you've heard. I want to be sure you have the correct information. First of all, I've neither the time nor influence to have arranged for that bit of vandalism. And if you would take a moment to speak to Henry Monroe, the manager of the winery, he could tell you that some young boys, bent on getting some free wine, were responsible. Henry saw them running off."

"And you believe Mr. Monroe's story?"

"It's not a story, Mr. Talbot, and it's not just me who believes him. Henry Monroe is a good man who tells the truth. You can ask Mr. or Mrs. Cochran right now. They both concur. The only reason Benjamin pointed the finger at me is because he's blind with rage over my wanting to adopt Maria.

"Once you understand how Benjamin's judgment has become clouded because of the adoption issue, I pray you will see how his anger could have a negative affect on our niece."

"When you put it that way, I suppose a child could very well be affected by his anger. I might also say the same of you, after that display yesterday."

"I apologize for my outburst, but you were questioning my integrity. As far as this matter of the break-in, do speak with Henry Monroe, Mr. Talbot. I'm sure he'll tell you the truth, removing all suspicion from me."

The man peered at Jessica through his thick glasses, stroking his mustache thoughtfully. "Of course. I'll speak to Henry this morning."

"You might also want to have a look at these sales reports," she said, handing the binder across to Talbot. "I know you've been impressed by Benjamin's wealth, but in these papers you can see the losses recorded this past year. Benjamin's financial problems have been escalating."

"Where did you—"

"Where I got them is no concern of yours. You're leaning heavily toward Benjamin for this adoption because of his business and this house, and that's why I've brought you these accounts." She stood and turned to the fourth page of the book, pointing out the notation in the margin.

"Read that, sir, written in Benjamin's own hand."

"Sell the house," Talbot said aloud. "My, my."

"In light of this new information, I hope you will reconsider me as the best parent for Maria."

The young man continued to shake his head and study the papers in front of him. When he looked up at Jessie again he said, "I am a novice at this job, Mrs. McAllister, and I find all this new information a bit overwhelming. I believe I will return to the mainland and speak to my superiors about all that's transpired here."

"Perhaps that would be best. Would you like to

take any notes before I return these papers to their proper place?"

"Yes, please." The man immediately withdrew his notebook. For several minutes he wrote in the book, then shook his head. "This is so hard to believe. The house . . . his business . . . it all looks so substantial, so solid."

"Things are not always what they appear to be, Mr. Talbot. Perhaps you should take this knowledge with you the next time you're blinded by outward trappings."

The man's face turned almost as red as his hair as Jessie continued. "I trust you will report all the facts to your superiors, with the recommendation that I, as Maria's maternal aunt, am the most logical person to assume responsibility for her care and well-being."

He peered at Jessie through his thick glasses for several seconds, then asked, "If the court found in your favor, Mrs. McAllister, would you take the child back to Indiana or remain here?"

"I've talked to Maria about the possibility of going to Indiana, but she convinced me that this is her home. She loves the island so much I could never take her away."

The man smiled. "That's good news, at least. But what of the place you call home, Mrs. McAllister? All those years in Indiana. Can you give up your home?"

"I'll repeat to you what I told Maria this morning, Mr. Talbot. My mother once told me that home is where your heart lies, and my love, my heart are here with my niece."

He nodded, then pulled a gold watch from his vest pocket. "If I hurry I can see Mr. Monroe and still make the noon ferry."

"I'll ask Margaret to have Samuel take you to the winery and then to the dock."

"Thank you. And thank you for bringing this new information to my attention. I might have made the wrong decision without it."

"As I said, Mr. Talbot, I hope it will make you more aware of not putting too much stock in outside appearances on your next case.

"Look into the hearts of the people who wish to adopt a child, sir . . . not into their purses."

Jessie turned and walked out of the room with as much outward calm as she could muster, but inside she felt as though a whole bevy of butterflies were loose in her stomach. The fluttering increased as she made her way to the kitchen. She'd invaded Benjamin's privacy, but in the process she'd turned the tide.

Margaret looked up from her work and when she saw Jessie's face, rushed over to her. "What is it?"

"Mr. Talbot believed me. He's going to talk to his superiors and . . . and Margaret, he thanked me for giving him the information. He said he might have made the wrong decision without it."

"That's wonderful, miss. It sounds like Maria will soon be yours."

Tears came unbidden to Jessie's eyes.

"There, there now," Margaret said, patting Jessie's shoulder. "It's no time for tears—it's time to cheer."

"You're right," Jessie said, brushing her tears away. "Oh, I almost forgot. Can Samuel take Mr. Talbot over to the winery and then see that he gets down to the dock to board the noon ferry?"

"Certainly. I'll go and fetch him. And you can

return that." She pointed to the leather binder in Jessie's arm.

"Immediately. I completely forgot I still had it."

Jessie rushed upstairs and was going down the hall toward Benjamin's room when she heard the front door slam shut. Benjamin's voice calling to Margaret almost paralyzed her.

Then she regained her composure, convincing herself she had enough time to return the book. She backed down the hallway, keeping her eyes on the stairs.

Crash! Jessica's movements jarred a side table and a vase of mums fell to the floor. The sound both startled and unnerved her, and without thought of the consequences she raced to Benjamin's door.

She heard him call up the stairs. "Margaret, is that you? Are you all right?"

As she opened the door to his room, she heard heavy footfalls on the stairs. In mere seconds she'd moved to the desk, opened the drawer, and slipped the binder in . . . just as Benjamin appeared in the doorway.

Her hand was still on the open drawer, and she slid it shut while he stood rooted to the spot, mouth agape, his eyes, hard and black, locked on hers, chilling her with his angry gaze.

"What are you doing in my desk?"

Jessica discarded several lame excuses that flitted through her head. Honesty would be best at this point. "I was searching for something to discredit you so that you would not get custody of Maria."

He continued to stand there in the doorway, staring at her. Despite all he had done, Jessie still felt drawn to him. But the lips that had thrilled her with a passionate kiss only days before were now curled in disdain.

Benjamin took two steps forward and closed the door behind him.

A shiver of fear shot through her at the sound of the door clicking shut. She came from behind the desk, trying not to show her trepidation. "I'll be going now," she said as she walked toward the door.

Benjamin's hands shot out and grasped her upper arms, biting through the sleeves of the cotton dress she wore.

"You're hurting me, Benjamin."

"And what are you doing to me, madame? First the destruction at the warehouse, now I catch you trespassing, stealing private documents."

"Henry has surely told you I was not responsible for the break-in. As for now, I suppose I am guilty of trespassing, but I have stolen nothing. I was replacing the documents."

"Oh, so you did find what you wanted. And what will you do with that information? Do you think Talbot will believe you after all you've done, the way you ordered him out of the house yesterday? He knows what a hotheaded woman you are and will not believe you when I tell him you are a liar."

"Mr. Talbot did believe me, Benjamin. He's gone back to the mainland to talk to his superiors. Now, let go of me."

Her words stunned him, and he relaxed his grip long enough for Jessie to break away from him.

"I'm warning you, Jessica. Don't even think of taking that child to Indiana. I have friends on every ferry that leaves this island. You'd never get away with it."

"I am not going to take Maria anywhere, Benjamin. This is her home. Why do you persist with this notion?" she asked.

"You forget how much my niece loves me, how close we've been," he said. "She came to me this morning, telling me about your talk of Indiana. She believes you're homesick, but I think you're planning to take her away from her home and from me."

Jessie tried not to scream at him, but her voice came out rather shrill nonetheless. "When will you understand I don't want to take Maria away from you? Since she confided in you, did she happen to mention that I promised her I'd stay on the island?"

"Oh, yes. She told me."

"Then why don't you believe that?"

"Because you're a liar."

"Stop it . . . please stop." Maria's plaintive wail brought them both around. The child had obviously heard them arguing and opened the door. She stood on the threshold, her eyes wide and filled with tears.

"Sweetheart," Jessie crooned, going to the child. "It's all right."

"You told me you wouldn't fight anymore, Aunt Jess."

"I know. I'm sorry. I just lost my temper."

Margaret, having heard the commotion, bustled down the hall. She gently ushered Maria out of the room. "Come, my little one. I have some jam cakes put aside just for you."

Jessie turned to Benjamin. "Did you know the child was in the house?"

He nodded, then slumped down on the side of the bed, his head in his hands. "I brought her home for lunch."

"How dare you let her hear another argument?"

His head shot up. "Another?"

"I tried to tell you this morning, she listened to us out in the yard yesterday. It frightened her badly. She heard you say you'd fight me and she took it literally. I told her I'd do my best not to argue with you again."

He shook his head, rubbing a hand back and forth across his forehead.

"I will not cause Maria another moment's pain," Jessie said softly. "There will be no more arguments between us, Benjamin, because I will never defend myself to you again, nor will I ever raise my voice in anger toward you again . . . no matter what names you call me or what you do to undermine me in the eyes of the court. Maria's well-being is the only thing that's important right now."

She turned and walked to the door, stopping with her hand on the doorknob. Without looking back at Benjamin, she softly murmured, "I imagine Frannie is truly disappointed in the two of us right now."

When Jessica was gone Benjamin lifted his head and looked out the window. "Dear sweet Fran, is she right? In doing what I thought best for Maria, have I only caused her more hurt? I wish you could answer me, dear sister. I wish I knew what to do next."

Chapter Eleven

After assuring Margaret there would be no more arguments between her and Benjamin, Jessie insisted on taking Maria home for lunch. "I think my niece and I need some time alone to talk, Margaret."

Maria had been sitting silently at the table, but at her aunt's words she spoke up. "I told Joanna I'd be back at the vineyard after lunch, and Willy's coming this afternoon too."

"Then I'll see that you get back . . . after we've eaten and had our talk."

As they rode home side by side, Maria was so quiet, Jessie's heart ached for the child.

"Sweetheart," Jessie began tentatively, seeking the right words to convince her niece that the fighting was over. "I'm so terribly sorry that you had to see your uncle and me arguing again."

"You said you wouldn't."

"I said I'd try my best, and I did, but something happened this morning that made me angry and it made me want to try even harder to adopt you legally."

"Why is this adoptin' so important?" Maria asked. "I just want to live in my house and have you take care of me like Momma said. I don't understand why Mr. Talbot had to come? And why he didn't listen to me when I told him I didn't want to live at Uncle Ben's house?"

How could she explain to the child, Jessie wondered. What were the right words to help her understand?

"Maria, there are laws which are important for your well-being. When a child's mother and father are both . . . what I mean to say is . . ."

"I am an orphan, aren't I?" Maria said with tears in her eyes.

Jessie wished she were sitting next to Maria in a wagon and not astride a horse. She wanted to gather the child in her arms and make her feel secure and loved. Instead she could only offer words. "Being an orphan isn't a bad thing, Maria."

"Tessa Kirby made it sound bad."

"Well, it's not. It's only a word used when a child has no mother or father. And that's why I thought the adoption was important. So you would know that you belonged, and not have to listen to Tessa Kirby or other people who don't know any better . . . people who hurt others by saying such foolish things."

When Maria didn't answer, Jessie asked, "Do you understand what I've said, sweetheart?"

"Yes, but I still don't like the arguing."

"I don't either. That's why I told your uncle

there'd be no more angry words between us. No matter what happens, I swear to you, I won't raise my voice in anger to him ever again, Maria. You have my word."

"Uncle Ben hasn't given his word. What if he still wants to argue?"

Jessie's lips curved upward in a wry smile, having thought the same thing when she left Benjamin sitting in his room. "Well, I'll just have to find a way to make peace with him, my sweet. He can't stay angry if I show him that peace between us is best for all concerned."

After Jessie and Maria left the house, Margaret went upstairs and found Benjamin sitting on the side of the bed, head in hands, rubbing his forehead with his fingertips as though he could rub away all the pain and confusion of the last two weeks.

When she saw him like that, her heart went out to him. She knew how much both Jonathan's and Miss Fran's deaths had affected him, yet he'd never broken down—had never shed a tear—at least not that she'd seen. And now with the dispute over Maria, on top of his problems with the winery, she couldn't help but wonder if it wasn't all taking a terrible toll on him.

"Are you all right, sir?" Margaret asked.

His head came up, and Margaret saw the tears in his eyes and the pain etched in deep lines in his face. "Why, Margaret? Why has everything gone wrong? First, the company my father established is threatened, then my brother is lost at sea, Fran's gone, and now . . . now this woman wants to take Maria away."

Margaret walked into the room and took the liberty of sitting next to her employer. "No, Mr. Benjamin, you're wrong about that. I spoke to both Miss Jessie and Maria today. She knows how much the child loves the island. She is not taking her to Indiana. But Miss Jessie was terribly disturbed by your threat to make her leave the island if you were awarded custody. The only reason she tried to discredit you was because she was afraid you would never let her see Maria again."

"She would do the same."

"No, sir. Knowing how much you love each other, Miss Jessie would never keep you from the child."

He shook his head sadly, wondering how Margaret could be so gullible in this instance. He'd always considered his housekeeper a good judge of character. She'd proven it time and again when it came to hiring workers at the wine company. He almost always introduced her to prospective laborers and asked her opinion of them afterward.

Is it possible that she's right about Jessica too? he thought.

"Do you honestly believe Jessica McAllister has no ulterior motives in trying to adopt Maria?" Benjamin asked.

"I believe with all my heart that she is a good woman who wants only to care for her sister's child. And if you weren't such a stubborn man, you would see it too."

"How do you know she's good, Margaret? How do you know she's telling you the truth?"

"For one thing, I know that she could have accepted Arthur Conners's generous proposal of marriage to aid in her adoption of Maria, but—"

"I told you Arthur was behind the destruction

at the warehouse," Benjamin shouted, coming to his feet. "I was right."

Margaret shook her head and sighed deeply. "No sir, you were not. Didn't you listen to Henry Monroe? There was no grand plot to destroy the wine. It was just two young men who were looking for some mischief."

"But you just said—"

"If you'd listen to me, I might be able to finish what I was saying."

"I'm sorry, Margaret. Please, go ahead."

"Arthur Conners was merely being the gentleman that he is, offering to help Miss Jessie in order to repay a debt owed to her sister. Surely you remember how Miss Fran took in his boys and straightened Arthur himself out."

Benjamin nodded. "Fran was a good person."

"And so is her sister," Margaret said emphatically. "She refused Arthur's proposal because she knows that marriage without love would not be good for Maria. She could have accepted, Mr. Benjamin. Having a husband would have given her much more substance in the eyes of the court. But Miss Jessie is more concerned about Maria's well-being . . . even if it causes her to lose the child."

Margaret left him then, and despite the weariness he felt clear into his bones, Benjamin knew that the thought of what he and Jessica were doing to Maria would not allow him any rest.

With Talbot gone, there was no other reason for him to be at home. The best thing for him now would be work.

By the time Maria had finished her lunch, Jessie saw a definite improvement in the child's demeanor.

"Well, now that your belly's full are you ready to go back to the vineyard?" Jessie asked.

"Yes. I don't want to get any further behind. Joanna picked five more baskets than me this morning."

"Dear me, we can't let that continue," Jessie said. "That does not bode well for the future manager of the Whittaker Wine Company."

Maria giggled, and her niece's girlish laughter touched Jessie deeply. *This is the way Maria's life should be, carefree and filled with little-girl pleasures, whether it be picking grapes or playing with puppets at Willy's.* Jessie vowed to strive her best to keep Maria's life on an even keel.

Impulsively she hugged the child, and her own laughter blended with Maria's, joyfully resounding into every corner of the house.

"Enough of this," Jessie finally said. "We better get you back to the vineyard. I surely don't want to have your uncle telling me I'm keeping you from your rightful place there."

"Now Aunt Jess," Maria cautioned in a tone much older and wiser than her six years.

"I'm just trying to keep peace between us, my little one. So go on now and get your warmest coat. There is a definite chill in the air and I won't have you catching cold. And while you're upstairs," Jessie added with a half smile, "I'll try and think of a good way to make peace with your uncle."

Upstairs, Maria immediately looked for her mother.

"Are you here, Momma?" she whispered. "Did you hear what Aunt Jess said?"

"I heard, my sweet . . . and I heard you both

laughing together. It was a glorious sound."

Maria turned toward the window and there, framed by bright rays of sunlight, glowing in her white robe, stood her momma. The little girl skipped over to the window. Although she knew Momma couldn't hold her like she used to, Maria derived the same comfort from the light encircling the heavenly being as she had from her mother's earthly embrace.

Maria wasn't quite sure how she knew these things, or why she felt the warm, coziness there in the heavenly glow, but she accepted the feelings without question.

"Aunt Jess wants to make peace with Uncle Ben, Momma."

"I know, my little one, and you're going to help her do it."

"Do you have an idea, Momma?"

"There has to be a way to make the two of them see that they can care for you together, Maria."

The little girl smiled from ear to ear. "I told Uncle Ben that must be what you meant when you told him to watch over me. I told him maybe you wanted both of them to take care of me."

"Indeed. If only the two of them could see it as easily as you."

"How can we get them to see?" Maria asked, sitting cross-legged in front of her mother, bathed in the shimmering radiance that emanated from her maternal angel.

"In order for them to understand how much they have in common and the bond they share in their love for you, they must first see past their hostility."

"Aunt Jess said she's never going to raise her

voice in anger to Uncle Ben again," Maria said with conviction.

"I know she did," the angel said with a smile. "But that might not be as easy as your Aunt Jess thinks. As you and she discussed, your uncle still has not yet released his angry feelings, and if he persists with this attitude it will surely test your aunt's promise to you. My sister can be feisty when others refuse to conform to her standards."

"What can we do to make Uncle Ben stop being angry?"

"Your uncle is blaming your aunt for something she didn't do, Maria. So that must be our first concern. Then perhaps we can move on from there.

"You must get your aunt to take you to the winery. I know your uncle is going there to talk to Mr. Monroe. Somehow, there in your uncle's office, Jess must learn of Benjamin's difficulties. I'm certain she will then think of some way to help him and bring about peace between them."

"All right, Momma, I'll try my best."

"I know you will, my little one. Until later."

The light faded, and Maria quickly donned her coat, trying to think of a way to get her aunt into Uncle Ben's office.

"Maria, are you ready?" Jessie called upstairs.

In answer, the little girl appeared at the top of the stairs. "All ready, Aunt Jess." She came down the steps and took her aunt's hand. "You're going to stay at the vineyard too, aren't you?"

Jessie crinkled up her nose. "I'm not sure your uncle would be happy to see me there after our . . . discussion."

"Stop making faces, Aunt Jess. You said you wanted to think of a way to make peace between you. I think working at the vineyard would be a good start."

The child seemed so determined, Jessie could not refuse her. "All right, I'll go and work with you. Perhaps it will indeed be a good start."

As she and Maria rode past the warehouse on their way to the vineyard, Jessie saw some of Benjamin's men repairing the broken doors.

"Aunt Jess, look, something must have happened at the warehouse."

"There was a break-in last night. Your uncle told me about it early this morning while you were still asleep."

"So that's what he blamed you for," the child said with conviction.

Jessie glanced at her niece, wondering if she'd heard their quarrel this morning, but Maria didn't seem disturbed by her statement.

"Were you awake when your uncle came by this morning?"

Maria shook her head. "No, but Momma told me he blamed you for something you didn't do."

A sigh escaped Jessie's lips. Evidently Maria had not been sound asleep that morning and had heard some of what Benjamin said, blaming her for the vandalism at the warehouse. Somehow, the child had once again incorporated what she'd heard into a dream about her mother.

"He did blame you, didn't he?" Maria asked.

"Only because when we were having that silly argument yesterday, I said something about—"

"You said he'd regret what he'd done," Maria said. "I heard that part from my window. And Uncle Ben said you were threatening him."

She'd heard more than Jessie thought. There was no use denying it. "That's right, and when this happened, in his anger, your uncle blamed me. That's part of the reason I was arguing with him when you walked into his bedroom this afternoon."

"Well, I'll just tell him you were at home with me."

"He believes I arranged for the vandalism, sweetheart."

Maria sighed and looked wistfully at the vineyards, then turned her pony toward the winery.

"Maria, where are you going? I thought we were going to pick grapes."

"Maybe later, Aunt Jess. Right now you and I have to go to Uncle Ben's office."

"I'm not sure that's wise."

"You have to, Aunt Jess. If you want to make peace with him, you have to come with me."

Again, Maria's determination was so strong that, rather than upset her anymore, Jessie did as her niece asked. Leaving their horse and pony in the company stables, they went inside the winery, past the presses and the bottling area, then up a long pair of wooden stairs that led to the upper floor and Benjamin's office.

"Maria, I'm not sure this is a good idea," Jessie whispered as they neared the landing.

"Momma thought it was," Maria whispered in return.

Since they were already stepping onto the landing outside Benjamin's office, there was no time to comment on Maria's words about her mother. Jessie immediately heard raised voices and pulled Maria to a stop beside her, just outside the office door.

* * *

Henry stood in front of Benjamin's desk, waving a sheaf of papers in his face.

"We can't keep on like this, Benjamin. You have to make that trip to the mainland today as you'd planned. I understand that it's not a good time for you personally, but you have to take care of your business affairs . . . before it's too late."

Benjamin began pacing behind his desk. "Why did that woman have to start this fight over Maria?" Benjamin growled. "And cause me more grief on top of it with this break-in."

Henry shook his head. "I wish you'd get that ridiculous notion about Jessica McAllister out of your head. You know damn well it was just some young men who'd had too much to drink looking to get into more mischief . . . or some free wine. It's clear that they were just trying to tap the barrel for their own pleasure and merely went too far."

"The woman threatened me, Henry," Benjamin said, realizing as soon as he'd uttered the words that he was again ignoring his manager's theory and forgetting Margaret's words in Jessie's defense. "I know you—and even my housekeeper—do not believe Jessica's responsible, but I'm still not convinced. Arthur Conners has proposed to the woman. This could have been his way of getting back at me for my angry remarks to him last week."

"That's just a crazy notion, Benjamin. I know Arthur Conners. He was not here last night. You're letting this adoption issue get in the way of your common sense."

"The woman's doing her best to destroy me, Henry. She even broke into my desk in order to prove to Talbot that I'm not as financially secure as I led him to believe."

Henry shook his head. "Is that so different from you redecorating your entire home to impress the man with a wealth you are no longer secure in?"

Benjamin ignored Henry's words. "I don't trust her. I still think she's capable of this destruction."

"You are as obstinate as everyone's ever told me. And you persist in your distrust of women who try to get close to you, even after all these years. Because of the things your wife did years ago, you would rather think a woman as lovely as Jessica is capable of arranging for a break-in than listen to the truth. It was a prank, Benjamin. That's all it was. Stop being so stubborn and listen to—"

"All right . . . enough, Henry." Benjamin rubbed his forehead hard.

"I am sorry if I've spoken out of turn," Henry said. "But I don't like what's happening to you, nor what it's doing to your business sense. I don't want to see this company fail. It meant too much to your father and your brother."

"It means a lot to me too, Henry, and it's Maria's inheritance."

"Then fight for it. You have to make that sales trip. We're running out of time, Benjamin. The steamers to the mainland will be stopping their daily runs after the harvesting. You must get to Port Clinton and Sandusky before that happens. It's imperative that you speak to the restaurateurs . . . and you need to collect from those shops that owe us money."

"You know I can't leave right now, Henry. I have to be sure the warehouse is secure no matter who was responsible for the break-in."

"Then send someone else."

"I cannot forget what happened the last time I let someone else go to do my job."

"That was an accident, Benjamin. No one could have predicted the storm. It came out of nowhere."

"I should have been on the boat."

"Stop it! It does no good to dwell on what might have been. Your brother knew what needed to be done. Will you let his death be in vain?"

"That's cruel, Henry, and you're not a cruel man."

"I'm only saying what you must be thinking. Frannie and Jonathan gave their lives trying to keep the company from ruin. If you lose the winery now and prevent Maria from attaining her rightful inheritance, their deaths were indeed in vain.

"Benjamin, I'm not as good at sales as you, but if necessary I'll go. Someone must. If we can get the owners of a few of those restaurants to compare our wine to the new company's, they'll see our product is superior. We have to get some of our business back, Benjamin, and we must collect the debts owed us for past shipments. It's our only hope. If you won't go, let me at least try."

"No. You're needed here, Henry. Give me some time to think. Perhaps in another day or two . . ."

Jessie had stood silently, finger to her lips so as to hush Maria too. But it had been an unnecessary caution. The child had not moved during the exchange inside Benjamin's office.

Not every word could be heard through the glass-paneled door, but enough came through to confirm that Maria's inheritance was indeed in serious trouble.

As Benjamin and Henry continued the debate, Maria tugged at Jessie's sleeve and the two of them descended the stairs.

"It sounds like the company's in trouble," Maria said as they left the building.

"Yes it does."

But he's brought much of it on himself, Jessie thought. He should have tended to his business instead of getting so distracted and upset by the adoption. But it was too late to change what had already transpired. Jessie must do as she'd promised Maria. She had to find a way to peacefully coexist with Benjamin on this island . . . for Maria's sake.

"Are you still thinking of a way to make peace with Uncle Ben, Aunt Jess?"

"I did say that's what I wanted to do, didn't I?"

"Uh-huh, and Momma said if I brought you here, you'd think of something."

"Oh, Maria . . ." Jessie stopped herself. She'd told Maria often enough that she was imagining her mother. There would be no use saying it again.

"Well? Have you thought of a way yet?" The child's innocent question suddenly gave Jessie an idea.

"Perhaps, Maria. Perhaps I have. What would you say to a trip to the mainland to sell your uncle's wine?"

The child's broad smile was answer enough. "Momma was right. You figured out a way. And remember what I told you Poppa and Uncle Ben said that night . . . before the accident?" She smiled as though indeed recalling her father's words.

"I remember, sweetheart. They said that a woman could probably sell more wine than either of them."

Jessie couldn't help but return the child's smile.

"If a woman can sell wine, Maria, think how much more can be sold when the woman is accompanied by a sweet little girl."

Almost immediately, though, Jessie's enthusiasm was dampened as she recalled her last scene with Benjamin. He was still angry with her, that had been apparent in his conversation with Henry Monroe. He would never agree to let her take Maria to the mainland on a sales trip.

"What's wrong, Aunt Jess? You look so serious."

"I'm thinking your uncle will probably not allow me to take you off the island. He still doesn't trust me."

"We won't tell him then," Maria said simply. "And once we've sold lots of wine and collected all the money owed the company, he'll be so happy he won't ever be angry again."

Jessie smiled down at Maria. "You could be right, sweetheart. I daresay those who owe money to the Whittakers might have difficulty turning away a woman and child."

"Especially an orphan," Maria said.

Jessie stopped and looked at the child, expecting to see tears again, only to be surprised by a mischievous grin on the little girl's face.

"Maria Whittaker, you are a bit of an imp."

The little girl covered her mouth with her hand, trying hard to suppress a giggle. "I'm not an . . . imp . . . whatever that is. I'm a Whittaker and will do what I must to keep the company solvent. It is after all my company too, Aunt Jess."

"Solvent? How do you know such words, young lady?"

"I've been raised with talk of the winery, Aunt Jess. I've learned all sorts of words when Poppa and Uncle Ben and Henry discuss business affairs."

"I hope you can distinguish unladylike language from business terms."

Maria giggled again. "I know the difference. Poppa used to warn Henry about certain words, and Uncle Ben always stops himself from saying anything bad when I'm in the office."

"All right then, let's figure out how to put my plan into action," Jessie said as they approached the stable. "Even if we do as you suggest and keep this a secret from your uncle, how in heaven's name can we get the wine for sampling and the names of those who owe the company money?"

"Henry will help," Maria cried out, her excitement apparent. "I know he will."

Recalling the desperation in the man's voice, Jessie thought Maria was probably right.

Chapter Twelve

An hour later, Jessie approached Henry Monroe with her idea and found him quite receptive. "This is exactly what the company needs, Jessica. And it will go far to heal the breach between you and Benjamin."

He immediately set Jessie's plan in motion, arranging to meet her and Maria later that afternoon in the company stables, promising to have everything in readiness for their sales trip.

Jessica and Maria went home to pack some personal belongings and to let Ann Weldon know that they would be away for a night. They got back to the stables as Henry and John Thomas were loading the older man's wagon with crates of wine.

Henry's face was aglow as he greeted Jessie. "My dear Jessica, I'm so excited about your suggestions for this trip. I'm certain you will be successful and turn the tide for the company."

He then scooted down to Maria's level. "You know enough about the wines to help your aunt with specifics, Maria. I've packed bottles of the Concord, Catawba, and Sauterne along with some of the new, sweet wine made from the Ives grapes. That one does seem to be a favorite with the ladies, and I'm sure you'll draw many women to your sampling. I've also included bottles of grape juice for those that prefer a non-alcoholic beverage."

Looking up at Jessie with his hand still on Maria's shoulder, he said, "I have no doubt the two of you will be apt representatives of the Whittaker Wine Company."

"Thank you for your confidence, Henry," Jessie said. "I only hope we can get off the island without Benjamin's knowledge. I'm afraid he would not see this trip in the positive light that you do."

"Don't worry. I'll keep him busy. As soon as you told me your idea, I gave him stacks of papers to read to keep him in his office. Once we get you on your way, I'll try and stay with him to be sure he doesn't leave the winery."

Henry handed Jessie a packet of papers, a small leather purse, and a large, oversized binder. "The accounts past due and the addresses of each shop or restaurant that owes the company a debt are all written here for you. And there is enough money to pay for your lodging tonight in Port Clinton and for all your meals tonight and tomorrow. In addition, I've had the printer who does our labels make you some signs announcing the sampling tomorrow in Port Clinton and the next day in Sandusky."

He then handed her another envelope with a name and address printed on the front. "This is a note of introduction to a good friend of mine in Port Clinton. He will see that you get safely across the bay to Sandusky tomorrow. You should be able to complete all the business we discussed in plenty of time to board the last steamer back tomorrow afternoon."

Jessie hugged Henry in a spontaneous gesture of appreciation. "Thank you, dear Henry. I hope we can warrant your faith in us."

"I have no doubt, Jessica. The strength of a determined woman and child combined with a good product are powerful sales tools."

Henry then went to help John Thomas finish loading the wooden crates of wine onto his wagon. Jessie overheard him telling John that the contents of the crates were not to be divulged. "Mrs. McAllister is on a serious mission, John, and we're trusting you to keep the purpose of her trip confidential."

"You and Mrs. McAllister have my word on that, sir," John replied.

Soon, everything was ready. Henry told Jessie he would care for her horse and Maria's pony in his own barn so Benjamin would not see the animals. "He probably won't even know you're gone until tomorrow when Maria doesn't come to the vineyard," Henry said. "By the time he discovers you've gone to the mainland, you'll be well along with your planned wine sampling."

"And I'm hoping we can collect most of the past-due monies this afternoon and evening," Jessie said. "Which will leave us plenty of time to talk to some individual restaurant owners before the sampling."

"The idea you've come up with to invite women to take orders to stock their cupboards and cellars for the holidays is brilliant, Jessica. Innovative ideas such as this are exactly what the company needs right now. If we lose some customers in one area, we must gain them in another."

"I'll continue thinking of new ways to sell wine on the trip to Port Clinton," Jessie said, pleased by Henry's praise. She picked up her satchel, took Maria's hand, and with Henry's help boarded John Thomas's wagon.

As the steamer cut through the water toward its destination, Jessie's mind paralleled its movements, cutting through the bad scenes that had passed between her and Benjamin. She glanced down at Maria, who had laid her head in Jessie's lap and fallen asleep soon after the boat pulled away from the dock. This day had been rather full already, and she was glad Maria was napping.

The smell of fuel combined with the sea air drew Jessie's memory back to the day she'd arrived, so filled with hope for her sister's recovery.

Dear Frannie, she thought, as she stroked Maria's hair. If only you'd been able to tell Benjamin that you wanted me to raise Maria, how much easier my life would be.

"I did try, dear sister."

Jessie's head turned at the sound, but no one was near her on the long wooden bench that lined the side of the ship.

Although it had sounded like words, Jessie knew that was a foolish thought. Maria was asleep, and the nearest passenger was at the prow of the ship. Most likely, the wind passing through the open deck had imitated a human voice.

Jessie promptly pushed away any other explanation, and set her mind back to the task before her. The goals for this trip were clear, to end the bickering between her and Benjamin and to stabilize Maria's life. If she helped to secure business for the winery, those goals would be met.

Smiling, she tried to imagine what Benjamin's reaction would be. Would the lips that had awakened her desires finally speak kindly to her? Would he look at her with gratitude and see that she truly cared about him? Through the love they shared for Maria could they, in time, come to love each other?

Her mind whirled with the thought of love between them. If she were honest with herself, though, Jessie knew there already was love in her heart for Benjamin. Although the notion disturbed her, there was no other explanation for the feelings he aroused in her.

Wouldn't Frannie be pleased if Benjamin and I could raise Maria together as a family? she thought.

"Oh, yes . . . dear Jess, yes."

Jessie rubbed her hand across her ear, wondering why the wind sounded so strange today. Then quickly, she dismissed the thought and went back to speculating about the three of them as a family. The concept intrigued her, even though it seemed a bit farfetched at the moment.

Yet if all went well on this trip and Jessie proved to Benjamin that she cared about the company . . . and about him, there was a possibility that they could resume the path they'd taken right after Frannie's death. His kiss that day and the way he'd looked at her betrayed his true feelings. There was no denying the force that drew them together.

If only Benjamin had believed her when she told him she'd never meant to keep the adoption from him, this animosity between them might never have begun. Perhaps, as Margaret had said, this lack of trust could be blamed on the things his ex-wife did. If she could restore his faith in women, they might have a chance at a future together.

Soon, she thought, as the horn sounded their approach to land. Soon you will understand how much I care, Benjamin. Then perhaps we can move on to a better life . . . for Maria's sake.

"Stop stammering, William," Benjamin shouted at his employee, who stood before him twirling his hat nervously in his hands. "What is it you're trying to say?"

"Sir, you're frightening the man," Benjamin's foreman said. "If you'll calm down and listen, I'm sure William can give you all the facts."

"I . . . I'm not sure what you want me . . . me to say, sir," the man said timidly.

"A minute ago, when I asked if you'd seen my niece in the fields, you mumbled something about seeing her at the dock."

The man nodded his head in agreement. "She and Mrs. McAllister were boarding the steamer."

The impact of the man's words hit Benjamin square in the chest, knocking the wind out of him as surely as if he'd been hit with a fist. "Are you certain of this, William?" he asked as his heartbeat accelerated.

The man nodded again.

"Could they have been seeing someone off?"

"No, sir. Mr. Thomas was carrying their belongings onto the boat. There were several crates and a large satchel. After everything was loaded, Mrs. McAllister thanked Mr. Thomas, took the child's hand, and went aboard."

"Damn! You should have stopped them."

"Excuse me . . . me, sir?" William stammered.

"She's done exactly what I've said she'd do. That infernal woman's stolen my niece from me." Benjamin turned to his foreman. "Daniel, go into town and tell the marshal to meet me at the town dock. Tell him it's an emergency and I want him to accompany me to the mainland."

"Begging your pardon, sir," Daniel said. "The steamer's made its last trip for today."

"Then I'll take my own boat."

"I don't think that would be wise, Mr. Whittaker," Daniel said. "It's near dark and the winds have grown stronger in the past hour."

Benjamin paced back and forth in front of the wine barrels. He couldn't concentrate. Knowing he'd been right, and Margaret and Henry wrong, about Jessica gave him little consolation.

Finally, he made his decision. "Daniel, please ride to my home and tell Mrs. Cochran I will not be in tonight. You needn't tell her anything else . . . do you understand?"

"Yes sir, I understand exactly."

"And William, Mr. Monroe is dealing with some problem in the warehouse. On your way past, please tell him I had some business to take care of in town—nothing more, not a word about Mrs. McAllister or my niece."

Within minutes Benjamin was mounted and on his way into town. He would speak to the marshal tonight and be ready to move in the morning. Of one thing he was sure, Jessica did care about Maria, and he knew she would not push the child to travel at night. If he planned well, leaving just before dawn, he could find her before she left Port Clinton.

As Benjamin rode into town, he spied John Thomas's wagon outside the tavern. Since the man seemed as fond of Jessica as others on the island, Benjamin would have to watch his temper and question him carefully.

Before Benjamin dismounted, though, John came out of the tavern.

"Good evening, John," Benjamin said as pleasantly as he could.

"Evening, Mr. Whittaker."

"Did you get Mrs. McAllister and my niece off all right?"

Benjamin could see the confusion in the man's eyes.

"Excuse me, sir?"

"You heard me, John." Benjamin's voice rose, his resolve vanished in his distress over Maria's abduction. "What was in those crates you carried on board the steamer for her?"

"I'm not one to pry, Mr. Whittaker."

"But you don't deny she took my niece aboard?"

"You evidently already know that, sir."

"John, I've known you for many years. How does this woman command your allegiance in so short a time?"

"My allegiance is to no man . . . or woman, Mr. Whittaker. I am a businessman, albeit not as important as you, but I do transport travelers and local people alike to and from the docks and earn a decent wage."

Benjamin stared at the elderly man for several moments, then turned and walked away. He needed no more from John. The crates obviously held Maria's belongings. Jessica had had nothing but her satchel when she'd arrived, so it was a simple conclusion.

He went on his way to speak to the marshal, his anger growing with each hoofbeat. How dare the woman be so bold? What did she think she was accomplishing by taking the child? She had no money. From what Fran had told him, Jessica lived in a boardinghouse and worked as a sales clerk in a general store. Did she believe he would go after her and beg her to return?

If she did, she was sorely mistaken. He'd see Jessica McAllister in jail before long.

"What do you mean?" Benjamin shouted at Marshal Sinclair. He'd arrived at the marshal's a few minutes before, and already the man was telling him he couldn't help him.

"She's broken no law, Benjamin."

"Stealing my niece is a crime, George."

"Unless I've missed something since Mrs. Whittaker's death, the child's not yours, Benjamin, so Mrs. McAllister cannot be accused of kidnapping. Maria is as much her niece as she is yours."

"First John Thomas defies me, and now you. That woman must be a witch to have you all defending her."

"I've only met the woman once. I'm not defending her, I'm explaining the law. Kidnapping involves forceful abduction and a demand for ransom."

"Well, I'm telling you she took the child by force," Benjamin lied.

"Do you have proof of this?" George Sinclair asked.

Benjamin was pacing back and forth in front of the marshal's desk. "What sort of proof do you need? The child is gone and I wasn't consulted. She should at least have consulted me."

"Perhaps, but it's not a crime because she didn't."

"Then I'll go alone," Benjamin said, jamming his hat on his head.

Marshal Sinclair's arm shot out and caught Benjamin's as he strode toward the door. "Surely you're not going to take your boat out tonight? You know the dangers."

"I'm well aware of the dangers, George. I know I'm responsible for the loss of two lives because I didn't heed the dangers the night my brother went out on the lake."

"Your brother knew the risks as well, Benjamin. You were not responsible for his death."

Benjamin shrugged the marshal's hand from his arm. "Good night, George."

"Benjamin, hold on. I may not be able to help you officially, but I'll go along with you in the morning. Maybe I can keep you from doing something you'll regret."

"I'm going to retrieve my niece. If Jessica McAllister cannot be held accountable for this reprehensible act, she can go on to Indiana. I'll not do anything foolish, George. I'll be glad to be rid of her."

Yet even as he said the words, Benjamin's heart felt empty at the thought of her loss. He'd not allowed himself to think beyond his hurt, beyond the pain he'd suffered from his wife's betrayal. There'd been such a strong attraction between him and Jessica years ago, and it had been reawakened with her appearance on the island. Benjamin could still feel the heat of her lips on his, her heart beating against his chest.

What kind of woman was this who could kiss him with such passion and then take his niece from her rightful inheritance?

"I'll meet you at the town dock at dawn, Benjamin."

The marshal's words brought Benjamin out of his reverie just in time. He mustn't think of that woman's kiss or her touch. He needed no distractions. He wanted only to bring Maria back home and he would do so, even if he had to go all the way to Indiana to retrieve her.

"Fine, George. Perhaps seeing you will make her aware of what she's done . . . even if it's not a crime."

"I am a peace officer, Benjamin, and I'll keep the peace without taking sides. I want that to be clear before we embark on this trip."

"Your purpose is perfectly clear," Benjamin said, gritting his teeth to keep from adding the words that ran through his head. Without knowing how she'd done it, Benjamin had no doubt that Jessica had managed to hoodwink all of his friends on the island.

He left the marshal's home making plans to leave before dawn. He certainly didn't need someone along who believed the woman was some kind of saint.

Clenching his fists at his side, Benjamin walked to his horse. As far as he was concerned, Jessica McAllister had committed a crime. By taking Maria off the island she'd committed a crime against her dead sister . . . and he would deal with her in his own way.

Chapter Thirteen

"Oh, Aunt Jess, we're going to have such fun. I've never stayed in a hotel before."

The steamer had just pulled up to the dock, and Maria was as excited as any little girl could be. For once, Jessie felt she was seeing the child in Maria. She so often acted like a miniature adult, and Jessie truly wanted her to enjoy her childhood more.

"I'm sure we'll have a lovely stay," Jessie said, "and I'm so pleased that Henry let us have the opportunity."

Maria immediately grew serious again. "Of course, we do have to conduct our business first."

Jessie wished she'd not mentioned Henry, and quickly tried to reestablish Maria's good mood. "I've already arranged for our things to be taken to the hotel, sweetheart, so we can see the people who owe the company money right now. Then before the sun goes down, we'll go to our hotel and have a fine dinner and a good night's sleep. Tomorrow morning we'll do our wine sampling here, and then go into Sandusky for the afternoon sampling there."

"Then we should put up the signs that Henry gave us on the way into town," Maria said.

"You're right. I almost forgot we had those." Jessie smiled down at her niece. "You are a better businesswoman than I, little one."

Jessie retrieved the signs, which had been rolled and placed with the crates of wine. She then took Maria's hand and they disembarked, threading their way among the stacks of crates, barrels, and sacks that lined the dock waiting to be loaded onto the boat.

Having been on the island for nearly a week, Jessie promptly noticed the difference in the air on the mainland. The smell of fuel and smoke from the businesses in the city dulled the fresh scent of the lake that was so noticeable out on the island.

As the thought occurred to her, she found it difficult to believe that she'd only been there such a short time and had already changed her feelings about the place . . . and about Benjamin. She wondered how she could possibly have come to care so much about him during her brief stay—especially since he was so hardheaded and distrustful.

Yet, there were times when she believed she might have fallen in love with him many years ago, ignoring her feelings because of her engagement to Michael.

"Come on, Aunt Jess," Maria called out, running

along the dock in front of her. "We have lots of work to do."

And work they did. For the next two hours, with a rented carriage to transport them, Jessie and Maria went about Port Clinton to collect the debts owed the Whittaker Wine Company. And Maria had been right . . . none of them could resist the widowed sister-in-law of Jonathan Whittaker nor his orphaned daughter.

By the time they were on their way back to the hotel, though, Jessie found herself a bit nervous. They'd collected considerable monies, and she prayed there were no undesirable elements to worry about.

The hotel was lovely, and Maria quickly reverted to being a little girl again, excited by their beautifully appointed room and the enormous dining room where they went to have dinner.

"Look, Aunt Jess, those are gas lamps along the wall. Henry told me they had them in all the fancy places on the mainland, and even in some rich people's homes." She looked up at the soft glow around the room. "You never have to fill these lamps, did you know that?" she asked a bit incredulously.

"I have indeed heard exactly that. The gas is fed through pipes that start under the ground and are laid up through the walls somehow. It is quite an amazing feat."

Soon they were seated at their table and enjoying a fresh fish dinner. The tall flickering tapers on the dining tables in the room added a romantic touch, and Jessie wondered what it would be like to sit down in such a place with Benjamin beside her. She hoped Henry was right and that this trip would heal the disunity between them. She was weary of fighting him, and would prefer to call a truce.

Maria was ready for dessert before Jessie had finished her meal. And after eating two pieces of apple pie, Maria leaned across the table and whispered, "Where did you put all the money, Aunt Jess?"

"It's safely tucked into my camisole."

The little girl covered her mouth with her hand trying hard to hold back her giggles.

"What's so funny, young lady?" Jessie asked.

"I thought you looked rather plump tonight."

Jessie had no choice but to join in Maria's laughter.

After they'd settled down, they talked a little longer while Maria finished her milk.

"I've never been outside of Ohio, Aunt Jess," she said between sips. "Wouldn't it be wonderful to go to the Exposition. It's going to be a grand celebration of our country's birth."

There were many notices posted around town about the upcoming Centennial Exposition in Philadelphia and the talk they'd heard about it had fascinated Maria.

"Well, perhaps we can talk your uncle into taking you."

"Will you come too, Aunt Jess?"

"We'll see, sweetheart," she said, already wondering if wine would be needed at the Exposition. "Right now, I believe it's time for all six-year-olds to be asleep. Come, sweetheart, you must be tired."

As though confirming Jessie's pronouncement, Maria yawned.

Soon the child was safely tucked into bed. Jessie kissed her good night and told her she was going back downstairs for a bit. "I believe I'd like to try selling some wine to the owner of this fine establishment."

Maria smiled a tired smile. "Do you need my help, Aunt Jess?"

"No. You sleep, sweetheart. Tomorrow is going to be another busy day."

As Jessie closed the door, she heard Maria talking. She reopened it a crack, and saw the little girl leaning up on one elbow, a beatific smile on her face. She was nodding. Then ever so softly she said, "You were right, Momma. Aunt Jess knew just what to do, and when Uncle Ben sees how well Aunt Jess can sell our wine, I know everything will be all right."

Jessie shook her head and pulled the door shut and locked it. She wondered how long this fantasy of Maria's would continue.

Going back into the dining room, Jessie spoke to the wine steward. After learning which wines they had in their cellar, Jessie then went in search of the owner of the hotel.

An hour later she walked back into their room with an order for five cases of each of the wines Henry had sent along with them. After sampling them, the owner had sat there shaking his head.

"Is something wrong with the wine, Mr. Moore?"

"On the contrary, my dear. It is far above what we've been buying from the Put-in-Bay Wine Company."

After he'd placed the order, Jessie took a deep breath and told him they'd need half of the money now, with the balance due upon delivery. "We've had some problems collecting debts, Mr. Moore. I hope you understand."

He assured her it was no problem, and Jessie went upstairs with more money tucked into her bodice. Before going to sleep she got out her sewing kit and sewed a pouch into the bottom of her satchel. Once the money was safely hidden there under her clothing and personal effects, Jessie gave herself up to sleep.

Dawn brought with it a penetrating chill, and a heavy mist hung over the shoreline as well as the lake.

Jessie stood by their hotel window watching the fog drift inland like a slithering snake, dampening her spirits.

"Don't be sad, Aunt Jess," Maria said as she finished dressing.

"But we've planned this wine tasting for the park, Maria. There won't be much of a crowd in this weather."

Maria tugged at her aunt's hand. "Go and finish dressing. You should know a little about our weather by now. As soon as the sun burns through the fog, it will be a beautiful autumn day."

"You have such faith, Maria."

"I know our weather, Aunt Jess, and I also know there's someone on our side today."

"Your guardian angel, eh?"

Maria nodded, her cheeks creased in a broad smile.

They went to the dining room for a light breakfast. Then Jessie called for a carriage and had one of the boys from the hotel staff load the crates and her satchel on board.

By the time they got to the park where they planned to conduct their sampling, the sun had burned off the fog and as Maria had predicted, it was indeed a glorious day.

* * *

Benjamin arrived at the dock well before dawn, but unfortunately Marshal Sinclair was there waiting for him.

"I knew you'd try to get off without me, Benjamin, but it won't work. I'm going along." The marshal tried talking him into waiting until the fog dissipated, but Benjamin refused to listen.

"Hope we don't run aground because of your stubbornness," Marshal Sinclair said as they cast off.

"George, I'm just a bit tired of people calling me stubborn and bullheaded and other words to that effect."

"Then perhaps you should change your ways."

Benjamin shook his head and sighed. He had no time for arguments this morning. He'd have to stay alert to keep his boat on course.

Within minutes, the heavy mist had soaked through his shirtsleeves. His vest offered the only protection from the elements. He'd not taken time to go back to the house to get warmer clothing for the trip. He had not wanted to alert Margaret to this voyage. She'd probably try to find a way to help Jessica if she knew what he was doing.

But this time he'd go home with proof of Jessica's treachery. Then Henry and Margaret would have to admit they'd been wrong about the woman.

George had evidently sensed his mood, and Benjamin was grateful that the marshal was leaving him alone.

Only when the fog cleared and Port Clinton could be seen ahead did Benjamin speak. "George, you take off that rain slicker. I want her to see your uniform and badge when we confront her."

"And what makes you think she's still here?"

"I don't think she'd risk traveling with Maria at night, and the fog was so heavy this morning, they might have delayed the next leg of their journey."

"You really believe she's taking the child back to Indiana?"

"She's obviously taking Maria somewhere, George. She snuck off the island without a word, like a thief. What other reason would there be for her to leave, loaded down with crates of Maria's belongings?"

Benjamin's astute questioning of the dockmaster who had forwarded Jessica and Maria's belongings to their hotel led him straight to the owner of the hotel where they'd spent the night.

"Do you know if they were going to continue their journey by train?" Benjamin asked the owner of the hotel.

The man seemed a bit puzzled by the question. "Your sister-in-law and niece have gone to the park, Mr. Whittaker. They'd hardly need a train to go there."

Benjamin called out to the marshal. He had a wry smile on his face as he told him where they were headed. "Can you imagine? She thought I'd give up without a fight. She's not even rushing to get away."

There was quite a crowd milling about the park for mid-October, and a festive air prevailed. Benjamin wondered how he'd find Jessica and Maria amidst all these people, most of whom appeared to be women.

He moved along the outer fringe of the throng with Marshal Sinclair following. Then he began threading his way into the center of the most concentrated area of people. He was now curious as to what the attraction was.

Marshal Sinclair came up alongside him, and they finally managed to break through the crowd.

Benjamin was dumbfounded by the sight before him. There, in the center of the crowd, stood a lace-covered table set with a silver candelabra, flowers, and crystal goblets, along with a large supply of Whittaker wines. Jessica sat behind the table, her dark hair tumbling in long, curled tendrils about her rather flushed face. Maria stood in front of the table passing out glasses of wine.

There appeared to be a long line of women waiting to see Jessica as she busily wrote in what appeared to be a company order book.

George tapped Benjamin on the shoulder and handed him a sign he'd just pulled off a tree.

Benjamin read it, marveling at Jessica's ingenuity. She'd invited the women of Port Clinton to sample all the Whittaker wines and grape juice and to place a large enough order to fill their cellars with wine for the upcoming holidays.

And he could see she was taking no chances. She was obviously collecting a down payment on each order.

As he stood there in awe of what she was doing . . . for his winery, she happened to glance up and catch his eye. She began to smile, and then her gaze shifted to Marshal Sinclair. She looked back at Benjamin and her smile was gone, replaced by an angry glare.

But when another customer stepped up to the table, Benjamin saw her force a smile back on her face. She was doing a good job of selling his wine, letting not even his stupidity keep her from her task.

And it was just as he and his brother had said just weeks ago, a beautiful woman could sell more wine.

Over an hour later, the line dwindled and Maria ran to Benjamin. "You came. Did you see what Aunt Jess has done? She's gotten so many orders, Uncle Ben, and a truly big one from the hotel where we stayed last night. And yesterday afternoon we collected all the money owed you." Maria's excitement kept her sentences running one right after another. "And Aunt Jess has been gathering in so much money she had to tuck some of it into her camisole for safekeeping."

Benjamin had scooped Maria up in his arms to listen to the end of her tale. And when she told him where the money was, Benjamin had to smile.

Watching Jessica gather up the orders, he felt a warmth pushing its way inside him, cracking open and melting the icy cold shell that had encased his heart for such a long time. She'd done so much to help him, and he'd come in anger to accuse her of a terrible deed. He knew she was angry that he'd brought the marshal and tried to think of a way to explain why George was with him. In the end, though, he knew he must be honest. There'd been enough secrecy between them.

When she'd finished the last order and packed up her folder, Jessica marched right up to Benjamin. He put Maria down and asked the child to take the marshal for a walk through the park.

"You still don't trust me," Jessica said as soon as Maria was out of sight. Anger bristled about her every movement.

"Jessica, I could try and talk my way out of this, but you'd know I was lying. Yes, I brought the marshal because I thought you'd kidnapped Maria . . . and I'm sorry. I'm sorry I didn't trust you."

"It's not only that you lack trust, Benjamin. It's that you fly off at the slightest provocation. All you had to do was ask Henry or Margaret. They both knew of our plans."

"You told Henry and Margaret?"

"I had Ann Weldon tell Margaret where we'd be, and I had to confide in Henry. I had to have wine for the sampling, and I needed to learn the names of those who owed the company money. Henry trusted me to do the job."

"But you couldn't come to me?"

She laughed, a bitter, high-pitched laugh. "Oh, I'm sure if I'd told you I wanted to bring Maria on a sales trip to the mainland, you'd have just given me your blessing and sent us on our way, wouldn't you?"

Benjamin looked down at the ground, unable to meet her eyes. "No, I suppose I wouldn't have."

"I know you wouldn't have. You'd probably have flown into another of your angry rages."

"Jessica, no more anger. Let's resolve this right now, today . . . or we'll destroy our niece."

Tears welled in Jessica's eyes. "That's all I wanted, Benjamin. I wanted to make peace between us and that's the reason I planned this trip . . . but it didn't change things. You were still angry with me and you still don't trust me. My God, Benjamin, you brought the marshal with you. Did you plan to have me arrested, dragged back to the island to be punished?"

"No. And I've already apologized for bringing the marshal, Jessica. I truly am sorry. It will be different now. I promise."

Jessica stood looking into Benjamin's eyes,

tears threatening to spill from hers. He'd said he was sorry and made a promise—two things she'd never heard from his mouth before. Perhaps this could end here and now.

Maria and the marshal returned just as Jessie blinked sending tears cascading down her cheeks.

The little girl ran to Jessie, crying out, "Uncle Ben, how could you make Aunt Jess cry again after all she's done?"

Jessie scooted down to Maria's level as she brushed her own tears away. "Hush, sweetheart. I'm crying because I'm happy."

"You're happy?"

"Yes. Your uncle apologized for doubting me and he—"

Benjamin interrupted, also getting down to Maria's level. "Your aunt's happy because we're going to the courthouse right now to remove my petition for adoption from the record." He looked at Jessie and added, "Your aunt's free to adopt you, Maria. And I know she'll stay on the island with you and make you a good home . . . and I hope she'll allow me to see you often."

"Every day, if you'd like," Jessie said, unable to stop her tears, unable to believe the offer Benjamin had just made.

"Now I understand," Maria said with a smile, putting an arm around each of them, drawing the three of them together in a circle of love. "Aunt Jess is crying happy tears. Momma always told me they were the best kind."

"She was right," Jessie said, giving her niece a hug as she stood. "If we're going to the courthouse, though," she added, smiling at Benjamin, "we best do it quickly. There's a wine sampling scheduled in Sandusky for one o'clock."

* * *

They found Mr. Talbot in his office, and the three of them entering together appeared to shock him.

"Good day," he managed to stammer, as he rose to greet them. "I must say this is a surprise."

"I've come to settle things, Mr. Talbot," Benjamin said. "I wish to remove my petition for Maria's adoption. We all agree that Jessica is the best person to care for her. She and Maria will remain on the island and live in Maria's home. And we've agreed that I will see my niece often, as I always have."

Mr. Talbot stood there, nodding his head. Finally he sat down behind his desk and made a notation on a pad of paper.

"I'll take care of this immediately," he said.

"When will I be 'dopted, Mr. Talbot?" Maria asked.

"Soon, Maria. I'll take this new development to my superiors and let you know their decision as quickly as possible."

Maria smiled as she stood holding Jessie's hand. Then she took Benjamin's hand in her other one, forming a human link between them.

For the first time in a very long time, Jessie felt connected . . . felt whole . . . felt happy.

Chapter Fourteen

The three of them had returned to the island, pleased with the outcome of Jessica and Maria's efforts on behalf of the winery.

After their visit with Mr. Talbot, Benjamin could visibly see the effect on Jessica. Her facial muscles relaxed, she smiled more often, her eyes sparkled. She was once more the woman who'd enchanted him so long ago, the woman who'd haunted his dreams of desire, the woman whose lips had sought his in sorrow and taken away the sting of Fran's death by sharing her own grief and reawakening amorous feelings he'd thought were dead forever.

They'd worked side by side at the sampling in Sandusky, although Benjamin did let Jessica take the lead in presenting their product. The women had listened to every word she said and asked questions of her they'd most likely never have asked him. He'd wondered how Jessica had become so knowledgeable about each of their wines and had been surprised and delighted to learn that Maria had given her a quick lesson in winemaking and how to differentiate between sweet and dry wines.

The monies she and Maria had collected would see the company through the slow winter months, and they would be able to intensify their sales efforts both on the island and the mainland come spring.

The trip had indeed been a grand success.

Back in Maria's home, the three of them spent a pleasant evening together. After Maria finally went to sleep, Benjamin poured a glass of wine for Jessica and himself, and they discussed how they would share in Maria's upbringing.

The conversation led Benjamin to think about the many opportunities he and Jessica would have to spend time together in the months ahead. He found the thought quite appealing.

As he was leaving later that night, Jessica reached up and kissed his cheek. "Thank you for ending the terrible strain between us, Benjamin."

"You have nothing to thank me for. I was being my usual stubborn self, as Margaret so often tells me. By going to the mainland with Maria and so unselfishly giving of yourself, you showed me what a fool I'd been. I can only thank God that you've chosen to forgive me and are willing to allow me to be a part of Maria's life."

He kissed her cheek then, knowing that someday, when the time was right, they would once again share a more passionate kiss.

* * *

The next day, after leaving the winery, Benjamin rode across the island to visit Maria and Jessica. He found himself whistling, something he'd not done in years, and he suspected his newly found sense of well-being had to do with the ending of the feud between himself and the woman he'd probably loved from the day they'd first met.

He tethered his horse at the hitching post and made his way to the front door, experiencing an unfamiliar ache in his cheeks . . . obviously from smiling more today than he had in a long time.

At the door, he knocked on the oak frame, then waited anxiously for Jessica's appearance.

Through the oval glass in the door, he could see her approaching, and walking close behind her was Arthur Conners.

As soon as Jessica opened the door, Benjamin pushed inside. "What are you doing here, Conners?"

"I came to call on Mrs. McAllister and it has nothing to do with you, Mr. Whittaker."

"Anything concerning Jessica or my niece has something to do with me, sir, and I'll thank you to leave now before our words get out of hand."

Arthur glanced at Jessica and she nodded. "We'll talk again, Arthur. Thank you for coming and for your generous offer."

As the door shut behind Arthur, Benjamin spun around, coming face-to-face with Jessica. He'd been ready to lash out again, but hesitated, seeing what appeared to be a confusing combination of pain and anger in her eyes.

Remembering his promise to make things different between them, he bottled his angry retort about Arthur's presence in his brother's house.

His frustration at finding another man with Jessica eased even more as he noticed her puffy, red-rimmed eyes.

"Did that man insult you in some way, Jessica?"

She shook her head, turned, and walked down the hall, with Benjamin at her heels.

"Then what's wrong? Where's the happy woman I left here last night?"

"My happiness was short-lived," she murmured, moving slowly into the sitting room. She stood at the window, but he was certain that she saw nothing beyond the lace curtains. Although she maintained her carriage, her back straight, her head held high, he could see the slightest tremor in her shoulders, and knew she was trying to stop her tears.

"Jessica, what is it? Things went so well yesterday. I thought we'd worked everything out quite amicably."

She issued one long sigh, and he saw her shoulders slump before she turned to him. She'd been unable to stop the torrent of tears—they still flowed down her soft pink cheeks. A sense of foreboding gripped him as he realized she had not cried this much after her own sister's death.

Tentatively he stepped closer. "Please tell me what's wrong." Then a shudder of fear shot through him. "Where's Maria? Has something happened to her?"

"No . . . no." She shook her head vehemently, and extended her hand to touch his arm. "She was tired this afternoon and fell asleep, thank God." Jessica looked up into his eyes and began to speak, each word punctuated with a sob. "Mr. . . . Talbot . . . sent a message."

For a brief moment, Benjamin relaxed. "These are what Maria called happy tears then? The decision has been made already?"

Jessica shook her head. "No . . . I mean, yes. The decision has been made but these are not happy tears, Benjamin."

He grasped her by the shoulders and looked at her sternly. "You are confusing me, Jessica. I have a right to know what's going on. Tell me . . . now."

Her voice was almost a whisper and filled with anguish. "Your efforts were in vain, Benjamin. Mr. Talbot has received explicit instructions from his superiors to find a married couple to adopt Maria."

For a moment, Benjamin stood there trying to absorb the words. The silence hung ominously over them like a black cloud, threatening to swoop down and blot out the sunshine forever.

"Why?" he finally asked. "I don't understand why."

Jessica shrugged her shoulders and shook her head. "Single women or men are not considered to be the best choice in adoptions," she said. "And I'm sure our bickering didn't help matters any. Mr. Talbot said his superiors felt it would be in Maria's best interest to have two parents."

"And did they say how *two* strangers could possibly become parents to a six-year-old girl?"

Jessica continued to shake her head, but seemed unable to speak.

Benjamin saw the utter hopelessness that had overtaken her. The woman who had come to the island with such fire and determination—first to make her sister well, and failing that, to do anything to adopt her niece—now appeared beaten. Watching the once feisty woman sit slumped in a chair, looking totally defeated, tore at Benjamin's heart.

In that moment, Benjamin knew with certainty that he loved her. And this knowledge had come at the worst possible time. She had made no mention of love in her time with him and had been distressed by the one kiss they'd shared. He could not risk declaring his love for her . . . another rejection would be too much. If he could not declare his love, though, he could at least give her hope.

Taking her hands in his, he pulled Jessica to her feet. "We'll fight this, Jessica. They can't just take her away. You know that. Dear God, you fought me for her—are you just going to give up and let her go to strangers?"

He was rewarded by a spark deep within her eyes.

"Do you think there's a chance?" she asked softly.

"Yes, there is a chance."

She continued to gaze up into his eyes, and all the emotions Benjamin had kept bottled up since the funeral—all the loving feelings he now realized he'd buried beneath his anger—came rushing out. The heat where her hands rested in his was almost unbearable, like a hot poker sizzling into his skin, and to look into her eyes was to be lost in their depths—like a drowning man.

A moment later she blinked as though awakening from a trance and leaned against him, her head on his shoulder, their fingers, still entwined, pressed between their bodies.

He could smell the soft, sweet fragrance of her hair, could feel her heart beat against his own chest. Without thought, he pulled his hands from hers and wrapped his arms around her, wanting to console her and wanting her warmth to console him as well.

Her head moved from his shoulder, tilting back just enough to look up at him. "Is this another instance of a comforting embrace?" she asked.

"Yes," he murmured, wanting to lower his head and place his lips on hers, wanting to caress her, to hold her, to carry her off and make love to her. Instead he ran his thumb along her lips, felt the softness, and imagined the taste of them. He must restrain himself, though, as he was unwilling to have her run off and retreat again as she did after their first kiss.

She sighed, lowering her head, leaning against him. He didn't realize she'd started crying again until he felt his shirtsleeve damp from her tears.

He tilted her head up with his thumb, and with a finger, wiped away her tears. "Why are you crying? We'll figure something out. We must," he added.

"There is a way," she said. "I've been thinking about it and I believe it's the only way."

"That's good news," Benjamin said. "Stop crying and tell me. I'll help in any way I can."

"Arthur came here to reiterate his proposal of marriage. It would mean he and I could adopt Maria. I'm sure the court would see him and his sons as a stable family. You can help," she added, "by keeping your word and letting me have Maria, even though I'd be married to someone you obviously are not fond of."

Benjamin felt the pain in his chest as surely as if she'd plunged a knife in his heart.

"If it's such a good idea, Jessica, why does it make you cry?"

She blinked, and another flood of tears spilled from her eyes. "Because I don't love him and . . . and if I marry him, there would always be a strain between the two of you when you come to visit Maria."

A sudden inspiration occurred to Benjamin, and the simplicity of the idea made him wonder why neither of them had thought of it sooner.

"Then marry me, Jessica."

For a brief instant, Jessie was certain her heart had stopped beating. Her breath caught in her throat and she could barely speak, but she had to know if she'd heard him correctly. "Marry you?"

"Yes. It's the perfect solution. You love Maria, and you've shown an affinity for the family business. If there's no love between you and Arthur, why marry him? You don't love me either, but it would be far more logical for us to marry and give Maria two parents who truly love her."

Jessie's disappointment nearly made her knees buckle. For a brief moment, she'd almost believed it had been an honest proposal, not just one of convenience. Benjamin's offer of marriage proved his love for Maria—if only he could love her too.

She hesitated, recalling her vow not to marry without love, yet she'd been ready to accept Arthur's proposal for Maria's sake. If she accepted Benjamin's offer, at least she would be marrying for love, even if he were not. Jessie knew that for a successful marriage love should be given as well as returned, but perhaps, in time, he could come to care for her.

Benjamin drew her down onto the divan to sit beside him as he continued to speak rationally about the legalities and the logistics of a marriage between them, yet Jessie barely heard him.

Her mind played back all the moments she'd spent with him, beginning with the clear remembrance of their dance at Fran's wedding . . . his hands on her waist as he helped her down from his horse that first day back on the island . . . the tingles that shot through her when their hands touched . . . the deep longing she'd felt when they kissed . . . the comforting warmth that had enveloped her when his arms held her just minutes ago.

Abruptly, Benjamin's voice broke through.

". . . of course we would have to put on a loving facade for the court's benefit. I'm sure Mr. Talbot would want to assure himself we are sincere. We could tell him we'd let our differences get in the way of our true feelings. I'm sure we could make him believe we care for each other."

Oh, yes, Jessie thought. I can make him believe I care for you, Benjamin.

She watched him as he spoke, but saw no emotion on his face and had trouble reconciling this picture of Benjamin with the man who'd kissed her the day of the funeral. Perhaps it had been just as he'd said that day—perhaps, for him, the kiss had been only a source of comfort.

How could I ever expect him to love me? she thought. Especially after he caught me in his bedroom, prying into his private affairs, trying to discredit him? Although she did believe that the good she'd done on the sales trip might help to ease that memory from his mind eventually.

Benjamin watched Jessica as he outlined his plan. She seemed lost in thought for a large portion of the time, but never spoke. He was almost afraid to stop talking for fear she would say no to his proposal.

At last he ran out of words and simply sat back in his chair and looked into her sea-green eyes. Suddenly, marriage to Jessica had become the most important thing in his life. He knew it had been his secret dream since the night he held her in his arms at his brother's wedding.

He'd never acknowledged his feelings, but the dreams, the desire she stirred in him, his response to her every look and touch should have made him aware of his growing love for her. Wedded to Jessica, spending each day . . . and night with her would bring all his dreams to fruition.

"Well, what do you think of my idea, Jessica?" he asked, silently praying she would not decline.

Still she did not speak. She walked again to the window as though the answer might be somewhere out on the lake beyond.

Or perhaps she was trying to think of a kind way to say no to his proposal. Perhaps she cared more for Arthur Conners than she let on. He supposed the man's good looks might appeal to a woman. And Arthur was much younger than he was, by at least seven or eight years. Possibly that was the reason Jessica was leaning in Arthur's direction.

Benjamin was doing a good job of working himself into an inner turmoil.

As she finally turned toward him, he tried desperately to remain impassive, to not show her his concern over her answer.

"It is a good proposal," she said. "I believe marriage would put us in an excellent position to adopt Maria . . . if we can convince Mr. Talbot we are sincere and do truly love each other."

Benjamin merely nodded, but his blood was pounding in his veins. Oh, yes, Jessica, he thought. It won't be at all difficult to convince Talbot of my sincerity.

She looked up at him, and in a barely audible

voice she said, "For Maria's sake, I accept your proposal."

Silently, Jessie wondered how far their "loving facade" would go.

Maria quietly moved back up the stairs, tears pooling in her eyes. She'd fallen asleep after returning from the mainland, and when she awakened she'd heard her aunt and uncle talking. She knew it was wrong to listen in on other people's conversations, but since they were talking about her, it seemed like a good idea.

Now she was sorry she had. She'd almost cried when she heard her aunt saying that the court wanted a married couple to raise her. She'd told Mr. Talbot that she was happy with Aunt Jess, and even Uncle Ben had finally agreed. Everything had been fine. Now it was all changing again.

Maria didn't understand grown-up things at all. How could Uncle Ben suggest that he and Aunt Jess marry? She remembered her momma's sweet voice telling her about the special feelings she and her poppa had had for each other before they wed. Her aunt and uncle didn't have those special feelings. Until today all they'd done was argue.

She'd heard often enough about Uncle Ben's terrible first marriage. Momma had often said it was because there was no love in the union and that her uncle had become a bitter man as a result of it. Maria couldn't let that happen to him again . . . and she didn't want Aunt Jess to turn into a bitter woman either.

Maria was lacing her shoes when the soft light filtering in through the window grew brighter. She looked up with joy in her heart. If ever she needed to talk to her mother, it was now.

The glowing figure in white took shape, and it

took all of Maria's willpower to keep from running to it. She wanted her mother's comforting embrace, and for the first time was sad because she couldn't be picked up in her mother's arms.

"Momma . . . I need you," she said softly, tears still wet on her cheeks.

A gentle breeze blew past the child, drying her tears. The light surrounding the figure fanned outward, enfolding Maria in its midst.

"Hush, my little one. No more tears now."

"But Momma, they've decided to get married so they can 'dopt me."

"That is not a bad thing, Maria."

"But they don't have those special feelings you told me about."

"No one but God can know what's truly in someone's heart."

"If you'd heard them arguing this past week, you'd know they didn't love each other," Maria said. "People who love one another don't yell at each other like that. You and Poppa never did."

"Your aunt never had the same temperment as I, Maria. She can be sweet and even tempered, but at other times her strong nature battles against those traits and she says things she doesn't always mean."

Maria smiled. "That's true. And she and Uncle Ben did kind of make up today on the mainland. She did really well for the company."

"I know, my sweet. I was quite proud of all the two of you accomplished."

Abruptly, Maria grew solemn again. "But I still don't want them to get married just because of me. I don't want Aunt Jess to grow bitter like Uncle Ben did because his wife didn't love him."

"People can grow to love each other."

"Uncle Ben's wife didn't."

"Maria, my time is short. Please trust me and don't worry about this needlessly. I need to know that your life is safe and secure, my little one. And if Benjamin and Jessica marry and adopt you, I would always know you are all right."

The light began to recede and the angel's face was no longer clear.

"Don't go, Momma. I'm still not sure about this. I don't want Aunt Jess to be hurt."

"Don't worry . . . please, my sweet . . . don't . . ."

The words faded along with the light. Maria knew her momma couldn't stay very long, and in fact each visit seemed to be shorter. But she had not finished her discussion. She had not told her mother what she planned to do.

Maria sighed deeply, chilled now that the light was gone. Quickly she donned her warm gray cape and bonnet and penned a note to her aunt. She propped it up against her pillow, then gathered up the doll her mother had made her from scraps of material and a quilt, adding them to the other items she'd already placed in her cloth sack.

"If I'm gone," she whispered to her doll, "Aunt Jess won't have to marry Uncle Ben."

Maria tiptoed out into the hallway. She could hear her uncle talking downstairs.

"All right, it's settled then. We will wed at St. Paul's with Reverend Weldon officiating."

A minute later, Maria heard her uncle going out the back door, and as their voices grew distant, she knew Aunt Jess had gone out on the service porch to speak to him. She slipped out the front door and around the side of the house.

After Uncle Ben leaves, Maria thought, *I'll go through the woods beyond the field and find the* cave Momma and I discovered last summer. They'll never find me there.

And as long as she stayed away, Aunt Jess wouldn't have to marry Uncle Ben. But she'd have to hurry. The sun would be setting very soon and she'd not find the cave in the dark.

Chapter Fifteen

When Benjamin left, Jessie returned to the warmth of the kitchen. She stood in front of the cookstove warming her hands.

"Mrs. Benjamin Whittaker," she murmured, a smile creasing her cheeks. "It's a beginning. We'll make Maria a good home . . . and perhaps, one day he will learn to love me too."

Jessie decided to have a cup of tea before preparing dinner. She had assured Benjamin that she would find the right words to tell Maria of their plans. It would take some thought, but Jessie was sure she could make the child understand.

Until the setting sun's rays streamed through the window, warming her back, Jessie hadn't realized how long she'd sat at the table.

Maria had been so tired after their busy day, she'd gone up to take a nap, and now as the day grew shorter, Jessie was tempted to allow her to sleep straight through the night. She'd been a busy little girl this long day, and might easily sleep till morning. But the child hadn't eaten since lunchtime in Sandusky, and Jessie didn't want her waking during the night with a hungry belly.

So Jessie went upstairs, calling out, "Come on, sleepyhead, it's time for supper. What would you—"

When Jessie opened the door, she saw immediately that Maria wasn't in bed. The next thing she saw was the note.

Jessie rushed to the bed and picked up the lined paper. The words, printed in Maria's best hand, tore at her heart:

Dear Aunt Jess,
I am going away so you don't have
to marry Uncle Ben and be sad.
I love you.
Maria

Jessie's mind reeled with a multitude of thoughts. Maria must have heard them discussing her and their plans to marry. The poor little thing—where would she go? No time to waste. Must get Benjamin.

Hastily, Jessie donned her cape, uttering a silent prayer that Maria did indeed have her guardian angel to watch over her. The sun would soon be setting, and Jessie didn't like to think of the little girl out alone at night.

Minutes after she'd found the note, Jessie had saddled her horse and was headed for Benjamin's house, sidetracked only for a moment to alert Ann Weldon of her predicament. Ann and her husband told her they would immediately set out to search the area between their two homes.

"We'll concentrate on that wooded area where Willy and Maria like to play," Ann had told her.

Jessie was glad someone was searching, because she felt the need to alert Benjamin. It was important for him to know of Maria's disappearance.

"Benjamin! . . . Benjamin!" Jessie rushed into the house without even knocking.

Margaret came down the hall, wiping her hands on her apron, looking a bit puzzled by Jessie's abrupt appearance. "What is it, miss?"

"Where is he, Margaret? Where's Benjamin?"

"He left several minutes ago. What's wrong?"

"I have to find him," Jessie cried out, turning back toward the door.

"Miss Jessie, what's wrong?"

Jessie stopped, suddenly unable to think what to do next. She pulled the note from her pocket and handed it to Margaret. "She must have heard us . . . Benjamin decided we should get married in order to adopt her—"

"Dear God in heaven . . . Samuel! Samuel, come quickly," she called.

Mr. Cochran appeared at the top of the steps, and a minute later—having read the note and heard Jessie's hurried explanation of what had transpired—was on his way to find Benjamin.

"He's gone to Henry's home to talk over some business matters," Margaret explained after Samuel left.

"Margaret, try and think . . . where would she go? Where would a little girl go to hide on the island?"

"Do you think she's hiding, or would she try and leave?"

Jessie had a momentary flash of Maria on the steamer—alone—crossing to the mainland. Then she shook her head. "The last boat leaves before dark so she'd not have had time to board, and besides, I doubt the captain would allow a child her age aboard without an adult."

"You're right," Margaret said.

"And I don't think she'd ever leave the island anyway," Jessie added. "It's her home and she loves it dearly. You should have heard the way she talked about it yesterday.

"Margaret, that's the answer. All I have to do is remember all the places she told me about. She's bound to be in one of her favorite places."

Jessie headed for the door, remembering Maria's words: ". . . watching the little egrets . . . West Shore . . . the caves."

"That has to be the place," Jessie said, turning back to Margaret and almost running into her.

"She mentioned the caves . . . that would be a perfect hiding place."

Margaret was nodding her head. "There are several, though. You'll need help searching all of them—and light."

Jessie was torn between rushing off and stopping to prepare so as not to go off haphazardly.

Margaret was the calming influence she needed. "Come, we'll get you something more appropriate to wear. You can't go off in the caves holding your skirts up. And you'll need lamps."

Jessie followed Margaret like an obedient child as the older woman listed their needs.

By the time Jessie had changed into a pair of Mr. Cochran's trousers and a cotton shirt, Margaret had gathered the other supplies she felt would be needed.

She was trying to convince Jessie to wait for the men when the front door burst open. Benjamin's dark eyes met hers, and she saw the fear and anguish of her own heart reflected there.

"Why?" he asked plaintively.

Jessie went to him, pulling the note from the pocket of the jacket Margaret had given her to wear.

Benjamin watched her as she approached, the paper held out in her hand. He was torn between the grief of his niece's disappearance and his desire to pull Jessica into his arms and comfort her.

Their eyes met once again. It was discomforting to Benjamin, as he read things into Jessica's glance that he could not be sure of. There seemed to be such longing in her eyes, yet he wondered if it was his own desire that he saw mirrored there. Earlier today, he'd wanted to go and take her in his arms. But years ago his love had been rebuffed soundly by his wife, and even Jessica had pushed him away when they'd kissed after the funeral. How many times could a man's pride endure rejection?

Although he knew it took but a moment, her movements seemed to slow to a snail's pace, making him aware of the men's clothing she wore, her hair pulled back with a piece of green ribbon, the anguish etched in her face, her eyes darkened with fear, her trembling hand outstretched.

He took one step forward and reached for the note.

Jessica stood silently before him as he read Maria's words.

"My God . . . Maria," he whispered, crumpling the paper in his hand.

"Benjamin . . ." Jessica's hand touched his arm and he looked into her eyes. "I think Maria's in one of the caves . . . she told me about all her favorite places yesterday, and it seems as though a cave might be—"

"Of course," he said, turning to Mr. Cochran, who stood behind him in the open doorway. "Samuel, go and get some of the men . . . Henry, Daniel . . . neighbors. We'll need more help if we're to search all of the caves."

Then he turned back to Jessica. "Please, I know you're anxious about her, but it would be best if you stayed here with Margaret . . . prepared some food for the men—"

"No!" Jessie shouted. "I'm going with you. Don't even try and stop me."

"I can handle things here, sir," Margaret quickly added. "I'll have everything ready when you get back."

"It may take some time, Margaret . . . darkness is already upon us."

"I understand . . . just go."

Benjamin looked at Jessica. "Please reconsider."

"I'm going."

From her stance and the determined look in her eye, Benjamin knew it was no use arguing with her.

"Let's go then," he said.

When her uncle had ridden away from the house, Maria had gone swiftly across the field and into the woods beyond, where she and Willy so often played in the summer.

She remembered the walk she and her mother had taken last summer, and how they'd stopped to rest by an enormous pine tree. They'd been watching a lizard which had moved languidly by them, when it disappeared under some hanging vines. Maria had been fascinated by the spotted reptile, and had moved the vines to see where it had gone.

Seeing the large opening beyond the vines, Maria had called out to her mother, who'd been truly surprised by her discovery.

And Poppa had been even more surprised when she showed him the next day. Poppa had lived on the island since he was a young boy and had never seen the cave. They'd taken a lamp and gone a little ways inside. Maria could still recall Poppa explaining how the limestone caves had formed and how the temperature in the caves was constant.

She moved the sack to her shoulder, hoping the quilt she'd brought would keep her warm.

As she went along the path, trying to recall the place she and her mother had rested, she became confused. The summer's growth was gone, the trees almost bare. Several large pines looked familiar, but when she moved toward them she saw there was no vine-covered ledge beyond.

The sun had almost gone down, and long shadows darkened the area where she searched for her cave.

She had to find it quickly before it was completely dark. Not that the dark frightened her. Her parents had taught her long ago that nothing lurked in the night shadows that wasn't there by day.

Dropping to her knees in a crisp heap of fallen leaves, Maria set her sack down beside her, folded her hands, and closed her eyes tight. "Momma, please help me find the place," she whispered into the stillness of the forest. "I have to go there and hide so Aunt Jess doesn't make a terrible mistake. Please, Momma, show me the way."

Maria remained there for several seconds waiting, her rust-colored skirt blending into the bronzed leaves where she knelt. She expected to see the brilliant light again, expected to feel its warmth, but no light came and she was still cold.

When she opened her eyes and looked up, though, she saw the tall pine some distance in front of her, and moved with assurance toward it.

Lifting the browned, bare vines, denuded of their summer leaves, she sighed with relief. "Thank you, Momma," she whispered before opening her sack and rummaging inside to find one of the two candles she'd brought. She'd been afraid to bring a lamp as it seemed more difficult to light.

Moving into the opening, out of the cold and the wind, Maria rummaged in the cloth bag to find the box of matches she'd also packed. She'd never lit one herself, but had watched her mother and aunt. So she took one of the wooden sticks out of the box and rubbed it alongside the box as she'd seen them do.

Nothing happened. Rubbing harder the second time, Maria was startled by the sudden flare and spark from the match head. With shaky fingers she lit the candle, then raised it to look about the cave. It was a small opening, but she recalled that when her father had come with her, they'd found a large cave just beyond the sloped hilltop that tapered into an opening toward the back. She located it quickly, and was soon inside the vast expanse.

The candle flickered as Maria walked, casting

eerie shadows on the walls of the cave. When she found a smooth area alongside a jagged structure that resembled the mountains she'd once seen in a picture book, she pretended she was camping near the mountains and was going to take a nap. Although she'd slept for a bit this afternoon, Maria still felt tired. And if she slept, she knew she wouldn't have to think anymore about her aunt and uncle right now.

She tipped her candle, forming a small puddle of wax on the lower edge of her little mountain. Then she stuck the candle upright in the puddle of melted wax until it held firmly.

The shadows were more stable now, and with the knowledge that her parents were watching her from heaven fixed firmly in her mind, she rolled the quilt into a sort of sack and slid down inside like a butterfly in a cocoon. She held her dolly close, and with the flickering candlelight reflecting against her closed eyelids she fell sound asleep.

Hours passed and there was still no sign of the child. Jessie had ridden beside Benjamin, entered two caves with him, crawled over rocks and through narrow openings with him, and climbed limestone steps into hillsides of rock. In the process she'd managed to scratch her face, tear the top of one fingernail off, catch her hair in a bramble bush, and bruise her shin on a rock—an excruciatingly painful experience, though she'd not admitted it to Benjamin when he'd inquired if she was all right.

They met as prearranged with Henry and several other men who worked for Benjamin near the second cave the men had searched.

When they arrived, Samuel was already there with bags of bread and cheese that Margaret had sent to give them sustenance. He also had jugs of water and grape juice to quench their thirst.

Jessie refused to eat, but did drink some of the juice. The fruity sweet taste immediately brought back Maria's list of favorite things on the island.

"I was so sure," she whispered.

"Did you say something, Jessica?" Benjamin asked.

She shook her head. "Nothing . . . it's just that I was certain she'd be in one of the caves. She described many places, but the caves seemed a logical place to hide."

"Try and relax a moment," Benjamin said, leading her to sit down near the fire Samuel had built to help dispel the chill from their bodies. "Perhaps if you think back to your talk, you can recall other places she told you about."

Jessie sat cross-legged in front of the dancing flames. She stared into the fire, recalling Maria's smiling face as she described each of her favorite things and places.

"Go ahead, Jessica," Benjamin encouraged. "Just say them out loud."

"She talked about the sunsets at West Shore and watching the birds . . . she loves the vineyard and tasting the juice as it comes fresh from the press . . ."

As Jessica recited Maria's favorite things, Benjamin couldn't help but think of Maria as a baby cooing at the egrets as they pecked between the rocks, gooing at the sight of the sunset, and as a toddler, reaching up with an empty cup for juice from the press.

He hadn't realized he was crying until Jessica

reached up and brushed a tear from his cheek.

He turned away, clearing his throat and swiping at his dampened cheeks. "What else did she say?"

"She talked about skipping rocks, and fishing, and of course the caves . . . and of long walks in the woods picking wildflowers with her mother . . ."

Jessica paused, and Benjamin caught the look in her eye.

"What? . . . what is it?" he shouted.

Jessie jumped to her feet. "She and her mother discovered a new cave last summer. She said even Jonathan was surprised as he'd never seen it in all his years on the island."

Benjamin was instantly beside her, smiling, holding her hands in his. "Of course. Jonathan told me . . . he was going to take me to see it but . . . did she say where it was, Jessica?"

"Only that they'd found it on one of their walks through the wooded path to pick wildflowers."

"Between her house and the Weldons'," he said. "It has to be . . ."

His words were cut off by the sound of horses' hooves thundering toward them. All the men rose and watched as Ann Weldon rode up, calling out before fully stopped. "We found something."

Ann dismounted quickly and hurried over to Jessie and Benjamin. "Look, Jessie . . ." She held out a button and a piece of ribbon that were unquestionably Maria's.

"Where did you find them?" Benjamin asked.

"We were searching the woods between our homes. William found the button along the path from your house and the ribbon was a little further in. William's still searching, but now that it's full dark, the search is going at a much slower pace. He told me to come and get more help to cover the area."

As they mounted their horses, Jessie told Ann about the cave Maria had described. Ann too had heard about it from Willy and wondered if Maria might have showed him the opening.

While the men spread out in the wooded area to continue the search, Ann and Jessie rode to the Weldons' to talk to Willy, who was at home with an intestinal upset.

Jessie approached the child, who looked as white as the pillowcase he rested on. She did not want to disturb him, but knew he might have the key to Maria's hiding place. It was already late, and Jessie couldn't bear to think of Maria being alone all night.

"Hello, Willy. I'm sorry you're not feeling well."

He nodded weakly. "Mother says I shouldn't have eaten so many apples off your tree."

"Your mother's probably right." Jessie hesitated, forming her thoughts into words. "Willy, I was wondering if Maria ever showed you the cave she and her mother found in the woods last summer."

Again Willy nodded. Jessie's heart beat faster. "Do you think you could find the place again?"

The little boy continued to nod. "I went there once, but I'm afraid of the dark, so I didn't go in."

Jessie looked at Ann, uncertain of what to do. The child looked so sick she couldn't ask his mother to take him out of bed.

Ann came forward and sat on the edge of her son's bed. "Willy, do you think you could tell us where to find the cave?"

The little boy raised one blond eyebrow and

turned his head to look up at Jessie. "Is something wrong?"

Jessie looked at Ann, who nodded in answer to her unspoken question. Jessie knelt down beside the bed and smiled so as not to frighten the child. "Maria heard something that disturbed her and she's run away from home. We think she might be hiding in the cave."

Willy closed his eyes a moment, then looked at Jessie and said, "She was worried about you and her uncle arguing."

"I know, Willy, and we've finally solved our differences. We just haven't had a chance to tell Maria."

"Can you tell Mrs. McAllister where the cave is, son?"

Willy shook his head. "I don't think so. It's off the path. In the summer there were lots of flowers nearby, but it might be hard to find it now, and I don't know how to tell you where to look."

Jessie's eyes met Ann's in a plaintive cry for help.

Ann looked down at her son. "Willy, do you think, if I bundled you up and took you on my horse, that you could direct us to this place?"

"My tummy hurts bad, but if it would help find Maria . . ."

"Oh, Ann," Jessie said. "I can't let you take him out. Maybe I can—"

"He isn't mortally ill, Jessie," Ann said. "If we have to stop we can. It's just those apples in his stomach."

They bundled the little boy up and got him outside. Ann mounted her mare first, and Jessie handed Willy up to her. His mother settled him in front of her in the saddle, and they started down the road.

Mr. Cochran rode up just as they were heading toward the woods. "Miss Jessie, Mr. Benjamin is distraught. He's concerned about little Maria out here in the dark and the cold. I told him to keep searching and I would check with you and see if Willy remembered anything."

Jessie quickly explained that Willy indeed had been to the cave Maria and her mother had found.

"Thank God," he said, looking at the little boy, who leaned against his mother. He rode up beside them and said, "I know you're not feeling well, Willy, but Maria needs your help."

The little boy nodded, a blond curl slipping from under the blanket his mother had wrapped around him.

Samuel reached out and patted the child's shoulder. "I'll go on back and tell Mr. Benjamin the area where you'll be searching.

The women rode slowly so as not to jar the boy, and Jessie held a lantern aloft as they went along the route Willy had pointed out. Occasionally he'd crane his neck, then shake his head. After several stops where he thought he recognized the place, only to be disappointed on closer inspection, he suddenly leaned forward and appeared to be searching for something.

"There," he said, pointing with one tiny finger. "Near that big pine. It should be beyond the tree . . . vines covering a hillside . . . you . . . have to move them."

The child sounded so weak, Jessie insisted Ann take him back home.

"We'll wait a moment to make sure he's right about the entrance," Ann said.

Jessie quickly slipped off her horse carrying the lantern with her.

She reached the hillside beyond the pine, and moved the dried vines that hung down over a portion of it. "It's here!" she shouted, turning back to Ann.

"Do you want us to wait?" Ann called out.

"No. Get Willy back to bed. Benjamin and Samuel should be here soon."

Jessie stuck her head in the opening and called Maria's name. There was no answer—in fact, she could hear no sounds at all. It appeared to be a rather small opening, but judging from the other caves she'd been in tonight, she was certain the space toward the back would lead to a larger area.

Before entering, she went back to her horse and lit the other lantern, leaving it on a large rock so Benjamin and Samuel could find their way. The possibility of her niece being lost inside a cave made a shiver of apprehension creep up Jessie's spine, and there was no need for anyone else to be lost out here tonight.

Silently she made a vow that if she found Maria alive and well, she would do everything in her power to make her marriage to Benjamin a good one and to convince the little girl that they could indeed be a happy family. Perhaps she'd even tell Benjamin of her love for him . . . and damn her foolish pride. It was what Maria needed to hear and Jessie needed to tell.

She carried the lantern in one hand, moving the vines aside with the other. Toward the back of the small enclosure she had to bend down and go through a narrow opening, which led into a much larger cave. There was a sort of alcove toward the back and in the flickering light of a candle, Jessie immediately recognized the quilt from Maria's bed. She was across the cave in seconds, on her knees beside the still form. "Maria . . . Maria, my sweet, are you all right?"

The little girl sighed and rolled onto her back, her doll still in her arms.

Thank God, she's just asleep, Jessie thought. She leaned down and gently kissed her cheek, not wanting to frighten her.

Maria's eyelids fluttered open and Jessie said, "Hello there. We've missed you."

Maria looked around, her gaze settling first on the candle, then going back to Jessie.

She rubbed her eyes with one tiny, balled-up fist. "I didn't want you to find me."

"We were worried about you, little one. Everyone's out looking for you all over the island."

"You didn't have to worry. That's why I left the note. And I ran away so you wouldn't have to marry Uncle Ben."

"But I want to, sweetheart. Your Uncle Ben and I both want to make you a good home. We'll be a family."

The little girl shook her head.

"We love you, Maria. Both of us love you very much."

Maria sat up, looking at her aunt for several silent moments before speaking. "I know you both love me—but you don't love each other." Tears suddenly filled the child's eyes, and Jessie tried to pull her into her arms.

"No," Maria said, shaking her head and pulling away. "You can't marry him, Aunt Jess."

"But it's the only way to make us a real family," Jessie said.

Maria still shook her head. "No. Momma told

me about getting married. She told me lots of things about it, but the one thing she told me to always remember was that two people should only get married if they loved each other so much they couldn't go on without each other. She told me that's why Uncle Ben often got so sad . . . because he'd married a woman who didn't love him. I don't want you or Uncle Ben to be sad anymore. I don't want you to have to get married just because my momma and poppa died."

Jessie wished she could say the words to assure Maria that she and Benjamin loved each other, but she couldn't lie to her niece about her uncle's feelings. Instead, she took Maria's hand in hers. "Maria, my sweet, please believe me when I tell you that two people can learn to love each other." Jessie wanted to tell Maria of her own love for Benjamin, but felt he had a right to hear of it first. So she had to do her best to console the child for the time being.

"Your uncle and I have you in common now, and by marrying and making us a family, we will grow closer . . . and someday, perhaps we will have what your mother described to you."

Seeing the doubt in Maria's eyes, Jessie knew this marriage was not going to be easy for the child to accept. And only after much prodding and cajoling was Jessie even able to convince Maria to return home with her.

Later, Jessie began to worry about Benjamin and Samuel. They never had come back to the cave, and Jessie had taken Maria home, unwilling to have her out in the night air any longer than necessary. There she'd heated water on the stove, and after she'd carried bucket after bucket to warm the water in the washtub, Maria sat in the tub soaping herself while Jessie continued to try to convince the child of the prudence of their wedding plans.

Maria barely spoke during her bath, and mutely allowed her aunt to dry her and put her in a soft, muslin nightdress. Her lethargic state concerned Jessie. The independent little girl Jessie knew would never have let her aunt dry and dress her.

"Why don't you hop into bed and I'll go down and heat you some milk and perhaps a piece of cinnamon bread?"

"I'm not sleepy, Aunt Jess. I've taken two naps already and I can't sleep anymore."

"Well, you need to get warmed up and rest a bit at least. I don't want you getting sick like Willy."

"Willy's sick?" Maria's concern was immediately evident.

"His mother thinks he ate too many apples yesterday."

Maria nodded, then climbed into bed. "He did," she said matter-of-factly. "I only ate two."

"That was very wise," Jessie said.

Maria sighed, then said, "I guess cinnamon bread would be good, and maybe some of that cheese that Mrs. Cochran sent over. I didn't take any food with me and my tummy's kind of hungry."

"Well, I suppose there was no need for me to come looking for you then. You would have come home to eat sooner or later."

Jessie's small attempt at humor did nothing to ease Maria's gloomy countenance.

"I'll be right back, sweetheart," Jessie said.

As she cut bread and buttered it for the child, Jessie suddenly heard horses approaching the house. She went out front, and was surprised to see Samuel and Henry.

"Samuel, why hasn't Benjamin come? Maria needs to speak to her uncle. We need to convince her of—"

"Miss Jessie," Samuel interrupted. "I'm afraid there's been an accident."

Jessie's blood turned cold. She knew without asking—it was Benjamin. Looking at Samuel's somber face, Jessie wondered why she'd let her silly pride keep her from telling Benjamin that she loved him. If anything happened to him, he would never know of her love, and that thought pierced her heart like a cold shaft of steel.

Chapter Sixteen

"Is he—"

Samuel must have seen the fear in her eyes, interrupting with the words she needed to hear. "He's unconscious, Miss Jessie. We were riding to the cave and Mr. Benjamin got ahead of me. He was riding faster than he should have at night. A branch caught him across his forehead and temple and knocked him to the ground. He's not come around since."

"Where is he?"

"At Dr. Rittman's," Henry answered.

"I have to go to him. Would one of you stay with Maria?"

"I'll stay, Miss Jessie," Samuel said. "Henry can escort you to the Doctor's home and then go on and inform Margaret of all that's transpired—if he doesn't mind."

"Not at all, Samuel," Henry said. "Shall we go, Jessica?"

She nodded, trying not to cry, praying with all her heart that Benjamin would live. "Let me tell Maria and I'll be right out, Henry."

After explaining to Maria that her uncle had an accident and that Mr. Cochran would be staying with her for a little while, Jessie left with Henry. They didn't speak on the way, and Jessie wondered if Henry was praying too.

A biting cold wind cut through Jessie's heavy cape, and as they rode along she could hear the waves battering the shore. As they neared the doctor's house, her heartbeat raced and she prayed even harder that Benjamin would still be alive. She had to tell him of her love, even if it was the last thing she ever said to him.

Henry helped Jessie down from her horse, and she raised her skirts and raced up the steps to the wide front porch. Dr. Rittman's housekeeper immediately ushered her in, and she was upstairs moments later.

The doctor stepped away from the bed as Jessie entered the room. Jessie knew he'd said something, but his words never reached her ears or her brain. The shock of seeing Benjamin lying so still and white against the pillows paralyzed her—she saw nothing, heard nothing, was unable to move or speak. Tears blurred her vision, and she stifled a sob, certain that Benjamin was dead. She felt her own heart break, knowing she'd never declared her love to him.

And only at that moment, did Jessie realize exactly how much she did love him.

Dr. Rittman came and put an arm around her. His blue eyes focused on hers. "Come closer, dear. Perhaps he'll know you're here."

"He's not dead?" she whispered.

"Of course not. He took a good bump to his head, and he most likely sprained his elbow or shoulder from the fall as he is badly bruised in both of those areas."

"But . . . he . . . he looks so still." Jessie couldn't help but remember the way Frannie had lain unconscious. "Is there any possibility that he may not waken?"

Dr. Rittman's lips curved in a half smile. "No one can ever be certain with a head injury, my dear, but Benjamin is quite hardheaded and I don't think a tree branch is a match for him. I'm sure he'll be all right."

Dr. Rittman patted her shoulder. "Why don't you sit with him for a bit while I check on my other patients."

Jessie nodded, grateful that Benjamin was still alive, thankful that she still had a chance to tell him of her love. It no longer mattered whether he loved her or not—her love would be enough for both of them.

She sat in a chair near the bed, staring unashamedly at his precious face. For the first time, she gave full vent to her feelings for him and gently touched his cheek, stroking the stubble of his beard. She stared at his dark eyelashes, willing his eyes to open. Brushing back a lock of hair that had fallen across his broad forehead, Jessie began to whisper words of love without even being aware of it.

"Benjamin, I was so afraid I'd lost you." Her voice was soft as she continued to stroke his hair. "I couldn't bear the thought of losing you without telling you of my love. I think I've always known there was something between us—even all those years ago when you held me in your arms as we danced at Frannie and Jonathan's wedding.

"And even in my grief over Frannie's death . . . when our lips met, I knew I loved you. I've fought these emotions because I was unsure of how you felt. Then, after our conflict over Maria—I was afraid you'd never return my love."

Jessie stopped for a moment to wipe the tears from her cheeks. Then she leaned forward and gently brushed her lips across his, wanting to touch him more intimately, needing to feel connected to him, longing to breathe life into him, yearning with every fibre of her being to make him well.

Her pulse beat accelerated and she continued talking. There was a need inside her, a desire to say the words that welled up from deep in her soul. "Dear Benjamin, I want you to be all right. I want you to know how much I love you. When you asked me to marry you—even though it was only to keep Maria—I could hardly still my excitement. The thought of being your wife caused my heart to leap inside my chest. . . . "

While continuing to talk to him, she had grasped his hand, and her head was bowed. She had to say it all, pouring out all the feelings that she'd kept locked inside.

"When you are well, my dear Benjamin, I will tell you of my love. Even if you cannot return that love, I am certain we can make a good home for Maria and . . . at the very least we will be a family."

As Jessica went on with her declarations of love, Benjamin began to rouse from his state of unconsciousness. He could hear her voice and tried to pull himself up from his disjointed state, wanting desperately to answer her pronouncement of love with one of his own. Although the pain in his arm throbbed with a vengeance, it faded with each word she spoke.

Jessica loved him. The words were like a soothing balm healing all the hurts of the past.

When she paused, he opened his eyes and looked at her bowed head. Her hair hung loose, covering her face like a veil. The thought made him realize she would soon be his wife and he would see her like this often. An overwhelming sense of joy and love flowed through his body.

She was holding his hand, and he could feel her teardrops on his arm. He found it difficult to believe this wonderful woman was crying over him. His other arm was immobilized, so he gently pulled his hand free from hers and brushed the tears from her cheeks.

Her head came up immediately, and when her eyes met his, it was plain to see the love there. "We must marry soon, my love," he whispered. "So I can show you how much I truly love you."

She shook her head in disbelief, wondering if the blow to his head had made him incoherent. Unable to respond, she stood and said, "I'll get the doctor."

Benjamin grasped her arm, pulling her back down beside him on the bed. "No, don't run away. It's true," he said. "I do love you . . . I've loved you for years. The first time we met, something special passed between us." Benjamin paused, taking her hand and placing it against his chest before he continued. "And it's been here in my heart ever since."

With a slight smile on his lips, Benjamin's eyelids drooped and his grip on Jessica's hand loosened. He opened his eyes again and murmured, "I do love you," then drifted off to sleep again.

Tears of joy filled Jessie's eyes. Her hand still rested on his chest, and she could feel the sure, steady beat of his heart.

Abruptly his eyes came open again. "Is Maria all right?"

"She's fine, home asleep in her bed. She was only concerned because she didn't believe people should marry unless they truly loved each other. Now we can assure her that we do."

She stroked his hair and smiled down at him. "Sleep now, my love. You need your rest." Then she leaned forward and tenderly kissed him once more. Even such a chaste kiss made her tingle inside, and she could hardly imagine the wonders their love would bring after their wedding day. The thought of being in the same bed with Benjamin every night sent shivers of delight throughout her body.

"Soon, my darling," she whispered. "Soon we'll be together always."

Jessie sat for a long while watching this man she loved. When she was certain he was breathing regularly and had entered into a truly restful sleep, she went downstairs to find Dr. Rittman.

The doctor told her Benjamin's waking and talking to her was a good sign. After examining him again, Dr. Rittman assured Jessie that he was sleeping soundly, and would probably do so throughout the night unless the pain from his injured arm should wake him.

"I promise you, Jessica," the doctor said, "if he wakens in pain, I will give him a bit of pain medication and it will help him sleep again."

"Are you sure he's going to be all right?" she

asked for what she knew must be the fifth or sixth time.

"He'll be fine," the doctor said reassuringly. "He can even go home in the morning if you or Margaret will care for him and see that he rests."

As much as Jessica would have liked to take Benjamin home with her, she knew it would not be proper. "I'll see that he gets back to his home in the morning, and I'll send word to Margaret so she'll be prepared for his return."

Torn between staying with Benjamin and wanting to get back to Maria, Jessie finally made the doctor promise to tell Benjamin she would return in the morning.

Once that was settled, Jessie was anxious to go and tell Maria the good news. She could now assure the child that their marriage would be exactly as her mother told her marriage should be.

Back at home, Jessie quickly apprised Mr. Cochran of Benjamin's condition, assuring him that he would recover completely.

He smiled at Jessie after she finished. "You must be pleased to have him on the mend," Samuel said. "Your eyes are sparkling and your cheeks are aglow."

"Of course I'm pleased, Samuel" Jessie said. "You know we're going to be married."

He nodded. "Yes, I know. And Margaret is delighted by the news. She is anxious to help you plan the wedding."

Jessie went on to tell Samuel about her plans to take Benjamin home in the morning, and he assured her all would be in readiness. He also agreed to stop by the Weldons' and ask Ann if she could look after Maria the next day and also allow Jessie to use their wagon to take Benjamin home.

After Samuel left, Jessie went upstairs. Quietly she opened the door to Maria's room, surprised to find her still awake.

"Why aren't you sleeping, sweetheart?"

"I had a bad dream, and then I couldn't go back to sleep until I knew how Uncle Ben was. Is he all right? I'd feel just awful if he got hurt bad because of me."

Jessie sat down on Maria's bed, quickly reassuring her. "Your Uncle Ben is going to be just fine. And you don't have to feel awful. He was just riding too fast in the dark and didn't see the tree branch. His arm is hurt and he has a bump on his head, but Dr. Rittman assures me he will heal. Now, do you want to tell me about this bad dream that woke you?"

Maria shook her head.

"You know, sometimes, if we talk about our bad dreams," Jessie said, "it makes them go away and never come back again."

Maria's face scrunched up, and Jessie thought the child was going to cry. "I just dreamed that you turned into an ugly old woman who yelled at me all the time because you had to marry somebody you didn't love."

"Oh, sweetheart," Jessie said, holding her close. "I'd never yell at you no matter what happened in my life. But you musn't worry anymore because something wonderful happened tonight."

"Uncle Ben got hurt. That's not wonderful."

"No, but because he was hurt, it gave us a chance to talk about our real feelings for each other. Maria, I've always felt drawn to your uncle from the first time we met years ago. But I was not free to explore my feelings."

"Why not?"

"I was to be married to another."

Maria nodded. "That's why you moved to Indiana."

"Yes. And when my husband died, I was so busy trying to keep our farm, I didn't have time to think about your uncle.

"But tonight I finally told him of my love, and he told me that he feels the same. Don't you see, sweetheart, this is what you wanted. We've declared our love for one another, and now when we marry, the three of us can truly be a family."

Maria shook her head. "You don't need to make up stories, Aunt Jess. Mrs. Weldon stopped by to see me while you were gone, and she explained everything. If you and Uncle Ben don't get married, I'll have to live with strangers. And I don't want to live with anybody but you. So I understand why you have to marry Uncle Ben."

The distress visible in Maria's eyes pierced Jessie's own heart. She continued to try to convince the child of her love for Benjamin, but no amount of talk would make Maria believe that she was telling her the truth.

At last the little girl slept, and Jessie again tucked the covers around her before extinguishing the lamp. "Someday you'll understand, my little one," Jessie whispered as she kissed the child's forehead.

But as Jessie lay in her own bed, she knew how difficult it must be for Maria to understand how their love could suddenly be real. She was having great difficulty believing it herself. Yet she'd heard the words. Benjamin had said, "I do love you."

Jessie recalled the smile on his face as his eyes

fluttered shut. She'd never seen such a smile on Benjamin before.

Abruptly intruding on Jessie's pleasant thoughts was the sudden notion that Benjamin might indeed have been disoriented because of the blow to his head. And having heard Dr. Rittman mention pain medication, she couldn't help but wonder if the doctor had given Benjamin any before her arrival.

Could it have been drugs that caused the sublime look on his face? Could it have been the blow to his head that made him declare his love? Perhaps his loving words were said in a drug-induced fantasy . . . and his thoughts had been of someone else, perhaps even his first wife, whom he must have loved at one time.

Her glorious dreams of loving Benjamin suddenly did not seem so secure. And she would have to wait for morning to discover the truth.

Jessie wondered if sleep would ever come this night.

Chapter Seventeen

Sleep did finally come from sheer exhaustion, but it was a fitful sleep, and she woke long before dawn.

Twice during the night, she'd wakened from bad dreams—dreams of Benjamin declaring his love to a woman whose face was a terrifying blank.

Lying back on her pillow, she tried to recall the scene at Dr. Rittman's exactly as it had happened. But all she could remember were Benjamin's fluttering eyelids as she once again heard his dear voice saying, "I do love you."

Try as she might, though, Jessie could not recall him saying her name—not once. And although he'd said something special had occurred between them when they first met, he had not mentioned meeting when she'd arrived for her sister's wedding.

By five o'clock she could not lie in bed another minute. She washed and dressed and brushed her hair with extra care.

Looking at her reflection in the mirror of the dressing table, Jessie remembered how Benjamin had looked at her the day he'd seen her with her hair down. The recollection caused her to leave her long tresses loose, pulled back only with a white satin ribbon. Jessie also decided the gray silk dress she'd brought with her would not be too outlandish for a woman in mourning, considering the fact that she was now engaged to be married.

The silk frock had a lovely white lace collar and cuffs, and although it was not as colorful as she'd like, she knew it was more becoming than her black cotton.

Maria had just come into the room when they heard a wagon coming down the road. "That must be the Weldons," Jessie said. "They're going to take you to their house for the day, so I can get your uncle Ben settled."

Maria glanced out the window. "I'll go and get dressed," she said.

From her listless tone, Jessie didn't know if she was happy or unhappy about going to the Weldons'.

"You don't mind, do you, sweetheart? I thought you might enjoy playing with Willy. Or perhaps you could read with him if he's still not feeling well."

Maria nodded her head as she went out the door.

Jessie sighed. She hated seeing the child so disheartened, but knew she could do nothing more until she saw how Benjamin behaved this morning after sleeping off his medication. If his loving declarations had not been the effect of the drugs, and Benjamin did indeed love her, they would together convince Maria of their love.

An hour later, Ann had left with Maria, and Jessie was on her way to get Benjamin.

As Jessie approached the doctor's white-frame house, her heartbeat accelerated.

She got down from the wagon, trying to slow her rapid pulse and keep her hands from trembling as she tethered the horse to the hitching post out front.

The doctor's housekeeper ushered Jessie inside, took her cape, and told her to go on upstairs.

Jessie found herself as nervous as a schoolgirl, patting her hair back on the sides, adjusting the white ribbon that held it in place, and straightening her dress so it hung smoothly.

She approached the door to Benjamin's room and felt as though she might burst from the anticipation of seeing him again. After rapping softly, she heard his voice. "Come in."

Taking a deep breath, Jessie opened the door and was instantly rewarded by a broad smile on Benjamin's face. He was sitting up in bed, pillows propped behind him. His dark brown eyes sparkled with warmth, and his hair had fallen across his forehead, giving him a rakish appearance.

Jessie just stood there in the doorway devouring every detail. It was obvious that he was happy to see her, and she relished the moment.

"Come in, please. We have so much to talk about."

She closed the door and moved forward as though in a dream.

His eyes followed her, and when she drew closer he murmured softly, "You are so beautiful."

"It's the dress," she answered nervously. "You're not used to seeing me in anything but black."

"No," he said. "It's you, not the dress, although it is lovely. And you've left your hair down."

She nodded, enjoying the look of yearning in his eyes.

"It's becoming that way," he said. He continued to apprise her, and suddenly blurted out, "I'd like to see you in a bright aqua-colored dress to match your eyes."

Jessie smiled at his request. "I don't own a dress that color, and besides, I am still in mourning. I even hesitated wearing this one."

"Then why did you?"

"I suppose it's because you've only seen me in black, and I wanted to look attractive to you this morning."

Benjamin smiled. "Such candor is refreshing."

"I should be in black, though, out of respect for my sister."

"Frannie hated black," Benjamin said. "She wore it only to burial services, and I'm sure she wouldn't mind if you didn't wear it anymore. Soon we'll be married, and you will not wear black after our wedding day."

"Are you asking me or telling me?" she inquired playfully.

"I merely suggested that it would be a good day to discontinue wearing your mourning dress." His dark eyes practically dared her to dispute his rational thinking.

She shook her head slowly, a slight smile playing at the corners of her soft pink lips. Benjamin could only imagine what she was thinking. One thing he knew for certain—life with Jessica would never be boring.

"You're right, of course," she said. "Thank you for your suggestion." A smile once more tugged at the corners of her lips. "Our wedding day will be a good day to stop wearing black. Unfortunately, I have no suitable dress for a wedding."

"There's a dressmaker in town—Mrs. Allnock. I'm sure she can make you a lovely dress."

She stood back aways from the bed, and Benjamin wondered what she was thinking.

"Have you had any pain medication?" she asked hesitantly.

Benjamin shook his head and smiled again. "I refused to take any. It was interfering with my dreams of you."

He could see the relief in her eyes and wondered why she was so concerned about his medication. She moved toward the chair beside the bed, but Benjamin shook his head and patted the bed beside him. "Please, sit here beside me."

His politeness was quite a novelty. "What? No orders?" she asked. "Could this be the same Benjamin Whittaker who usually tells me what to do?"

"It's the same Benjamin Whittaker who met and fell in love with you seven years ago," he said with a smile.

Jessie sighed. He did remember. She sat down beside him, and he immediately clasped her hand in his.

"The man who's been telling you what to do and causing you so much anguish has been an imposter," he said.

"So that's the answer. I knew there had to be some plausible reason for that man's rude behavior."

"I apologize on his behalf."

They looked at each other for several long, silent

moments. Then Jessie had to ask, "Benjamin, did you mean what you said last night? Or were you delirious from the bump on your head?"

His broad smile was all the answer she needed, but he said, "Come here and kiss me, my love."

She smiled and pulled back a bit. "Giving orders again? Could this be the imposter back once more?"

Abruptly their bantering was over. His eyes met hers, and in an instant she moved forward and their lips joined, gently at first, until a surge of desire melted whatever resistance remained. Soon Jessie was lost in the kiss giving in to the swell of emotions that swept over her like waves crashing over the rocks on the shore.

"Ahem . . . ah . . ." Slowly Benjamin moved her away from him. Jessie heard the sound behind her, but couldn't force herself back to reality.

"Jessica . . . Jessica," Benjamin said. "Dr. Rittman's here."

Jessie forced her eyes open.

"I apologize for disturbing you," said the doctor.

Jessie turned quickly. She could feel her cheeks flaming red. "I'm sorry, Doctor. I didn't hear you come in."

"No need for an apology, my dear. You are, after all, engaged to be married, from what Benjamin tells me."

"Yes, we are," Jessie said, beaming with pride and pleasure.

"Well, if you're ready to take him on home, I thought I'd help him get dressed and you can be on your way."

Jessie almost said she would be happy to help, before realizing it would not be appropriate. But the very thought of dressing Benjamin, or undressing him, made her all the more anxious for their wedding day.

"Of course," she said, her cheeks still flaming. "I'll wait downstairs for you." She leaned forward and kissed Benjamin lightly on the lips before leaving.

The ride to Benjamin's house was a little rough by wagon, but Benjamin barely felt the pain the jouncing caused his arm. He need only look at the woman beside him—his betrothed—and his pain diminished.

All the way between the doctor's house and his own she inquired as to his well-being. "Are you cold? Is your arm paining you? Shall I slow down?"

He reached over with his good left arm and covered her hand with his briefly. "I'm fine, as long as you're beside me."

Margaret's husband, Samuel, was waiting at the bottom of the hill with two horses. He helped both of them up and told Jessica he'd take care of the wagon.

When they got to the house, Margaret came rushing down the path, clucking like an old mother hen. And James Weldon came running from the stables, enlisted by Samuel to help Benjamin and Jessie with their horses.

Walking toward the house, Margaret scolded Benjamin for "racing around in the dark."

"You're right, of course, Margaret. I never saw the branch that knocked me from my horse."

"Come along now," she said. "No more talking. You come in and get into bed and I'll bring you some—"

"Oh, please, Margaret, couldn't I just sit in the

library by the fire for a bit. I've been in bed too long already."

"Dr. Rittman sent word that you were to rest."

"I promise to rest in the library. You can get me a hassock for my feet, and I'll drink your herbal tea and whatever else you've prepared."

Jessie saw the effort it took for Margaret to suppress her smile. "All right, if Miss Jessie will sit with you while I fix a tray."

"I think she could be persuaded to do so," Benjamin said, his good arm protectively around Jessica's shoulder.

Margaret's blue eyes twinkled, and Jessie had no doubt that the woman was thoroughly enjoying her employer's new found happiness.

After Margaret added logs to the fire and admonished Benjamin once more to rest, she bustled off to the kitchen.

"You certainly didn't have much to say in my defense," Benjamin said.

Jessica laughed merrily. "I didn't have much of an opportunity. And it did me good to hear Margaret at least try to give *you* some orders. You certainly did wheedle your way around her, though."

"I've had years of practice. Come and sit on my lap now."

"There he is again—that imposter—telling me what to do."

"Please, Jessica. I need to feel you close to me—to know I haven't dreamt it all."

Gently she sat, leaning back against his good arm and shoulder, carefully avoiding his right arm, which was in a sort of sling, immobilized against his side and across his stomach.

Benjamin sighed as she settled against him. "My

God, it's true. You are real."

Jessie placed her hand on Benjamin's cheek in a tender caress. Then she slowly drew her fingers along his strong jawline, over his chin, and across his lips.

Benjamin felt her touch deep within. He closed his eyes as her fingers explored his face. He felt her shift slightly, and then her soft lips were on his, tenderly brushing at first, until her ardor seemed to ignite, and she pressed herself against him.

Benjamin wanted to pull her close with both arms and groaned when he unintentionally tried to move his injured arm.

Jessica immediately sat up. "Dear Lord, I've hurt your arm," she cried.

"No, no, my love. It's all right. I merely forgot my injury for a moment. I wanted to hold you so badly."

Margaret came in, clucking in disapproval, yet a smile was on her face as she said, "You best be careful, or he'll not be fit to marry, Miss Jessie."

Jessie slipped off Benjamin's lap and helped Margaret maneuver the large tray to a table in the center of the room.

There were several varieties of tea sandwiches and Benjamin's favorite jam cakes, biscuits dripping with butter, and a jar of strawberry jam. There were two pots of tea, one of which, Margaret assured Jessica, was especially brewed with herbs to help Benjamin heal more quickly.

"Everything looks delicious," Jessie said.

Benjamin agreed, and after sampling a jam cake, he asked Margaret to do him a favor.

"Anything, if I can, sir."

"There's a small box in the top right-hand

drawer of my desk," he said. "Would you mind getting it for me when you have a moment?"

She smiled broadly, said she'd be delighted to bring it down, and left.

"Margaret seemed awfully pleased about this box you asked her to get. Is it something special?"

"You might say so. Now come and eat something with me."

After they'd sampled each of the sandwiches and a jam cake, Benjamin picked up a biscuit and spread jam on it. "Aren't you having one of these?"

"Benjamin, I am filled to the brim. There is no room for one more bite, but I will have to get Margaret's recipe for the jam cakes. They're truly delectable and since they're your favorite, I should learn to make them."

"Do you mean to cook for me even after we're married and Samuel and Margaret come to the house to work for us?"

"I'd like to do many things for you. But I had for a moment forgotten that we'd talked about the Cochrans coming to work at the house. It will be wonderful to have Margaret there when you're off at work. But the house is so much smaller, Benjamin. Where will they stay?"

"The third floor could be made into adequate quarters for them. Their needs have always been simple."

"But what of this house? I'm not sure I can ask you to give up your home."

"You didn't ask. Besides," he said, gesturing around the room, "this was never really my home. It was a place I built for someone else—to try to please her, to make her want to stay—but she was as cold as the stone in the house. She didn't appreciate my efforts, nor my love."

"It must have hurt you terribly when she left."

Benjamin shook his head. "By the time Helene walked out of this house, there was no love left between us—if there ever had been. Even when I learned of her death years later, there was no heartache. I naturally was saddened that one so young should die, but there was no real pain or sorrow in my heart. Perhaps I never knew love before you."

Margaret came back at that moment, forestalling any further discussion of love. She handed a small box to Benjamin.

"Thank you, Margaret."

"Will you be needing anything else?"

"Not right now. In a bit, I will be going up to my room. Perhaps Samuel could get the fire started."

"He's already seen to it."

Benjamin nodded his thanks and Margaret left the room, closing the door behind her.

"You're looking very much like a cat who's just feasted on a forbidden meal of the mistress's favorite bird," Jessica said as Benjamin's eyes fastened on hers.

He reluctantly pulled his gaze from Jessica's and looked down at the box he held in his hand. "This was my mother's, and she told me to keep it until I found someone I truly loved to give it to. Helene and I were married for almost a year when I happened to come across it in a drawer. I remember wondering how I could have forgotten it when we decided to marry. But after thinking about it for several minutes, I knew the true love Mother spoke of was not what was between my wife and me, so I returned it to the drawer.

"Before you came into my life, I thought I might

give it to Maria someday. Now it belongs only to you."

Benjamin opened the hinged lid and removed a golden ring.

"Oh, Benjamin, it's lovely. Does it have some special meaning?"

"It's a betrothal ring made in Ireland many years ago. It was my grandmother's. She left the ring for my father to give to his bride-to-be, just as my mother left it for me to do the same. The two hearts represent the couple who are to be joined in marriage. The crown above them signifies that love will always rule the hearts of the two lovers."

"What a beautiful thought," Jessie said.

With great tenderness he slipped the golden band on Jessica's finger.

"See there," he said. "It's a perfect fit. That's a sure sign we were meant to be wed."

Benjamin cradled her with his good arm, and when she smiled up at him, he lowered his head and covered her lips with his. He'd never known such bliss, and he tried to restrain himself to keep from overwhelming her. Slowly he passed his tongue over her lips, probing gently until they yielded. She gasped when his tongue met hers, exciting him even more.

When at last they paused for breath, Benjamin moaned from the sheer ecstasy of the kiss.

"Is it your arm? Are you in pain?" Jessica cried out in alarm.

He smiled down at her, pulling her close with his good arm. "No, my love. The pain I am in can only be cured by sharing a marriage bed with you."

She felt her cheeks redden, but returned his

smile. "Perhaps we should begin to make plans for this wedding then?"

"Most definitely," he agreed.

"I'd like to include Maria when we make our plans," she said. "It may help her accept our marriage."

He nodded and continued to smile up at her.

"I think a formal wedding would be best for all concerned . . . don't you?" she asked.

"Unquestionably. Not only is it more appealing, I believe it would be the best way to show the court our sincerity, and I'm sure Maria will be more apt to get caught up in the festivities of a formal wedding."

Jessica nodded. "I agree. So, it will be a formal wedding, at St. Paul's, of course, with Rev. Weldon officiating. I'll enlist Margaret and Ann's help in planning the reception. Maria probably would be pleased if we had the reception in her house, if that's all right with you?"

He nodded again, his eyes still focused on her face, the smile remaining on his lips.

Jessie cocked her head to one side and reprimanded him. "You're not listening at all, Benjamin Whittaker."

"I'm trying, my love, but I can't seem to concentrate. Why don't you go ahead and make the plans—with Maria's approval—then let me know what you've decided. But please," he added, "make it as soon as possible."

Later, after Margaret insisted that Benjamin go up to his room and rest, Jessie went back to the kitchen to talk to Margaret about the wedding plans.

"Benjamin said to make it as soon as possible," Jessie said, blushing as she spoke.

"Can't wait now that he finally realizes he loves you, I see," Margaret joshed.

"Oh, Margaret, it's so wonderful to be in love, but do you think people will talk if we marry so soon after my sister and brother-in-law's death?"

"I believe everyone is aware of your concern for your niece, and once the word is spread that you've loved each other for many years there should be no—"

"Excuse me," Jessie interrupted. "Who said we'd loved each other for years?"

"Anyone who saw you at your sister's wedding could see the feelings you both tried so desperately to ignore. I personally had an ache in my heart knowing what might have been, knowing how desperately Mr. Benjamin needed someone. If I could have had more time to work at my matchmaking you might never have left the island."

The thought gave Jessie a strange, melancholy ache of her own. So many lost years.

"All right, perhaps there always has been something between us, but how would people know of this if they didn't have your special powers of observation?"

"I told you, the word would spread . . . I have my ways. And if anyone doesn't understand your desire to make a home for Maria, then they aren't worthy of your friendship or your concern."

Jessie smiled and hugged Margaret enthusiastically. "You are so wise and such a good friend."

Margaret appeared a bit flustered at the praise, and immediately changed the subject.

"Well, now that that is settled, when shall the wedding take place?" Margaret asked.

Jessie sat down at the table where Margaret had

been preparing pans for bread dough. "I'd like to give Benjamin a few weeks to recover, and I'll need to have a dress made—"

Margaret interrupted. "You must let Dorrie Allnock make your dress. She does excellent work."

"Benjamin did mention a dressmaker on the island, but I don't remember her name."

"Dorrie's the only one, miss." Margaret looked at Jessie and smiled. "You're going to be a beautiful bride."

"Thank you, Margaret. I hope Benjamin will think so."

"There's no doubt in my mind."

"What color do you think I should wear?"

The housekeeper wiped her hands on her apron and appraised Jessie for several seconds. "You can wear most any shade with your coloring. Ivory would be the choice of most brides of a second marriage, I suppose, but with your black hair and fair complexion, I believe you'd look outstanding in a rose or green-colored gown."

Jessie considered Margaret's words, remembering what Benjamin had said about an aqua dress. "I suppose aquamarine would be a bit too bright for a wedding?" Jessie asked.

"Ah, yes, but it would be lovely with your unusual eye color."

"Well, a soft sea-green would be close enough," Jessie said. "I'll go into town and see Mrs. Allnock tomorrow."

"And what day do you think would be good for the wedding?" Margaret asked as she covered the pans of dough for their second rising.

"A Saturday, of course, so all of Benjamin's employees can attend. Don't you think that would be wise?" she asked.

Margaret nodded. "Saturday is a good choice. Now you must choose the date."

"Well," Jessie said, "I want Benjamin to be able to enjoy the festivities. The grape picking will be finished this week, and the doctor said to give his arm at least two or three weeks to mend." Jessie glanced at a calendar hanging on the wall. "Perhaps the sixth of November would be a good date."

Margaret agreed. "And that will give Rev. Weldon ample time for the reading of the banns as well," she added.

"I hadn't even thought of that. Oh, Margaret, there's so many things to think of—I'm going to have to rely on you to help me."

The old housekeeper beamed. "Let's get paper and pen and begin a list," she suggested. "Starting with your dress and Maria's."

By the time Benjamin came downstairs, the women had quite a list made and the aroma of baking bread filled the kitchen.

Jessica rose from her chair and went to him. He marveled at the love in her eyes as she approached.

"Did you sleep well?" she asked, standing on tiptoe to kiss his cheek.

Benjamin pulled her closer with his good arm and lowered his lips to hers. When their lips parted seconds later, Benjamin said with a smile, "Kisses on the cheek are for grandmothers and babies."

"But . . . Margaret," Jessica whispered.

The housekeeper's laughter bubbled out. "My, my, miss, don't ever worry about me. You forget I spent the early years with Benjamin's parents. If he's anything like his father, I'll be likely to see more than a kiss on the lips."

Benjamin noticed Jessica's peachy complexion color brightly with each word Margaret spoke.

"Don't ever be embarrassed by your love," Margaret said, before moving back to the stove to take the freshly baked bread from the oven.

"You know, Margaret," Benjamin said, "you are responsible for waking me from a sound sleep."

Margaret turned from the stove, a stricken look on her heat flushed face. "Me and my big mouth," she grumbled. "I'm sorry if I got too loud, Mister Benjamin. Talking about your wedding is just so exciting, I can't help—"

"No, no, no," Benjamin said, shaking his head and going to the stove beside her. "It was the smell of this bread baking that roused me. Is it ready for butter and jam yet?"

Margaret and Jessica laughed in unison.

"You women dare to laugh at my hunger? How cruel." Benjamin rubbed his stomach like a little boy anticipating a treat. "The doctor starved me. I thought I could at least count on my own housekeeper to feed me."

"Dr. Rittman told me you ate a fine breakfast before I arrived," Jessica said. "Not to mention the tray Margaret served before you went up to rest."

"But, surely some bread and jam . . ."

"You should wait and have the bread with your evening meal," Margaret said sternly. "Or you'll spoil your appetite."

"Margaret, you know it never tastes as good as fresh from the oven."

"Oh, Margaret, give him a slice or he'll never let you have any peace."

Again the two women joined in laughter as Benjamin watched them work together. Soon they were all sitting at the kitchen table with tea and thick slices of fresh bread slathered with butter and jam.

With groans of pleasure, Benjamin bit into the bread. He could see Jessica watching him as he licked the jam from his lips. From the blush on her cheeks, he thought she might be remembering his tongue on her lips earlier.

The very thought of it made him anxious for their wedding day . . . and night.

"Have you ladies planned the day of our wedding yet?" he asked, his eyes on Jessica.

"November sixth," Jessica answered.

Benjamin banged his fist on the table. "Absolutely not."

He saw Jessica's eyes widen and quickly changed his scowling countenance into a smiling one. "Sorry, there's the old Benjamin coming out again."

"What's wrong with the sixth?" Jessica asked, her feistiness coming to the fore again.

"This is only mid-October. I refuse to wait till November to take you as my bride. I'm not getting any younger, you know." He leaned forward and whispered, "Besides, I can't wait that long."

"Benjamin, restrain yourself," Jessica said, glancing at Margaret, who was trying to muffle her laughter.

The housekeeper got up and carried her cup to the sink, shaking her head and muttering, "Just like his father."

"Perhaps we should have a talk about Benjamin's father, Margaret."

"Nothing much to say. He was forever chasin' that poor woman around the house, hugging and kissing no matter who was present—Mrs. Whittaker used to say he would scandalize them before the entire population of the island." Margaret was unable to stop her laughter. "Mr. Whittaker . . . he said . . . well, there's less than a hundred people here, my love . . . so let's get started. And he pulled her into an embrace and kissed her right there in the general store."

"And were people scandalized?" Jessie asked, trying to keep the smile off her face.

"Oh, my, yes. The Whittakers were the talk of the island. And when new people came, one of the first things they heard was, 'Don't mind those Whittakers.' They were known as the lovebirds of the island. At least until young Benjamin here came along. They continued with their shenanigans until the first time he toddled in to find them in a . . . shall we say, compromising position in the dining room and . . ."

"The dining room?" Jessie blurted out.

Benjamin burst into laughter at the wide-eyed expression on his bride-to-be. "The table's quite sturdy," he chuckled.

"Benjamin—stop this talk. I won't have you embarrassing Margaret."

Margaret lowered her head, covering her mouth with her hand to again tone down her laughter.

"What happened after that, Margaret?" Jessie asked, trying to retain her composure.

"They restricted their antics to the bedroom . . . at least when the boys were in the house."

"As I recall," Benjamin added, "my father once told me a ship at sea was one of their favorite places."

"Your father spoke to you of such things?" Jessie asked.

"Only when I was older. Before that they were

relatively good at keeping things from Jonathan and me."

By the time Margaret and Benjamin finished, Jessie's cheeks were flaming. The very thought of being with Benjamin . . . in the dining room or on a ship, sent her heart into a rapid staccato beat; the kitchen grew warmer even though Margaret had tampered the heat from the oven. And deep within her, Jessie felt the stirrings that only a husband could satisfy.

She looked across the table at her husband-to-be and without preamble said, "Perhaps November is too far off."

Her words set Benjamin and Margaret off into gales of laughter.

After a few moments trying to ignore the two of them, Jessie had no choice but to join in their laughter.

"What in heaven's name is going on in here?" Samuel asked as he entered the kitchen.

Margaret went to him and put a hand on his arm. Making an effort to still her mirth, she said, "It seems we're going to have a wedding very soon."

Her words only served to set the three of them off again, while Samuel tried to congratulate the couple.

Finally, after getting himself under control, Benjamin shook Samuel's hand and thanked him for his good wishes.

"Now," Benjamin said, "If you'll excuse us, my bride-to-be and I have a wedding to plan."

Jessie proudly took Benjamin's arm and smiled at Margaret as they started out of the kitchen.

"While you're choosing a date, mind you," Margaret said with a grin, "there are a few things that need done before a wedding, like writing out invitations, preparing the food, and baking a wedding cake, to mention but a few."

"We'll remember," Jessie said.

They returned to the library, where the fire was still warm from morning. Benjamin went toward the log bin, but Jessie put a restraining arm on his.

"You are supposed to be resting. I'll fix the fire."

"I can lift a log, Jessica."

"Bullheaded, just like Margaret said. Well, I have a bit of that in me too. Now sit down and rest. I am perfectly capable of fixing the fire. Besides," she added with a mischievous grin, "I want you to heal as fast as possible so you can perform your husbandly duties." She lowered her long, dark eyelashes, then turned to fix the fire.

Benjamin came up behind her. "One injured arm will not prevent me from 'performing my duties,' " he whispered huskily in her ear.

"Really?" she asked, turning with another smile in place. "I can't imagine how you'd split logs with only one hand."

He shook his head, returning her smile. "I had no idea my intended could be such a tease. But may I assure you, my love," he said, tightening his arm around her waist, "I can do many things with only one hand."

The look Benjamin gave Jessie before his lips claimed hers went straight through to her core, exciting her almost as much as his touch.

His kiss was passionate, yet tender, and she marveled at the sensations his tongue created as it stroked her own.

When, finally, Benjamin ended the kiss, he did not speak, but drew her close, and she rested her head against his chest, hearing the rapid tempo of his heart.

A brief thought played through Jessie's mind. In all their time together, Michael had never kissed her so.

"What are you thinking, my love?" Benjamin asked.

"Must I tell the truth?"

Benjamin drew back to look down into her eyes. "Always. There must never be a lie between us."

She nodded. "Then the truth it will be. I was thinking that I'd never been kissed as you kiss me."

"Never? . . . your husband—"

Jessie put a finger to his lips and shook her head. "Never."

"Did you find the kiss . . . satisfactory?" he asked.

"I found the kiss . . . delightful, in every way. And," she murmured, lowering her eyelids as she felt a flush spread to her cheeks, "I look forward to learning more wonderful new things from my husband."

Benjamin lowered his cheek to Jessica's head, feeling the soft silkiness of her hair against his skin, while her hands gently caressed his back and shoulders. The fragrance of summer flowers drifted from her raven tresses, and Benjamin gloried in the wonder of her smell and her touch.

"My love," he murmured as his lips tenderly touched her forehead. "I look forward to learning with you."

"But you were wed—"

He stilled her words with a light kiss. "My . . . wife was not pleased by my kisses . . . nor my embrace. And in truth, there was no deep emotion on my part when we kissed."

"Then why did you marry?"

"And why did you?" he asked in reply.

"Because I did not know love could cause my insides to quake . . . I was not aware of the fact that love could bring such excitement." Jessie paused and looked up at him. "I settled for a warm, contented feeling instead."

"You had more than I then."

Jessica's sparkling eyes explored his face, and he felt every movement inside as surely as if her fingers glided along his skin. When at last her eyes met his, she murmured, "Life is often unfair, my darling."

"But no more," he said, his lips lifting into a bright smile. "We have found each other at last—life will be good for us, Jessica."

"Then let's begin our plans," she said, moving toward the table. She took the papers that she and Margaret had worked on and spread them across the tabletop.

Benjamin remained standing near the fire, following her every movement, marveling at her beauty and grace. Soon she would be his always.

Dipping her pen, she held it midair and asked, "When shall the wedding be, my darling Benjamin?"

"Tomorrow," he replied with a husky breath.

Jessica stopped the smile that would come to her lips, pursing them in disapproval instead. "My, my, you men just don't understand anything about weddings, do you?"

In two strides he was across the room and on one knee beside her chair. "We men concern ourselves only with the legality of the vows and the awesome responsibility of pleasuring our wives on their wedding night."

Jessie had watched his impulsive move, and his words sent a shiver of delight through her body. She wanted to lean forward, to pull his head to her breast, but knew there might be no stopping if she did so.

Instead, she lifted his chin with her fingers and felt his jaw clenching and unclenching. "I look forward to our wedding night . . . but," she said with mock seriousness, "you did promise me a suitable dress for the ceremony and I haven't seen the dressmaker yet."

He shook his head and could not restrain his laughter. "You are incorrigible, my darling." He stood and said, "How long does it take to have a dress made?"

"I will speak to Mrs. Allnock about my dress tomorrow, and I would also like to have one made for Maria. I've been trying to think of a way to include her, because I do believe we must make her a part of the wedding."

"I agree," Benjamin said.

"I thought perhaps she could follow me down the aisle, carrying a bouquet. Then she will be there with us as we take our vows. I also thought if I took her to the dressmaker's with me, she might become more excited about the wedding."

"Of course. But do tell Mrs. Allnock speed is of the utmost importance." Jessie saw the mischief in his dark eyes as he added, "I will pay extra if she rushes the job."

Jessie continued to write. "Despite your impulsiveness, I don't see how we can have this wedding in less than two weeks." Jessie leafed through the papers on the table. "Since Margaret and I have agreed that a Saturday is best, that would put it at the end of the month."

Benjamin looked over her shoulder. "This is only Monday. Why not put all our plans in action, have the banns read on Sunday, and be married the following Saturday—the twenty-third of October."

"You are a man of swift decision, sir," Jessie said.

He caressed her shoulder and murmured, "Not at all—I'm a man anxious for his wedding night."

"If you continue discussing it . . . I will not be responsible for my actions."

Again, he bent to one knee beside her. "Then perhaps, we should discuss it more."

She heard as well as felt his fingers as his hand moved up under her dress, rustling the folds of her silk skirt. His appeal was enhanced by his vulnerability, with the sling immobilizing his injured arm. His touch on her bare skin caused her to utter a moan of desire, but as Jessie began to give herself up to the pleasure as he fondled her, she suddenly remembered Maria . . . and Mr. Talbot.

"No, Benjamin," she said, rising and pushing the chair back in one fluid movement. "We must maintain our respectability. No hint of scandal must reach Mr. Talbot's ears."

"But if by some wild chance he should discover our indiscretion, he would at least know our love was real."

"He will see that soon enough. We'll invite him to the wedding. It's only twelve days, my darling."

Benjamin sighed and rose to stand beside her. "All right. We will wait . . . until the day I can legally take you to my bed."

Jessie reached up and touched his cheek, drawing her fingers down his jawline. After a moment's hesitation, with fingers resting on his lips, she murmured, "Then I must go home now and prepare for that day."

After one last brief kiss she turned away and called to Samuel as she went out into the hall.

"You little vixen," Benjamin muttered under his breath, a smile playing across his lips. Left with the uncomfortable results of her touch and her kiss, he lowered himself into a chair and sighed deeply. "Ah, but soon, my love . . ."

Benjamin heard Jessica call out again to Samuel, and when he responded, she asked him if he would bring a horse around for her.

Minutes later, Benjamin watched her come through the doorway, pulling on her leather riding gloves. When she raised her eyes and saw him looking at her, she lifted her skirt and ran to him, her cape billowing out behind her.

Reversing their earlier position, she knelt beside him and taking his hand in hers, she placed her head against his thigh, her body shuddering with desire. "How can I leave you?" she murmured.

He eased his hand from hers and gently stroked her hair. "I'll come to the house tomorrow."

She leaned back on her heels and looked up at him. "No, Benjamin, promise me you'll rest for a few days at least. I'll take Maria to the dressmaker's and perhaps, if there's time, we'll stop here so Maria can visit with you."

His eyes held hers, but he didn't speak.

"Promise me, Benjamin, please."

"All right, my love. I promise. I will remain in the house like a sickly old woman."

"It won't be so terrible." She gestured around the room. "You can read some of these wonderful books that you never have time for . . . and I'm sure Margaret will take good care of you and keep you well fed—"

"Indeed I shall, Miss Jessie," Margaret said as she bustled into the room. "And I'll see that he naps in the afternoons as well," the housekeeper added as she carried over a tray.

"Jessica, save me," Benjamin cried in mock distress, grasping her hand in his. "She'll treat me like a child."

"Only if you behave like one," Margaret said, hiding her grin behind an upraised hand. She began to pour, and the aroma of fresh-brewed coffee drifted from the cup. "Since you are acting like an adult at the moment, I've brought you a pot of coffee, but you'll have the herbal tea before bed."

Jessica reached up and kissed Benjamin, then rose. "I see you are in capable hands," she said, smiling down at him before turning to leave.

His heart constricted at the thought of her leaving. He reached out and grasped her hand. "I'm going to miss you desperately, my love."

"And I you, but the faster the days go by the sooner we will be together . . . always."

"Don't you worry, Miss Jessie," Margaret said. "I'll keep him busy enough so he won't even know you're gone."

Benjamin looked up at his housekeeper and said, "That, my dear Margaret, would be impossible."

Samuel came to the doorway, hat in hand. "Your horse is ready, miss."

Jessica leaned down and brushed her lips gently across Benjamin's. "Till tomorrow, my darling," she whispered.

After Jessica and Samuel had gone, Benjamin turned to Margaret.

"How do you think Samuel would feel about the two of you working at my br . . . at Jessica and Maria's house? That is, after the wedding, of course, when it will be our house."

He saw the surprise in his housekeeper's eyes. "But what of this house?"

Benjamin glanced around the library, which had become his favorite place since Margaret's redecorating. "This house was never a real home for me, Margaret. You have done wonderful things here, and perhaps in other circumstances the place could truly become a warm home. But my association with it is a rather cold one, and I can walk away from the place without regret. The money from its sale will give the business a solid foundation again.

"I'd always felt badly about having such a pretentious house when Jonathan's was so much smaller," Benjamin continued. "He did wisely in putting his extra money away for his daughter."

"He understood why you built this house, though," Margaret said.

"Yes, I suppose he did, though we never talked about it. But getting back to my moving there. Jessica and I are both agreed that Maria will do best in her own home, and we'd certainly be pleased if you and Samuel would come and work for us."

"It's a much smaller house, Mr. Benjamin, and you'll be wanting your privacy."

"I've given that some thought," Benjamin said, walking to the window. After looking outside for several moments, as though lost in thought, he finally said, "The third floor hasn't been used much, other than for storage. But there are two large rooms and one small one up there. With a little work, they could be made into comfortable quarters. For the time being, you and Samuel can use the room at the end of the second-floor hall. It is large enough to be both bedroom and sitting room and should accommodate your furnishings nicely. You might both want to go over there tomorrow and see what you think. Everything should be in place by our wedding day."

"May I suggest you might wish to have a day or two alone," Margaret said.

Benjamin rubbed his chin thoughtfully, a smile tugging at the corners of his lips. "You may have a point there, Margaret . . . a very good point."

After Samuel saw her down the hill and hitched the horse to her wagon, Jessie told him there was no need for him to see her home. "I'll be stopping at the Weldons' for Maria, and will probably spend some time talking to Ann about the wedding."

"Take care then," Samuel said, "and give Maria my love."

"I will, and please thank Margaret for everything. I know she'll take good care of Benjamin."

He nodded, remaining in place until Jessie reached the bend in the road and turned back to wave.

Jessie let the horse have free rein, and as the wagon jostled along the road, she marveled at the changes in her life. The love she felt for Benjamin was a source of amazement and joy such as she'd never known before.

If she could only convince Maria of their love, life would be very good indeed. It truly was a shame that Maria had heard the petty arguments they'd had before realizing how much they meant to each other. Jessie wondered if indeed their many arguments had been an excuse to release some of the tension building between them.

She smiled at the thought. Kissing and touching each other was infinitely better than arguing. Although these activities brought a new, exciting tension to their relationship. "Which shall be relieved on the twenty-third," she said aloud.

Her face felt as though it were permanently molded in a smile as all her thoughts focused on the fact that she would soon be Benjamin's wife.

A thick bank of clouds blocked the sun's rays, and the chill reminded Jessie that winter was not far off. She wondered what it would be like to spend the entire winter here on the island, isolated from all outside influences. Remembering that she would have a husband to keep her warm on cold nights, though, suddenly made the season so much more appealing. She urged her horse to a faster pace, wanting to get to the Weldons' quickly, anxious to talk to Ann and Maria about their wedding plans.

As she neared the house, Ann came outside to greet her, and from the expression on her face Jessie could see that Ann appeared to be worried.

"Ann, what's wrong?" she asked, getting down from the wagon.

"I wanted to catch you before you went inside. Maria and Willy are busy playing with the puppets now, but we had quite a talk when she first arrived."

"About the wedding, I suppose?"

"Yes. After you told me this morning about Benjamin declaring his love for you, I tried explaining that all the things I said to her last night were irrelevant."

"But she didn't believe you."

Ann shook her head. "She is so concerned that both you and her uncle are going to become bitter people because of this marriage and that some day you will blame her."

"How can I convince her, Ann? It's so unfair to the child, especially when Benjamin and I are so happy."

Ann smiled. "I could see the radiance in your face as you were coming up the road and I hated to even approach you with this problem. You deserve some happiness in your life."

"Do you think we should postpone our plans?"

"No. The sooner you are settled as a family, the better it will be for Maria. Once she sees the affection between you, she'll come to understand that you do love each other." Ann smiled again and took Jessie's arm. "Come, let's go in and make some plans for your wedding."

Chapter Eighteen

Although Willy was more than happy to get involved with plans for the upcoming nuptials, Maria showed no interest. By the time they reached home that evening, Jessie was disheartened by her niece's lack of enthusiasm.

As she tucked the child into bed later, though, she decided not to bring it up again. Perhaps if they just proceeded without making a big show of it, Maria would come around gradually.

The next morning dawned bright and clear. Jessie wakened early, unable to go back to sleep because of the many thoughts of Benjamin and her wedding day swirling about in her head.

When breakfast was ready and Maria still hadn't come downstairs, Jessie called up to her. "Come on, sleepyhead. It's a beautiful autumn day and we're going for a walk down by the lake before we go into town."

Maria appeared at the top of the stairs rubbing the sleep from her eyes. "Aren't we going to the vineyard today?" she asked.

"Not today, my sweet. Today we must go to see Mrs. Allnock, the dressmaker. You and I are to have lovely new dresses made."

"What for?"

"Have you forgotten that I'm going to marry your uncle soon? I need a bridal gown. And you, my little one, are going to carry flowers down the aisle of the church and stand with your uncle and me as we exchange our vows. We want you to be a part of the ceremony, Maria, so you will need a fancy dress as well."

Jessie saw a curtain drop over Maria's face.

The child's continued distress over their marriage made Jessie feel guilty. It seemed strange that the child who'd brought them together, the little girl who'd led them to find their true happiness in each other, could not be happy for them.

As Maria ate her bowl of oatmeal, Jessie tried again to involve her in the plans for the wedding. Jessie thought that talk of a wedding celebration in her home, with all of Maria's friends and neighbors present, would spark her interest. But the little girl just stared into her cereal bowl without making any comment.

Later, walking along the shore, Jessie tried again.

"Perhaps you and I will have matching gowns, Maria. Would you like that?"

Maria shrugged as she looked out over the lake, which was placid and still as glass that morning. "Whatever you want, Aunt Jess."

Jessie continued to prattle about the menu Margaret had begun planning. In all her talk, though, the only time the child made any comment was when Jessie mentioned the tiered wedding cake Margaret would be baking.

"What flavor will it be?" Maria asked.

"Whatever flavor you'd like, sweetheart," Jessie said, pleased that finally something had sparked the child's interest. "Perhaps, one layer of that delicious yellow batter Margaret makes and two of chocolate . . . how does that sound?"

She was disappointed as Maria merely shrugged her shoulders again.

"Maria, I love you very much, and it's important to me that you help me with plans for my wedding . . . even if it's only to help me decide the flavor of the wedding cake."

"All chocolate would be better than two flavors," the child said without additional comment.

"Then chocolate it will be," Jessie said, hoping this small beginning would grow into Maria's total involvement in their plans.

As the morning progressed, though, it was plain to see Jessie's hopes would not be realized. In Dorrie Allnock's dress shop, Maria exhibited even less interest in the matching gowns Jessie planned for them.

"Do you like this pale green color?" Jessie asked Maria.

"Whatever you want, Aunt Jess. It's your wedding."

Later, as they left the dressmaker's shop, with the promise that the gowns would be ready for the twenty-third, Maria finally asked about her uncle.

"He's improving, sweetheart," Jessie answered. "He still has some pain in his arm, but it should ease in time. Wait till you see him, though—he looks quite dashing with his arm all done up in a sling." Jessie smiled at the memory of him.

"How does he manage with just one arm?" Maria asked.

Other memories came to mind, and Jessie had to control her emotions when she answered. "Your uncle does quite well with one arm. But you'll see for yourself when we visit him after lunch."

"I thought we might be able to pick grapes this afternoon," Maria said. "There are very few days left for the harvesting and I want to do my share."

"You are, in fact, correct. Your uncle talked to Mr. Monroe yesterday before I took him home from the doctor's, and Henry told him the picking is almost finished. So, I thought you would do more good cheering up your uncle with a visit this afternoon."

Maria sighed. "All right, I suppose I really should do something nice for Uncle Ben. If it weren't for me hiding in the cave, he wouldn't be hurt at all."

When they arrived at Benjamin's home, Maria was a bit more animated, asking her uncle questions about his sling and how he did things with only one arm.

Minutes later, though, after Benjamin had answered all his niece's questions to her satisfaction, she was off to the kitchen to see Margaret.

"At last," he said, with a wicked gleam in his eye. "We are alone."

Despite Jessica's apparent eagerness to come into his arms, Benjamin noticed a difference in her kiss . . . much less passionate than yesterday's kisses.

He held Jessica at arm's length and looked into her eyes. "What's wrong, my love? You look exhausted . . . and somehow troubled."

She tried to smile, but he could see the concern in her eyes. "It's Maria. She shows no interest in the wedding. She refuses to believe we love each other. She persists in the belief that we are only marrying so she will not have to live with strangers."

Benjamin embraced her, pulling her close with his good arm, leaning his head on hers. "It'll be all right, love. I've sent Samuel to telegraph the news of our nuptials to the mainland, specifically to Mr. Talbot. Once the legalities are taken care of and we are wed, Maria will see for herself how much we mean to each other. Everything will be fine."

Jessie nodded. "I want to believe that. More than anything, I want the three of us to be happy."

"Then believe it, my sweet, and it will come to pass."

She finally relaxed in his arms. They remained so for several moments. Then Benjamin spoke. "Did you give the date of our wedding to Reverend Weldon?"

"Yes. I stopped there on my way home last night, and Ann marked our nuptials in his book for October twenty-third."

Benjamin smiled and once more pulled her close. He loved the way her body seemed to mold to his as though they had indeed been made for each other.

"I'm not sure I can wait till then, my love," he murmured. "Now that I know you're going to be mine, I can barely stand to be away from you. Your face was with me all through the night, and I ached to have you in my bed."

She reached up, kissed him lightly, then gently withdrew from his embrace. "Then perhaps I should not see you before our wedding day? I don't want to be a temptation and cause you distress."

"There's that tease again," he said, drawing her back toward him, holding her snugly against his body in a one-armed embrace.

She looked up at him, and he could see the desire in her eyes. "You are not the only one who aches, Benjamin," she said breathlessly. "If you continue holding me against your body this way, I may forget that I'm a lady."

Her eyes deepened in color and the underlying passion was easily visible there.

"No woman should have eyes such as yours. No man could resist when you cast your spell with such a magical gaze."

"There is no magic in my eyes . . . it's love you see reflected there, my darling Benjamin."

He bent forward capturing her lips, wanting to possess her entire being. She responded eagerly, her body pressed firmly against his.

"Maria, it's not polite to stare."

Margaret's voice yanked Jessie from Benjamin's arms as surely as if a strong arm had pulled her from his grasp.

She and Benjamin just stood there as the child looked from one to the other.

Benjamin was the first to speak. "Margaret may be correct, Maria. But I am not sorry that you were watching us. I love your aunt very much and I'm sure you know kissing is a way for grown-ups to express their love."

"Benjamin," Jessie said. "She's only six years old. I don't think any more explanation is necessary."

Jessie bent down to the child's level. "Is there

anything you want to ask me, Maria?"

The child shook her head.

"Well then," Benjamin said, obviously ready to change the subject. "Did Margaret stuff you with goodies?"

She nodded. "I ate the last jam cake, Uncle Ben. I hope you don't mind."

"Not at all. I'm sure Margaret will bake more very soon."

The rest of the afternoon went quickly as Jessie and Margaret continued working on the wedding plans. After a light supper with Benjamin and Maria, Jessie's exhaustion finally overwhelmed her. Although she hated to leave him, Jessie knew she needed a good night's sleep. He agreed, once again telling her to try not to be concerned about Maria.

When Jessie tucked Maria into bed that night she tried once again to interest her in the wedding plans.

"What kind of flowers do you think we should carry?" she asked the little girl.

Maria matter-of-factly answered, "All the flowers are dead."

"No, they're not all dead. Mrs. Cochran's garden still boasts some beautiful fall flowers, or we might order some from a florist on the mainland."

Maria shrugged, and slid down further into her bed. "I'm sure you and Mrs. Cochran can decide."

Before Jessie could speak again Maria's eyes closed, and Jessie knew her mind was closed as well.

"Goodnight, my sweet," Jessie whispered, gently kissing the child's forehead.

Looking down at Maria, Jessie's thoughts were of the woman who gave the little girl life. *Frannie, what am I to do? Help me know the right words to convince her of my love for Benjamin. Help us know the way to give her a good life.*

Jessie had no sooner left the room when a bright light appeared, drawing Maria's eyes open.

She sat up in bed, and for the first time that day felt truly happy. "Momma? Momma, are you there?"

The illumination took form and a hand reached out, sending a beam of light to touch the child. "I'm here, my sweet, but I haven't much time, so you must listen very carefully."

Maria's head bobbed up and down.

The heavenly figure was at the foot of Maria's bed, and the soft radiance that surrounded it stretched across the quilt and wrapped itself gently around the child.

"You must trust me when I tell you that your aunt and uncle will take good care of you. I'm pleased that they've decided to marry, and they need you to be happy for them too."

"Momma, remember I told you they didn't love each other?"

"Yes, and I told you no one but God could know what was in their hearts."

"I think I know now."

"And how did you receive this revelation?"

"I saw them kissing, and it wasn't like two friends kissing. It was quite a long kiss, and if Margaret hadn't corrected me for staring, I would have begun to wonder how they could breathe."

Maria's angel smiled, and the light grew warmer.

"Then be happy for them, my sweet. Help your aunt with her wedding plans. I need to see you settled so I can go on and be with your poppa."

Maria's eyes widened. "But Momma, I thought

you said you'd always be with me."

"I will. Yet my earthly ties will soon fade and you'll not be able to see me with your eyes."

"That's the only way I can see you."

"No, you can see me in your mind. You can carry my image with you always."

"How?"

"I'll show you. Close your eyes, Maria."

The little girl did as she was told, shutting them tight.

"Now think about the day we were picking wildflowers last summer . . . remember, we'd gone to the woods down near the edge of the lake?"

Maria nodded.

"All right, now I want you to think about how I looked when we were picking the flowers. Imagine that we are there in the woods and you look up and I'm there beside you. Can you see me?"

Maria smiled and nodded again. "You have on your green dress with the white collar and your hair is in a braid. I can see you, Momma!"

"Good. Now you understand. I'm always with you . . . in your mind and in your heart. You only need to think of me and I'll be there."

Maria's eyes came open and she sighed. "But do you really have to go?"

"Soon, my sweet, soon."

The light began to fade, and Maria waved as the figure receded.

Minutes later she was asleep.

"Maria, it's time to wake up."

Jessie grew concerned when Maria hadn't wakened after the sun rose high above the horizon. "Come on, sweetheart," she coaxed. "We have so much to do and I need your help."

The child lifted her head off her pillow and blinked her eyes. Then a broad smile lit up her entire face and she reached out and hugged Jessie.

"My goodness, what a lovely good morning this is," Jessie said. She looked down at her niece, who continued to beam. "You look happy this morning."

"I am. And I'm going to help you with your wedding because I know you and Uncle Ben love each other."

Jessie was astonished. "I'm so pleased, Maria." She hugged the child and felt tears prick her eyes.

Maria looked up at her aunt and touched a tear that had trickled down Jessie's cheek. "Are these happy tears, Aunt Jess?"

"Yes they are . . . oh, yes, Maria, they're definitely happy tears."

All through breakfast Maria talked about her aunt's wedding plans, and Jessie was overjoyed at her enthusiasm. Only when the child once again mentioned her maternal angel was Jessie's happiness dimmed.

". . . and Momma said I should help you because she needs to see me settled before she can go on to be with Poppa."

Maria's last words brought Jessie upright in her chair. "Your mother told you she's going to be leaving?"

Maria nodded, a sudden sadness apparent in her eyes.

"When is this to take place, Maria?"

"She said it would be soon." The child's eyebrows drew together as she scrunched up her forehead in thought. "Her times with me have grown shorter and I can't see her as clearly . . . sometimes it's as though a bright fog surrounds her."

Abruptly, a radiant smile crossed Maria's lips. "But the light is always so warm, Aunt Jess, almost like a blanket that's wrapped around me."

Just then Ann came to the kitchen door with her sons, and Maria's conversation about her maternal angel was ended. Yet Jessie kept all the child's words in her heart pondering their meaning. She would have to speak to Benjamin about this last angelic visit. Many things that Maria said sounded quite logical. And even if it was still her imagination, the child was evidently beginning to ready herself for her angel's departure.

Chapter Nineteen

The next week moved swiftly, and Jessie found herself caught up in a whirlwind of activity.

Jessie, Ann, and Margaret, with some help from Samuel, Maria, and even the Weldon boys, worked hard to prepare the house for the wedding reception.

The wood floors and furniture gleamed, windows and mirrors sparkled, and an ample supply of wood was brought onto the service porch to feed all the fires in the downstairs rooms. Linens were pressed, crystal stemware glistened, silver candelabras had been polished. Candlesticks for all the mantels were prepared.

The banns were read from the pulpit of St. Paul's, and people reacted with surprise and delight. Rev. Weldon was also kind enough to announce that all islanders were welcome to attend the nuptials at St. Paul's, and noted that the festivities following the ceremony would be limited to a small home reception.

Although to Jessie, as she spent hours addressing fifty-eight invitations, calling it small seemed incongruous.

"It would have been easier to invite the whole island," she said to Maria as her fingers grew cramped.

Maria giggled. "We're probably inviting half of them anyway, Aunt Jess."

Once those tasks were completed, the decorations had to be tended to. When Jessie began planning the floral arrangements, Margaret told her of a woman on the island who dried spring and summer flowers in a unique process that she had discovered after considerable experimentation.

"The process leaves them colorful, but softly muted," Margaret told her when describing the blossoms. "And they retain their fragrance for quite some time."

Knowing how much Maria loved the island flowers, Jessie took her to see the woman's work, and the child was enchanted by what she saw.

"Oh, Aunt Jess, the larkspur are beautiful, and look at the tiny trillium blossoms." She put her nose to them and sniffed, beaming at the result. "They even smell good. It's almost like they're still growing outside, but just not quite as soft."

"They are perfectly preserved," Jessie said. "You do lovely work, Mrs. Crandall. I believe our decision is made. We will definitely use these island flowers for the wedding."

After the floral arrangements had been chosen for the church, house, and bouquets, they went on to see Margaret in order to go over the menu.

Maria entered into those plans with great pleasure, especially when discussing the sweets.

"Mrs. Cochran is going to make raspberry and strawberry jam cakes and tiny round cakes with gooey icing," Maria told Jessie after spending some time in the kitchen. "And she's baking all sorts of cookies, and there's even going to be a punch that was served at my grandmother's wedding. It's made from grape juice and other ingredients, and Mrs. Cochran found the recipe for it in a small wooden box in the attic."

Jessie was so pleased with the child's enthusiasm, she asked if there was anything else she'd like to add to the menu.

Maria scrunched up her face as she often did when thinking seriously and said, "I do believe, since it's Uncle Ben's wedding too, there should be ample wine from the Whittaker Wine Company for the adults and grape juice for the children who don't care for punch . . . white grape juice of course. Children do spill, you know, and Momma told me grape juice could leave a nasty stain."

Jessie laughed aloud at the child's remarks. "Maria, sometimes I believe you are an adult in disguise. Your suggestion is a good one, and I will see that your uncle receives those instructions exactly."

When Benjamin stopped by two days before the wedding, Jessie told him about Maria's menu suggestion. She tried to remember it word for word with the childlike inflections in place. Evidently she succeeded, as Benjamin laughed aloud when she finished.

"I don't believe she'll have any trouble running the company, Jessica," he said after he stopped laughing.

"Perhaps you should start her now," Jessie said

with a smile. "She could probably make some improvements over there."

"No doubt," Benjamin said. He's been standing with his arm around her waist, and Jessie had grown warm at even that light touch. She turned and faced him, aware of her growing desire.

"I'm glad you moved our wedding date closer," she said, keeping her eyes fixed on his.

"And why is that, my love?"

"Because I can't bear to be without you much longer. If Maria wasn't asleep upstairs right now . . . I don't know if I could restrain myself."

His lips curled upward in a smug smile. "And I thought you were ignoring me, letting all these wedding preparations come between us."

"I thank God for the hectic pace," Jessie said with a deep sigh. "If I hadn't been kept so busy, falling into bed exhausted each night, I might never have resisted you this long."

"I believe the reason you have resisted me," said Benjamin with a grin, "Is the fact that we have not been alone once since we set our wedding date."

Jessie leaned to one side, looking around Benjamin, then turned to look behind her. When she looked back up at him, her arms snaked around his waist and she whispered, "We seem to be alone now."

It was all the excuse Benjamin needed. His desires had been keeping him awake at night, and this evening's ride in the cold night air had begun as an excuse to slake his passion. But his horse had somehow found its way to Jessica's and with her aqua eyes fixed on his, he could no longer fight his passionate desires.

With a low moan, he drew her closer, his lips crushing hers in an intense kiss filled with passion and hunger. Her arms tightened around him, moving upward. Benjamin reached up, his hand entangled in the silky hair at the nape of her neck.

And for the first time, Jessica's tongue passed his lips, meeting his own with a rhythmic stroke. He made a pleasurable sound in response and with her arms now clutching his neck, he was able to slide his good arm under her and lift her against him, balancing her with his injured arm.

She broke the kiss momentarily, gasping for breath. "Your arm—"

He instantly recaptured her mouth, cutting off her concern. With sheer willpower he carried her to the sitting room, kicking the door shut with his boot. The rug in front of the fireplace was warm as he laid her gently back. They were both breathing hard from the lengthy kiss.

He lay alongside her, propped up on his good elbow, his eyes taking in every inch of her. Her hair had loosened from its bow and fanned out on the deep green rug beneath them. Her cheeks were flushed, her lips slightly parted. He could see her chest moving with each breath.

Her body was tense with unreleased passion, and when his eyes at last found hers, he saw his own desire mirrored there. "I can't wait any longer, my love. I need you."

Her eyes remained focused on his, sparkling in the firelight. "It's only two more nights, my darling," she murmured breathlessly.

Benjamin did not speak. Gingerly, with a feather-light touch, he moved the fingers of his injured arm slowly across her shoulder, then traced a fiery path up her neck, along her jaw, and around her ear. By the time his fingers moved to brush tantalizingly across her lips, no resistance remained in Jessica's body. Her lips opened as if of their own accord and she licked the tips of his fingers.

He groaned with desire and in one smooth movement, he rolled her sideways until he was on his back and she rested atop him. "Benjamin, your arm. You'll—"

She never got to finish as he raised his head, pulling hers down to meet him, and captured her mouth with his.

Jessie felt Benjamin's arm, complete with sling, just below her breasts. She felt the movement of his fingertips beneath her, first cupping, then moving to gently knead her nipple. His mouth still ravaged hers—his tongue like a viper striking over and over until she could no longer think or feel anything except her need for him.

"Aunt Jess . . . Aunt Jess . . ." The voice came through disjointedly at first, chipping away at her subconscious until finally breaking through the wall of passion that had surrounded her.

She pushed away. "Benjamin . . . it's Maria." Quickly she rose to her feet. Pushing her hair back from her face and straightening her dress, she moved toward the door.

"Coming, Maria," she called out. Turning back to Benjamin, she put her finger to her lips and whispered, "I'll be back when I get her settled."

Benjamin watched her leave, aching to have her back. He sat on the rug, leaning forward on one knee, staring into the sizzling flames as they curled from under the logs, devouring the bark with their red-hot heat.

As he studied the flames intently, Benjamin thought about Jessica's willingness to come to him tonight. The wedding he had once thought of as a convenience was now to be the highlight of his life. To have found such a love was almost beyond comprehension.

He recalled all their movements, relishing the remembrance of her touch, her lips, her tongue, her glorious hair as it rippled over him . . . and he recalled her words, the only words she'd spoken. "It's only two more nights, my darling."

Respectability had been the one thing holding them apart until their wedding day. Jessica was determined to have no stain on their love—nothing that Mr. Talbot could use to say they were unfit to adopt Maria.

And he had almost spoiled it, for lack of self-control.

Minutes later Jessica returned. Benjamin stood near the fireplace, observing her movements as she closed the door and came to him.

"Is Maria all right?" he asked.

She nodded. "Just thirsty."

Her arms went around his neck and she kissed him tenderly, stirring his emotions once more to the boiling point.

"I'm ready, my darling Benjamin," she said.

His dark eyes met hers. For a moment, they stood immobile, barely breathing. Then Benjamin kissed her forehead and stepped away from her. Slowly he walked to the door, barely able to force himself to leave. He turned before going out into the hall and said, "Only two more nights, my love, and then you'll be mine."

Jessie was so surprised when he walked out the door that he had almost reached the front door before she roused herself to go after him.

"Benjamin!"

He stopped at the front door when she called his name.

She stood on the threshold and asked simply, "Why?"

"Because you were right. Mr. Talbot is coming in for the wedding and to give us his decision about Maria. If we had . . . if I had . . ." Benjamin looked down at his boot tips as he restlessly fingered his hat. "There would be no way to hide the truth," he continued. "He'd need only look at me to know. Some people have very strict standards, Jessica. If for some reason Mr. Talbot found out we'd been intimate before the wedding, who can predict how it would affect his decision. Better to wait and know we've done everything right," he said. He stepped out the door, then turned back and kissed Jessica's cheek.

She moved forward in an instant, placing her hands firmly on either side of his face. With a hearty grip she lowered his face to hers and kissed him soundly on the lips.

"Someone once told me, 'Kisses on the cheek are for grandmothers and little babies.' Good night, Benjamin."

With those words she closed the door and slid the latch firmly in place.

It took only a second for him to react. "Jessica!" he shouted, banging on the door.

Jessie leaned against the door, peering out through the glass. She had to smile at the look on his face. "Only two more nights," she repeated.

He found himself laughing at her words. "You little minx," he said, shaking his head.

"Good night," she mouthed through the glass, blowing him a kiss.

Benjamin bowed slightly and put on his hat. "Good night, my sweet."

Through the glass, Jessie watched Benjamin go down the path and untether his horse. He mounted effortlessly, even with his arm in the sling. She thought his arm must be healing quickly or else he was very good at hiding the pain.

Straight and tall in the saddle, he rode away without a backward glance. Jessie could not move from the window until he was gone from view.

After banking the fires and extinguishing all the lamps except the one she carried upstairs, Jessie checked on Maria one last time. The child was sleeping soundly, and Jessie couldn't help but think that if the child hadn't wakened Benjamin would have made love to her tonight.

The recollection brought an instant flush to her cheeks and a quiver deep within. Benjamin's body beneath hers had been firm, and even now her breast tingled at the remembrance of his fingers stroking her nipple. She'd felt his need when he rolled her on top of his body, and she'd wanted him to love her more than she'd ever wanted anything in her life.

As Jessie started to undress, her eyes were drawn to the four-poster bed across the room. Her imagination put Benjamin in that bed, and when she crawled under the coverlet, the very thought of his body next to hers sent an exciting shudder of delight through her.

She clasped the extra pillow against her chest with both arms, trying to recall the look of desire she'd seen in Benjamin's dark gaze.

"Two more nights, my love," she whispered into

the darkness. "Two more nights until you share this bed with me."

Jessie heard the surf rhythmically lapping at the shore. The sound had lulled her to sleep many a night with its consistent soothing movement . . . in and out the water rolled . . . in over the rocky shoreline, then rolling back out again, only to be repeated over and over . . . never ending. As her eyes began to drift shut, Jessie wondered what it would be like to make love while the waves beat out their soft, rhythmical song.

Chapter Twenty

The next two days flew by in a flurry of activity. There were last-minute fittings on Jessie and Maria's gowns, tons of food to be prepared, cakes and cookies to be baked, and what seemed an endless supply of wine brought into the cellar.

Samuel practically lived at the house, polishing all the brass, cleaning out the fireplaces, bringing blocks of ice from the ferry to chill the wine, and even helping with the decorating.

Two of Benjamin's distant cousins arrived for the wedding, and Jessie thanked God and Margaret that they were staying at the house on the hill. Mr. Talbot had declined an invitation to stay overnight and was to arrive on the first ferry in the morning.

The night before the wedding, Samuel also moved some of Benjamin's things into what would soon be their bedroom.

At last, it was the morning of her wedding day, and Jessie had again awakened before dawn. The anticipation had been almost too much to bear. She was nervous and a bit scatterbrained, which was unusual for her.

"Margaret, I don't know what I'd do without you," Jessie said as Margaret carried a breakfast tray into her room.

"It is a bit early for breakfast, miss, but I heard you moving around up here and thought a cup of tea and some cinnamon bread might calm you down a bit. I've put plenty of warm milk in the tea—it will help soothe you."

Jessie nodded, but Margaret knew she hadn't heard a word she'd said.

"Sit down," Margaret said a bit sternly.

"Excuse me?"

"Well, at least I got your attention. I said, sit down and drink this tea and eat something. Then we'll talk."

"I don't think I can swallow, Margaret."

"Try."

Margaret sat silently while Jessie sipped the steaming hot brew and nibbled at the bread as she stared out the window at the sea beyond.

There was no doubt about it, with Miss Jessie's coal-black hair spilling over her shoulders, those sparkling eyes, and a flush on her cheeks, she was indeed a beautiful woman. It was no wonder Mr. Benjamin had been pacing the floors the past week and yelling at everyone for at least two days.

The man was beyond caring about anything but marrying this woman, and Margaret could understand his desire. She wasn't too old to remember the days before she and Samuel were wed. Sure enough, there were many things to do to carry off a wedding, yet beneath all the preparations remained the true reason for the tension that gripped the bride and groom. The fulfillment they both desired and waited for was within their grasp. The vibrations between two lovers just before they'd consummated their love was palpable.

Margaret had felt it bouncing off Mr. Benjamin the past two days, and even Samuel had commented on Miss Jessie's behavior when he was at the house. He'd told her stories of Miss Jessie racing up and down the stairs, issuing orders about things that had already been done, fussing at Maria to clean her room when it was already spotless, then apologizing endlessly for being unreasonable.

"I'll be glad when this wedding's over, Margaret," Samuel had said last night. "Then we can get back to normal activities."

She recalled smiling at her husband and saying, "I don't believe it will be normal for some time to come, Samuel. Those two are going to set the sparks flyin' for a bit."

Samuel had smiled in return and pulled her into his arms. The comfort she felt in his embrace had not changed in the 38 years they'd been wed. She hoped Miss Jessie would find the same joy in her marriage.

". . . Margaret . . . you will, won't you?"

Jessie's voice brought Margaret out of her reverie.

"Will what, miss?"

"Margaret, you weren't even listening. Here I am depending on you and you've gone off into another world."

The housekeeper smiled broadly. "I was indeed. Recalling my own wedding day."

Jessie stood up and hugged her. "I'm glad," she said. Stepping back, Jessie looked into Margaret's clear blue eyes. "From the looks of you, the recollections are happy ones."

"They most definitely are, and I hope yours and Mr. Benjamin's will be even happier."

Again Jessie hugged the woman. "Thank you for everything," she whispered, her eyes suddenly welling up.

"What's this?" Margaret asked, pulling out a handkerchief from her apron pocket. "Tears on your weddin' day?"

Jessie dabbed at her eyes. "It's all right. I'm just so very happy. Benjamin is to be my husband, hopefully Mr. Talbot will tell us we can raise my sister's child, I have found wonderful friends like you and Samuel and Ann, and . . . and I'm so happy . . . I . . . don't know . . . what to do."

Jessie could do nothing to stem the tears that coursed down her cheeks. She was grateful to Margaret for attempting to calm her down, patting her shoulder and telling her everything would be all right.

Somewhere between a sob and a laugh, Jessie nodded. "I do know that. I'm just not sure why I'm acting like a simpering female—because I'm not."

"It's the wedding, Miss Jessie. Everyone's a bit on edge—you and Mr. Benjamin in particular. That's the way it is with a bridal couple. They're so anxious for the day, then don't know what to do when it finally arrives."

Jessie laughed, effectively wiping away the last of her tears. "You're absolutely right. By tonight everything will be perfect." The implication of her words caught her off guard, and she felt her cheeks redden.

"No need to be embarrassed, miss. We all know exactly what you and Mr. Benjamin are waiting for."

"Margaret!"

"You know it's true." Margaret gestured in the direction of the house on the hill. "He's over there pacing the floors, thinkin' about his beautiful bride and how it will be tonight, and you're over here thinkin' about how handsome and strong he is and how he'll be—"

"Margaret, that's enough . . . please."

"Sorry if I overstepped my bounds, miss, but the two of you are driving everybody to drink. I thought maybe if you realized what the problem was you could calm down a bit."

Jessie sighed deeply. "You think that's all it is then? I'm anxious to have the wedding over?"

"Yes, ma'am . . . and him in your bed there," Margaret added, nodding towards the bed.

Jessie felt her cheeks flaming, but couldn't keep her eyes from the bed. If indeed she admitted the truth, it was exactly as Margaret said.

She knew Margaret had seen the glance and felt she had to defend herself. "All right, I admit my wedding night's been on my mind a bit."

"More than a bit, from the way Samuel tells it."

"Samuel? Samuel thinks I'm anxious for my wedding night?"

Jessie was sure she would die of mortification. No proper woman should let such intimate feelings show. "Margaret, how? I never said anything to Samuel."

"Neither of you need say a word," Margaret said, a wide grin creasing her wrinkled cheeks. "It's written all over you . . . it's in your eyes, the way you walk, the way your mind wanders. You're both shooting off sparks of desire whether you're aware of it or not."

"Benjamin too, eh?" Jessie said with a grin.

"Oh, yes, ma'am. He's been good for nothin' these past two days. He just . . ."

"Two days?" Jessie asked.

Margaret nodded her head. "It seems he started actin' just about impossible—let's see—uhm, yes, it was that evening he came over here to talk with you about something to do with the wedding. He's not been right since."

Jessie smiled a secret smile, turning toward the window so Margaret wouldn't see. Good, she thought. It serves you right for walking away after exciting me to the point of oblivion.

Suddenly, the dark clouds parted and the sun seemed to rise from the lake itself. "Look, Margaret, the sun . . . the sun's going to shine on my wedding day."

Jessie parted the lace curtains and stood at the window. Margaret came up beside her and together they silently watched as the sun moved above the water, painting the tips of the foaming waves with colorful orange and red sparks.

"My mother always said if the sun shone on your wedding day, the marriage would be long and blessed with much love," Margaret murmured.

"Was it shining on your wedding day, Margaret?"

Margaret smiled and nodded.

A knock came at the door, and Margaret hurried to open it. Jessie continued to look out at the lake, glistening in the morning sunlight.

"Miss Jessie," Samuel said, poking his head in the open door. "Mrs. Mills is here. She'd like you to come down and supervise the decorating."

"All right, Samuel, I'll be down in a few minutes."

Margaret took the tray and started out after him. "Oh, by the way, miss, what was it you were askin' me when I was daydreaming before?"

"Oh . . . I just wanted to be sure you were planning to come to the church. I don't want you here in the kitchen while we're exchanging our vows."

"I wouldn't miss your vows for anything, miss. I have a good friend comin' in to handle the kitchen while we're at the church. She's a good worker and will have everything ready for us when the ceremony's over."

For the next few hours the house was a beehive of activity as everyone busily prepared for the reception. Maria's excitement was joyful to see as she helped Mrs. Mills with the decorating.

Greens were hung, flowers arranged, extra chairs put in place, cookies and cakes arranged on platters, and the final touches were put on the wedding cake.

By noon, the house had been changed into a wonderland. Mrs. Mills, a woman Jessie had become acquainted with at church, had hung garlands of shiny greens from the mantles, looped them down the banister, and edged the tops of all the downstairs windows with them as well.

The dining room looked especially lovely, with an enormous bouquet of dried spring and summer flowers centered on the pristine white tablecloth. And Mrs. Cochran had been right about the flowers retaining their fragrance—the smell of spring filled the room. Additional flowers adorned the mantle and buffet, and greens decorated the doorways and window tops. The crystal stemware sparkled on the sideboard, and wine buckets were ready to be filled after the ceremony.

Candles would be lit on their return from the church, and Jessica could imagine how lovely their home would look bathed in candlelight.

Even the sitting room and parlor had been decorated, as Mrs. Mills felt people would move throughout the house. Jessie was pleased that the woman had offered to help with these details as she'd done a marvelous job.

Everything is perfect, and it will all lead me to this special night . . . the night I will spend with Benjamin.

"It's time for you to get ready, Miss Jessie," Margaret said, interrupting her thoughts.

Jessie smiled. She was going to be Benjamin's wife. "Yes, Margaret—it's time."

The organ in the rear of the church seemed to play on and on. Benjamin paced back and forth in the anteroom to the right of the altar.

He had never been more nervous in his life, yet he couldn't understand the reason. Jessica was going to be his wife, and it was the happiest day of his life.

Then why am I pacing like a caged animal?

Samuel came to the doorway. "Miss Jessica's arrived, sir. She's in the vestibule with Maria. Rev. Weldon said it will be a few minutes yet."

"Thank you, Samuel. Do you know if Henry Monroe's arrived yet?"

"Yes, he has. I believe he stopped to see someone in the back of the church, but he should be here momentarily."

Benjamin sighed. Although Henry was a good friend as well as his company's manager, he wished his brother Jonathan could have been here to stand beside him.

Henry came in a moment later and smiled broadly. "My, my don't you look splendid. Tails and a silk cravat certainly suit you."

"Don't say another word. You know how I hate dressing in these fancy clothes."

"I do indeed. But when you see your bride, you will be glad you made the effort."

Benjamin grasped Henry's arm. "You've seen Jessica?"

Henry nodded. "She is the most beautiful bride I've ever seen, Benjamin. You will be the envy of every man on the island."

He smiled at Henry—and kept on smiling—he couldn't have stopped if he tried.

Instantly, the nervousness was gone. A sense of peace descended over him like a fresh spring shower. Jessica was here . . . his bride was coming to him. Soon she would be his wife and he could take her into his arms . . . and his bed.

"I can't imagine what you're thinking," Henry said with a grin. "You might want to at least get the wicked gleam out of your eyes, though. This is, after all, a church."

A rousing blast from the organ caught Benjamin by surprise. "Wha—"

"Let's go. That's our signal to move to the altar."

Benjamin felt like a child on Christmas Eve, anticipation stimulating every nerve ending in his entire body.

Henry led the way and Benjamin followed. They stood side by side near the altar, and when the wedding march issued from the organ, Benjamin's eyes moved to the back of the church.

A smile came unbidden at the sight of Maria,

looking like a tiny angel floating in a soft green cloud. Benjamin couldn't help but think of how proud his brother would have been to see her walking down the aisle at her uncle's wedding.

With that thought Benjamin's eyes scanned the crowded pews—it seemed the entire population of the island had come to the ceremony. After a moment, he located Mr. Talbot's red hair towards the back of the church and was pleased to see the smile under the official's bushy mustache.

Ann had followed Maria and now took her place across from Benjamin and Henry. He smiled at her and hoped he would remember to thank her for being a good friend to Jessica and for agreeing to be her attendant today.

She returned his smile just as the organ reached a crescendo and all eyes turned once again to the back of the church.

Benjamin knew Jessica had asked Samuel to escort her to the altar, and had been surprised at how dashing the older man looked when he'd tried on his wedding finery the previous day.

When Jessica stepped through the doorway, Benjamin's eyes devoured her. It was as though no one else existed on the face of the earth. She too had on a dress of soft green material, scooped into a bustle at the back that trailed behind her as she walked slowly toward him. A sheer ruffled cape of the same material flowed from a high, lace-trimmed neck band, and as she walked, it fluttered about her like a butterfly's wings.

Benjamin caught her gaze. Her eyes sparkled and a smile creased her rosy cheeks. Her dark hair had been brushed back on the sides and pulled up into long spirals that cascaded down her back, secured by a lacy green bow.

The music continued, and Benjamin felt Henry nudge him forward. A moment later, Samuel relinquished Jessica's arm and she slipped it inside his. Her radiant smile ignited a fire in Benjamin's chest and he tucked her arm securely around his.

He was glad he'd insisted on not wearing the sling. A bit of discomfort was worth the freedom of two hands.

The smell of the gardenias Jessica carried drifted upward, and he was pleased to see they'd arrived in time. He'd ordered them, as well as the basket of roses that Maria carried, from the mainland.

Maria and Ann stood to Jessica's left and looked properly solemn. Benjamin glanced from the child to his bride, and was suddenly overwhelmed by the fact that he now had a family.

All through Rev. Weldon's readings and the choir's songs, Benjamin kept his eyes on his bride.

Jessie felt as though she were in a dream. Ever since she'd stepped through the doorway at the rear of the church and saw Benjamin she'd been lost. Trim and dashing in his formal wear, he appeared taller and more handsome than ever. His dark hair had been brushed till it actually shone in the candlelight, and his eyes . . . his eyes had met hers and she floated the rest of the way down the aisle.

She could hear the music drifting through the church. The sunlight still poured through the tall, arched windows, and Jessie was vaguely aware of the many people on both sides of the aisle, but she could not move her eyes away from Benjamin's. It was as though his dark gaze pulled her along like a magnet, until at last she stood beside him, her arm in his, his hand covering hers.

Jessie heard snatches of Rev. Weldon's words. She heard him talk of the first miracle Jesus ever performed—turning water into wine at a wedding feast. She heard him quote from Genesis: "And the Lord God said, it is not good for man to be alone . . ."

The songs the choir sang struck a chord in her own heart as Benjamin stroked her hand and smiled down at her.

When at last they'd exchanged their vows, never once separating their eyes from each other, Jessie listened as Rev. Weldon pronounced them husband and wife and ended the ceremony with words from the book of Matthew: "What therefore God has joined together, let no man put asunder."

Benjamin's kiss took her away from the church momentarily. Only the crescendo from the organ and Henry's nudging brought her back.

She turned to see Maria watching them, a broad smile on her face. Jessie reached out and squeezed her hand, and Maria pulled her down and whispered. "Momma came to see you married, Aunt Jess."

Maria's words jarred her momentarily, yet in the next instant a warmth flowed through her and the thought of her sister's presence was comforting.

"Mrs. Whittaker," Benjamin said, "it's time to greet our friends."

Jessie bent down to Maria and answered with a whispered "I'm glad." Then she sent Maria down the aisle and turned to Benjamin. "Mr. Whittaker, I'm ready."

At the back of the church, Benjamin, Jessica, and Maria stood, acknowledging the good wishes of friends and neighbors. Jessie was so happy with the way Maria had accepted their marriage. The little child's face was wreathed in smiles as her parents' friends and neighbors leaned down to hug her. And when Willy Weldon kissed Maria's cheek, she giggled, warming Jessie's heart.

As the crowd moved outside the church, lining the steps, the last of the guests came out. When Jessie saw Mr. Talbot approaching, she sobered instantly. This was the last step between her and complete happiness.

Benjamin greeted him first. "Mr. Talbot, my wife and I are so glad you could come for the celebration."

"My pleasure, sir, and congratulations to you, Mrs. Whittaker." Jessie saw him glance down at Maria and smile at her.

"There will be papers to sign, of course, but we do feel the child is best left with her own people. The wedding was a wise move, although I must say you look exactly like two people in love."

"That's because we are, Mr. Talbot," Jessie said.

He nodded and went out the door.

Benjamin reached down and scooped Maria up in his arms. "Did you hear, little one? We are to be a real family."

Jessie thought Maria's excited shout of "Hurrah!" was a fitting end to the ceremony.

Chapter Twenty-one

Back at the house, the celebration began in earnest. The sun had begun its swift descent as the guests filled the house, and Margaret and Mrs. Mills quickly lit all the candles and lamps. Samuel had the fires blazing to ward off the autumn chill, and the rooms glowed with warmth and cheer.

Benjamin introduced Jessie to so many people she could barely remember one name.

There were toasts to the bride and groom, to a long life, to their good health, for good fortune, and on and on. The food was served, and exclamations were forthcoming on the delicacies Margaret had prepared.

Each time Benjamin squeezed her hand or put a proprietary arm around her waist or caught her eye, Jessie knew this marriage was the best thing that had ever happened to her.

The crowd and the conversation gave them little

time to talk, but near the end of the evening, Benjamin took her hand and pulled her into the kitchen, where mountains of dishes and remnants of the wedding feast remained.

Benjamin drew her into his arms and kissed her passionately. When he released her lips, he whispered, "They'll all be gone soon, my love."

The words almost made her knees give way. The desire she'd suppressed for so long had made her weak.

"Very soon," she whispered.

Ann Weldon happened to come into the kitchen carrying a tray of wine glasses. "Oh . . . excuse me, I didn't know the bride and groom were in here."

"Just trying to have a moment alone," Benjamin said.

"Then I'll set this down and be out of your way."

"Benjamin," Jessie admonished. "How could you speak to Ann that way after all she's done for us?"

"I do beg your pardon," he said, bowing to Ann.

"No need . . . I certainly understand. It's been a hectic day." She started out of the kitchen, then suddenly turned, a mischievous gleam in her eye. "Oh, I did want to ask you if it would be all right for Maria to spend the night with us."

Jessie started to protest, but Benjamin interrupted. "I think that would be a very wise idea, Ann, and I thank you for suggesting it."

Two hours later, after bidding their guests good-bye, Jessie hugged and kissed Maria and gave Margaret and Samuel one last embrace. Then she found herself standing on the threshold, alone with her husband.

Benjamin's arm was around her waist, and they

watched Margaret and Samuel's wagon until it was out of sight.

They stepped in out of the cool night air, and Benjamin closed and locked the door. The sound of the latch sliding into place sent a ripple of anticipation straight to Jessie's core.

When Benjamin turned to her, she saw her own emotions mirrored in his eyes.

"Come here and kiss me, woman."

Drawing her skirt up on one side, she deftly moved around him and bounded up the stairs. "Not until I've changed out of this dress."

Just as quickly, Benjamin dashed up the stairs, and when he caught up with Jessie on the top step, he scooped her up in his arms as easily as he did Maria.

"Benjamin, put me down. You'll reinjure your arm."

"My arm is fine, and I'll never put you down. We have all night and all day tomorrow, and I mean to take full advantage of our time alone."

Jessie's laughter bubbled out. "I only want to change into my nightgown. If your ardor is as passionate as the other night, I'd prefer not to take a chance on ruining my beautiful wedding dress."

Suddenly, as Benjamin held her in his arms and stared down into her eyes, all humor left Jessie. Her heart began to pound furiously and her skin tingled. Deep inside her body, the insatiable yearning for fulfillment that had gripped her for days spasmed in anticipation.

Holding her eyes with his deep, smouldering gaze, Benjamin walked slowly to their bedroom door and murmured huskily, "I want to undress you myself . . . and I don't want you in a nightgown."

Benjamin's words excited Jessie as much as his touch, and she knew there was no reason to don the lacy, white nightgown Ann had given her.

"I look forward to having you undress me," she whispered, "if I may return the favor."

A pleasurable moan escaped his lips just before they covered hers, assuring Jessie that he too looked forward to the experience.

The next few minutes were lost in a deluge of sensations as Benjamin carried her across the room, never releasing her lips until he gently stood her next to the bed.

Without a word, his eyes focused on hers, and he began to unfasten the lace collar of her sheer cape. The cloth grazed her arms as it fluttered down to the floor sending a delicious shiver along her spine.

Benjamin bent his head and brushed a gentle kiss across her lips, then took her by the shoulders and turned her so that she faced the bed. The thought of them soon together there on the soft mattress set her heart racing.

"Benjamin," she murmured breathlessly.

His mouth was beside her ear, and he whispered, "Let me enjoy this, my love." He gripped her shoulders for another moment before releasing them in order to unfasten the row of buttons at the back of her dress.

With each one he undid, he kissed her neck just below her ear—first one side and then the other. Jessie closed her eyes and surrendered to the exquisite feelings he aroused in her.

By the time Benjamin had undone the bustle at her waist Jessie's breath was coming in ragged gasps. His lips had traced a red-hot trail down her neck and back and she could feel herself melting inside.

Still standing behind her, he slowly pushed the dress over her shoulders and down her arms, teasing her as his fingers caressed her skin, ending with the final tantalizing strokes across her palms. He reached forward and undid the bow and clasp of her undergarments, releasing her breasts, which he cupped gently in his hands. As the work-roughened skin of his thumbs circled each of her tender nipples, he set her body aflame. Inside and out, she burned with desire.

When she thought she could wait no longer, his hands moved away from her breasts, causing her to moan and again murmur his name.

"We have time, my love," he said softly as his fingers moved to undo the bow and hairpins that held her locks of hair at the back of her head. Dropping each pin to the floor as he removed it, he let her hair fall softly down her naked back.

Jessie found the effect of her own hair moving against her bare skin extremely sensuous. She realized she'd always left it up when she undressed for her bath, and Michael had always made love to her with her nightgown on.

For a moment she stood silently, enjoying all these new sensations. Then Benjamin turned her to face him. As his eyes glistened in the candlelight, he leisurely moved his gaze from her face to look at her body.

"You are exquisite."

Jessie thrilled to his touch as he once more brushed his thumbs across her nipples. Before she had time to absorb all the excitement his touch elicited, though, he dropped down on one knee, gently sliding her dress and undergarments from the lower half of her body, scorching her skin with his touch.

By the time he gently eased her onto the edge of the bed and began to remove her shoes and stockings, Jessie wasn't sure she'd be able to undress him when the time came. She had never done such things before, and each new movement brought with it an increase of her desire and an almost unbearable need for fulfillment. She trembled in anticipation.

When Benjamin had thrown both her shoes behind him, he stood, taking her hands in his. "Let me look at my wife," he said as he tenderly pulled her up from the bed.

His eyes slowly explored her entire body, and the effect was as incendiary as if he'd touched every inch of her.

Flushed with pleasure, Jessie felt no embarrassment as she stood naked before her husband in the flickering candlelight.

Without a word, she moved her hands to the diamond pin that held his black silk tie. Dropping the tie and stickpin to the floor, she then slid his jacket from his shoulders while he stood tall and stiff as a ramrod. She unbuttoned his collar and as she continued to loosen each button, she could feel the rapid increase in his heartbeat.

Benjamin moaned as Jessica undid his trousers. Her touch had brought him close to losing his self-control.

As he had done with her only minutes before, she gently urged him to be seated on the edge of the bed. When she knelt before him, the sight of her glorious hair tumbling over her firm naked breasts was almost unbearable.

She pulled off each of his boots in one smooth

motion, then had him stand while she remained in her kneeling position to slide his trousers off.

He stood before her, clad in his last remaining item of clothing. She seemed hesitant, then bent to remove it. She did not gasp as Helene had on their wedding night. And she did not ask him to extinguish the candles.

Jessica appeared to glory in their nakedness, and he could not wait a moment longer. He picked her up in his arms and cradled her against him, his mouth devouring her moist lips.

At last he laid her on the bed, covering her body with his, moving only to capture her breast in his mouth, bringing moans of pleasure from her lips.

Moments later, almost breathless, she cried out for him to come to her. "Please, Benjamin," she cried a second time.

He glorified in Jessica's plea and, unable to curb his desire any longer, he quickly parted her long, slender legs and entered her easily in her eagerness.

Jessica amazed Benjamin many times that night with her willingness to open herself to him and to fulfill all his needs. In turn he responded by giving her all he knew how to give. When at last he could no longer stay awake, he pulled her close and wrapped his legs and arms around her, holding her fast as sleep overtook him.

When Jessie felt Benjamin's grip relax and heard his deep easy breathing, she realized her new husband had fallen asleep. She stroked his cheek and smoothed his hair back from his forehead, glorying in the sight of him there beside her.

Unable to sleep, Jessie couldn't help but think of her first wedding night. A sadness came over her with the knowledge that what she and Michael had shared had not been a true mature love. There would always be a place in her memories for Michael, but she knew that Benjamin had claimed her heart forever. Jessie silently pledged her love for him, knowing there could never be another man in her life.

As though he was aware of her thoughts, Benjamin's eyelids fluttered open and he smiled before once more demonstrating his love.

The sunlight woke Benjamin, and for a moment he found himself disoriented. But it took only a moment to realize the warmth molded against him was his bride's extraordinary body. Her head still rested on his arm and his other arm lay across her breasts.

He dared not move as he listened to Jessica's deep even breathing. They'd slept little and, despite his growing ardor, he wanted to let her rest a bit longer.

Her long hair tickled his chest, and he found the sensation enticing. Remembering their night together, he marveled again at her willingness to share herself with him in every way.

He'd known Jessica was a passionate woman, but even in his wildest dreams he had never expected a wife who would bring him such joy.

Even when he'd thought Helene loved him, it had never been like this. He'd never even seen his first wife unclothed.

"I love you, my darling wife," he whispered in her ear.

She immediately stirred, moving her body against him, a smile slowly inching across her face.

"Good morning," he murmured, kissing her ear

and her neck with tiny, light movements.

"Uhmm . . . yes, it is," Jessica murmured, rolling over to face him.

And once again they consummated their love.

"Dear God, woman," Benjamin said later as he stroked her hair. "If we keep this up, I'll not be able to work to support you."

"We'll live on love alone then," Jessica said.

Benjamin's laughter delighted Jessie.

"It's true," she said, raising up on one elbow to look down at him, reveling in her ability to make him laugh. "Couldn't you?" she asked, teasing him with a light flick of her tongue on his lips.

"Live on love?" he mused, laying his head back against the pillow. "Indeed, you might kill me at this rate."

"Did I do something wrong?" she asked.

"Wrong? Dear Lord, no, my love. You did everything just right—more than right."

"I pleased you?" she asked with a naughty grin.

"More than pleased . . . overwhelmed. I've never known such love was possible, Jessica."

"Nor I, my darling," she said, once more delighting in the touch of his lips on hers.

Hours later, a gnawing feeling inside Jessie made her aware of yet another sensation. "I'm hungry," she said, smiling at her husband. "Perhaps we should have something to eat. To keep up our strength," she added with a grin.

"You stay here and rest," he said, kissing the tip of her nose. "I'll cook you breakfast."

He slid out of bed, shivering as his bare feet hit the floor. "I think it might be wise to rekindle the fires in the house first," he said, quickly slipping on his trousers. He padded over to the wardrobe to get one of the shirts Samuel had brought for him.

"Could you hand me my dressing gown?" Jessie asked.

"No. I meant what I said, woman. I want you to rest. When the house is warm, perhaps I'll let you up . . . for a while. Then it's back to bed."

"You mean to keep me in this bed all day? What if someone comes to call?"

Jessie watched as a mischievous grin lit up Benjamin's face. "Ah, but Margaret has taken care of that. She decided we needed at least two nights and a full day alone, so she informed everyone not to call on us until late tomorrow."

Jessie suddenly thought about their niece. "What about Maria?"

"Ann is taking Maria and Willy to the mainland today and promised to keep Maria for another night."

"Oh, Benjamin, I hope she doesn't feel abandoned."

"Come now, you know how much she enjoys being with the Weldons. She'll be fine. We need some time alone, Jessica. There'll be years for us to be a family, but these two nights are ours. Maria will be delighted to see the love pouring from us."

Benjamin leaned down to kiss Jessie once more, then went to the fireplace. Jessie watched her husband, his every movement fascinating her. Barely able to believe this man could truly be hers, she called out, "I'm not dreaming, am I?"

Without a word, Benjamin approached the bed. Slipping his hand under the covers, he pinched Jessie's backside.

"Ow!" Jessie cried out, her hand rubbing the spot he'd pinched.

"You're not dreaming, my love," he said.

"You could have just told me."

A half hour later, delicious aromas drifted upstairs, and Jessie could no longer remain in bed. Fastening her new dressing gown of peach silk around her, Jessie reveled in the feel of the silk against her bare skin. "Hmmm," she murmured aloud. "So many new sensations to discover."

Satin slippers to match the gown were a gift from Margaret, and Jessie slipped them on before going quietly downstairs.

In the kitchen, she tiptoed up behind Benjamin, who was busy at the stove, and wound her arms around his waist. "Something smells wonderful," she said as he turned spoon in hand.

"You were supposed to stay in bed, woman."

"I couldn't stand to be apart from you another minute."

He smiled, leaned down, and kissed her nose, then turned back to the stove.

"Breakfast is almost ready. If you want to be of some help, get the dishes and silver and set the table."

Their first full day as a married couple brought even more surprises to Jessie. She discovered Benjamin was a marvelous cook. "Learned from Margaret," he told her as he prepared breakfast and then a late lunch.

Near midnight, Jessie realized that they'd skipped dinner. But she also discovered there were more ways to satiate hunger than food.

They'd spent most of the evening relaxing in the sitting room, stretched out on the thick carpet in front of the fire, talking about the things they'd do together as a family.

Abruptly Benjamin kissed her and said he'd be back shortly.

"You can't leave me alone," Jessica said.

"It's a surprise. You have to stay here. Just rest—you've certainly earned it."

He came back a bit later, assuring her she had to wait a little longer for the surprise. They enjoyed a glass of wine and talked about their childhood and so many other things they didn't know about each other.

Benjamin left once more, then returned with a bright smile. "Come, my love."

As Benjamin led Jessie down the hall, she shivered. "It's chilly out here."

"Well, no wonder, with that flimsy bit of cloth on."

"I thought you liked my dressing gown."

"I like what's under it better."

"Benjamin, you best watch your tongue. When Maria returns tomorrow we will have to watch what we say . . . and do."

"Correct," he said, opening the doors to the dining room with a flourish. "That's why we must take advantage of tonight."

Jessie was surprised to feel the warmth that poured from the room, evident from the roaring fire blazing in the fireplace. Even more surprising was the dining room table, which had been completely cleared.

As she stood there watching the fire reflected in the gleaming mahogany table, Margaret's conversation popped into her head. She turned to Benjamin, her eyes wide.

"Surprise," he said as he picked her up in his strong arms and carried her to the table.

"I cannot believe we did that," Jessie said later as they started back up the stairs to their bedroom.

"Which, my love, the dining room table or the rug in the sitting room?"

"Both! Until you and Margaret talked about your parents' escapades, I never dreamed anyone made love anywhere but in their bedroom with the door closed and locked."

"It's Whittaker tradition, Mrs. Whittaker. And with Maria coming home tomorrow, I thought we should take double advantage of our privacy."

After a second of bliss, a morning filled with love, and a wonderful breakfast which Jessica insisted on cooking, Benjamin looked across the kitchen table at his wife and said, "You are the most wonderful wife any man could ever have."

She smiled back at him and answered, "Only because I make the best biscuits and ham gravy you've ever eaten."

"If you never cooked again, it would not matter. I could, as you said yesterday, 'live on love.' "

It was Jessica's turn to laugh, and she did so with a lilting sound that warmed Benjamin's heart.

"I love everything about you—your laughter, your smile, your glorious hair, your lips, your body—"

"Stop that," Jessica said, rising to clear the table. "Or we'll never leave this house."

"I never want to leave," he said, standing to help. "We could stay locked inside forever, growing old without ever getting dressed again."

Jessica's laughter bubbled over him. "It does sound wonderful, my darling," she said. "But we do have Maria to consider. She is, after all, the reason this marriage came about."

Benjamin wrinkled his forehead in thought. "It did start out that way, didn't it?"

Jessica nodded and held his gaze for a long moment, her eyes taking on a rather serious look.

"What are you thinking, my darling Jessica?"

"I was wondering what would ever have become of us if there'd been no Maria. Where would we be without her, Benjamin?"

He looked at her with such love it almost took Jessie's breath away.

"We would be exactly where we are right now, my love, because we were meant to be together. Even if there'd never been a Maria, you and I would have come together . . . it was destiny . . . a plan made in heaven." He kissed her tenderly, then added, "Or perhaps it truly was Maria's angel who nudged us together."

They shared another kiss, and Jessie's eyes teared with happiness.

"No more tears, Jessica," Benjamin said, brushing them from her cheeks.

"You're right, my love. It's time to pick up Maria so the three of us can begin our life together."

Epilogue

A week after their wedding, Jessie surprised Benjamin by announcing that they would be celebrating their first anniversary with a dinner party.

"Anniversary?" he asked with a puzzled expression. "I thought anniversaries usually began after the first year of marriage."

"My dear Benjamin," Jessie said playfully. "You should know by now that your wife does not do the usual. We have had one full week of wedded bliss and our life with Maria has been so perfect, I feel the need to celebrate."

"Then celebrate we shall," he said, kissing her soundly on the lips. "But since the dining room has many place settings, may I assume others will be joining us?"

"Of course. I've invited Henry and the Weldons, and I've even managed to coerce Margaret and Samuel to sit down at the table with us."

"Quite a feat, Mrs. Whittaker."

"I'm looking forward to entertaining our friends," Jessie said. "In fact, they'll be here any moment. I wonder what's keeping Maria? I sent her upstairs for some candles, and it seems to be taking her forever."

Benjamin called upstairs, but there was no answer.

"Perhaps she's fallen asleep," he said with a slight smile. "You've been working her so hard to prepare for this dinner party, she's probably exhausted."

"Or she's talking to her mother again," Jessie said.

"Still?" Benjamin asked. "I thought you told me these times were lessening?"

"They have, and I took it as a good sign, since Maria appears to be settling into our life together so well."

"Why don't we go up and check on her?" Benjamin said, putting his arm around Jessie. "She may just be napping. And even if she's not, you mustn't fret over her talks with her mother, Jessica. I'm sure it will pass in time."

They went upstairs together and sure enough, when they entered Maria's room, she was kneeling near her bed, a look of rapture on her face as she looked upward.

Jessie's eyes unexpectedly filled with tears. She had so hoped Maria was comfortable enough in their new life that the visits would stop.

Her vision blurred with tears, Jessie suddenly felt Maria's tiny hand holding hers, stroking it in a comforting gesture.

"Please don't cry, Aunt Jess. Everything's all right now. Look, Momma's here."

Jessie raised her head, wishing she could see her sister one last time, but she saw nothing.

"Oh, Maria, she's not—"

"Shh . . . Momma doesn't have much time, Aunt Jess. She has to leave very soon."

Benjamin scooted down to Maria's level. "Do you really see your mother here now, Maria?"

The little girl nodded. "If you both do like Momma told me to, you'll be able to see her too. Just close your eyes and picture her, and she'll be with you."

Sighing in resignation, Jessie thought, why not? She closed her eyes, trying to remember her sister's beautiful image on the day she was married.

A smile instantly tugged at Jessie's lips. Maria was right after all. She could see Frannie's face clearly, the wreath of flowers atop her head. She could almost feel the warmth Maria described.

"Can you hear her, Aunt Jess?"

Jessie started to say no, but hesitated. It was a vague, faraway sound, much like the wind she'd heard on the ferry weeks ago, but it sounded like . . . *Everything's all right now, Jess*.

Jessie's eyes flew open. Still she refused to believe she'd actually heard the words, yet when she felt a sudden warmth on her shoulders, Jessie looked to her niece. "Maria?'

The little girl was sitting on the floor in front of her, looking upward.

"Momma's saying good-bye, Aunt Jess. She's telling you not to worry because the three of us are going to be just fine now."

Benjamin was still down beside Maria, and he suddenly reached upward and clasped Jessie's hand in his. With tears brimming in his eyes, he spoke barely above a whisper. "I heard her too, my love. Frannie said we're a family now, Jessica, united not only by law, but by love as well."

As Jessie tried to absorb Benjamin's words, an abrupt, all-encomposing sensation of warmth radiated throughout her body from a central point on each of her shoulders.

She had to ask, she had to know. "Maria, where is your Momma right now?"

Maria's smile was purely angelic, reflecting the vision she obviously could see before her. "She's standing behind you, Aunt Jess, with her hands on your shoulders."

"Good-bye, Jess. Take good care of my little one. I love you."

The words seemed to vibrate through Jessie's body as tears of joy filled her eyes. "I love you too, Frannie. Good-bye, sister," she whispered.

Maria beamed as she rose along with Benjamin and took her aunt's other hand in hers. "You finally believe," she said.

Jessie nodded, knowing that the three of them were indeed blessed by an angel's touch.

LORI HANDELAND

On the run from his past, Charlie Coltrain never plans on rescuing a young nun in the desert. Charlie tells himself he wants only the money she offers him to take her to the convent. But hiding away such shimmering beauty is a sin he couldn't abide, and he yearns to send her to heaven with his forbidden touch.

Hoping to find happiness, Angelina Reyes is ready to follow her calling and dedicate her life to the Church. But the first soul she finds that needs saving belongs to a gunslinger wanted by the law, not the Lord. Determined to help Charlie at any cost, Angelina discovers that he is far more than a mere man—he is her mission, her temptation, her greatest love.

_3776-9 $4.99 US/$5.99 CAN

Second Chance is a small Missouri town where the people believe that anyone who has done wrong deserves another shot. All the condemned man needs is someone to take responsibility for him. And that someone will never be Katherine Logan. With a bad marriage behind her, and the bank note on her horse ranch coming due, the young widow has neither the time nor the inclination to save a low-down bandit.

But the sight of the most wickedly tempting male ever to put his head through a noose changes her mind real quick. Although the townsfolk say Jake Banner will as soon shoot Katherine as change his outlaw ways, she won't listen. Deep within Jake's emerald eyes lie secrets that intrigue Katherine, daring her to give him a second chance at life—and herself a second chance at love.

_51966-6 $4.99 US/$5.99 CAN

Dorchester Publishing Co., Inc.
65 Commerce Road
Stamford, CT 06902

Please add $1.75 for shipping and handling for the first book and $.50 for each book thereafter. NY, NYC, PA and CT residents, please add appropriate sales tax. No cash, stamps, or C.O.D.s. All orders shipped within 6 weeks via postal service book rate. Canadian orders require $2.00 extra postage and must be paid in U.S. dollars through a U.S. banking facility.

Name ______________________________________
Address ____________________________________
City ______________________ State ______ Zip ______
I have enclosed $______ in payment for the checked book(s).
Payment must accompany all orders. ☐ Please send a free catalog.

"A wonderful, magical love story that transcends time and space. Definitely a keeper!"
—Madeline Baker

Patrick is in trouble, alone in turn-of-the-century Chicago, and unjustly jailed with little hope for survival. Then the honey-haired beauty comes to him, as if she has heard his prayers.

Lauren has all but given up on finding true love when she feels the green-eyed stranger's call—summoning her across boundaries of time and space to join him in a struggle against all odds; uniting them in a love that will last longer than forever.

_52042-7 $5.99 US/$7.99 CAN

Dorchester Publishing Co., Inc.
65 Commerce Road
Stamford, CT 06902

Please add $1.75 for shipping and handling for the first book and $.50 for each book thereafter. NY, NYC, PA and CT residents, please add appropriate sales tax. No cash, stamps, or C.O.D.s. All orders shipped within 6 weeks via postal service book rate. Canadian orders require $2.00 extra postage and must be paid in U.S. dollars through a U.S. banking facility.

Name____
Address______________________________________
City ____________________________ State______ Zip______
I have enclosed $______in payment for the checked book(s).
Payment must accompany all orders. ☐ Please send a free catalog.